P9-DIY-267

Dear Reader,

Things at the schoo[illegible]n my young ladies marrying at a dizzying pace. Poor Lucy Seton, however, one of my favorite graduates, has had a most difficult year ever since that scoundrel Peter Burnes broke her heart by choosing a rich heiress for his betrothed. To keep her mind off the matter, I asked her to step in when one of my less reliable teachers quit without notice. So Lucy will be teaching drawing at the school for now.

I can only hope that keeping her busy will distract her from her troubles. At least now she fully understands what I have been drilling into my students from the beginning: Any man who puts his purse above his heart is not worth the having. It is very important for these young ladies to separate the fawning fortune-hunters from the genuine gentlemen. Young women are so easily swayed by flattery that they can overlook the glint of avarice in a young man's eye.

I do wish Lucy hadn't had to learn this lesson the hard way, however. She is such a passionate young woman—I would hate to think that dreadful Burnes has broken her spirit. If anyone deserves to find love, it is young Lucy. Her loyalty to her friends—and to my school—speaks to her fine character. I only wish I could find a man good enough for her.

Perhaps I should ask Cousin Michael, my anonymous benefactor, for help in that regard . . . or perhaps not. His letters have been rather sharp of late. I don't know quite what to make of him.

But one way or the other, I intend to see Lucy Seton happily settled. What sort of friend and instructor would I be if I did not?

Most sincerely yours,
Charlotte Harris
Owner and headmistress
Mrs. Harris's School for Young Ladies

"Anyone who loves romance must read Sabrina Jeffries!"
—*New York Times* bestselling author Lisa Kleypas

**Praise for *New York Times* and *USA Today*
bestselling author
SABRINA JEFFRIES
and her delightfully enticing series
THE SCHOOL FOR HEIRESSES**

LET SLEEPING ROGUES LIE

"Consummate storyteller Jeffries pens another title in the School for Heiresses series that is destined to captivate readers with its sensuality and wonderfully enchanting plot."
—*Romantic Times* (4½ stars)

"Scandal, gossip, greed, and old enmities spice up the pot in this fast-paced sexy romp that bubbles over with Jeffries's trademark humor and spirit.... Sparkling dialogue, stirring sexual chemistry, and an engrossing story."
—*Library Journal*

BEWARE A SCOT'S REVENGE

"Irresistible.... Larger-than-life characters, sprightly dialogue, and a steamy romance will draw you into this delicious captive/captor tale."
—*Romantic Times* (Top Pick)

"Expertly entertaining and splendidly sexy."
—*Booklist*

The SCHOOL FOR HEIRESSES titles are available as eBooks

ONLY A DUKE WILL DO

"Bringing together a bold heroine and a scarred hero while incorporating political scandal into a tightly woven romance, Jeffries once again proves her mettle as a first-rate Regency author."

—Publishers Weekly

"Marvelous, powerful, and sensual. . . . Jeffries fans will devour this treat."

—Romantic Times

"Politics and passion prove to be a particularly potent combination. . . . Expertly crafted and delectably sexy."

—Booklist

NEVER SEDUCE A SCOUNDREL

"Jeffries delivers lively lovers in an entertaining, sensual historical romance."

—Booklist

"Jeffries carries off this cat-and-mouse game of mutual seduction so cleverly that you'll be turning the pages at lightning speed. . . . Warm, wickedly witty, and brilliantly plotted, this is a must for anyone who just wants a fast, intelligent read."

—Romantic Times

Sabrina Jeffries

Don't Bargain With The Devil

POCKET BOOKS

New York London Toronto Sydney

The sale of this book without its cover is unauthorized. If you purchased this book without a cover, you should be aware that it was reported to the publisher as "unsold and destroyed." Neither the author nor the publisher has received payment for the sale of this "stripped book."

Pocket Books
A Division of Simon & Schuster, Inc.
1230 Avenue of the Americas
New York, NY 10020

This book is a work of fiction. Names, characters, places, and incidents either are products of the author's imagination or are used fictitiously. Any resemblance to actual events or locales or persons, living or dead, is entirely coincidental.

Copyright © 2009 by Deborah Gonzales

All rights reserved, including the right to reproduce this book or portions thereof in any form whatsoever. For information address Pocket Books Subsidiary Rights Department,
1230 Avenue of the Americas, New York, NY 10020

First Pocket Books paperback edition June 2009

POCKET and colophon are registered trademarks of Simon & Schuster, Inc.

For information about special discounts for bulk purchases, please contact Simon & Schuster Special Sales at 1-866-506-1949 or business@simonandschuster.com.

The Simon & Schuster Speakers Bureau can bring authors to your live event. For more information or to book an event, contact the Simon & Schuster Speakers Bureau at 1-866-248-3049 or visit our website at www.simonspeakers.com.

Front cover and stepback illustration by Alan Ayers
Handlettering by Dave Gatti

Manufactured in the United States of America

10 9 8 7 6 5 4 3 2 1

ISBN: 978-1-4165-6081-4

To my wonderful Puerto Rican sister-in-law,
Erika Martin, who helped me with the Spanish in this book.
Thanks for being such a doll!

Chapter One

Richmond, Surrey
Late April 1824

Dear Charlotte,
  How thoughtless of your drawing instructor to
quit just before the Easter term begins! At least you
have Miss Seton to help you until you can replace
the irresponsible woman. Though I do hope she has
grown out of what you called "her inability to think
before speaking."

                            Your friend and cousin,
                            Michael

Lucinda Seton needed an impressive suitor, and she needed one *now*.

A prince would be her first choice, but she'd settle for a duke or even a marquess, preferably one who was filthy rich.

Not that she cared about riches, oh no. Expensive phaetons tearing neck-or-nothing through town made her retch, and hothouse roses made her sneeze. Jewels were rather nice, but a lot of trouble to watch out for when strolling with one's maid in the parks.

No, she wanted an impressive suitor for one reason only: to make Peter Burnes eat his words.

Tears stinging her eyes, she paced the bedroom at Mrs. Harris's School for Young Ladies that would be hers for the next few weeks. Fie on that wretch! She jerked a shawl from her half-unpacked trunk. How could she still be crying over him? And how could that heartless blackguard choose some milk-and-water miss over *her*?

The memory of their humiliating exchange at last Saturday's ball made her cringe as she tucked her shawl into the chest of drawers. Bad enough that she'd foolishly asked him how they stood. But his answer . . .

Given my new position in society, Lucy, I require a more suitable wife. Someone of a settled and responsible disposition, not a hot-blooded hoyden who says the first thing that pops into her head.

Hunting through her trunk, she found her pencils and the sketch pad containing the drawing she'd done of him a year ago, back when he'd thought *she* might be a suitable wife. She stared at the tousled curls and beatific smile that always made her heart turn over, then drew a pair of vile-looking horns on his head. She wasn't an irresponsible hoyden. She *wasn't!*

All right, perhaps she was a trifle outspoken. But what was wrong with that? He'd enjoyed it well enough when they were children running about the regiment.

You're the kind of woman a man dallies with, not the kind he marries.

Dallies with! She gnawed on her pencil, remembering the first time Peter, a seventeen-year-old general's son three years older than she, had laughingly stolen a kiss from her. Had he been dallying even then? Had she assumed it meant something when it had meant nothing to him?

And after she'd waited months for him, too! She'd been so sure Peter would marry her. Before his departure on the Grand Tour, he'd even called her his "one true love." He'd kissed her again, so sweetly it had seemed a declaration, especially when he'd told her to wait for him.

But once he'd returned, that was all forgotten. Instead, he'd called on her dressed in costly splendor, sporting a fine gold watch and talking down to her.

You're too impassioned, too curious about things no lady should deign to notice. You can't help it—it's in your blood.

Her *foreign* blood. Peter knew that Lucy had been adopted by Colonel Seton, the man she called Papa. Her real father had been an English soldier, her mother a Spanish woman of uncertain background. Not that Lucy could remember, since they'd died in the war when Lucy was only four.

But Peter didn't care about that, did he? Oh no, he only cared about the precious *blood* that her mother had passed on, which he seemed to think seethed with Spanish wildness and passion and fire.

Well, she'd show *him* wildness and passion and fire! With quick slashes of her pencil, she added a pointy tail that curved out from behind the modest frock coat he'd worn back when he was plain old Mr. Burnes, before he'd unexpectedly inherited the earldom of Hunforth.

That's when he'd become "too good" for her, too conscious of his precious lineage and important connections. That's when he'd become exactly like every other man in English society.

Although most people assumed Papa was a widower and Lucy his daughter, they soon learned otherwise from the gossips. Lady Kerr, her stepmother, had gently warned her that her odd parentage might prove an issue for high sticklers, especially since she wasn't a great heiress like her friends. And though men had shown her some interest during her first season, she'd had no offers. Not that she'd encouraged them—she'd been waiting for Peter. But she would have thought *one* would have made an offer anyway.

Unless . . . Oh, Lord, what if Peter were right about her? What if *everybody* thought she was some hussy not good enough to become a respectable man's wife? Was that why men were always eyeing her bosom and trying to kiss her on balconies? They never seemed to do that to the other girls.

They certainly never did that to Lady Juliana. Rich, elegant, boring Lady Juliana, whom Peter had apparently chosen as sufficiently suitable to be his bride.

Fresh tears sprang to her eyes. How dared he spurn her? The other men didn't surprise her; half were sheep who did what their mamas said. But Peter was supposed to be . . .

Hers.

She'd make him rue the day he'd rejected her. She had started to sketch a knife protruding from his treacherous heart when a knock came at the door. Hastily, she thrust the sketch pad beneath a pillow and bade the person enter.

Her stepmother glided into the room with her usual grace, another trait Lucy lacked. "Your father has finished his discussion with Mrs. Harris." Lady Kerr, who'd been married to Papa for little more than a year, surveyed the harum-scarum pile of clothing on the bed. "So we're leaving. And he'd like to say good-bye."

"I'll be along shortly."

Lady Kerr glanced at the open trunk. "Shall I help you unpack first?"

"I don't need your help!" Lucy snapped, then regretted it when Lady Kerr flinched. Lucy softened her tone. "It's kind of you to offer, but I can handle it alone. There's no reason for you to alter your plans."

Lady Kerr's halfhearted smile pricked Lucy's conscience. The woman had tried hard to be her friend. Papa had even hinted at how much it would mean to Lady Kerr to have Lucy call her Mother, but Lucy couldn't bring herself to do it. She chafed at Lady Kerr's constant reminders to lower her voice and mind her tongue and not laugh at men's rough jokes. If all a mother did was chide, perhaps she was better off without one.

At least Lady Kerr improved *Papa's* life. Though she didn't always approve of his blustering, she did love him. And she was right for him, too, strong and calm to balance his impetuous nature, and never daunted by the addle-brained things he did when distracted. Lady Kerr would make certain he didn't forget his hat.

Of course, managing Papa had been *Lucy's* job until she'd left for school. She missed that—and the dinners when he'd spun tales of India or the evenings when she'd practiced her sums for his approval. Life had been simple then.

A sigh escaped her.

As usual, Lady Kerr mistook it. "You don't have to stay. Your father and I would love to have you go with us to meet Venetia in Edinburgh. Surely another instructor can teach drawing until Mrs. Harris can replace the teacher who quit."

Lucy returned to unpacking. "Actually, I look forward to the teaching. Edinburgh is such a bore, and I should stay busy until the Season is in full swing."

And she needed to show Peter Burnes that she wasn't irresponsible. After she impressed him with her levelheaded behavior as a teacher, he would grovel at her feet, admitting he'd been wrong and begging her forgiveness.

She might forgive him. She might not. But she could do neither if she were stuck up north while he pranced about town with Lady Juliana.

Taking her stepmother's arm, Lucy guided her toward the door. "You should go. You know how Papa is about waiting." Besides, she wanted them both off so she could wallow in her misery.

They walked down in silence to find Papa pacing before the stairs. When he heard them and looked up, his irritation altered instantly to pleasure.

Most of it was for Lady Kerr. And the countess's blush further illustrated their bond.

A painful yearning pierced Lucy. Would a man ever look at *her* like that and make *her* blush? Even Peter hadn't managed that. She wasn't the blushing sort.

"There's my lassies!" Papa boomed. His manner of speaking was one thing Lady Kerr hadn't civilized out of him. "Come now, Maggie, no dawdling. We must make haste while the weather is fine, eh, Lucy?"

"No rain is our gain," Lucy parroted his oft-used remark, left over from her childhood in Spain and Portugal during the war, when long marches in bad weather meant pure misery.

"You're all settled, then?" he asked Lucy as Lady Kerr took his arm.

Papa and Lady Kerr were going off together. Without her. It was all she could do to manage a smile. "I'm fine."

With a frown, he looked her over. "You don't look fine to me. It's that idiot Peter Burnes, isn't it?"

She blinked. "How did you—"

"I'm no fool, lass. I know ye had yer heart set on him, and I saw yer face when he and that snooty Lady Juliana danced together three times at Saturday's ball. I always thought him a bit of a fribble, but I never took him for a fool until now. Ye're better off without him, d'you hear?" He chucked her under the chin. "Don't be wasting another thought on that jackanapes."

The fact that her unobservant Papa had noticed what had gone on between her and Peter was so unexpectedly sweet she burst into tears.

He stood frozen in shock until Lady Kerr nudged him. Then he hastily drew Lucy into his arms. "There, now, lass, didn't mean to make you cry. It's not so bad as all that, is it? Sh, sh, hush now."

The familiar scent of Guard's Bouquet on his collar calmed her, reminding her that he was still her dear Papa, no matter whom he'd married.

Lady Kerr held out a handkerchief, and Lucy took it gratefully, casting her stepmother a tremulous smile as she dabbed at her eyes and nose.

"As I told you," Lady Kerr said, "we'd be happy to have you come with us."

The kind remark nearly brought back Lucy's tears, but she stifled them ruthlessly. When had she become such a watering pot?

Steadying her shoulders, she pulled away. "I can't. I need to keep busy, and Mrs. Harris could use the help. I'll be fine. Really, I will."

"We'll be back in three weeks," Papa said, "but if you need us sooner, just send word."

"Thank you, Papa." Lucy kissed his cheek, then, on impulse, kissed Lady Kerr's. The bright smile she received in return made her wish she hadn't been so sharp with her earlier. "I'll miss you both," she said, and truly meant it.

She accompanied them to the coach and followed it to the end of the drive. As she strolled back, she balked at facing her unpacking. It would only provoke more tears, and she was sick of crying.

She made a sharp turn and headed across to the blooming cherry orchard that separated the school from its neighboring estate, Rockhurst. According to Mrs. Harris, Mr. Pritchard had been trying to sell it, but no one would meet his exorbitant price, since the house was nearly beyond repair. So Rockhurst had lain vacant for the past three months, which was why she felt free to wander into its orchard.

As she entered the trees, a breeze sent blossoms tumbling about her like snowflakes, and her heart lightened. Unable to resist the enticement, she kicked off her kidskin slippers and began to twirl amidst the falling blossoms as she'd done when she was a girl. The more she twirled, the less her heart ached. Her hair pulled loose from its pins to fall about her, twirling with her.

For the first time in days, she felt free to be herself, without Peter's nasty words taking her to task. When she was gasping and too light-headed to make another turn, she threw herself to the ground. Tucking her hands beneath her head, she stared up at the branches and lifted her face to the blossoms drifting gently onto her gown.

If only life could always be like this, just cherry blossoms and spring. Or even as it was during her blissful student days here, when she and the other girls learned geography and the waltz and how men could deceive you—

A sigh escaped her. She should have heeded those lessons. Instead, she'd let her imagination run away with her, soaking up the nonsense in that scandalous book of harem's tales she and the girls had read in secret. She'd convinced herself that one day she and Peter would marry and try . . . all those . . . naughty . . . things . . .

The previous night's tear-torn sleep caught up with her, and she fell into a doze. She was dreaming of a harem where the women were in charge and the sultan had to do *their* bidding, when a deep male voice penetrated her haze.

"What have we here? A local lady come to welcome me to the neighborhood? Or a goddess descended from Mount Olympus to sport with a mere mortal?"

Lucy's eyes shot open. Was she still dreaming? The devilishly handsome man standing at her feet could easily be a sultan, with his olive skin and eyes the color of roasted almonds. He'd clearly just come from a bath, for his glossy black hair lay damp on his neck. Shockingly, he wore only a white shirt tucked into black pantaloons tucked into a pair of top boots, with no waistcoat, coat, or cravat.

She had to be dreaming. No man hereabouts would leave his house in shirtsleeves. Or leave his shirt open at the throat to reveal a smattering of chest hair. Or wear pantaloons so tight they showed every well-defined muscle in his thighs. He was such a delicious specimen of manliness that he fairly took her breath away.

Meanwhile, *his* gaze slid down her body in an intimate and decidedly wicked perusal. It paused at her breasts before moving to where her gown dipped between her parted legs. After casting her stocking feet a pointed look, he smiled, his thin black mustache quirking up.

"A goddess, most assuredly," he said in faintly accented English. "No local señorita would walk about without her shoes."

Señorita? Oh, no. He wasn't her dream sultan. He was very real. And foreign. And a complete stranger.

Belatedly, she scrambled to a sitting position. Lord, what must he think of her? Before she could struggle to stand, he held out his hand. She hesitated half a second before taking it, although the moment she was on her feet, she snatched her hand free.

A chuckle escaped him. "I should beg your pardon for disturbing your siesta, but I do not regret it. You make an enchanting picture lying in the cherry blossoms."

His amusement sparked her temper. "Who are you, sir, and why are you on private property?"

He arched one finely groomed black brow. "I could ask the same of you."

"I'm a teacher at the school that adjoins this orchard." She smoothed her skirt, trying to make herself look more teacherly. It was woefully hard to do with her hair tumbled down about her waist.

"Ah, yes, the girls' academy." He cast her a speculative glance. "But that is *what* you are, not who. What is your name?"

Oh, dear, she wasn't supposed to be here, and if he were to mention it to Mrs. Harris . . . "I shan't give my name to a stranger. Especially when you haven't given me yours. *You* are the intruder here."

"Intruder! What a suspicious little thing you are," he

said without rancor. "As it happens, you already know my name. It's on my calling card."

The comment threw her into confusion. "I-I . . . haven't seen your calling card. If you left it with our school-mistress—"

"No need to dissemble, señorita. You have it right there." He reached up to pull something from behind her ear, then held it out with a flourish.

Caught off guard, she took the gilt-edged calling card from him. "How did you . . ." She trailed off as she read the printed card.

Diego Javier Montalvo, Master of Mystery.

Master of Mystery? She lifted her gaze to him, seeing nothing in his half-smile to enlighten her. It didn't sound like anything a normal person would put on a card. It almost sounded like . . .

The truth dawned. "Oh, Lord, you're a magician."

"Indeed, I am." He gave her a mock frown. "You don't seem very pleased to hear it."

Hardly! She had a weakness for magicians—their swirling black capes, their intriguing smiles, their astonishing ability to surprise at every turn. Coupled with her weakness for devastatingly handsome Continental gentlemen, Diego Javier Montalvo was the perfect temptation.

But Peter would never eat his words if he learned she'd been flirting with a stranger.

"Why is a magician wandering around Rockhurst?" she demanded. As a teacher, she would be most irresponsible if she didn't find out.

"Are you worried I have come to steal your neighbor's valuables?"

"Have you?" she asked archly.

That made him grin. "I would hardly tell you if I had." The words rolled off his tongue melodically, turning her knees to butter.

None of that! she chided herself as she glanced about for her shoes, which were nowhere to be seen. *You must be responsible. Mature. Not swayed by good-looking men. Not the sort of woman a man only dallies with.*

"Perhaps I am here to steal something else." His voice had turned calculating. "The heart of a beautiful lady like you, for example."

She burst into laughter. That sort of nonsense she could handle perfectly well. "Do you rehearse such compliments when you rehearse your tricks? Or do flatteries simply come naturally to you?"

He looked genuinely surprised. "You are very jaded for one so young."

"Young! I'll have you know I'm more than twenty years old."

His eyes seemed to mock her. "Ah, then you are clearly a woman of the world. My mistake."

She crossed her arms over her chest. "I'm certainly worldly enough to tell when a man is trying to turn me up sweet for his own purposes."

Some unreadable emotion swept his angular features. "And what purposes would those be?"

"I have no clue." She blew out an exasperated breath. "You still haven't told me what you're doing here."

"Very well, if you must know, I am the new tenant at Rockhurst."

Pure shock kept her motionless. "Oh, dear," she murmured, mortified anew.

Laughter glinted in his gaze. "So you see, Señorita Schoolteacher, *you* are the intruder. I saw you from the window upstairs as I was dressing and came down to learn who was invading my property." He reached up to pluck a leaf from her disordered hair. "*Now* will you allow me the pleasure of your name?"

Definitely not. For one thing, just the brush of his fingers over her hair had already quickened her pulse most dangerously. For another, it would be a great deal easier for him to complain of her to Mrs. Harris if he knew her name. "I-I didn't think the house was even habitable."

"It will suffice until I decide if I want to buy the estate."

But weren't conjurers nomads, living in inns and lodging houses? He was too young to retire, and even London theaters couldn't pay well enough for him to afford a property the size of Rockhurst. "What would you do with it?"

His gaze grew shuttered. "It depends."

Something in his evasive manner sparked her concern. "On what?"

"Whether it and its environs meet my stringent requirements."

Its environs? Did he mean the school? "What sort of requirements? Surely, once it is put into shape, Rockhurst would be sufficient for your family."

"I am not married." He cocked his head, dropping one raven lock over his eye, then smoothed it back with the nonchalance of a man sure of his exotic appeal. "And you? Does your position as a teacher mean you have no husband?"

She caught herself before answering. "Why are you avoiding my question?"

"For the same reason you are avoiding mine, I would imagine." His eyes gleamed with mischief. "To prolong this intriguing conversation."

A laugh bubbled up inside her that she struggled to tamp down. "Actually, I find it less intriguing than frustrating. You are purposely being mysterious."

"As are you, Señorita Schoolteacher. Indeed, your reluctance to divulge your identity fascinates me." He bent his head close enough that she caught a whiff of soap and hair oil. "You stand in my orchard and interrogate me bold as brass, yet you will not tell me something as small as your name. Are you hiding a secret? Acting as a spy?" Seeing the smile rise to her lips despite her struggle to prevent it, he lowered his voice to a throaty murmur. "Waiting for a lover, perhaps?"

She jerked back as an unfamiliar heat rose in her cheeks. Good Lord, did she give off some scent that led people to make assumptions about her character?

Then again, he *had* found her shamelessly lolling about on the ground of his orchard. She would have to set him straight.

"That's a very impertinent suggestion, sir," she answered in her loftiest tone. "Especially when we haven't been properly introduced."

A slow smile curved up his finely carved lips. "And do such trivialities matter to you, *cariño?*"

Cariño? Oh, but that was too wicked of him. Her Spanish was rusty, but she did remember that *cariño* was an endearment. A trill of pleasure skirled along her nerves. He should never have used it with her, whether he thought she understood it or not. And she certainly shouldn't let it do funny things to her insides.

She answered sharply, "This is not the Continent, sir. 'Such trivialities' matter to everyone in England. So if you hope for success in your ventures here, you'd best start showing some concern for propriety yourself."

Her remark darkened his gaze to a dangerous glitter. "I forgot how obsessed you English are with propriety," he bit out. "Except, of course, when you are invading other people's property."

He was right to chide her for that. And she'd been rude indeed to point out his improprieties when she'd been the one trespassing. Though she couldn't fathom why it angered him now, when he hadn't seemed to care earlier.

"Forgive me for intruding," she said, wanting to escape with her dignity—and identity—intact. "I must go."

She whirled toward the school but had taken only two steps before he called out, "Aren't you forgetting something?"

When she looked back, he was dangling her slippers from two fingers, his features smoothed into a charming mask once more.

"Thank you, sir," she murmured, but when she reached for the shoes, he held them out of reach, easy enough for him to do with his great height.

"Your name, señorita," he said softly, a smug smile playing over his lips.

She hesitated, weighing her choices. But there was none.

"Keep the shoes," she retorted, then ran.

Better to lose her slippers than have him inform Mrs. Harris of her shameless behavior. If Peter should hear how she'd reclined on the ground like a "hot-blooded hoyden" while some stranger looked her over, she'd simply die. As long as Señor Montalvo didn't know her name, this incident need never reach anyone. Their paths weren't likely to cross again.

Still, she wanted to warn Mrs. Harris about the man. It wouldn't do to have the girls trailing after him like lovesick puppies. Besides, something wasn't right. Why would a magician rent an estate the size of Rockhurst just for himself?

If she hadn't been so busy reacting to his flirtations, she might have pressed him for more information. But when he'd cast his hot gaze down her body and had spoken Spanish endearments in a voice of warm honey . . .

Lord help her. Continental gentlemen were the worst. Or the best, depending on how one looked at it. They knew exactly how to warm a woman's blood.

Perhaps Peter was right about her, after all.

She frowned. All right, she found the foreigner appealing, but he was a performer, for pity's sake. He made love to the audience every night—he'd honed his abilities for years. Of course she was tempted. What living, breathing female wouldn't be, when a man that sinfully attractive looked at her like that?

Peter's new love wouldn't. Lady Juliana would be appalled.

Gritting her teeth, Lucy cut through the garden while twisting her hair up in a knot. She'd best pray she never saw him again. She was much too susceptible to his charms.

She'd nearly reached the steps to the entrance when a female voice asked, "Feel better now, dear?"

Startled, she whirled to find Mrs. Harris sitting at a table, reading the newspaper. "What do you mean?" Lucy asked guiltily.

"A good walk always cheers one, doesn't it?" she said without looking up.

"Oh." She relaxed. "Yes."

Itching to get inside before Mrs. Harris noticed her missing shoes and disordered hair, she hurried forward. But the schoolmistress's cry of alarm stopped her short.

"What is it?" Lucy hastened back, all thought of her own disarray banished by the woman's stricken expression.

Shaking her head, Mrs. Harris finished scanning an article in the paper. When she threw down the paper with an unladylike oath, Lucy grabbed it up. Front and center was the headline, "Magician to Build Pleasure Garden in Richmond."

Curse it—she'd known that smooth scoundrel was up to something! She greedily read the article as Mrs. Harris rose to pace the flagstone walk.

"He means to turn Rockhurst into another Vauxhall!" Mrs. Harris exclaimed. "Can you imagine? It's a disaster! Pickpockets hiding in the orchard, watermen lounging on our river landing, music playing at all hours, and fireworks at midnight. The girls will never be able to sleep. Not to mention the scandalous goings-on that always occur at such places at night."

Between the article and Mrs. Harris's outraged recitation, Lucy gleaned the facts. Apparently, the twenty-eight-year-old Diego Montalvo was no ordinary conjurer. He was famous all over the world, performing his tricks to great acclaim before the kings of Sweden and Denmark. He'd even spent a year touring Russia, impressing the tsar with his astonishing illusions.

Now the talented fellow had come to England to raze the house next door and build a public place of amusement. Good Lord.

Mrs. Harris paced in increasing agitation. "I don't even allow my girls to visit Vauxhall strictly chaperoned. How am I to protect them with a Vauxhall rising practically at our very steps?"

Lucy glanced over at Rockhurst. She'd heard of the licentious activities occurring in Vauxhall's darkened walks while the magicians and orchestras performed. And judging from Señor Montalvo's wicked flirtations—and the newspaper description—that was exactly the sort of place he would establish.

No wonder he'd been so mysterious. The devious wretch was worse than Peter, dallying with her even as he plotted against the school she loved.

"I must write Cousin Michael at once," Mrs. Harris said. "He will know how to stop this." She whirled toward the steps, then halted to glare at the other property. "I swear, I shall have Mr. Pritchard's head. He has gone too far this time, bringing such trouble into our midst!"

Indeed, it would mean the end of the school.

Never! Lucy couldn't stand by and watch everything Mrs. Harris had worked for be destroyed with such careless disregard. This school meant too much to too many, including her. She wouldn't let Señor Montalvo get away with this. She was tired of men trampling over her and her friends.

Somehow, she'd show that scheming magician that he couldn't transform Rockhurst into a pleasure garden as easily as he thought. Then, after saving the school, she would make Peter eat his words about her being an irresponsible hoyden. Just see if she didn't.

Chapter Two

Dear Cousin,

Disaster has struck. That weasel Mr. Pritchard
plans to sell Rockhurst to that conjurer in the
newspaper, who is looking for a site for his pleasure
garden! You must stop him. If ever there was a time
for you to reveal yourself, it's now. Or I fear that the
school's future is doomed.

Your frantic friend,
Charlotte

Still clasping the slippers, an annoyed Diego Montalvo entered Rockhurst and stalked past the new servants
who were opening the essential rooms for his use. It had
been half a lifetime since he had lived in a house this size,
and he had forgotten how much work it took to maintain even a run-down place like this. Of course, he would
be gone by the time the task became too onerous . . . or
expensive.

That thought increased his annoyance as he climbed
the stairs. *Dios mio,* he was sick of the constant travel, sick
of dragging his belongings "from pillar to post," as the
English would say. He had hoped to be settled by now.
Sometimes he felt so close to regaining his family's estate,

Arboleda, that he could almost see its vineyards and feel the cool mountain breezes wash his cheeks.

But there always seemed to be an impediment—if not money, then something else. Life had a habit of biting a man in the ass when he least expected it.

Not this time. Not if he could prevent it.

He strode into Rockhurst's master bedchamber to find Gaspar, his aging mentor, unpacking the trunk and setting out the rest of Diego's attire for the day with gnarled and twisted hands.

"Stop that," Diego said, knowing how even such simple actions caused the man pain. "I can do it perfectly well myself."

"If you don't leave it to me," Gaspar retorted, "the servants will suspect that I'm not what I seem. And you know how servants talk."

Gritting his teeth, Diego threw the slippers onto the bed. "I suppose I do."

Gaspar had chosen to play his valet on this extended trip to England because it better enabled them to gather information from the staffs of the households they watched. Still, Diego hated putting the old man in such a humiliating role, even if their success would benefit them both in the end.

Gaspar had been a talented magician until arthritis set in years ago, forcing him to give up the profession. Fortunately, by then, he had already begun training Diego in the conjurer's art. Diego had become his whole family, since Gaspar had no one else to look after him—no wife or children or relations.

Exactly like Diego himself.

A shudder wracked him. *No, not me.* He was not meant for the rootless life of a performer. How his parents would have cringed to see what their only son had become. After what they had sacrificed, it was a mockery. He would not let their sacrifice be in vain.

He had been raised for something better, and he would take up his birthright again as soon as he and Gaspar found the Marqués de Parama's granddaughter. Then he could honor the vow he'd made to his father to regain Arboleda and restore his family's reputation and position. Gaspar would have a place of comfort in which to end his days. Diego could even marry and raise a family. He wanted none of this life for any wife or children of *his.*

Walking to the window, Diego drew out the ivory ball he used for practice and manipulated it through his fingers as he surveyed the adjoining property. When he spotted two women talking on the steps, his heart began to pound.

Yes, it was long past time he married. He needed a woman of his own. Why else had he let that lovely female standing down there rattle him so badly?

The other woman didn't interest him—he assumed she was "that red-haired virago who owns the school," as Pritchard had described her. But Señorita Schoolteacher . . .

An image of her stretched out on a bed of cherry blossoms flamed into his memory. He was not likely to forget *that* anytime soon. With her fine bosom rising and falling with each breath, her dark hair spread around her, she'd been a picture to fire any man's blood. She had smiled in her slumber, her succulent mouth parting so temptingly that he had half considered playing the prince to her Sleeping Beauty and kissing her awake.

He should have done it. She might have slapped him for it, but it would have been worth the risk. Because her lush eyelashes had parted to reveal lovely hazel eyes, and in those first few moments, the look in those eyes had been utterly without guile or fear.

That had changed soon enough.

Even now, Señorita Schoolteacher looked belligerent as she tucked a newspaper beneath her arm, then glanced up at his window. Though the sun glinting off the glass prevented her from seeing him, he jerked back.

Hostias, he could not believe she was still rattling him.

Yet he had not rattled her in the least. He had used that "card behind the ear" maneuver a thousand times. It never failed to amuse the ladies and soften their tempers. Why had it not worked with her?

I can tell when a man is trying to turn me up sweet for his own purposes.

He grimaced. She had seen right through him. Women rarely did. It was irritating to have some twenty-year-old slip of a teacher do so—and intriguing, too. He seldom met women that perceptive. He was not certain what to make of it. What to make of her.

Thumbing his mustache, he watched as she gestured at Rockhurst. She was probably complaining about his lack of "propriety."

He stiffened. If she hadn't set off his temper, he might still be in the orchard with her, enjoying more than mere conversation. For a moment near the end, when a delicious smile had tugged at her lips and her eyes had grown suspiciously bright, he had been sure he had succeeded with her at last.

Until she had insulted him. Haughty female, citing the

English as the model of propriety. Like most English ladies, she had no idea what her countrymen were really like when their masks were off.

The next time he encountered Señorita Schoolteacher, he would manage himself better. And her.

"So?" Gaspar asked. "What happened with the servant we saw from the window? And how did you acquire a pair of lady's slippers?"

"As it happens, she wasn't a servant but a teacher."

"Then she's no use to us," Gaspar said dismissively.

"I do not agree. We need a source inside." That was why he had hurried down in the midst of dressing—to see if the lovely woman lying in the grass might provide them an entrée to the school.

After tossing his practice ball onto the bed, Diego drew out the miniature given him by the *marqués*. As Diego stared at the serene face of a beautiful young Spanish woman dressed in an outmoded fashion, Gaspar muttered a curse. "Don Carlos's granddaughter may not look like her mother, you know. She might resemble her father instead, and we have no miniature for him."

"Or worst of all, she might look like her grandfather."

They laughed. The *marqués*'s squinty eyes, bulbous nose, and sour mouth gave him the appearance of a very cranky toad. Diego could not fathom how the rich old grandee had spawned as lovely a creature as Doña Catalina.

"Father or mother, it matters not," he said. "Both are Spanish. The girl will surely stand out among these pasty-faced English."

"Not even all of the Spanish look Spanish. Better not to rely on that image to find her." Gaspar hung up one of Diego's shirts. "I wouldn't trust that teacher's word, either. Teachers must be discreet. Servants, however, can be bought."

"Fine," Diego said irritably. "Feel free to establish a connection with a servant if you think that's best. *I* intend to work on the schoolteacher."

He and Gaspar had perfected their technique during two months of trailing about Britain, pretending to seek out sites for a pleasure garden. First, locate the daughter of the next man on their list of soldiers who'd served in Gibraltar. Then glean whatever knowledge they could about the female from servants and acquaintances. Finally, insinuate themselves into the lady's intimate circle to determine if she was the one they sought.

It had not helped that the *marqués* had given them so little information to go on. All he could tell them was that his granddaughter's nurse had run off with a soldier from the Forty-second Regiment fifteen years ago, stealing his four-year-old granddaughter in the process. He'd had no name for the man, no description, and little description of the nurse. Only recently had he even learned that the nurse's lover was an English soldier.

Diego and Gaspar had laboriously compiled a list of possible names. The four women they had already investigated had lacked backgrounds that fit the facts. Their sources had said that the daughter of the next soldier on their list was presently enrolled at Mrs. Harris's School for Young Ladies.

Their sources had damned well better be right. He was tired of this madness.

With a flick of his fingers, Diego returned the miniature to his pocket. "I believe the teacher will be more useful for our purpose than any servant."

Liar. It had nothing to do with her usefulness. Diego was simply galled that he had not succeeded better with her. She had actually laughed at his compliments!

When Gaspar snorted, Diego turned to find the man watching him, eyes as sharp as ever. Gaspar pointed his chin at the window. "So, what's her name?"

Diego gritted his teeth. "I did not . . . catch it."

Understandably, Gaspar raised an eyebrow at that. Diego always "caught" people's names. His memory for them was part of his appeal. The audience, particularly the ladies, loved it when he could call their names from the stage.

Yet he had not gained Señorita Schoolteacher's. Although he might have, if not for ending the conversation prematurely by losing his temper.

That, too, galled. He rarely lost control in such a manner. Rage was too volatile and dangerous an emotion to allow. Give it free rein, and you ended up dead, either at the hand of another or at the hand of the hangman.

Lately, however, his temper had been plaguing him. With each new failure to locate Don Carlos's grand-daughter, his anger grew a little more. If the ailing *marqués* died before Diego and Gaspar fulfilled their part of the bargain, they got nothing. So Señorita Schoolteacher looking down her pretty nose at him and lecturing him about proprieties had provoked his temper more than usual.

"You will have to discover the woman's name yourself," Diego told Gaspar, "but that should not be too hard. How many teachers can there be in such a place?"

"What does she teach?" When Diego groaned, the old man laughed. "You didn't get that either? I'll have to find out what this English paragon eats that makes her impervious to your attractions. She must be a rare bird indeed."

"I did learn that she is twenty," Diego shot back, annoyed. "That seems young for a teacher, so that is something to go on. *You* are the one who claims to be able to weasel information out of a stone. Why not put your talent to good use?"

"Don't carp at me," Gaspar grumbled. "I swear, you are as surly as a bear these days. And I know why."

"Because we keep running into obstacles?"

"Because you need a woman, that's why. How long has it been?"

"Not that long," Diego lied.

"A year." When Diego's startled gaze shot to him, he said, "Yes, I have noticed. You ignore even the fine ladies who cast you come-hither looks, and you take no one to your room."

"I have more important things on my mind these days than rutting."

"Nonetheless, you should spend your pent-up energy on something besides work. Why not just tumble a whore and be done with it? It will do you good."

"*Dios mio,* I do not *want* to tumble a whore!" he snapped. "I am sick of whores. For that matter, I am sick of fine ladies. They only wish to share my bed to say they have lain with the 'great' Diego Montalvo. Or to provoke their husbands."

"You didn't used to mind that."

"I didn't used to mind a great many things." He threaded his fingers through his hair. "Plowing every field that came my way was fine when I was too young and stupid to know any better, but now I want . . . I want . . . ."

He wanted so very much. He wanted to go home to Villafranca to blot out all memory of the charming trickster he had played for the past fifteen years. He wanted the life of dignity and honor that the English and French had stolen from him, the life he should have had. And that life did not include bedding whores.

"I know what you want," Gaspar said softly. "But are you sure that having the *marqués* sign Arboleda back over to you will satisfy you? It's been years since you lived there. You may find it isn't the Eden you remember."

"That does not matter." Diego could hardly speak for the turmoil churning in his chest. "What kind of man would I be if I did not keep my vow to Father?"

"A sensible one, that's what. When you promised him you'd restore it to what it once was, neither of you could have anticipated that your mother would have to sell the estate. You've done your best to fulfill his dying wish. Perhaps it's time to let that dream pass." Gaspar slid Diego's shirts into the tallboy. "This life has its compensations, doesn't it? Especially for a conjurer as talented as you."

But its compensations paled beside his failure to accomplish his life's dream. Gaspar did not understand that.

Gaspar turned for the door, then paused. "I almost forgot to tell you. Have you seen today's *Times*?"

"Not yet. Why?"

Gaspar picked up a newspaper, opened it to a page, and shoved it under Diego's nose. Diego read the headline, then read it again.

He shook the paper. "What is this?" Another obstacle, damn it.

Gaspar shrugged. "Perhaps Pritchard talked to the press."

"But I only told Pritchard that nonsense to get him to lease us the place! If I had wanted the papers to know, I would have told them myself." The press had its uses when advertising one's appearances. But when trying to hide one's true purpose, it could be damned inconvenient.

"We were free enough with the tale everywhere else— why should it make a difference here? No one will care."

Diego scowled. "Are you mad? No one will care that a foreigner is building a garden of sin and iniquity next to a girls' academy? Think, man. Would you send your gently bred daughter to a boarding school with a pleasure garden abutting the property? If the owner is wise, she will soon be up in arms over the prospect. If she is not already," he added, remembering the newspaper he had seen in Señorita Schoolteacher's hand.

He picked up the ivory ball again, working it in a frenzy. "Damn the press. I have to cajole them into mentioning an upcoming performance, but tell one white lie to an idiot Englishman, and they blast the news everywhere."

"You could deny it," Gaspar suggested. "Offer them an interview. State that you are only here to plan a future tour of the country."

Diego shook his head. "Pritchard will evict us if we change our tale. He only agreed to lease Rockhurst if I was reasonably interested in buying. No, we will have to find another way to lessen the damage. Perhaps if we live here quietly for a while before we begin asking our questions . . ." He paced the floor, still working the ivory ball. It helped him to think. "Then again . . ." His mind raced ahead, considering possibilities.

"Then again, what?" Gaspar prodded.

Dropping the ball onto the bed, Diego wheeled to face his mentor. "This could work to our advantage."

"How? Trying to gain information is a business of discretion. We do not want to call attention to ourselves."

Diego laughed, startling Gaspar. "That is *exactly* what we want to do. I gave Señorita Schoolteacher a vague story about trying to determine if the area would suit my purposes, but what if we turned it into the truth? What if we were to visit local businesses, make a show of our plans to build a place of amusement?"

"I don't see—"

Diego seized Gaspar by his stock with one hand, while relieving him of his handkerchief with the other. "What is the magician's most beloved precept?" When Gaspar just stared, Diego waved the handkerchief in his face. "Misdirection. Draw the observer's attention one place while you work elsewhere."

With a scowl, Gaspar snatched his handkerchief back. "But if you're right about the school's owner, then the attention focused on us won't be friendly. They'll watch our every move with distrust."

"But they will be looking for the wrong thing. Besides, if I know women, they will not just watch. They will try to change our minds. That gives us a chance to ingratiate ourselves with them."

"Ah, you intend to charm them."

"With a vengeance."

Gaspar arched one gray eyebrow. "This has naught to do with that teacher turning up her nose at you, does it?"

"Do not be absurd. I am only thinking of how to solve our problem." He cast Gaspar an earnest glance. "And this will work, I am sure of it."

"It does sound promising."

"Excellent! Then we're agreed. We shall take a couple of days to settle into our new home and let the news circulate. Then we take Richmond by storm—beginning with our neighbors at the school."

He allowed himself a private smile. *Particularly Señorita Schoolteacher.*

Chapter Three

❧

Dear Charlotte,
    I knew nothing of this until now, but I will
do my best to find out how this Montalvo can
be stopped. I am appalled that Pritchard could
countenance selling his property for such a purpose.
I will see what I can discover about the project and
let you know what I learn.

                                Your outraged cousin,
                                Michael

$\mathcal{T}$wo days after Lucy's encounter with Señor Montalvo,
the school's formal parlor filled up with graduates attend-
ing Mrs. Harris's monthly tea. Since the students wouldn't
arrive until later that afternoon, the older women had the
place to themselves.

And they were preparing for war. As the daughter of a
decorated colonel, Lucy knew that war required plenty of
recruits and lots of space.

The news about Mr. Pritchard's tenant had shot across
town like a cannon ball, even drawing ladies who'd long
been happily married. The teas were intended to help eligible heiresses learn how to avoid fortune-hunting scoundrels, so only a few married women generally attended to

visit their friends and give advice. Today, however, nearly everyone was here.

Just as the ladies gathered in the parlor, Mrs. Harris was informed of an unexpected arrival—Mr. Pritchard himself. As she left to find out what she could from the horrible little man, the schoolmistress instructed Lucy to begin the meeting herself.

Lucy stood there stunned. Mrs. Harris was entrusting *her* with such a task? What an honor!

And what a responsibility! The weight of it settled heavily on her as she surveyed the parlor full of distinguished graduates.

Viscountess Kirkwood stood chatting with the wife of the Lord Mayor of Bath. Near them sat Lucy's former teacher, the newly married Lady Norcourt. And was that the Duchess of Foxmoor on a settee near the door? Panic seized Lucy. Good Lord, when had *she* arrived?

Not that it wasn't wonderful to have her. Her charitable works were legendary, and she had the influence to be effective in the campaign against Señor Montalvo. But although Lucy had been introduced to her at a ball last week, they'd spoken only a moment. Why in the dickens should the duchess listen to *her*?

Lucy wiped her clammy hands on the skirts of her best day gown. Mrs. Harris wouldn't have given her the responsibility if she hadn't thought Lucy could handle it. She must not let Mrs. Harris down. She could do this.

Stay calm. Don't say the first thing that pops into your head. That's what always gets you into trouble.

Drawing in a measured breath, Lucy walked to the podium. But before she could rap the gavel, a peal of laughter sounded from one end of the room, and a monkey scampered across the back of a sofa.

Oh no, the duchess had brought her husband's famous pet, Raji. He leaped onto the Viscountess Kirkwood's lap, eliciting a startled shriek that sent him flying under the duchess's chair to cover his ears. Everyone laughed—except Lady Kirkwood.

"Merciful heavens, Louisa," the viscountess complained, examining her satin skirts. "Would you please cage that annoying creature? I just bought this gown, and if that vile animal tears it, Kirkwood will restrict my allowance again."

The Duchess of Foxmoor arched an eyebrow. "And here I'd thought that your husband restricted your allowance because of your fondness for faro, Sarah."

A strained silence fell across the room. Everyone knew that the duchess and Lady Kirkwood disliked each other, despite their husbands' friendship. The truth was, no one else much liked the snooty Lady Kirkwood either. She'd been called Silly Sarah in her day, and some still called her that behind her back, because she insisted on gambling away her pin money. Mrs. Harris had tried to instill a dislike of gambling in her students, but it hadn't worked with Lady Kirkwood.

The viscountess flipped open her fan. "You ought to try faro yourself, Louisa. I should think your little jaunts to the prison to help the poor convict ladies would get tedious. What's the point of marrying a duke if you don't enjoy what his position can give you?"

"And repay his generosity by spending him into the poorhouse?"

Lady Kirkwood pouted at the duchess. "My husband wouldn't have *any* money if not for me. I don't see why I shouldn't get a bit of it for myself. You really should learn how to coax your duke into doing what *you* please." She scowled over at Raji, who lolled in another lady's lap. "The first thing you should do is inform him that his disgusting pet is not allowed in polite company."

Apparently, the duke's "disgusting pet" knew an insult when he heard it, for he promptly turned around and presented Lady Kirkwood with his naked bottom.

The other ladies burst into laughter.

"I believe Raji has just told you what he thinks of your opinion," the duchess said, eyes twinkling.

Lady Kirkwood glared at her. "If that nasty animal doesn't watch it, he'll find himself dead at the bottom of a privy one day." There was no mistaking who meant to put him there, either.

When the duchess's face darkened, Lucy figured she'd best take matters in hand. "Your concern for Raji is admirable, Lady Kirkwood," she put in. "But I'm sure he's much too clever to fall into a privy."

The silence in the room thickened.

Lucy gripped the edge of the podium. "Still, given his tendency to wander off, Raji might be safer if he spent the meeting in Mrs. Harris's office." She cast the duchess a pleading glance. "Don't you agree, Your Grace?"

Fortunately, the duchess was too astute not to notice Lucy's consternation—and too kind to add to it. "I'm sure he would, Miss Seton," she said graciously. "I'll take him there myself." Picking up her pet, the duchess left the room.

"Now then," Lucy said, taking advantage of the lull in

conversation. "I believe you've all heard about Mr. Pritchard's new tenant."

That shifted everyone's attention to the proper subject. Swiftly, Lucy sketched out what they'd probably read in the papers. By the time the duchess returned, Lucy was explaining what else she and Mrs. Harris had learned. Señor Montalvo hadn't yet applied to the city's licensing magistrates.

"Our best course of attack is to sway public opinion to our side." Lucy handed out the sheets of foolscap they'd prepared. "We are starting a petition to keep him from gaining a license, and we're asking you to spend the next few days gathering names from the good people of Richmond. It shouldn't be difficult to convince them that a pleasure garden in our midst can only lead to disaster."

Lady Kirkwood snorted. "That's rather overdramatic, Miss Seton, don't you think? At least a pleasure garden would give people something to do in this dull town. The theater here is pathetic."

"Pathetic it may be," Lady Norcourt said tersely, "but it doesn't draw roués and rakehells next door to the school, where they can prey on our girls." As always, the former teacher's main concern was for the students' welfare.

"You're exactly right, Lady Nor—" Lucy began.

"Perhaps Mrs. Harris should just speak to this Montalvo fellow," the naive lord mayor's wife spoke up. "I'm sure she could persuade him to ban unsavory men from his establishment. They do it at Almack's."

"Almack's is not remotely like—" Lucy began.

"Speaking of that magician," said another lady in an eager-to-gossip voice, "has anyone actually seen the man? I'm told that he left a string of brokenhearted princesses behind him on his Russian tour."

Lucy found that vaguely annoying. She wasn't sure why, since it was exactly what she would expect of Mr. Too Charming for Words.

"Oh, he's very handsome," said a banker's wife with sly assurance. "And quite dashing. He made all the ladies swoon when I saw him perform in Italy."

When that got everyone's attention, she went on gleefully. "And his tricks are every bit as amazing as they say. He had someone choose a card without telling him what it was and then returned it to the deck, which he tied up with string. Then he tossed the bound deck up in the air. When it came back down, the chosen card was attached to the ceiling. It gave me shivers, I tell you. Even my husband couldn't figure out how the man did it. And then Señor Montalvo—"

Lucy rapped her gavel. "While I'm sure the man excels at his profession, what he intends to build next door would ruin all that Mrs. Harris has worked for."

For a moment, the ladies sat blinking at her, and she thought she'd regained control. Then they turned back to the banker's wife.

"Is he married?" asked one.

"What other tricks did he perform?" asked another.

"Ladies, please," Lucy cut in, but they paid her no mind.

"Do you know how old he is?" asked an unmarried lady.

"Is it true he can catch a bullet in his teeth?" asked the lord mayor's wife.

"It doesn't matter if he can catch a bullet in his *nose!*" Lucy cried. When everyone gaped at her, she realized she'd shrieked the words. But she didn't care.

"Señor Montalvo is a menace to everything we hold precious," she went on fervently. The drawing-room door opened behind her, but she was too caught up to pay it any heed. "And if you succumb to his tricks and physical attractions without a protest, you might as well consort with the devil himself!"

For a moment, the words echoed in the immense silence. Then it was punctured by a low male laugh that sent her stomach plummeting.

She whirled to find Mrs. Harris and the Spaniard himself standing there.

"'Better the devil you know,'" said Señor Montalvo, his eyes glinting with fiendish amusement. "Or so I'm told."

Lucy wanted to sink through the floor. Especially when everyone in the room laughed, as if it were all a grand joke. As if *she* were a grand joke. Bother it all, how was she to save the school if she couldn't even hold her tongue?

Mrs. Harris wore a pained smile, but as always in situations when her charges made public fools of themselves, she pretended it hadn't happened.

"Ladies," Mrs. Harris said as she approached the podium. When Lucy moved aside, the schoolmistress grabbed her hand to stay her, then squeezed it reassuringly. "Mr. Pritchard was kind enough to come introduce our new neighbor, who has asked to address you. So please welcome to the school Mr. . . ." She glanced at the magician. "Forgive me, but I'm not sure exactly what to call you. Is it Señor or Mister?"

"Diego will be fine," he said smoothly. "I am not one to worry overmuch about proprieties." Looking over at Lucy, he had the audacity to wink.

That chilled her. There was nothing to stop him from telling everyone about finding her splayed on the ground like a doxy. Oh, she'd simply die if he did!

Could she claim he was lying? Anyone could see he was an unconscionable scoundrel.

She sighed. Not anyone, judging from how the women had gushed over him. And not when he looked like *that*. He was almost more spectacular fully dressed. Lord help her, how did such a dastardly fellow manage to cut such a fine figure?

It was more than the excellent tailoring of his dark blue Saxony coat or the fine sheen of his understated silk waist-coat. It was the tall, muscular body they contained. Like a sleek panther, he padded carelessly among the pigeons. His longish hair marked him instantly as being different from other men in society, with their elegant curls. So did his whisper of a dark mustache. Englishmen simply didn't look like him. And he not only knew it but used it to cap-tivate his audience.

Just as he used his tricks. Lucy scowled when he plucked a silk rose from thin air, then presented it to Mrs. Harris amid a smattering of applause.

"Thank you for the opportunity to speak with your lovely ladies," he said in that husky tone designed to lull any woman into doing as he wished.

But although Mrs. Harris accepted the rose in one hand, she squeezed Lucy's hand hard with the other. Could the woman have some plan in mind?

When he moved to the podium, Lucy turned her gaze to the audience to find the duchess and some others openly frowning. Perhaps all wasn't lost.

Señor Montalvo offered the audience an amiable smile. "I should like to assuage your fears regarding my plans for

Rockhurst. It is true that I mean to develop the property into a pleasure garden." He ignored the low murmurs provoked by that comment. "But I assure you that I shall take your concerns into account. I have no desire to harm this admirable institution, if I can prevent it."

When someone snorted loudly, he arched one brow. "Have you any questions? I am happy to answer them."

"You insult our intelligence, sir." The duchess shot to her feet. "We know that men generally ignore our wishes where business is concerned."

"And you, madam, insult my honor," he countered with quiet dignity. "Did I not just say I mean to take your concerns into account?"

The duchess's lips thinned. "Have you considered that your establishment will draw men of every stamp, who will surely accost our young ladies?"

"While your students would undoubtedly tempt any man, you need not worry about the gentlemen who will visit my gardens," he said with an ingratiating smile. "Unlike other popular amusement places, mine will be open only in the evenings, when your pupils are ensconced in their beds."

The quick burst of laughter in the room seemed to take him by surprise.

Lady Norcourt rose to stand next to the duchess. "This is no Continental convent school, where we pack our charges off to bed at dusk," the former teacher chided. "Our girls have lessons on astronomy in the evenings in our garden. Some read aloud in the parlor; others perform music. And if you think that on a hot summer night, they'll wish to keep the windows and doors locked up against your visitors, you're quite mad."

"Then I will build a wall. I can wall off the entire place if need be."

"But surely you do not expect your visitors to limit themselves to approaching the park from the river," the duchess said. "Many will use the road, so they'll be forced to leave their carriages alongside it for miles. What is to keep the gentlemen—if such they can be termed—from strolling down our drive?"

"Perhaps I will build a wall around the school as well." Exasperation showed in his handsome features. "Though it would seem to me that gently bred pupils should not be allowed to roam freely without a male escort, pleasure garden or no."

"So now we'll need male escorts on our own grounds out in the country?" Lady Norcourt shot back. "And where can we find the men to accommodate our young ladies? We can hardly find enough town lads to attend our assemblies as it is."

"I think Señor Montalvo is saying that the school will require more footmen," the duchess remarked slyly.

"But someone would have to pay these footmen," Lady Norcourt pointed out. "And all to protect our girls from unsavory gentlemen who attend these gardens?"

"I did not mean that the school should hire additional servants," Señor Montalvo protested.

He was ignored. "We have more than unsavory gentlemen to worry about," the lord mayor's wife remarked. "Ladies of ill repute inevitably flock to pleasure gardens, and we certainly do not want *them* about."

A smile tugged at Lucy's lips. Señor Montalvo's expression grew more annoyed by the moment. She doubted that he found their observations quite to his liking. Apparently, Mrs. Harris had planned this outcome all along.

"There are other concerns as well—" the duchess began.

"Thank you," he said with an air of finality, looking exactly like grandees Lucy had seen in Spain: arrogant, proud, and formidable. "I will carefully weigh your concerns." He bowed to the ladies. "Now, if you will excuse me, I must return to Rockhurst. You have given me a great deal to think on."

"You have given *us* a great deal to think on as well," Mrs. Harris said as she cast him a considering look. "It will help us know how to act."

He nodded with an air of nonchalance that seemed at odds with his purpose. Didn't he realize he'd just lost the first skirmish? Why wasn't he more upset?

"Miss Seton will show you out." Mrs. Harris winked at Lucy and added, "I'm sure she can answer any questions you might have. She knows more about the school than anyone."

And Mrs. Harris was clearly counting on Lucy to voice her opinions.

Lucy would do so, too . . . after she made sure that Señor Montalvo wasn't going to tell anyone about finding her in the orchard.

She didn't trust him. Something in his manner made her wary, and it wasn't only his charm and smooth compliments. Some instinct told her that he posed a threat to more than just the school, though she wasn't sure what or how.

But she would find out. She would be calm, rational, and determined. She meant to uncover the nasty details of his plan, no matter what he pulled out of his sleeve.

Chapter Four

Dear Cousin,

We plan to thwart our new neighbor by petitioning the licensing magistrates to refuse him a license. It was Miss Seton's idea—she has proved quite an asset. She has matured so much. Granted, she is still outspoken, but I do not find that nearly as annoying in a teacher as in a pupil. Teachers <u>should</u> be opinionated. And it will serve her well in navigating society's treacherous waters.

Your harried relation,
Charlotte

Miss Seton? Diego stood frozen, trying to gather his wits. He could not have heard correctly. Señorita Schoolteacher was his quarry? Could he possibly be so fortunate?

When she hurried to the door, he struggled to mask his surprise as he followed her. But once they left the parlor, he could no longer restrain his need for information. "Your name is Seton?"

She nodded.

"Spelled S-e-t-o-n?" He had to be sure. The next soldier on their list was a Colonel Seton.

"Yes, that's how I spell it." She narrowed her eyes. "Why? Do you know the name?"

"No," he said hastily. *Watch what you say, man. You must not give anything away until you are absolutely certain of the facts. Too much is at stake.* "After you were so stingy with it two days ago, I merely want to be sure I have it right."

As expected, that reference distracted her sufficiently. She slowed her steps and looked as if she meant to say something, but before she could, a young girl cleared the top of the stairs and stopped in front of them.

Miss Seton broke into a smile of genuine pleasure. "Why, Tessa, aren't you looking all grown-up these days?" she said, and opened her arms.

"Lucy!" The girl rushed into her embrace. "My aunt said you were here!"

He stood back watching, his mind awhirl. Lucy. Her Christian name. That was short for Lucinda, wasn't it? Lucinda Seton was the colonel's daughter, according to their sources in Edinburgh.

Lucinda also just happened to be the name of Doña Catalina's daughter. That had been one reason they had placed her so high on the list—on the chance that the nurse had not changed her name after stealing her.

So Señorita Schoolteacher *was* their quarry, and he had stumbled upon her almost immediately.

Take care, he cautioned himself. *Remember what the marqués said. This is a delicate situation.*

Even if she was the Lucinda Seton they sought, it merely meant she was next on their list. He must be sure of the facts before he revealed his purpose.

Besides, Lucy might be short for Lucia or Lucretia. He did not know enough about English names to be certain. And Miss Seton did not look remotely Spanish. Nor was she a student, as their sources had claimed.

While the girl named Tessa babbled on, he surveyed her teacher, searching for some hint of the woman's foreign blood.

She lacked any olive tone to her skin, and her eyes were not dark. Her features did not resemble Doña Catalina's, though both women were beautiful in their own ways. Where Doña Catalina's image evoked the serenity of a Madonna, Miss Seton's evoked the sensuality of a Mary Magdalene. Her features were rounder, softer, her nose less narrow. Her full lips tempted a man to taste and plunder.

God preserve his soul. He must not think of her in such terms. If she proved to be the *marqués's* granddaughter . . .

But today the silken female witchery she wore showed off her lush hips and ripe breasts only too well. The slender span of her waist made him itch to put his hands on it and draw her close.

Then there was her hair—a rich chestnut brown, the texture of rumpled velvet. When down, it had fallen in undulating waves about her slender shoulders, reaching to her hips. What he would give to see it like that again . . .

A pang of regret stung him that he ruthlessly shook off. It did not matter how pretty she was. It did not even matter if she roused his blood. She had a more important purpose: she could be the key to his escape from this dreary life of odorous hotels, tasteless inn meals, and cold theaters in icy climes. The key to home, to restoring his family honor. He would not jeopardize that.

"And who is this?" young Tessa asked as she turned to him. She had been shooting him curious glances. "A new teacher?"

"Hardly," Miss Seton said. "This is Señor Diego Montalvo, our new neighbor. Señor Montalvo, this is Miss Tessa Dalton. She's a student here."

The girl sketched a pretty curtsy beneath the approving eye of Miss Seton.

"Delighted to meet you." Diego reached out and pretended to pluck a sixpence from behind the girl's ear.

When he presented it to her, she seized it with a laugh of delight. "That was amazing!" the girl exclaimed. "How did you do that?"

"It is nothing for a man like me," he quipped. "Ask Miss Seton—she has already determined that I am the devil himself."

He had the very great pleasure of seeing the teacher blush to the roots of her pretty hair. "I-I did not mean to call you the devil," she stammered.

"I think you did." He chuckled. "But do not worry. You would not be the first to call me such, nor the last. Conjurers often bring forth such responses."

"You know perfectly well I was not referring to your profession."

Tessa's eyes went wide. "You must be that magician my aunt and uncle have been talking about! The one who wants to ruin the school!"

He gritted his teeth. "I have no desire to—"

"Tessa's aunt is Lady Norcourt," Miss Seton explained with a mischievous expression. "She was the woman who joined the Duchess of Foxmoor in criticizing your plans. Lady Norcourt taught here before she married a viscount."

If Miss Seton thought to intimidate him by citing the rich and titled friends of the school, she was in for a surprise. He had dined with kings—he could handle a few English lords. Especially when he meant the school no harm anyway.

But he must play his role, so he smiled at Tessa. "Please tell your aunt and uncle that they should not listen to idle gossip about my intentions. I merely want to enhance the adjoining property, not ruin your school."

Miss Seton snorted. "Tessa, if you go to Mrs. Harris's office, you'll find a surprise there."

Tessa's face lit up. "What surprise?"

"Go and see. I think you'll be pleased."

Young Tessa looked torn between wanting to stay and hear the gossip and the temptation of her "surprise." The latter apparently proved too much. "I hope we can talk later," she told Miss Seton. Then, after a quick curtsy for him, she raced off.

"I see that bribery still works as well on pupils as it did in my youth," he remarked as Miss Seton headed for the stairs once more. "Do you even have a surprise for that poor girl? Or was that merely a ploy?"

She eyed him askance. "It just so happens that the duke's pet monkey is in the office. Since Tessa adores animals, I knew she'd enjoy keeping him entertained." Lifting her skirts, she descended the stairs. "Unlike you, Señor Montalvo, I am forthright and honest in my dealings with people."

She was using her "proper" voice from two days ago, but he began to wonder if it was her real one. Her impassioned remarks in the meeting suited her more than this formal façade.

"How have I not been forthright and honest with you?" he teased.

She shot him a mutinous look. "When we first met, you didn't say one word about what you really intended for Rockhurst. You were purposely evasive."

He had to restrain a laugh. "Ah, yes. But as I recall, you were equally evasive."

Her face clouded over as they reached the bottom of the stairs. "I do hope you aren't planning to mention to anyone where . . . that is, *how* we first met."

"Why should I?" That wouldn't suit his purposes.

When relief spread over her face, he remembered how prickly the English were about their propriety. *Dios mio,* that must be why she hadn't told him her name—for fear that he would speak to her employer about something as inconsequential as finding her in the orchard behaving with the exuberance of any other young woman.

He wanted to laugh. No wonder he had failed to charm her then. She had probably hoped that withholding her name would protect her.

Little did she know. Now that he knew her identity, nothing would protect her from him. Especially if she turned out to be the *marqués*'s granddaughter. Already, he could taste his success.

And her English propriety could be used to his advantage. "Since you would not want your employer to hear how I found you on my property in such fetching disarray, I will expect compensation for my silence, of course."

Paling, she halted to face him. "What sort of compensation?"

"More time spent in your company."

With a look of sheer outrage, she crossed her arms over her chest. "And I suppose you want this time to be spent . . . privately."

Any other woman would be flattered. But not Miss English Propriety, oh, no. It should not annoy him, yet it did. "I am not so much a devil as to expect *that*. I merely wish to see more of the school you prize so highly, and I thought you might be willing to show it to me."

"Really?" she said warily.

"Absolutely." It would give him an excuse to question Miss Seton further about her background; he needed time and opportunity to confirm her identity.

"I have invested a large sum in coming to England and surveying sites to find the right one for my purposes." That was why they had chosen the ruse of the pleasure garden. It gave them reasons to travel as they pleased, ask questions in insular communities, and spend time in popular watering spots without rousing suspicion. For a foreigner in England, that was essential.

It also ensured that they could stay as long as necessary. Although a tour of performances would have allowed that as well, it would have restricted them to certain cities and times, making their task more difficult.

"So despite what you think," he went on, "I am none too eager to launch into a scheme that might anger you and your neighbors. On the other hand, if I am forced to abandon this site, I will sustain a substantial financial loss: the three-month lease I signed with Mr. Pritchard, the expenses of travel, the funds I do not earn while I wait to open my business. You see my dilemma."

She softened a fraction. "I suppose."

"This is your chance to convince me I should change

my plans," he said as a footman brought him his hat and coat. "Show me how the school operates. Accompany me to one of those assemblies the ladies mentioned." He shot her a smile of challenge. "What could it hurt?"

As usual, she was stubborn. "Why not ask Mrs. Harris to show you? Or even Terence, her personal footman?"

Diego fought a grimace. Mrs. Harris had a formidable footman, rumored to be a former boxer. He had met the surly fellow going in, and the last thing he wanted was to deal with *that* belligerent ass.

"Mrs. Harris's financial interest in the place ensures a certain bias, as does her footman's. But you seem to have an attachment that runs deeper than money." He shrugged. "Though I cannot imagine why a mere instructor should be so devoted."

"Actually, I was a student here before I became a teacher."

Aha, that explained the confusion in that regard.

"I came here when I was twelve," she added. "It has largely been my home ever since."

That gave him pause, though it fed certain suspicions he'd had about her upbringing. If her "father," the colonel, had been the nurse's lover, as he and Gaspar suspected, he might not have been keen to raise a child not his own. Especially since the nurse, who must have pretended to be her mother, had apparently died before she came to England.

Diego played dumb. "You have no parents?"

"Of course I have parents. Well, a father. And a step-mother, but—" She caught herself. "The point is, when I have not been with my family, I've been here. I would hate to see it harmed."

Ah, she was so easy to provoke into saying too much. He rather liked that about her. She was exactly what she seemed, which was more than he could say for her treacherous countrymen. "Then the matter lies in your hands." He slid into his greatcoat, trying not to let her see how much her answer mattered. "I have not yet bought Rockhurst. My mind can be changed. Who better to change it than you?"

A tiny frown formed between her nicely shaped brows. "And if I agree to this scheme, you'll keep quiet about finding me in your orchard?"

"Exactly."

"I have to speak to Mrs. Harris and determine if she will allow me—"

"I would advise you to make sure that she does."

She stiffened. "You really are the devil, you know."

"Merely an astute businessman, *cariño*."

A pretty blush touched her cheeks. "You shouldn't call me that."

"Do you know what it means?"

She refused to look at him. "It means sweetheart."

His eyes narrowed. "You speak Spanish." One more confirmation.

"I looked it up after you said it in the orchard."

"Ah." Too bad. But their earlier encounter had intrigued her enough to go to the trouble of finding out what he had called her, which gave him more pleasure than was wise. "So. Do you agree to my proposal?"

"You give me no choice, do you?"

"None." When she glared at him, he arched an eyebrow. "You act as if I ask you to throw yourself on a funeral pyre, yet I am the one accommodating *you*. I do not have to listen to your opinions on the matter of your school, you know."

A rueful smile touched her lips. "I know. Forgive me. I have been a trifle . . . cranky of late."

He would love to know why but had pushed his luck as far as he dared. "It is forgotten. Shall we begin our tour of the school?"

"I can't now; I'll be much too busy helping settle the girls in this afternoon. But tomorrow, after the term has officially begun and I have finished my first class, I'll have plenty of time to show you around. Assuming Mrs. Harris agrees."

He did not want to wait, but neither did he want to appear overhasty. "Very well, tomorrow, then." Clapping his hat on his head, he bowed to her. "Good day . . . Lucy, is it not?"

"How did you—Oh, yes, Tessa mentioned it. Actually, it's Lucinda."

He bit back a smile. He'd been right.

"Of course, *you* must call me Miss Seton," she chided him.

"But even your pupils call you Lucy."

"Tessa called me that because I was her friend before I became her teacher." She frowned. "I suppose I shall have to make her address me more formally in the classroom, or my students will never pay me any mind."

"They will pay you even less mind if they learn how I found you in the orchard." Heedless of her panicked gaze, he added ruthlessly, "And I have no reason to keep the tale to myself when you are being so prickly and formal." Why not blackmail her into that as well? The quickest way to gain her confidence was to demolish those walls of propriety that kept him out.

She scowled. "You are determined to have your own way, aren't you?"

He stifled a triumphant smile. "Always."

"And I suppose you mean for me to call you Diego."

"It is what my friends call me."

"We are hardly friends," she bit out. "And if anyone were to hear us, they would make the wrong assumptions about our association."

"So we will only be informal in private." That was actually better. The more secrets they shared, the more likely she was to trust him when it counted.

"Fine. Call me what you please." She smoothed her skirts. "Now, if you will excuse me, I have to prepare for our students' arrival. Good day, Señor Montalvo."

Her stubborn insistence on not using his Christian name goaded him into doing what he should not. He caught her hand, then bent to press a hard kiss to the back of it. "Good day, Lucy."

She froze but did not immediately snatch back her hand. With his blood thundering in his ears, he took advantage, turning her hand over to brush another kiss over her palm, which was neither necessary *nor* proper. She smelled of violets, so English. Yet so arousing that he let his mouth drift to her wrist for another brief kiss before he straightened, still holding her hand.

For a moment, they stared at each other, two uneasy adversaries trapped in a gesture that ought to have been awkward.

Except that it felt entirely different. Intimate. Intoxicating. Addictive.

Addictive? No, that must not be. He could not afford addictive.

With a swift press of her fingers, he let go, whirled, and walked out the door.

As he strode down onto the drive, he broke into a sweat. He could swear that when he had kissed her wrist, her pulse had leaped beneath his lips. That tiny reaction had resonated through him, shaken him somewhere deep inside.

For despite all her blustering and her fiercely loyal defense of the school, Lucy Seton was still a woman, susceptible to the touch of a man. To *his* touch. As he was susceptible to hers.

Por Dios, he could not let himself be susceptible. It made it harder to continue the charade. It would muddy his perceptions, ruin his concentration—and concentration was everything. One must never take one's eye from the prize, or everything fell into chaos.

Like a wraith, Gaspar came out of some hedges and fell into step beside him. "You won't believe what I found out from the school's cook about that teacher."

"I know," Diego said irritably. "She is the one. Lucinda Seton."

"It's a good omen, meeting her right off. It bodes well for our success."

"A lucky coincidence, I will grant you. But we make our own success—omens have naught to do with it." He slanted a glance at Gaspar. "You, of all people, should know that. How often have you said that anything can be done with a trick? That miracles only last until the source of their illusion is revealed?"

"I used to think so." Gaspar veered toward the orchard. "But the older I get, the less certain I am. I'm not as ready to dismiss the hand of Fate as I once was."

Shaking his head, Diego quickened his pace. If this was Fate, then Fate was cruel. To offer Diego a chance at obtaining his dream, while forcing him to keep at arm's length the first woman to attract him in a very long while . . . it was damned unfair. A very *un*lucky coincidence.

Unless she proved *not* to be the one, after all.

He shoved his hand into his coat pocket to draw out the miniature. "I hate to discourage your new philosophy, but we thought we had found our quarry before, and we were wrong. Miss Seton might be only another dead end." He gazed at the picture of the young Spanish woman. "She does not even resemble Doña Catalina."

"I warned you she might not."

"And she mentioned nothing about having Spanish parents."

"She may not know. No telling what tales the colonel has spun for her."

That was certainly true. "She is twenty, not nineteen as the *marqués* said."

"Can't you just take what Fate has handed us and be happy?" Gaspar grumbled as they reached the orchard. "You ought to be rejoicing." He paused, his gaze boring into the side of Diego's head. "Unless—" He blocked Diego's path. "I know why you don't want her to be the one. You want to bed her, and you can't if she's the granddaughter of Don Carlos."

Bed her? He wanted to do more than that. He wanted to ravish her, devour her, incite her to passions beyond her wildest dreams.

Diego neatly sidestepped Gaspar to stalk through the trees. "That is absurd."

"Is it?" Gaspar hurried to catch up to him. "I watched

the two of you on those steps. You kissed her hand. *After* you knew who she was."

Diego strove for nonchalance. "I kiss a lot of women's hands."

"Not these days, you don't," Gaspar said. "And I saw how you looked at her. You've never looked at a woman like that."

"Like what?" Diego snapped.

"Like Antony seeing Cleopatra for the first time."

Why did Gaspar have to know him so well? "A whimsical notion. But utter nonsense. I hardly know her."

Though what he knew, he liked. Her passionate outbursts amused him, and her loyalty to her school impressed him. She called him the devil for what she felt was a good reason, but she looked at him as if she didn't think him the devil at all.

That made him yearn.

Yearn? He was mad. The only thing he yearned for was Arboleda, and she was the key to regaining it. So she was out of his reach. "You know I will not jeopardize my bargain with the *marqués*. If she is the one we seek, I will persuade her to return to Spain with us, as I promised. That is all."

"I want to see you regain your family's home, but life is not meant to be lived alone. So if you really want this woman—"

"Then what? Throw away everything I have worked for? Dishonor my vow to Father? Because that is what taking up with Miss Seton would mean. The *marqués* made it very clear—we are not to lay a hand on her."

"Except for confirming her identity." A dark expression flitted over Gaspar's features. "Perhaps *I* should be the one to examine her thigh for her birthmark. *You* are too eager to get inside her drawers to be trusted with that."

"I am not remotely interested in getting inside her drawers," Diego growled.

Hostias, how he wished Gaspar had not put it that way. Now he had *that* image in his head to plague him.

The *marqués*'s granddaughter had a butterfly-shaped birthmark on her thigh. His instructions had been clear. They had to see it with their own eyes, at the exact moment of revealing its importance. A great deal of money was at stake, after all. Their quarry must not have the chance to create a similar birthmark. And if a servant were paid to look, the truth might be manipulated.

Diego had easily agreed to the stipulation. But that was before their quarry had turned out to be a lovely creature capable of rousing his desire. Even knowing it was madness, the very idea of lifting Lucy's skirts, either stealthily or with her permission, fired his blood unbearably.

He gritted his teeth. "I will do whatever I must to make sure that the *marqués* gets his granddaughter exactly as planned."

"And it does not trouble you that he means to find her a titled husband to bear him his heir, now that his son is dead?" Gaspar's tone grew skeptical. "That some other man will be 'plowing her field'?"

He steeled himself against the image of Lucy in another man's bed. "Why should it? It has naught to do with me. I do not qualify as a husband for her."

"Your father was—"

"Nobody, compared to the *marqués*. Don Carlos would never agree to let her marry me. His aspirations are higher. He would cut her off first—and refuse to give me back Arboleda as he promised, too. If I relinquish my estate, it will be back to performing and endless travel—no Arboleda, no nothing. I will not risk that just to bed some female."

He strode up the Rockhurst steps and headed for the brandy. This perplexing attraction to Lucy would pass if he kept a tight rein on it. He had weathered hard times before; he could do it again.

Even if it meant relinquishing his chance at the lovely Lucinda Seton.

Chapter Five

Dear Charlotte,

I am surprised you tolerate anyone else being as opinionated as you. We both know you don't take well to having your ideas contradicted. And I would not pin your hopes on such a petition. The licensing magistrates are notoriously fickle about their choices, not to mention susceptible to bribery.

Your cousin,
Michael

Early the next afternoon, Lucy herded several twelve-year-olds down the path through the oaks behind the school. With the weather still unseasonably warm, it was far too lovely to sit inside and draw.

Bearing their smocks, sketch pads, and charcoals, they quickly reached the old river landing, which had four spectacular views. Before them was the Thames with the countryside beyond, behind them lay the oak copse, to the left was the school's boathouse, and to the right was the cherry orchard.

That cursed cherry orchard. As the girls donned their smocks, she strolled over to gaze at it. Was Diego Montalvo out there now, or was he still abed?

The idea sent an unwelcome warmth flooding her belly. Would he wear a nightshirt? Or sleep in his drawers, like some men in the regiment?

She didn't want to know. Because the thought of him bare-chested, wearing only drawers, set her pulse pounding, and she was going to see him later today. How was she supposed to react after yesterday's kisses?

Her fingers curled automatically into her palm, and a groan escaped her. The first had been bad enough, but the second and third . . .

No man had ever kissed her palm or her wrist, not even Peter. It had nearly turned her to ash right there. How strange that such kisses felt so much more intimate, so much more sinful, than one to the back of the hand.

Or was it just the way he'd stared at her while doing it?

She shivered. His eyes, warm and coffee-brown, had met hers in a look that held more than mere admiration, something wild and wanton and very, very wicked.

That licentious look, those unwise kisses, had fed last night's dreams in the most shocking manner. She'd spent half the night imagining that dark gaze poring over her naked body, those possessive lips burning a path down her chin and upper chest and . . . and breasts . . .

"Miss Seton?" asked a pupil, jerking her from her thoughts.

She whirled to find the girls seated on the aging plank bench that circled the landing, with their charcoals and sketch pads at hand and their faces expectant.

She struggled to regain her composure. "Ah, I see you're ready. Very good." This was her first drawing class. What in the dickens was she doing allowing thoughts of that wretched magician to intrude? If she weren't careful, she would forget why she was here in the first place.

And why *he* had come to Richmond, too. That was probably why he'd kissed her hand so scandalously: to make her forget about his devious plans.

With matter-of-fact efficiency, she donned her smock and set out her sketch pad and charcoals. "Now then, ladies, according to your previous teacher's notes, you left off with landscapes. Is that correct?"

"Yes, Miss Seton," the girls said in unison. Then Tessa's hand shot up.

"Miss Dalton?" Lucy asked.

"She told us we would start on figures next."

Lucy bit back a smile. The girls were always eager to go right to figures, so they could sketch their parents and beaus and friends. But it wasn't wise to rush them beyond the limits of their competence too quickly, no matter how eager they were for it. It would merely frustrate them.

"Let's leave the figures until a day when the weather is not so fine."

Another girl raised her hand, followed by two others.

Suppressing a sigh, she called on the first. "Yes, Miss Pierce."

"Our teacher *promised* that if we practiced drawing hands enough last term, we could go on to figures this term," she protested. "And we've been drawing our left hands for weeks and weeks!"

"And you'll be drawing them for weeks more if you keep complaining," Lucy said with a teacherly scowl.

The other two girls' hands went down.

"Now then," she said firmly, "today you will draw one of the views surrounding us—there are plenty to choose from."

Eleven heads bent quickly to their sketch pads.

That went rather well, she thought as she settled herself on one end of the landing, where she could observe all of her pupils.

Fortunately, only Tessa knew her as a friend. The others were too young to have attended here when she had, which would make it easier to maintain the proper distance. But for tomorrow's class with the older girls, she'd have to make it clear that she was Miss Seton, drawing teacher, and not Lucy, the colonel's daughter famous for never holding her tongue.

She flipped through her own sketch pad, hurrying past the sketch of Peter to find an empty page. After her shameless response to yesterday's hand kisses, she needed no more reminders of her flawed character.

Today she would do better.

"What a fine picture you ladies make," said a male voice.

Startled, she looked up to see Señor Montalvo striding up to the landing. Just the sight of him in a chocolate-hued riding coat, tight buckskin riding breeches, and well-polished Hessians sent her pulse racing. And a racing pulse didn't augur well for good behavior.

"What are *you* doing here?" she snapped.

He laughed, the throaty sound making her go all shivery. "Such a welcome! You told me I might come, remember?"

"I said *later!*" She rose to her feet. "After our lessons are done."

"I wanted to see you teaching your class," he said smoothly.

"But Mrs. Harris—"

"I spoke to her when I entered. That's how I knew where to find you. She thought my joining you a fine idea." A devilish smile curved his mouth.

A likely story. When Lucy had broached the possibility of taking Diego around the school yesterday, she'd had to twist Mrs. Harris's arm to get her to agree. But apparently, even though Mrs. Harris wasn't entirely sure that Señor Montalvo could be trusted, she did trust Lucy. Of course, that was only because she didn't know about their previous encounter.

"Very well, sir," she said, determined not to let him intimidate her. "Feel free to watch, but I'm afraid you'll be bored. The young ladies and I will merely draw for a bit, and then I'll stroll around to observe and make comments."

"May I ask what you're drawing?"

"We were *supposed* to draw figures," Tessa grumbled.

"Miss Dalton—" Lucy warned.

"I suppose you can't draw figures without a model," he jumped in, eyes twinkling. "Why not let me be your model? I might as well make myself useful."

Eleven pairs of hopeful eyes swung her way. She would have refused, except for one thing: being a model required utter stillness. He couldn't distract her with magic tricks or flirtation, so she'd have a chance to extol the school's virtues. And he'd have to listen.

Besides, she could also ask *him* questions. She still felt that he was even more a Master of Mystery than he seemed, and this would give her the chance to unveil his secrets. It was crucial in any war to know the enemy well. Surely the man had *some* vulnerability.

"All right, Señor Montalvo. We'd be delighted to have you as a model."

As the girls cheered, he flashed her an arrogant smile and strode to the bench at the other end of the landing.

Enjoy yourself while you can, sir, Lucy thought smugly. *Those planks will get uncomfortable very quickly.* Even half an hour of holding the same position was sure to wipe that self-satisfied expression from his handsome face.

When she resumed her seat, he called out, "How shall I pose?"

"However you wish." She picked up her charcoal, annoyingly eager to sketch him.

"How's this?" He stretched out on the bench on his back, crossing his ankles and tucking his hands under his head.

When the girls giggled, she scowled. He thought he was so clever. "Planning to take a nap while we sketch you, sir?"

"You did say I would be bored."

"Ah, but you're not allowed to move, even in sleep. I would prefer that you choose a pose that allows you more control."

He sat up to cast her a cheeky grin. "You're a harsh taskmaster, Miss Seton."

"I do try," she said. "The way you're sitting now is fine."

More than fine. He was leaning forward, with his hands planted at his sides and his legs splayed wide, like a man on the verge of rising. It not only lent the pose energy and action, but it flexed the muscles of his thighs beneath his tight breeches.

Perhaps this hadn't been such a good idea.

She should focus on a part of him that didn't tempt her. Not his broad shoulders straining against his coat. Not the well-shaped calves encased in fine leather. Certainly not those amazing hands that had haunted her dreams . . .

With a groan, she jerked her gaze to his face—where his sensuous mouth reminded her of how he'd kissed her hand yesterday. Nothing was safe with him.

Determined to resist his attractions, she forced herself to think of him as an object—a statue, perhaps, like the stuffy ones adorning town halls.

For a while, only the scratch of charcoals on paper pierced the silence.

Then he cleared his throat. "Am I allowed to talk?"

"As long as you move only your lips." She seized on the opening. "I'm sure the young ladies would enjoy hearing about your home in Spain."

"What makes you think I'm Spanish?"

"You speak Spanish."

"And English, Portuguese, and French."

"Fine." She tried not to be impressed that he spoke four languages. "Tell us about wherever your home is."

"I'm from León."

Her gaze shot up from the sketch pad. "That *is* a province in Spain, isn't it?"

"You know of it?" He didn't sound entirely surprised.

She knew of it better than she wished. Her mother had died in its frozen mountain passes. "As a girl, I traveled through Spain with my parents."

"Why were you in Spain, Miss Seton?" Tessa asked.

"My father served in the army." Both of her fathers had. Her real father, a British soldier named Tom Crawford, had died at the Battle of La Coruña, heartsick and weakened by the recent loss of his wife. But not before begging his superior officer, Hugh Seton, to take her in. According to the colonel, neither of her parents had possessed any other family.

"So you were on the retreat to La Coruña," Diego said, his tone oddly gentle.

Tears stung her eyes. "Yes, though I was too young to remember anything except being always cold. And hungry."

Years later, she'd pored over every document relating to that disastrous retreat, looking for information about Sergeant Thomas Crawford or his Spanish wife, Catalina, who'd died beside the road. There was none. But she now knew the horrors they'd faced in the British army's mad dash to reach the coast ahead of the French.

"The mountains of Ancares get very cold in January. The snow lay thick that year." An edge had entered his voice, but when she glanced at him, his expression was bland. "Or so I heard."

And the dead had littered the road. "If you're from León, you *are* Spanish," she said, eager to change the subject. "Why did you imply otherwise?"

"Because I'm Galician. We're an entirely different people, though Spain has . . . appropriated us, shall we say."

"How can there be snow in Spain?" Miss Pierce put in. "Isn't it hot there?"

"It depends on what part you're in. Where I come from, it's hot in summer, cold in winter. On one side are the mountains, on the other high plains. It's green but dry." A palpable yearning for home filtered into his voice. "At present it's spring. The cherries are in bloom there as well, and the grapevines are flourishing. The skies are clear and blue, and the days warm enough to doze in the courtyard."

Lucy caught her breath at his wistful tone. Why build his pleasure garden in England when he so clearly missed Spain?

Perhaps it had to do with being Galician. "What makes Galicians different from Spaniards?"

"We are descended from the Celts. Our ancient *pallozas* are much like the Celtic roundhouses in old Britain, and we play the *gaita*, which is exactly like the bagpipes your countrymen play."

Lucy stopped drawing. "What do you mean, my countrymen?"

His gaze bored into her. "You are Scottish, are you not?"

"But how—"

"Your accent. I hear the burr of Scottish r's in it."

A little shiver coursed along her flesh. Amazing that he should have heard it buried beneath the layers of her years abroad in an English regiment. "Not too much of a burr, I should think. But yes, Papa is Scottish."

"Even without the accent, I would have guessed you were Scottish." He paused. "Or perhaps even Spanish."

A tingle of wariness vibrated along her spine. How did he know about her Spanish blood?

He couldn't possibly. Unless he'd been talking to people about her. But why would he? And why did the calculated look in his eyes make her think of medieval renditions of Lucifer enticing an innocent?

Lucy shook herself. Now she was just being silly. "Why on earth would you guess I'm Spanish?" she said lightly as she forced herself to continue drawing.

"You have their fiery temperament."

She sighed. Was "hot-blooded hoyden" branded on her brow, for pity's sake? "Fiery temperaments are said to abound among the Irish and the Moors, too. You can't guess a person's lineage from her temperament."

"It was only an observation."

"An unjust one," she shot back, unnerved by his perception. She couldn't believe he'd just guessed at her lineage and gotten it right. "Is this another of your conjuring talents, to be able to detect a person's origins?"

"Actually, it is."

"Can you guess where *I'm* from?" piped up Miss Pierce.

"Wales, possibly," he answered. "And Miss Dalton is certainly from the south of England, though I cannot narrow it more than that."

He was right on both counts. Perhaps he *could* guess lineage. If so, she shouldn't blame him for using his ability.

Diego relaxed as he saw the suspicion subside on Lucy's face. He had nearly given himself away with that comment about the Spanish. Her startled expression had made it clear that she not only knew of her Spanish blood but was surprised a stranger should be aware of it. Certainly no one in Edinburgh had mentioned it when he and Gaspar had asked about her and her "father."

Then again, no one in Edinburgh had been all that eager to speak to them. The Scottish were suspicious of everyone.

"How did you guess I'm from Wales?" Miss Pierce exclaimed, bringing his attention back to his audience.

"He's a magician, you ninny," said another girl. "They can divine people's thoughts."

"No, we cannot," he said dryly. "And any magician who claims otherwise is only lying to get your money. I merely have a good ear for accents. When I was young and entertaining the regiments in Spain and Portugal, I met men from all over. I trained myself to notice how their speech reflected their origins. It has proved a useful talent for a conjurer."

"When lying to get people's money, you mean?" Lucy said archly.

Curse the woman—she knew exactly how to try his temper. "I am neither a cardsharp nor a thief, Miss Seton." Though he had briefly been both.

"Forgive me," she said without sincerity. "I didn't mean to imply that you were."

No, she had meant to imply that he was the devil. His role as villain already began to pall. He had always considered himself honorable, even while doing things to survive that he had not been proud of. He was not the sort of man to open a pleasure garden next to a girls' school, even one belonging to the hated English.

It gnawed at him that he must pretend to do so.

The girls let out a loud cry.

"What?" he asked, startled from his ill humor.

"You're to hold still, which includes your expression," Lucy reminded him. "No frowning. Or smiling, for that matter."

"Ah. Beg pardon," he bit out, resisting the impulse to point out that *she'd* been the one to provoke him into a frown.

She seemed to provoke him into many unwise things. Such as talking about Villafranca. He hadn't meant to chatter on about the town of his birth like some old man reminiscing about his youth.

He had only fallen in with her questions about Spain so he could determine if she had indeed been on the road to La Coruña with the Forty-second Regiment, as the *marqués* had speculated. When Diego and Gaspar had first begun to fix on her as their quarry, they had been perplexed to discover that the colonel had retired from the

Seventy-third Regiment, not the Forty-second. They had finally decided that he must have purposely changed regiments to cover his tracks.

Until she had spoken of the retreat to La Coruña, however, it had not occurred to him what it meant that she had been there at age four. How strong a little girl she must have been to survive deprivations that had killed sturdy members of the British army.

He could tell that the memories pained her. If she did prove to be the *marqués's* granddaughter, Diego might have to take a horsewhip to that colonel for having dragged her through such horrors, when she should have been at home being coddled by her true parents.

Leave it to the British to think themselves impervious to cold and hunger, to count on being able to take what they wanted from whoever dared to—

He gritted his teeth against the memories. He could not change what had happened to his family, but at least he could set to rights what the damnable British had done to her. A pity that Doña Catalina and her husband, Don Álvaro, had both died a few years after their daughter's abduction. But if Lucy did prove to be *Doña* Lucinda, she would at least be reunited with her grandfather, who would make her the sparkling jewel of society that she deserved to be.

Diego started to change position, then remembered it was not allowed. This modeling was none too comfortable. His left leg had gone to sleep, and his back throbbed. He tried shifting his leg, but the girls howled a protest. *Dios Santo.*

Lucy began to look smug. No wonder she had agreed to his proposal so readily. She did like to torture him.

"Ladies," she said primly, "since Señor Montalvo grows restless, we ought to entertain him. Why don't you tell him about our school? That is why he's here, after all. Each one of you can say why your parents wanted to enroll you and what you like best about it."

Diego groaned. Lucy had leaped into saving her precious school with the fierceness of a mountain lynx. Clearly, she meant him to endure many lectures.

As one young lady extolled the school's virtues, Lucy closed her sketch pad and rose to stroll about, commenting on the students' work. He tried not to watch her but couldn't help himself. Even with that utilitarian smock thrown over her poppy-colored gown, she had a way of moving that reminded him of fine wine swirled in a glass.

He would give much for a taste of that wine.

Hostias, that did not bear thinking on. Already his body was reacting to the lovely temptation she presented as she swept from one student to the next, but if he began to imagine *tasting* her . . .

He fought back his arousal; his pose displayed only too well the part of him he struggled to control.

Gaspar was right. He had indeed been too long without a woman if his body could be roused with such ease at the mere sight of Lucy prancing about. And with giggling girls watching, too! *Dios mio,* he would rot in hell for such behavior.

Better to concentrate on what she said to her pupils. That would surely put his randy self to sleep.

But it was difficult to notice her words when she kept flashing her ready smile to all and sundry—except him, of course. He found himself envying her pupils with astonishing virulence. She was quite a good teacher for someone new to it. She put the girls at ease without coddling them, critiquing their work without destroying their confidence. He marveled at such delicacy of feeling.

Gaspar would think it too gentle an instruction. He had been the sort to bark commands and slap Diego's hands whenever Diego dropped a card or picked up the wrong handkerchief. After a coddled childhood as the only son of a nobleman, it had been quite a shock. But being Gaspar's assistant had been safer—and more profitable—than thieving or cardsharping.

"Ladies, it's time to wash up," Lucy suddenly said.

Diego gaped at her. They were finished?

As he straightened and the girls hurried to wipe their smudged hands on damp towels, Lucy walked up to him. "Thank you, sir," she said very prettily. "You were quite helpful."

He rose, wincing as the feeling returned to his limbs. "Remind me to be more appreciative of artists' models in the future," he grumbled.

Amusement shone on her face. "I did warn you."

"You warned me I would be bored." He limped forward, his muscles cramping. "Not crippled."

This time a laugh spilled out of her. "You were a good sport about it, I must say. Most models are much grumpier their first time."

A girl asked her a question, and she returned her attention to the class, sending them off to dancing lessons. While she was distracted with cleaning her own hands, he wandered over to where she'd left her sketch pad, curious to see how she had drawn him.

But as he flipped through her surprisingly accomplished drawings of Scotland's heather-clad mountains and Richmond's cobblestone streets, it was the images of the people in her life that sparked his curiosity.

He turned a page, blinked, then let out a laugh, unable to believe his eyes.

When she whirled at the sound, he held up to her the picture of a handsome young gentleman with horns and a tail. "And who is this interesting fellow?"

An enchanting flush filled her face. "Oh, Lord," she muttered.

The other girls had filed off through the woods, leaving them alone on the landing. Since Mrs. Harris had told him this was her only class for today, he had her to himself at last.

And he meant to take full advantage. "How reassuring to see I am not the only person you deem the devil. Is that a common theme in your work?"

"Give me that, Señor Montalvo!" she snapped as she strode up to him.

Grinning, he held it behind his back. "I thought you were going to call me Diego in private."

"Fine." Two spots of color rose high in her cheeks. "Give me that, Diego, you unconscionable scoundrel."

"Not until you tell me who he is." He enjoyed watching her bristling with heat, her eyes ready to slay him. It made him wonder what she would be like in his bed, writhing beneath him in equal passion.

"Good Lord," she complained, "you are so . . . so . . ."

"Charming? Witty? Irresistible?"

"Annoying!"

"And persistent." He held the sketch pad high and gazed up at it. "Of course, your Mrs. Harris would probably be able to tell me."

"You wouldn't dare!" When he arched an eyebrow at her, she blew out a frustrated breath. "Very well, he's just . . . that is . . ."

"A fiancé perhaps?" he prodded. "Or more likely, a *former* fiancé, given the horns."

That thought instantly dampened his fun. Until this moment he had not considered that she might have a serious suitor. Such a person would almost certainly try to interfere with his plans.

"He's neither." Turning from him, she gazed out across the river. "At one time, I had hoped . . . Never mind, it doesn't matter. He's nobody to me now."

"Not nobody, judging from your blush." He was inexplicably annoyed that any pasty-faced Englishman could so affect her. "What is his name?"

"Why do you care?"

Because he needed to know who else might influence her decisions. Or so he told himself.

"I am curious to learn what sort of fellow earned horns from you. We both know you do not use that insult lightly."

"Very funny." She started off toward the path through the woods.

Tucking the sketch pad under his arm, he followed. "What did he do? Break your rules of propriety? Insult your pupils? Try to buy the property on the *other* side of the school to build a brothel?"

"He dallied with me," she shot back. Even as a rush of blood filled his ears, she stopped short just inside the trees to add in a more subdued tone, "No, that's not true. I-I didn't mean that how it sounds."

He steadied his anger at the unnamed stranger. "How *did* you mean it?"

"Peter . . . that is, Lord Hunforth and I grew up together in the regiment. I thought he meant to . . . I always assumed that he and I . . ." She shook her head. "It doesn't matter. I was wrong."

And it had obviously hurt her badly. She started to walk off, but he stayed her. "You thought this Englishman meant to marry you."

She nodded. "But once he ascended to his title, he decided he required a more proper wife."

"Ah," he said, the light dawning. "That is why you are so eager for the proprieties now." And that was why she would make the perfect wife for some high-ranking Spanish noble once she learned of her true lineage.

The thought rankled.

She glared at him. "I'll have you know I have always been eager . . ." When he arched an eyebrow, she pulled away. "Oh, why am I even telling you this? You already think me every bit the hoyden that Peter does."

"*Por Dios,* what gave you such a notion? If anything, you behave too properly for your true nature."

"That's what I mean!" she exclaimed. "You hardly know me, and already you've decided what my true nature is, which is apparently that of a . . . a—"

"You are passionate," he said. "There is nothing wrong with that."

"That is what *you* would think, of course."

The contempt in her voice grated. His eyes narrowed. "Ah, you mean I am not like your insipid Englishman. I am a devil by nature, so I think everyone else should behave the same."

She met his gaze with a stubborn look. "Well, you must admit that gentlemen like you are fond of certain vices, so of course you expect women to . . . to . . ."

"Cavort with abandon in my presence?" His temper gaining the better of him, he advanced on her. "Behave like animals to satisfy my lecherous desires?"

Color rising in her cheeks, she backed away. "I only meant—"

"I know exactly what you meant." His head filled with memories of that horrible night in Villafranca when he had lost so much to her countrymen, who *had* behaved like animals. Who had also apparently drummed into her their contempt for anyone but their own.

Dropping her sketch pad into the leaves, he stalked her. "Foreigners like me are only fit for shooting with your English rifles. Foreigners like me have no feelings, no morals, no rights."

"Foreigners? No, I was speaking of—"

"Foreigners like me devour young ladies for sport." When she came up against an oak, he lunged, trapping her against it by bracing his hands on the trunk on either side of her. "If I am to be painted that way for no reason, then I might as well enjoy the benefits of such a reputation."

"B-benefits?" she squeaked.

"You said I'm the devil." He bent his head, goaded by hot temper . . . and hotter desire. "And the devil always gets his due."

Then he seized her mouth with his.

Chapter Six

Dear Cousin,

    Señor Montalvo has asked that we let him observe the school so he can make a more informed decision about his pleasure garden. I agreed to Miss Seton's proposal that she escort him, since she is a fine representative of the sort of woman who benefits most from our classes. And unlike other ladies whom he cast under his spell, his charm and legerdemain do not seem to fool her.

Your harried relation,
Charlotte

It was every bit as luscious as Lucy had imagined, God rot him. There was none of Peter's playfulness or the damp ardor of the two men who'd stolen kisses from her at balls. This was hot and impassioned and bold, a kiss to dream on.

He tasted of coffee and smoke, a flavor so distinctly male that it sent her head reeling. So did the forceful way his mouth took hers. His kiss was hard but not hurtful, demanding but not bullying.

It was also far too brief.

He drew back, his eyes glittering, a hint of his anger still in their fathomless depths. "You kiss too innocently for a hoyden."

"You kiss too briefly for a devil," she shot back. Oh, why couldn't she hold her tongue? She might as well have thrown down a gauntlet.

And he picked it right up. Smoldering need flared in his face as he caught her head in one hand and said, "That can be remedied, *cariño.*"

This time when he slanted his mouth over hers, he coaxed it open for his tongue.

She'd heard of such kisses from the other girls, but she'd never dreamed that having a man slide his tongue into one's mouth could feel so pleasurable. So thoroughly sinful.

Her hands seemed to grab naturally for his waist and her body to sway naturally into his embrace. It all felt perfectly . . . natural. Which probably explained why his tongue dove so naturally into her mouth.

Then again. And again, until her heart thundered like a timpani, and her very skin came alive to his touch, to the caress of his fingers against the nape of her neck and the slope of her jaw. His thumb stroked the pulse that beat madly in her throat, and she arched her head back for more.

His kisses began to wander from her mouth, to her cheek, to her ear. "Ah, *querida,*" he rasped, enthralling her with his husky endearments, "your mouth would tempt any devil." He nipped at her earlobe, sending little shocks of delight to her senses. "Did it tempt your friend Peter? Did he ever kiss you?"

"When I was fourteen . . . and once later." But not like this. Never like this.

Diego dropped his lips to her throat, plundering it with open-mouthed kisses that turned her bones to mush. "I take it he was older than you."

"By . . . three years."

"For that he calls you hoyden? Because *he* took advantage of you?" He leaned into her, hard muscle against soft flesh. "I do not understand you English."

"I thought you claimed I was Spanish," she taunted him, though she could hardly think with his hand roaming down her shoulder and arm, onto her waist, down to her hips, up to her ribs.

"I do not know what you are anymore." His mouth now hovered a breath away from hers. "Except the most maddening woman I have ever met."

This time his kiss was deep and warm and leisurely, as if he meant to linger with her the rest of the afternoon, driving her to distraction.

She liked "maddening." It was vastly superior to "hot-blooded." She shouldn't believe him, but she liked the idea that she might entice a man as worldly and sophisticated as he, that she might tempt him to behave as he shouldn't, to kiss her so lusciously.

She hooked her arms about his neck, and he groaned somewhere low in his throat.

Then he slid his hand from her ribs to cup her breast.

She felt the shock of it to her toes, and when he kneaded her flesh through her gown, the thrill that shot through her held her motionless.

Until Peter's humiliating words came back to her.

"No," she said firmly, shoving him away. "You mustn't do such things!"

She slid from between him and the tree, poised to fight. Until she saw his dazed expression.

He stared at her a long moment. "*Dios mio* . . . forgive me . . . I did not intend . . ." His fingers raked through his hair, disordering it. Then he glanced about them and groaned. "I have lost my mind."

She hugged herself, trying not to remember the moment of bliss when his hand stroked her through her gown. "What were you thinking?"

"Thinking! Do you really believe thought was involved?" Backing away from her, he swore a string of Spanish words. "My temper got the better of me, and I . . . made a mistake."

She was a mistake? Why was she *always* a mistake? Anger and hurt roared through her as she bent to pick up her sketch pad. "You're as bad as Peter. You both think I'm only good for a dalliance."

When she headed for the path, he darted in front of her, eyes blazing. "I do not think any such thing. My behavior had nothing to do with you."

A harsh laugh escaped her. "Oh, I see. Any woman would have served your purposes."

"No, I did not mean—" He gritted his teeth. "I only meant that my loss of control was not your fault."

"I should say not." Never mind that her own loss of control had urged him on. It was probably unwise to delve too deeply into that. Her gaze locked with his. "So you weren't just dallying with me? You meant something more by it?"

"Something more?" He briefly looked perplexed until her meaning apparently sank in. Then he let out another Spanish curse.

Lucy went cold. "Of course not. What was I thinking?" Desperate to escape, she tried to go around him.

He caught her by the shoulders to prevent it. "Listen to me, *cariño*—"

"Don't call me that!" Tears welled, and she fought them ruthlessly. She refused to let a man do this to her twice in one week. "Don't you dare use your meaningless endearments on me as if I'm some . . . doxy you can tumble without a thought. Just because you found me in an orchard behaving—"

"Like any other young woman enjoying a spring afternoon?"

She blinked at him.

"I do not think you a doxy or hoyden or any other silly names." Releasing her shoulders, he stepped back, as if touching her taxed his control. "I never did. *You* are the one who clings to English propriety, not I."

"Then why did you threaten to tell Mrs.—"

"To get what I wanted, of course. A chance to see the school with an amiable guide so I could decide how to act."

An awful thought occurred to her. "Is that why you kissed me, too? To stop me from plaguing you about your pleasure garden?"

"My pleasure garden!" He let out a choked laugh. "Of course. I always settle my business affairs by kissing the nearest female into submission." When she glared at him, he added, "You cannot really think I worry about you and your ladies. If I decide to build it, you cannot stop me. But I am trying to make the right decision. That has nothing to do with my kissing you."

Now she was confused. "Then why did you do it?"

"I told you: you made me angry. When you started talking as if I were some unconscionable scoundrel just because I am foreign—"

"Not because you're foreign," she broke in. "Because you're bent on ruining the school! For pity's sake, I'm foreign myself."

The interest that sparked in his dark eyes gave her pause.

"Because you're Scottish?" he said.

"Actually, I-I'm not Scottish. Colonel Seton adopted me. My mother was Spanish. Like you."

"Was she?" he said hollowly. He looked rather displeased to hear it.

"My real father was English. He died at La Coruña." Unnerved by his intent stare, she babbled on. "My mother died during their retreat to the coast."

"You were present when your parents died?" He looked oddly perplexed and seemed inordinately interested in her answer.

She would sound like a ninny if she admitted that she scarcely remembered her own parents. "My point is, I have no quarrel with foreigners. Why should I? I spent half my girlhood in Spain and Portugal and other foreign countries."

His eyes narrowed. "Yet you clearly have a quarrel with me."

"Because of the school—"

"Not only because of your precious school," he countered. "There is more to it than that. You said gentlemen like me are fond of certain vices. And I doubt that you meant men of business, no matter how ruthless you consider them."

"I meant performers, magicians. You're a famous, smooth-tongued conjurer with a courtly manner, who, according to one of our ladies, left a string of brokenhearted princesses behind you in Russia. Who knows how many other women you have discarded in the course of your career?"

When he winced, she knew she'd hit close to the truth. "Admit it: you only kissed me because you assumed I'd let you."

"And why would I assume that?" he asked irritably.

This time, when she headed for the path, he followed right alongside.

"Because I'm the kind of woman a man dallies with, not the kind he marries. I must give off this air or something. Peter says it's my wild Spanish blood."

He snorted. "Your Peter is an idiot."

She conceded that with a shrug. "All the same, *you* dallied with me." Her voice grew bitter. "And clearly not because you had any notion of courting me."

"It's not that I . . . *Por Dios,* you have to understand, I am not free to—" With an oath, he shoved his hands into his coat pockets. "My situation does not presently permit me to court anyone."

"Then you shouldn't have kissed me." She clung desperately to her propriety to keep from railing at him and bursting into tears like a silly fool.

"No, I should not have," he said grimly. "That much is true."

She swallowed, hurt by how readily he agreed with her. "You won't do it again, I hope."

"Why? Was it so dreadful you do not wish to repeat the experience?" he clipped out with what sounded like wounded pride.

That was just ridiculous. He had women drooling after him wherever he went. Why would he regret the loss of her? "Whether I enjoyed it is immaterial. But if someone happened to see—"

"You would lose your position as a teacher."

"Oh, I don't care about that. I'm just filling in temporarily." She thrust out her chin. "But people do talk. And *that* I care about."

"You mean," he said, his voice dripping with sarcasm, "you do not want your Peter to find out you have been letting me kiss you in the woods."

"I don't want *anyone* to find out. It would ruin me."

He muttered some oath but did not try to dispute that.

"Surely you can see why I'm not eager to have my name dragged through the mud over some foolish indiscretion. I may not be a great heiress, but my dowry is decent. As soon as Mrs. Harris fills this position, I'll join Papa and my stepmother in London for the Season, and some respectable gentleman will offer for me . . . eventually."

"I am sure he will," he bit out as he strode along beside her.

She glanced over to find him glaring at the path ahead. Could he actually be bothered by the thought of her marrying someone else?

No, not likely. He was merely irritated that in a short while, she would be beyond his seductions. "Now you understand why you must not kiss me again."

"Certainly," he said flatly.

Annoyance spiraled in her chest. He could have put up more of a fight than *that,* for pity's sake. "You should also understand why it is probably best that you ask someone else to take you around the school."

His reaction was more satisfying now: he halted to stare her down. "I do *not* understand. I have agreed not to kiss you. I assure you, I am perfectly capable of restraining my lust when I choose, *cariño*."

"All the same—"

"No. It will be you, and that is final."

She *wanted* it to be her, which was all the more reason it shouldn't be. He might claim not to be interested in a dalliance, but his actions showed otherwise. And given how susceptible she was to his kisses . . .

"This time you have no say in it," she told him loftily. "And threatening to go to Mrs. Harris will do you no good. I'll just tell her that you kissed me. Then it will be open war." She tipped up her chin. "Mrs. Harris will walk through fire to protect one of her girls from censure."

He shrugged. "Fine. That makes my decision easy. A pleasure garden it is."

Turning on his heel, he strolled down the path with the easy confidence of a man who knew he'd just trumped her ace.

Ooh, he was so arrogant and infuriating and . . . thoroughly insufferable! And the fact that it thrilled some part of her was appalling. Only sheer stubbornness made him insist on her showing him around. What other reason could there be?

But if she persisted in refusing, then Mrs. Harris would think she'd failed to convince him, which stung her pride. She could not fail at this.

She ran after him. "Surely you're not daft enough to destroy the school simply because I won't spend time with you."

A tight smile crossed his lips. "I am the devil. I do as I please. And it is a perfectly rational business decision. If you will not endure my company even after I swear to behave properly, then this school is not as important to you as it seems. So I need have no compunction about building whatever I wish next door."

"You're being ridiculous." She tried to match his stride. "There's no reason I should be your guide over anyone else."

"I prefer you. That is reason enough." They'd reached the end of the path.

Clearly it would be harder to get rid of him than she'd thought. Lucy even began to doubt that showing him the glories of the school would do it.

There *was* the petition, but Mrs. Harris had already warned her that the licensing magistrates were notorious for taking bribes in exchange for licenses.

She gritted her teeth. Oh, how she hated the thought of losing to the man.

He halted to face her, ruthless determination on his face. "So, where do we go next?"

"The front lawn." She swept past him. "You can watch the archery lessons."

He fell into step beside her. "Are you hoping someone's aim goes astray?"

"It's a thought."

"Murdering me on the school's premises will not help matters."

"Who said anything about murder?" She shot him a baleful glance. "Maiming might be more satisfying."

A chuckle sounded low in his throat. "Careful, now. Your wild Spanish blood is kicking up again."

"Don't remind me," she grumbled.

"You do realize there are worse things I could build next door. Mr. Pritchard intends to sell his property regardless, and given his high price, the only people who can afford it are those who wish to make a commercial success of it. How would Mrs. Harris feel about a munitions factory or a hospital for the insane?"

He had a point. What if they ran him off only to have someone worse come in?

But what could they do?

The idea hit her like a rifle shot. Yes! It was brilliant! But why hadn't Mrs. Harris thought of it herself? Perhaps because it couldn't be done? She would have to ask.

And she would have to keep him busy and out of the way so the idea could be explored.

But there would be no more private moments. With luck, Diego Montalvo would be gone and out of her life soon. And she refused to let him take her reputation with him when he left.

Chapter Seven

◦◦◦

Dear Charlotte,

I am working on a solution to your dilemma, but I need more time. Meanwhile, Miss Seton's association with the magician can surely do no harm, assuming it is properly chaperoned. And if it actually softens him toward the school, it can only help.

Your concerned cousin,
Michael

Two days after kissing Lucy in the woods, Diego watched from the orchard as a succession of carriages headed down the drive shortly after dawn.

He cursed under his breath. Yesterday, Lucy had told him she needed to go over accounts with Mrs. Harris today, so she would not be able to see him. And on Sunday they would attend church, so she could not see him then either.

He had spent enough time in her company to recognize when she lied, so he had risen at this ungodly hour to see if he was right. It appeared that he was. Because he would wager every *peseta* he had saved through the years that the woman enveloped in a cloak who had hurried into the first coach was Lucy herself. And that the woman joining her moments later was her employer.

They were up to something, along with several teachers and pupils, judging from the number of carriages. It must be something they did not want him to discover. No doubt Lucy had assumed he would sleep past their leavetaking— but then, she always underestimated him.

Gaspar hurried up, having come the back way from the school's kitchens, where Diego had sent him after seeing the carriages gather at dawn.

"Did you learn anything from that cook you are sweet on?" Diego demanded.

Gaspar glared at him. "She has a name, you know. Sally. And do you think you're the only one who can turn a pretty woman's head?"

Diego fought mightily not to laugh. He had seen the woman in the kitchen gardens once. She was no beauty. But Gaspar loved large-breasted women. And anyone who fed him well. Sally was probably Gaspar's idea of a goddess.

"I am well aware of your prowess with women," Diego said. "Whom do you think I learned it from?"

"You're damned right, you did," Gaspar shot back, only slightly mollified. "What is it to you, anyway, if I *am* sweet on her? Unlike you, I don't hate the English, and I deserve—"

"Gaspar!" Diego chided. "What did you learn from Sally?"

Gaspar blinked. "Oh. Not much. They're headed off to a charity breakfast."

"Ah, that explains the early hour."

"Actually, no. It seems that English society holds breakfasts in the afternoon."

"So where the devil is this breakfast—Bath?" Diego said irritably.

"It's at the Duchess of Foxmoor's mansion, but they go early to help set it up. Apparently this is a regular affair. At the beginning of every term, one of the married ladies hosts what is called a Venetian breakfast. They invite the wealthiest members of society to raise money for various causes—a ladies' association that helps women in prison, an orphanage, political parties, whatever interests them. Sally did say the ladies were leaving earlier than usual."

"And we both know why," Diego bit out.

"You think they're up to something?"

Diego started for the house. "Why else did Lucy keep it secret from me?"

With a dry laugh, Gaspar hurried after him. "She's a woman. They love secrets. Perhaps she's nervous because she's already told you so much."

Diego snorted. "After two days of acting the perfect gentleman, I have learned nothing of worth."

"You learned she was on the road to La Coruña, thinks her parents died there, and believes her father to be an English soldier and her mother his Spanish wife."

"Yes, but I do not know what basis she has for believing it. I do not even know if she remembers their deaths. She remembers the retreat. If she remembers them being with her on it—"

"She was four," Gaspar said with a shrug. "She's probably remembering the nurse."

"But why did the colonel not just say *he* is her father? And why allow his mistress to steal a child in Gibraltar and carry her on a transport in the first place? That cannot have been easy for an unmarried soldier. Even if they married, why would he continue to care for her? Miss Seton's description of the colonel's stellar character contradicts what we have been told."

"Yes, but she fits so many of the facts. She is probably ashamed to admit the truth about his character. You must get her to talk about the couple she believes to be her real parents. Then perhaps she will feel comfortable telling you the rest."

"I have tried!" Scowling, Diego strode up the steps. "I cannot even get her alone. Mrs. Harris's burly footman accompanies us everywhere. Lucy has built a wall of English propriety between us, and everything is 'the school this' and 'the school that.'"

"She doesn't like you much, does she?"

He suspected she liked him too well. That was the problem: her attraction to him terrified her. After their reckless kisses, she had closed up like a morning glory at midnight.

Still, he couldn't regret those kisses. They had been a revelation. *Lucy* had been a revelation, a ravishing blend of inexperience and curiosity that made him want to show her everything she secretly yearned to know.

She had sensed the depths of his desire, which had alarmed her, since that fellow Peter had blamed the ferociousness of his own lust on *her* nature. He'd been right about her nature but wrong about her character.

Imbécil. How could the man not appreciate her love of the sensual? It enticed Diego. And when yoked to her firmness of purpose, it was intoxicating.

In Spain, men would recognize her fine qualities. They would not belittle her as these foolish English did. She would be admired, adored. She deserved better than she got from these English, and Diego meant to see that she received it.

Even if it meant watching some other man marry her.

He cursed under his breath. Why did he torture himself like this? He could not afford to marry her. Yet the tantalizing thought of her melting in his arms again had kept him on edge during their days together. He had found it harder by the hour to concentrate on trying to get information from her, when all he wanted was to carry her off to his bed and spend the night rousing her passions. Just the idea had kept him lying awake and frustrated for the past three nights.

Muttering a curse, Diego headed for the rickety staircase. "It is not that Miss Seton does not like me; she simply does not like what she thinks I mean to do to her precious school. That is why her behavior this morning strikes me as suspicious. She has no reason to lie about supporting a charity. You would think she would invite me, if only to squeeze money out of me for her favorite cause."

He took the stairs two at a time, not bothering to slow for Gaspar. By the time the old man joined him in the study, huffing and puffing, Diego already had the trunk half packed.

"*Qué demonios!*" Gaspar clutched his hand to his chest. "What madness has possessed you?"

"Miss Seton's sneaking off at the crack of dawn only makes sense if she is raising money for a cause that she does not wish for me to know about—probably something to do with stopping the pleasure garden."

Gaspar blinked. "Ah, yes. That does make more sense. But assuming you're right, what does it matter? It's not as if you really mean to build anything."

"No, but if she thinks she has found a way to thwart me, then she has no more reason to deal with me. I cannot have that."

He wished he could tell her the truth and let the cards fall where they may. But only think how much more secretive she would become when he said he believed she had been stolen from her real parents by her beloved Papa and the woman she knew as her mother.

If Diego did not have his facts exactly right when he admitted the truth, she might recoil, refuse to talk to him. Or worse yet, tell the colonel, who would enlist the authorities on his side to have them thrown out of the country before he and Gaspar could be sure of their facts. Then where would they be?

"I must change tactics." Diego threw his evening attire into the trunk. "I have played the gentleman with her, letting her dictate the terms of our association, thinking she would grow to trust me. But that is not working."

The only time she revealed anything of worth was when they fought . . . or kissed—when he made her forget her English propriety.

"With Miss Seton, it is all about rousing her temper." Or her passions. "She is more forthcoming with information when her emotions run high."

"What do you mean to do?" Gaspar asked.

"Shake her up. Attend her little breakfast. Make her dance to *my* tune for a change." Diego packed his rigged candles and special wine bottle, then grinned at Gaspar. "I think it is high time I give our good neighbors a charity performance."

Lucy was in the Duchess of Foxmoor's elaborate gardens, going over the musical selections with the orchestra, when

Mrs. Harris hurried up. "Lucy, dear, I have some news that . . . I don't want to distress you, but—"

Leaving the list with the players, Lucy drew Mrs. Harris off. "What is it?"

"Lord Hunforth has come. With Lady Juliana."

Lucy waited for the pain to hit.

None did. How odd. The last few days, she'd been so consumed with her campaign to save the school that she'd scarcely thought of Peter at all.

Of course, she'd been rather distracted by that cursed magician, but that shouldn't be a factor. He might be a devastatingly handsome villain, with a quick wit and a way of making her insides flutter, but that only put her more on her guard.

"I'm sorry," Mrs. Harris said. "I had no idea Louisa intended to invite them, or I would have cautioned her against it."

"Nonsense. Let them come. Their money is as good as anyone's." And thankfully she had dressed with particular care today, in a gown of ivory silk and gauze that showed her figure quite well. "Besides, it will give me the chance to prove I care nothing about Lord Hunforth anymore."

"I hope that's true, dear. Because he's headed this way."

That was all the warning she got before a familiar voice sounded at her elbow. "Good afternoon, Miss Seton."

She faced Peter with a forced smile, not surprised to find him dressed in an exquisite blue coat so adorned with gold braiding and gilt buttons that he outshone the sun. Predictably, his female companion wore a gown of pink satin and lace that had clearly cost three times what Lucy's had. They made a striking pair.

"Lord Hunforth, how nice to see you." Taking some satisfaction from how he winced at her formal tone, Lucy cast his female companion a cool nod. "And you, too, Lady Juliana. So lovely of you both to support our cause."

As someone called Mrs. Harris away, Lady Juliana drew her shawl more closely about her and sniffed. "It's rather chilly today for an outdoor party, don't you think, Miss Seton?"

"You must understand, my dear," Peter said to Lady Juliana before Lucy could answer. "Miss Seton is a sturdy sort of female. She does not feel the cold the way someone as delicate as you probably does." He gently patted Lady Juliana's hand, which gripped his arm rather sturdily for a "delicate" female's.

"I feel the cold well enough," Lucy said meaningfully. "I just choose to ignore it."

Lady Juliana glanced around with the pinched expression of a supercilious grande dame twice her age. "Well, it *is* very pretty out here, I suppose. The duchess does have lovely gardens, and Venetian breakfasts can be enjoyable under the right circumstances." She performed an elegant motion with her head and neck that Lucy couldn't begin to master. "Though we can't stay long, can we, Petey?"

Lucy had barely smothered her smile at Peter's horrified reaction to being called Petey when Lady Juliana added, "I'm sure you know, Miss Seton, how hectic everything is when one is planning a wedding. So much to do."

A wedding?

Lucy had expected them to marry eventually, but the tiny part of her that still clung to her girlish dream screamed in outrage. How could he countenance taking this . . . this patently false female to wife?

Worse yet, Lady Juliana's expression made it clear she'd mentioned the wedding intentionally. She must have learned of Lucy's hopes for a future with Peter, but how? No one knew except her family and Mrs. Harris.

Had *Peter* told her? Had that miserable worm laughed at her behind her back with this witch?

Apparently so, for he avoided her gaze. "I thought we were going to wait until our betrothal party to announce it," he muttered to Lady Juliana.

The woman tittered, covering her mouth oh so elegantly with one "delicate" hand. "I'm sorry, my love, I quite forgot. I'm afraid our secret is out now."

"Yes, it seems so." Still avoiding Lucy's eyes, he added, "I suppose you have surmised that Lady Juliana has kindly consented to be my wife."

Lady Juliana cast him an adoring smile, then cast Lucy a gloating one.

Lucy forced down the bile rising in her throat and somehow wished them joy, though she wanted nothing more than to wipe the gloating smile off Lady Juliana's face with a *sturdy* kick to her rump.

Fortunately, a reprieve came in the form of the duchess herself, who beckoned to her from a small knot of footmen. "I beg your pardon, my dear Miss Seton, but I'm afraid I need you."

"Certainly, Your Grace," Lucy said, profoundly grateful for the interruption before she did something awful, such as bursting into tears. Or stabbing Peter through the chest with her parasol.

Giving Peter and Lady Juliana a superior smile that she carried off much better than the younger woman, the duchess added, "Please forgive me for dragging Miss Seton away. We find ourselves in a difficult situation, and I require her advice on how to handle it."

Peter stood slack-jawed at the idea of a duchess needing Lucy's help, and Lady Juliana's smile vanished. "Pray excuse me," Lucy murmured to them before hurrying off.

When she neared the knot of people, she found Mrs. Harris wearing a smug smile that made it clear exactly who had prompted the duchess's effusive comments. As it turned out, though, there *was* a difficult situation.

"Your magician has shown up," Mrs. Harris told her.

Diego was here?

Her pulse gave a sudden leap, and a silly fluttering in her belly followed. *Idiot. Fool.*

The duchess arched one eyebrow. "He got in without anyone knowing. Apparently, he acquired an invitation somewhere."

"By sleight of hand, no doubt," Lucy said. "Though how he found out about it, I'll never know. The man has eyes in the back of his head."

"I can have him tossed out, if you wish." Her Grace wore a smile that reminded Lucy of a cat eyeing a plump carp. "Or we can make good use of him."

When Lucy blinked, Mrs. Harris added, "He has offered to perform."

"What?" Lucy exclaimed. "Why?"

"He thinks we're raising money for the Ladies' Association, since that is what's on the invitation," the duchess said. "He doesn't know that we changed it to a fund for purchasing Rockhurst out from under him."

"Are you sure he doesn't know?" Lucy had an uneasy feeling about this. "We sent notes to all of the guests so they wouldn't be taken by surprise."

"He told me that he wished to help us with our Ladies' Association," the duchess replied. "And if he didn't receive an invitation by legitimate means, how could he know? I say we let him perform. He'll look the fool, once everyone realizes he's raising money to ruin his own plans."

Lucy sighed. "He never looks the fool, trust me."

"We did a good job of taking him down a peg at the tea," Mrs. Harris put in.

"But this is his livelihood. Within minutes of beginning his act, he'll have everyone eating out of his hand and thinking that a pleasure garden in Richmond is a jolly fine idea."

"I still say we let him perform," the duchess retorted. "Half the people here never remember what we're raising money for, anyway. They just come to enjoy themselves. And if they have a chance to see the great Diego Montalvo? They'll be *pouring* money into our donation bowls. Did you know he's never performed in England? Why, I could have half the press over here in a trice just to see that. Their attention alone will raise funds for our cause, no matter what he says or does."

"I'm sure you're right," Lucy said. Who was she to question the woman who brought more money to their various causes than all the other ladies put together?

"Then we're agreed. We'll use the ballroom—apparently, some of his tricks must be done indoors. He told me he would need an hour to prepare, so I'll send a footman to the papers to coax them here. Once the press has arrived, we'll begin."

"Very well," Lucy said.

Meanwhile, she meant to find out just what he was up to. She didn't trust Diego, and she wasn't about to let him make fools of them in front of the press. Were men good for anything but making trouble?

It took her a while to slip away. By the time she entered the ballroom, she'd worked herself into such a state that she didn't even care he was alone.

Bolstering her righteous indignation, she marched up to where he stood with his back to her on a small stage that the Foxmoors sometimes used for theatricals. Before she could reach him, he said in a husky voice, "Good afternoon, Lucy."

Her heart fluttered insanely before she beat it down. She wouldn't let him affect her! Absolutely *not*. "How did you know it was me?" she asked, hurrying up the stage steps.

A low chuckle escaped him as he worked with something on the table, not even sparing her a glance. "I read minds, remember?"

"Hah! I am not as credulous as you think."

"Trust me, *cariño*, I do not think you credulous in the least."

Another thrill chased down her spine. He hadn't called her *cariño* since the day he'd kissed her. Trying not to think of that, she went to stand across the table from him.

He was cleaning a pistol, which explained why he was in shirtsleeves again and why his attire was not of the best quality.

"What are you up to, Diego?"

He finished his work with neat, efficient motions. "I am preparing for my performance."

"You know perfectly well that's not what I mean," she said irritably. "What are you doing *here*?"

"I was—" he began as he glanced up for the first time since she'd entered. Then he just stood there speechless. Staring.

Unlike Peter's cursory assessment or other gentlemen's sly glances, his gaze took bold liberties, eating her alive, rousing heat in every part: her mouth, her half-bare shoulders . . . her bosom. His gaze flared hot as it ran along her low neckline. Oh, dear, he'd never seen her in a ball gown, had he?

As if realizing where he was staring, he snapped his gaze back to her face. Then he set down the pistol, gathered up his cleaning materials, and headed into the wings.

She followed him on shaky legs, still determined to gain answers to her questions. "Diego, I demand to know why you came here and offered to perform."

"To help your cause, of course."

"And what cause is that?"

"Some Ladies' Association, I believe." Setting the rags and chemicals into an open trunk, he walked over to a washbasin, rolled up his sleeves, and began scrubbing his hands and forearms. "Now, let me ask *you* a question. Why did you lie to me about your plans for today?"

"I didn't lie," she shot back.

"You told me you would be going over accounts with Mrs. Harris."

"We went over them in the carriage." They had, but only to assuage her guilt over her evasion. Which was absurd, given his devious purpose.

"In the carriage." His voice dripped sarcasm. "Of course." Drying his hands on a towel, he strolled back toward her. "That does not explain why you felt the need to conceal your outing."

"I wasn't trying to conceal it." She tipped up her chin as he neared her. "I simply didn't think you would be interested."

"Why would I not be interested in a gathering designed to ruin my plans?"

At the sight of his smug smile, her temper flared. "Oh, I *knew* you had found out what we were about. I just knew it!"

"I am no fool, *cariño*." His gaze bored into her. "Not to mention that you lie badly. And the only time you lie is when you are plotting against me." He tossed the damp towel onto a chair. "Like today, when you and your friends are amassing money to buy the property out from under me."

Her stomach sank. "How did you hear about that?"

His face grew shuttered. "I have my sources."

"So what do you mean to do about it? Denounce everyone from the stage? Make us all look like fools?"

Pure temper shone in his black eyes. "What I do is up to you. I can tailor my performance however I wish. I can indeed make all of you look like fools, or—"

"Or what?"

"I can raise a great deal of money for your cause."

She eyed him suspiciously. "Even though that cause involves our trying to ruin your plans for Rockhurst."

He shrugged. "As I said, it is up to you."

"I'm almost afraid to ask what compensation you'll require of me for *that*."

"Fine. Do not ask. I shall simply return to preparing for my performance." A taunting smile curved his lips. "It will be one to remember, I promise."

"Oh, stop being the Master of Mystery, and just tell me what you want."

He cast her a searching glance. "There will be dancing later, will there not?"

Not sure what that had to do with anything, she nodded.

"I want one waltz with you." His expression had turned quite serious. "And a little conversation about anything other than your precious school."

A frisson of purely feminine gratification shook her. Coming on the heels of Peter's cruel betrayal, his asking such a thing was balm to her wounded heart.

If she could trust his motives. "That's all? Why?"

"For the same reason I have spent two days enduring countless tales of your school and subjecting myself to stray arrows and bad poetry and painful posing for your students. To have the pleasure of your company."

As much as she wanted to bask in that answer, she didn't quite believe it. "Just the pleasure of my company. Nothing more . . . wicked than that."

His face darkened. "Not once in the past two days have I overstepped the bounds of your propriety. That should speak for my character."

Guilt brought hot color to her cheeks. He *had* shown impeccable manners during their tours of the school. Even when she'd been awful to him.

"But I see that means nothing," he clipped out. "Since I am not quite the devil you think and have no desire to 'make fools of your friends,' as you put it, I will leave. That seems the only thing that will satisfy you."

He turned, but she caught his arm. "I'm sorry. You *have* been a gentleman these past two days. I'd be honored to waltz with you." When his stormy gaze shot to her, she managed a smile. "And I would love to see your act."

His rigid features softened. "Then I will perform for your friends. And your cause."

He glanced to where her hand gripped his bare forearm, and his expression grew strained. "If you wish me to continue to behave as a gentleman, *mi dulzura*," he choked out, "I suggest you release my arm."

It was an excellent suggestion. If he hadn't looked so torn about it, she might have complied. But in the privacy of the area behind the curtains, she found herself wanting something else entirely. Especially after he'd called her *mi dulzura*, "my sweetness." Like *cariño*, it made her ridiculous heart hunger for more.

"Perhaps I don't always want you to behave as a gentleman with me," she whispered.

He sucked in a breath, his gaze meeting hers in a brazen glance that told her exactly what he thought of *that* insane remark. Then he dragged her into his arms.

"Never say I did not warn you," he growled, seconds before he took her mouth with such feverish need that it reduced her very bones to ash.

She'd been craving his lips on hers for an eternity, and now she couldn't get enough. She sank into his kiss, reveled in it.

His possessive embrace swallowed her up, plastered her to the lean body that had haunted her dreams. Without his coat and waistcoat, she could feel the heat of his muscular body, and it fed hers like kindling to smoldering coals.

He drew her deeper into the shadows, still kissing her, until he had her pressed against the side wall. "You inflame me, *cariño*," he murmured between delectable kisses to her cheek, her throat, the swells of her breasts. "I have tried to put you from my mind, but I cannot. I have thought of nothing but touching and kissing you for two days."

"Diego . . . please," she said, not sure what she was begging for. He decided for her, his mouth delving lower into her bodice, scattering hot kisses where no man had ever touched her before.

By the time he had edged her bodice and shift down to free one breast, she was aching to see how it would feel to have him kiss her *there*. Her years of lessons clamored that this was wrong, and she tried to listen, even closing her hands in his hair with a righteous intent to pull him back.

Then his mouth covered her bare nipple, and all thought of stopping him died right there. "Oh . . . my . . . word," she whispered as he caressed her breast with deft strokes of his wicked tongue.

She didn't care why he desired her, or how wicked she was to let him dally with her. She just wanted to set her wild Spanish blood free.

Because being here with Diego suddenly seemed worth any censure.

Chapter Eight

Dear Cousin,

We have hit upon a solution of our own. We are raising money to purchase Rockhurst ourselves. We can only hope that if we show Mr. Pritchard we have a reasonable expectation of being able to pay for it, he will refuse to sell to Señor Montalvo.

Your friend,
Charlotte

*T*his was madness, Diego knew. It was unwise for so many reasons, and yet . . .

The intoxicating scent of violets on Lucy's skin and the moans she made low in her throat were too sweet to ignore.

Thank God the footmen had finished setting out chairs and Gaspar was off eating breakfast. Because Diego could not seem to satisfy his own hunger for the enchanting vixen clutching his head to her soft breast.

Dios Santo, how could he help wanting to taste her? When he'd seen her, all he could do was feast his eyes on her beauty. Her bewitching gown of creamy silk and gauze had served up the golden mounds of her breasts like those lemon cakes he'd coveted during his years of hunger.

Except that these cravings were more insistent, more powerful than a mere desire for food. "*Cariño*," he murmured against the flesh that was every bit as lush as he'd dreamed, "we must not . . . enjoy such pleasures here. It is too public."

"Yes . . ." She groaned as he tugged on her nipple with his teeth. "I mean, no . . . not here."

Yet she did not stop him when he cupped her other breast through her gown, fondling it in a futile attempt to assuage the rampant need stiffening his cock to iron. One more moment, just one more moment, and he would stop.

But then she would come to her senses, and he might never get to taste her again. And that was too great a risk to take.

"Ah, *mi dulzura*," he rasped as he dropped to one knee to caress her breast more in earnest. "I wish I could devour every part of you."

He was about to do just that, lifting her skirts, daring to go further, when the sound of boot heels on the wooden floor tapped into his fogged brain. He froze.

"Diego?" she whispered.

He covered her mouth with his hand, then cocked his head to listen, praying it was not Gaspar, who would walk up onto the stage without a thought.

Silently he rose and regretfully pulled up her bodice, fighting the desire that still swamped him with need, that still roused his cock.

He had taken quite a chance with her reputation, and judging from her widening eyes and her frantic attempts to set her clothing to rights, she realized that herself.

"Lucy?" a voice called out from somewhere in the ballroom.

It was sharp, insistent, male. And the intimacy that the man's use of her Christian name implied raised Diego's hackles instantly.

"I know you're in here somewhere," the man went on. "The footman told me you came to speak to that cursed magician. I'm not leaving until we talk."

Lucy cast Diego a look of half apology, half embarrassment, then called back, "I don't want to talk to you. I am helping Señor Montalvo prepare for his performance."

The sound of footsteps approached the stage. Although she was fully dressed, Diego was not. Lucy hurried to the end of the wings while Diego searched for his waistcoat and coat, donning them hastily over his filthy shirt.

As he tied his cravat, he heard her say firmly, "Go away, Peter. I have nothing to say to you."

The Peter? The roiling in Diego's belly intensified as he tightened his cravat. At least anger now banished his unwanted arousal.

"Lucy, I want to explain about Lady Juliana. You have to listen to me."

Muttering a curse, Diego strode out onto the stage beside Lucy. "You heard the señorita. She is not interested in your explanations." He glared down at the man who stood a few feet from the stage.

"This is Peter Burnes," Lucy said in a low voice. "The Earl of Hunforth."

"I gathered as much." Diego loathed him on sight.

The earl took a threatening step forward. "You'll stay out of this, sir, if you know what's good for you."

Diego smiled thinly. "A pity I never seem to know what is good for me. And I damned well know what is not good for *her*."

The two men took each other's measure. Diego wished Lucy's sketch had been a girlish exaggeration, but alas, the young earl was probably every Englishwoman's idea of perfection.

Lord Hunforth possessed the tousled golden curls, fair skin, and blue eyes that were the latest fashion in England. Even worse, he was broad-shouldered, well built, and nearly as tall as Diego. Not a milksop Englishman at all. Next to him, Diego felt every bit the dusky-skinned foreigner.

For a moment, he was catapulted back to the age of fourteen, before he'd grown an extra foot and put on some muscle, when his underdeveloped frame and brown skin had prompted the bluff English soldiers to dub him the Conjuring Crow.

Hostias, what had brought *that* to mind? No one had dared call him that in years—not since the day he'd bested a burly sergeant in a brawl that had left the man with two broken ribs and a bloody nose. If this pasty-faced Englishman thought Diego would back down at idle threats, he would soon learn otherwise.

Ignoring Diego's glower, Lord Hunforth appealed to Lucy. "Call off your dog. I want to speak to you alone. Tell him to go back to changing the colors of cards and drawing scarves out of his sleeve."

His sneering seemed to grate on Lucy's nerves as much as it did Diego's, for she tucked her hand into his elbow. "Anything you say to me can be said in front of Diego just as well."

"Diego? Don't tell me you've taken up with this . . . this . . ."

"Perhaps I should introduce myself." Diego put as much condescension into his voice as the earl. "I am Don Diego

Javier Montalvo, Conde de León. I do not believe we have ever met."

As Lucy gaped at him, Lord Hunforth let out a contemptuous snort. "Conde? *You're* a Spanish count?"

"A Galician count, actually," Diego retorted. Though he might as well be Count of Nothing, with his family's estate sold to pay his dead father's debts.

The earl looked skeptical. "I never heard that about you."

"I choose not to use the title."

He had not used it in fifteen years. At first, it had been a way to preserve the dignity of his family name until he could regain Arboleda. Then it had become something he aspired to be worthy of, something that would make his parents' suffering have significance.

So why had he trotted his title out now? Because that damnable Hunforth had strutted into the ballroom as if he owned it. As if he had the right to bully Lucy simply because he was an English earl. Diego did not like that. At all.

"Whoever you are," Hunforth said, "be a good fellow, will you, and leave us alone a moment? Lucy and I are old friends."

"Friends?" Diego uttered a harsh laugh. "Is that what you call it when you kiss a girl barely old enough to flirt, then call her a hoyden for it?"

The man cast Lucy an accusing glance. "You told him about that?"

Lucy released Diego's arm to march to the front of the stage. "Why not? You told your fiancée about . . . about our discussion at the ball."

The hurt in her voice made Diego want to leap off the stage and throttle Hunforth.

"I knew you would misunderstand." The earl's tone turned peevish. "I had no choice. At the ball, after Juliana saw you and me go off together, she had the impression that—I mean, I couldn't very well let her go on thinking that—"

"That you and I were *friends?*" Lucy said. "Of course not. Much better to laugh at me behind my back."

"Not a very *friendly* thing to do, Hunworth," Diego said darkly.

The earl glared at him. "Hunforth. And you stay out of this."

Lucy planted her hands on her hips. "Why do you care what I think, anyway? You have your perfect fiancée. What has it to do with me?"

Wondering the same thing, Diego watched Hunforth cast furtive glances at Lucy's lovely bosom, and the answer began to dawn on him. Why, that *cretino*—

"I want to preserve our friendship, that is all," Hunforth replied.

Diego could just guess what kind of friendship the earl meant. The kind a man hid from his wife. The kind that could ruin Lucy.

His temper near to exploding, Diego was about to tell the man what he could do with his offer of *friendship*, when a door opened and a footman hurried in. "Miss Seton, Her Grace would like to talk to you about the musicians."

Lucy looked relieved. "Yes, of course."

"I'll go with you," Hunforth said.

"Actually, I'd like a word with you in private," Diego put in. He was not about to give the *imbécil* any chance to insult Lucy further. She seemed oblivious to what he offered, and Diego preferred to keep it that way.

Hunforth hesitated, then lifted his chin with stiff pride. "As you wish."

As soon as Lucy was gone, Hunforth said, "What's this about, Montalvo?"

Diego strolled to the front of the stage, enjoying his two-foot advantage over the earl. "Just a warning. Since you are engaged to another and can clearly have no honorable intention toward Lucy, I suggest that you leave her be."

The earl's face darkened. "And your intentions are honorable? I've heard about your string of women and your smooth ways and your—"

"Ah, but I am not betrothed to anyone. I am free to court Lucy if I wish. *You* are only free to make her your mistress."

From the guilt flashing over Hunforth's face, he had at least considered the possibility. "Look here, you bloody arse. Here in England, married men can have female friends without its being dishonorable."

"*Unmarried* female friends?"

The earl stiffened. "When they are old family friends, yes. Lucy and I have known each other since childhood. We are very close."

"Does your future wife approve of this 'close' friendship?" Diego bit out.

The earl blanched. "My future wife is none of your concern."

"So, she does not know."

"She understands that Lucy is like a sister to me."

Diego crossed his arms over his chest. "You do not look at her as a man looks at his sister."

Hunforth scowled. "You can't possibly understand. Lucy and I grew up in the same regiment. Her mother washed my family's shirts for extra money. It was I who dried her tears after her father died in battle. So don't interfere between us."

The conversation abruptly shifted meaning for Diego. "You knew her father?"

"Didn't I just say that?" the earl snapped.

Yes, but it was impossible. Her "real father" had to be a fabrication of the colonel's, if the man had been the nurse's soldier lover.

"I do not believe you." He took a stab at the truth. "She does not even remember her real father."

"Of course not; she was only four when he died. But I had already turned eight. I remember Sergeant Thomas Crawford very well."

Diego's world tilted on its axis. Hunforth actually had a name for the man? How could that be? "And Lucy's Spanish mother? You remember her, too?"

"Catalina? Yes, why?"

His pulse quickened. Catalina? Could the nurse have had the same name as Lucy's mother? No, that was too much of a coincidence. But she might have taken her mistress's name to comfort the child.

Still, would that not draw attention to her and the girl she had stolen? It made no sense.

"If you and Lucy traveled with the same regiment, then you must have known Lucy in Gibraltar, too, where she was born."

"No, I was never in Gibraltar. My father's regiment was the one Colonel Seton transferred into. I first met her and her real parents in Spain when both regiments were on the same march."

That might explain the earl's strange memories. If Hunforth had only met her "real parents" in Spain, then they might have been anyone. Perhaps the colonel had not been the nurse's lover after all. Perhaps it had been some other soldier.

But why would an unmarried officer take on the stolen child of another soldier? And it still seemed odd that the nurse would have used Doña Catalina's name. Then again, perhaps she had felt safe to do so once they left San Roque outside Gibraltar. He sighed. This grew stranger and stranger. What if he and Gaspar had the wrong woman?

There was only one way to be certain. Get a look at Lucy's thigh to see if she had the birthmark.

"I say," Hunforth broke into his thoughts, "what the devil does this have to do with anything?"

"That should be obvious, given my interest in her." Remembering Hunforth's cruel words to Lucy about her "blood," Diego said, "I wish to know more about her real family, especially if one of them was Spanish. Her mother may have come from nobility."

Hunforth snorted. "I seriously doubt that. Sergeants don't marry so far above their station. Besides, judging from how her parents behaved around each other, their marriage wasn't particularly warm. I'm sure Catalina was just some little Spanish whore who got her hooks in Crawford when she went whining to him about being with child, and he was foolish enough to marry her for it."

Diego nearly choked on his sudden rage. He remembered all too well the soldiers calling his own mother a "little Spanish whore." And she, a lady! "Is that why you think it's acceptable to treat Lucy with disrespect? Because of her mother?"

"How I treat Lucy is not your concern."

"I am making it my concern." Diego glowered at the man. "You had your chance with her, and you were too foolish to see her worth. So leave her alone."

The earl sneered at him. "Or what?"

"I will tell your fiancée about your 'close friendship' with Miss Seton."

The color drained from Hunforth's face. "She wouldn't believe you."

Diego flashed the man a cool smile. "I have never had trouble persuading a woman to believe me before. I cannot imagine it being a problem now."

"Why, you bloody, scheming—"

The sound of a side door opening made the earl break off. Gaspar strolled in, wiping his mouth on his sleeve. "Diego, you have to try the food. I don't know where the duchess found her cook, but he can season a haunch of pork as well as any Spanish . . ." Gaspar trailed off when he spotted Hunforth.

"It's about time you got back," Diego said, ready to be rid of the earl. "We have much to do before the performance."

"This is not over, Montalvo," the earl growled as Gaspar climbed onto the stage.

"I did not think it was," Diego shot back. "Now, if you will excuse me . . ."

And turning his back on the earl, he headed for the wings.

He ought to be pleased that the earl had answered some crucial questions about Lucy's background, but he was too furious that the man thought to continue pursuing her while wedding another woman.

He could tell himself he was only angry because Hunforth's interference could ruin his own plans. Or that he considered himself Lucy's friend and did not want to see her misused.

But honestly, he simply didn't like that *cretino* going near Lucy. It was jealousy, pure and simple.

Besides, the earl would continue to be a thorn in Lucy's side if Diego did not take action, so Hunforth was in for a surprise. Once Diego was through with that damned Englishman, the man would never dare to trouble Lucy again.

Chapter Nine

Dear Charlotte,

  I don't know how to tell you, but Pritchard is unlikely to sell Rockhurst to you. There are things you don't know about the man, things I cannot reveal. All I can say is, be careful how you deal with him. He cannot be trusted.

                    Your concerned cousin,
                    Michael

*B*y the time Lucy returned to the ballroom, Peter had vanished, thank heaven. Diego and his assistant, whom she remembered seeing once, were so busy setting up for the performance that they didn't spare her a glance. She listened to them a moment, surprised to understand some of their Spanish quite well. Papa had said that her mother had often crooned to her in Spanish, and she'd certainly heard a great deal of it in the regimental camp, but she hadn't expected to remember it.

She wished she could stand there longer, but she had other matters to attend to. Regretfully leaving the delicious sight of Diego in rolled-up shirtsleeves, she headed for the gardens. Sighing over him would only encourage him to take further liberties, anyway.

Though she hadn't minded the liberties he *had* taken. What an amazing feeling to have Diego kissing her breasts! Even now, heat rose at the memory. The harem tales hadn't prepared her for the full glory of *that*; reading about it wasn't nearly as exciting as doing it.

She almost wished Peter hadn't come in and interrupted them. Though Diego had probably had many such encounters, it had seemed to mean more to him than a mere dalliance. Especially after Peter's arrival. Diego had seemed overprotective, possessive, even jealous. She'd actually feared they might come to blows. It made no sense. Peter had a fiancée, and Diego claimed not to be free to marry.

She didn't care why Peter had behaved like an idiot. After how he'd betrayed her to Lady Juliana, she could never forgive him anyway. And when he'd gone on about their being old friends, she'd realized that he meant to keep her dangling on a string forever, an admirer he picked up and discarded at whim. Which she would not allow.

Diego was another kettle of fish entirely. She'd assumed that his nonsense about not being free to marry meant he only wanted meaningless dalliances. But he didn't talk like a man who saw her merely as a conquest. Even before Peter had started insulting him, Diego had been downright rude to the earl, defending her as fiercely as Papa would have done.

And why had he wanted to speak to Peter? She fervently wished she could have heard their conversation. According to Mrs. Harris, men talked one way around women and quite differently around other men, but she hadn't explained why. What else had the schoolmistress left out about men?

Like why they were so confusing. Lucy sighed. Mrs. Harris often warned that they might have ulterior motives for their attentions, but she hadn't said it would be so very hard to figure out what those motives were.

Half an hour later, as people took seats in the ballroom, Lucy still hadn't figured out either man. Although Lady Juliana latched onto Peter like a barnacle to a ship's hull, he cast Lucy furtive glances that made her distinctly uneasy.

Diego stood deep in conversation with the duchess while also shooting Lucy glances, but his sent a jolt of excitement to her senses.

Why must he always look so fine? He'd changed into evening attire that sent her pulse stampeding like a cavalry charge. How did he manage always to be perfect? It wasn't as if he dressed to impress—his attire was spartan compared to the other gentlemen's flashy satins and colorful waistcoats. His figured waistcoat was plain white, as were his shirt and simply tied cravat.

But his attire was also of the highest quality, from his fine top hat and perfectly tailored black tailcoat and breeches to the black dress shoes with silver buckles. The ruby pin in his cravat, winking blood-red whenever it caught the sunlight, gave credence to his claim that he was a count.

A Spanish count—how could that be possible? Wouldn't someone in the press have discovered it if it were true?

She glanced around, noting half a dozen newspapermen with notepads ready. Even Charles Godwin, the owner and publisher of *The London Monitor*, was here. He'd probably attended only because he was Mrs. Harris's good friend, but if anyone could find out about Diego's past, it was Mr. Godwin.

Then again, it was one thing to uncover secrets in England and quite another to uncover them in Spain. The war, followed by a series of conflicts, had kept that poor country in turmoil for some time.

Besides, while Diego might tease and evade, he never lied. He seemed to follow a code of honor all his own. Perhaps he was indeed a count. At this point, it would scarcely surprise her.

Either that, or she'd badly misjudged his character. She prayed not, because if he didn't keep his promise not to make them look like fools . . .

Too late now. The duchess was signaling the footmen to turn up the gas lamps at the foot of the stage and close the curtains, dimming the sun's rays to a thin wash of light that instantly transformed the room into an enchanted hall.

Lucy waited tensely for Her Grace or Mrs. Harris to introduce Diego, but he apparently had persuaded them to let him introduce himself. He strode up the stage steps, and the audience broke into applause as he bowed and doffed his hat. "Good afternoon, ladies and gentlemen. I am told that you already know who I am"—more applause ensued—"so I won't bore you with an introduction. I will only say that I am happy to participate in raising money for such a worthy cause."

Around her, people began speculating about whether he actually knew what he was raising money for.

He continued, "I am sure it comes as a surprise to you that I am advancing a cause so opposite to my own aims. You have Miss Seton to thank for that. She has spent the past few days arguing so eloquently on behalf of Mrs. Harris's lovely academy that I sometimes quite forget what my aims even are."

That brought laughter and more applause, this time for her. Lucy's heart began to race, though she wasn't ready to let down her guard just yet.

"I have decided to be open-minded and let you voice your opinion about my pleasure garden in the only way that matters," he went on. "At the back of the room are two donation bowls. The contents of Mrs. Harris's will go to the fund to buy Rockhurst out from under me. The contents of Lady Norcourt's will go to the Newgate Children's Fund, an equally worthy cause."

Lucy wasn't sure what to make of this new turn.

Diego flashed the audience his charmer's smile. "I, of course, prefer that you fill the second bowl, but since Miss Seton and her friends hope you fill the first, I will be a gentleman and not try to influence your decision. In either case, the duke and duchess have agreed to match the amount in whichever bowl has more money. So choose well."

"And you, sir?" Lord Kirkwood called out, having managed to drag Silly Sarah to the breakfast despite the lack of card playing. "Will you agree to match the amount, too?"

Diego feigned a look of horror. "I said I was openminded, sir. Not insane."

That brought another round of laughter.

Fixing his gaze on Lucy, Diego struck a pose of exaggerated seriousness. "I know that there are some in this audience who think my character very bad. And to those people who call me the devil and such, I can only promise that . . ."

A fit of giggling at the front of the room made the others strain to see what was going on.

A pair of horns had begun to emerge from beneath Diego's hair. He talked on as if he didn't realize it, but the horns soon rose so high that everyone in the room could see, and laughter drowned out his words.

Several ladies who'd heard her comments at the tea turned to smile at Lucy, but she didn't mind his little joke at her expense since it brought such pleasure to the audience. And when he finished his speech with a formal bow, then turned to head upstage, displaying a long barbed tail that stuck out from beneath his tailcoat, the crowd roared with laughter.

That set the tone for his performance.

Lucy could only watch in awe as a succession of astonishing tricks followed. First, he took four cards chosen by audience members, restored them to the deck, placed the deck in a goblet, and then, from several paces away, made the chosen cards dance out of the deck at his whim. He poured a seemingly endless flow of different wines from one ordinary bottle into wine glasses, passing them out among the audience. All the while, he interspersed his tricks with amusing remarks that had people laughing with delight.

Then came more ambitious feats: coaxing eggs into strolling up and down a cane taken from someone in the audience, removing a man's shirt without removing his coat, making cards disappear from a deck only to appear again in the donation bowls at the back of the room.

Things got really interesting when he brought out his pistol. He had someone choose a card and restore it to the deck before he tossed the deck into the air and pinned the selected card to the ceiling with one pistol shot.

The audience was still gasping over that one when Diego motioned to his assistant, who brought out a waist-high pedestal and set upon it a candelabra with three candles. Diego picked up another candelabra, which he displayed to the audience. "For this next trick, I will need a volunteer."

Several female hands shot up, but he ignored them, fixing his gaze on someone to Lucy's left. "Lord Hunmouth, if you would be so kind?"

Lucy pivoted to see Peter's reaction, not surprised to see him stiffen with outrage—not only at Diego's deliberate slaughtering of his title, but also at being singled out for such an undignified role. It was all Lucy could do to suppress her laughter as Peter hesitated while others near him prodded him to go on.

"Then again," Diego went on with deceptive nonchalance, "I cannot blame you for not wishing to face a man with a pistol. Is there someone else who—"

"Nonsense." The implication of cowardice made Peter rise. "I'm perfectly happy to help."

As Peter strolled up, Lucy saw Diego's satisfied smile and swallowed hard. He was planning something that didn't bode well for Peter.

Why did those two despise each other? Could it really be just because of her?

That seemed unlikely, yet she'd swear Diego had never met Peter until today. Diego could have no reason for disliking the earl except jealousy. Over her. The very thought sent a thrill through her.

Once Peter was onstage, Diego went through the usual routine of having him check the articles—the pistol, the candelabras, the pedestal—to be sure they were in order. Then he directed Peter to stand three feet away from the pedestal. Handing the earl the second candelabra, he moved the man's arms until the candles were positioned in a line with the others.

"Now, my lord, I hope you have a steady hand." Diego strode back to the pedestal and lit the three candles on the candelabra. "Because I mean to transfer the flames on these candles to your candles with one pistol shot. And it will only work if you keep the candles perfectly aligned and do not move a muscle."

As it dawned on Peter that Diego meant to shoot in his general direction, the alarm spreading over his features was priceless. Lucy bit down hard on her lip to keep from laughing, though no one else seemed to have such restraint. And when a red flush of embarrassment stained Peter's pale cheeks, Lucy could have kissed Diego right there in front of everyone.

She couldn't have thought of a better—or more public— humiliation. It almost made up for Peter's pompous remarks about wanting to be her friend. As if he hadn't already given up the right to that by insulting her.

Diego called the duke's friend Lord Stoneville up to the stage to load the pistol, which only made everything worse, since it implied that Diego would be using a real ball, not a trick one. Peter's eyes widened, and his body stiffened until he looked like a rabbit cornered by a fox.

By the time Diego took his position, sighting down the barrel at the line of candle flames and empty wicks, Peter's candelabra had begun to shake uncontrollably. Lucy could almost feel sorry for him.

Almost.

"Steady, man, steady," Diego said with a decidedly devil-ish glint in his eye. "Wouldn't want to clip you instead of the candles."

Diego continued to sight and aim and adjust his position. To anyone else, it probably seemed as if he were merely drawing out the suspense, but Lucy recognized the dark pleasure shining on his face. He was reveling in Peter's fear. It was really too awful of him, but she couldn't blame him when she remembered Peter's nasty remarks about his abilities.

At last, a shot sounded. The first three candles were extinguished; the second three caught fire. And Peter looked as if he might actually faint.

Diego, however, looked intensely satisfied. As the applause sounded, he bowed to the audience and said, "Please give another round for my accommodating *friend*."

Lucy stifled a smile. It was clear from Peter's face that he'd caught Diego's sarcasm. As the audience applauded again, Peter headed for the stage steps, pausing to shoot Diego a venomous glance. Diego's chilly nod made Lucy shiver.

Good Lord. She would have to keep an eye on those two. She couldn't have the wonderfully successful charity breakfast end in a brawl. Or worse.

"For my final trick, I require the assistance of Miss Seton. Señorita? Will you please come to the stage?"

Nervous at what he had up his sleeve now, Lucy rose and joined him onstage amid enthusiastic applause.

With a wicked smile, Diego doffed his hat. "Here we have an ordinary hat. Is that not correct, Miss Seton?"

Lucy checked the hat and agreed that it was indeed a plain top hat.

He took it from her. "Now, if you will be so good as to give me one of your lovely earbobs."

She did so. He placed it in the hat, passed a handkerchief over it, and whisked away the handkerchief to reveal that the hat was empty. The trick seemed rather humdrum considering his earlier effects, but the audience clapped politely.

"Let's see if we can restore Miss Seton's property." Again, he covered the hat, but this time when he whisked the handkerchief away, he held the hat out to Lucy. "Miss Seton, your earbob."

She reached into the hat but instead of her jewelry found a handful of ten-pound notes. When she pulled them out in bewilderment, the audience clapped.

Diego feigned deep concern. "*Dios mio*, I knew I should not have bought one of your English hats. It lacks all magic."

Everyone laughed.

He peered into the hat and knocked it on his thigh. "That should do it. If you will hold those notes, señorita, I will see if I can produce your earbob this time."

He tried again. And again, each time varying his patter and producing more bank notes to increased laughter and applause from the audience. After the fourth miraculous appearance of ten-pound notes, he gazed hard at the pile in her hand and said, "Ah, I see the problem. Your earbob is in hiding."

Plucking a note from her hand, he crumpled it up, then opened his hand to reveal her earbob. As the audience applauded wildly, he handed it to her.

Then he gestured to the pile of notes in her hand. "Please accept these as my own donation to your cause," he announced with a bow.

She gaped at him, then stared down at the notes. "But sir, there must be more than two hundred pounds here."

He nodded. "For your fund."

She waited until the audience finished applauding, then said tartly, "But *which* fund?"

Eyes gleaming, he said, "Whichever you feel is more worthy." He turned to the audience. "And now it is your turn. You must not leave Miss Seton's donation to languish alone. If you enjoyed the performance, do be generous!"

The duchess swept onto the stage. "Ladies and gentlemen, Diego Javier Montalvo, Master of Mystery!"

Amid thunderous applause, he gave a bow, offered Lucy his arm, and led her off the stage. At the bottom, he released her arm and bent close to whisper, "Remember, Lucy. You owe me a waltz."

Then the press swamped him.

For a moment, she watched, her heart thundering in her chest, as Diego handled the press with expert ease. A waltz? She owed him that and more. A quick glance at the donation bowls showed that each already contained more money than the total generally raised at these affairs. Though the two funds were filling equally, his two hundred pounds would probably tip the balance in favor of the one to buy Rockhurst. And the duke and duchess would match it.

How astonishing. Why had he done this? Why risk his own plans for Rockhurst to come here and perform for them? Surely it wasn't just because of her. She dared not believe that. No matter how clever and handsome and amazing he seemed, this was but an interlude to him.

Or was it? After all, if he did buy Rockhurst, and he did settle next door to the school . . .

Best not to dream such things. Besides, if he stayed, it meant the ruin of the school, and she didn't want that, either.

With a sigh, she headed for the back of the room, where the ladies were busy emptying the bowls while the guests headed out to dine at tables in the gardens. She helped tally the funds as the footmen cleared the chairs in the ballroom and Diego finished dealing with the press.

Half an hour passed before she could get away, but when she exited onto a terrace on the side of the house away from the gardens, a man slunk out of the shadows, startling her.

"Peter!" She glanced nervously around, not the least pleased to see that they were alone. "Why aren't you eating with the other guests?"

The ugly look on his face struck a chill to her bones. "Juliana and I are leaving. She's waiting for me in the carriage with her maid." He stalked toward her, his face a mottled red. "But I had to talk to you first, to tell you I will never forgive you for sending Montalvo to humiliate me before my fiancée."

"What? I did not—"

"I knew you were angry about me and Juliana." He approached so close she could smell the brandy on his breath. "You never did understand the requirements of rank, that a man has to do certain things because of his position."

"Odd how you forgot all that when you called me your 'one true love.'"

His face darkened. "Things may have changed between us, but I still care about you. If you think I'll stand by while that bastard Montalvo tries to worm his way into your good graces by making fools of your old friends—"

"Friends?" she spat, trying not to be alarmed by his drunken anger. "You haven't been a friend to me in a year or more, Peter. You know nothing about me. I'm beginning to realize you never did. So go back to your fiancée."

She turned to walk off, but Peter grabbed her by the arm and jerked her up next to him. "I don't love Juliana, you know," he murmured in her ear. "But with this title came an estate I can ill afford, and she has the wherewithal to maintain it. You're the one I love—the only one. You're the one I want."

How long had she waited to hear those words again? And now that she had, all she wanted was to slap him. Bad enough to think he'd fallen out of love with her, but that he'd loved her and chosen someone else because of money? And then tried to make her think it was because of her own flaws?

How had she never noticed that Peter had lost his honor and his character somewhere on the Grand Tour? Or that he seemed to think she should take his excuses as a reason for letting him do as he pleased with her?

"Well, *I* don't want *you*." She swung at him with her ineffectual reticule as she struggled to free her arm from his grip.

He shoved her against the wall so hard he knocked the breath from her. "You wanted me a week ago," he growled as he trapped her with his body. "You wanted me well enough to ask my intentions, like the bold flirt that you are. What's happened since then? Decided to taste a bit of the exotic? Does your father know you're consorting with that dirty Spaniard?"

"I'm doing no such thing!" She pushed against his shoulders in a panic. Peter was stronger than she remembered, especially with some liquid courage inside him.

Pinning her hands against the wall, he flattened himself against her, making it impossible for her to move. "Do you really think a man like that has honorable intentions? A man who discards women when he's done with them?"

She writhed against him, now truly alarmed. "Get off of me, Peter!" she cried, praying someone would hear. But how could they, with all the noise?

"Or what? You'll tell your new friend to humiliate me? Don't worry—he'll never get that chance again. I'll see him dead first. But not before I remind you how you feel about me." He shoved his mouth against hers so hard she couldn't breathe, and she feared he might actually try to violate her.

Suddenly, he was yanked bodily from her and thrown to the floor of the terrace.

As Peter scrambled to his feet, Diego faced him down, balling his hands into fists. "You *maldito Inglés!* How dare you assault a respectable woman! Have you no shame?"

"I wasn't assaulting her! She wanted me to kiss her, didn't you, Lucy?"

"*Sí, sí,* that's why you had to hold her by force!" A string of Spanish curses left his lips. Then he cast her a concerned glance. "Are you all right?"

She could only nod, still shaken.

Without warning, Peter threw a punch at Diego, catching him so hard that he split Diego's lip. As blood dripped down his chin onto his cravat, Diego struck back: one swift blow to the belly, then another to the jaw.

It laid Peter out cold.

Chapter Ten

Dear Cousin,

*That is all you can tell me about Mr. Pritchard:
Do not trust him? I know the man has a sly
manner, but I would appreciate more concrete
evidence of <u>why</u> I should not trust him. You are
as impenetrable as our neighbor, the Master of
Mystery. It is most frustrating.*

*Your annoyed correspondent,
Charlotte*

His blood roaring in his ears, Diego stood over the prone
Hunforth with fists clenched. Just the memory of the bastard pinning Lucy to the wall made a red haze fill his vision.
"Get up, you damned English ass!" Diego kicked him in the
ribs. "Let us see how well you do when you fight fair!"

"Stop that!" Lucy grabbed him by the arm. "I will not
have you two brawling at the duchess's party like animals.
He's out cold, so leave him be."

"He deserves to be thrashed—"

"Yes, he does. But think what the press would make of
that." With troubled eyes, she drew a handkerchief from
her reticule and pressed it to his bleeding lip. "Please,
you've already got blood on your shirt. If you keep fight-

ing, someone will surely see. And I don't want my name plastered across the papers. Or yours."

That gave him pause. Especially since he could hear voices on the terrace. As he hesitated, Lucy stuffed her handkerchief into her reticule and yanked on his arm until he reluctantly let her drag him away. Diego heard Hunforth moaning behind them as he came out of it, but Lucy's implacable expression kept him moving as she half pulled, half shoved him along the terrace. She tried door after door until she found one unlocked. It led into what looked like a library.

"Wait for me in here," she ordered. "I'll take care of Peter."

He stiffened. "I am not leaving you alone with that ass."

"I won't be alone. I'm going to fetch two footmen to remove the very drunk Lord Hunforth, who passed out on the terrace." More voices could be heard. "Quick, before anyone sees you!" she commanded, giving him a little push. "If you don't have a care for your own reputation, at least have a care for mine."

Hostias, how he wished she hadn't said that. He itched to go back and beat Hunforth to a bloody pulp just for daring to touch her. But the press was still here, and if he was found brawling with Hunforth over Lucy, she *would* be ruined. If he was even found alone with her, with his lip busted and blood on his shirt—

He walked into the library and let her shut the door behind him.

But he could not stay still while awaiting her return. It was not in his nature to let a woman clean up his mess, and this mess was certainly his. If he had not stepped in earlier, or had not made a fool of Hunforth onstage . . .

A grim smile touched his lips. No, he could not regret *that.* Hunforth had needed someone to prick his pompous pride, and it had given Diego a great deal of pleasure to do so. He only wished Lucy had not suffered for it.

Pacing the room, he saw again the fear on her face at Hunforth's assault. What if Diego had not gone looking for her in the duke's study and then been sent in her direction? What if that drunken ass had really hurt her?

He could not bear the idea.

A different door opened, and he whirled around, braced for discovery. But it was only Lucy, bearing a glass of water, a sponge, and a small pot of what looked like ointment. She locked the door behind her.

"Take off your shirt and your cravat," she ordered. When he arched an eyebrow at that interesting command, she blushed. "I have to get the blood out of them, you dolt. Only imagine what the press will make of it if they see it."

"I have another shirt," he said.

Her face brightened. "Another dress shirt? And a cravat?"

"No, but—"

She sighed. "That won't do. When they see you've changed clothes, they'll be suspicious."

"Then I will say I spilled red wine on myself."

"That won't do, either. As the footmen carried him off, Peter mumbled that you had attacked him. I told them he was too drunk to know what he said, and he certainly reeked of brandy. Still, we don't know who else he might tell on his way to the carriage. So when you appear before the press again, you have to look exactly as you did before."

He touched his finger to his split lip. "What about this?"

"I brought some makeup I found backstage. If you stay out of sight until night falls and don't go near brightly lit areas, it should suffice. As long as you don't have big red stains on your clothes, you should be able to fool the press."

With a scowl, he removed his coat and waistcoat, tossing them across a settee. "I hate the press."

"Yes, I could tell," she said dryly. She set her items down on a writing desk and turned up the low-burning gas lantern sitting there.

"What is *that* supposed to mean?" he grumbled, untying his cravat.

"I saw how you were with them. You were masterful at keeping their attention, and you definitely enjoyed the verbal sparring." She smiled to soften her words. "Your ability to handle people is what makes you such a good conjurer. You're quite the showman. I daresay it comes naturally to you."

He stared blankly at her as she opened her reticule to rummage around in it. Should he be flattered or insulted by that odd observation? He had never thought of himself as a showman by nature. Conjuring was just something he happened to be good at, something he did to make a living.

Something he would quit doing one day to become lord of Arboleda and a respected member of society in Villafranca, as he had promised while Father had lain dying before the burning vineyards.

Pulling a small bottle from her reticule, she poured something into the water.

"What's that?" he asked as she stirred it with a quill from the writing desk, raising a foul odor in the room.

"Smelling salts." She held out her hand for his cravat, and he tossed it to her. "They work well on bloodstains when mixed with water."

"You are a very clever woman, *querida.*" He unbuttoned his shirt. "Though I am not sure whether to be pleased or alarmed that you know how to clean up blood. Does Hunforth make a regular practice of bloodying your suitors?"

She shot him a veiled glance. "Papa was in the army, remember?" She worked the liquid into the bloodstain with a sponge. "Learning how to deal with blood was a necessity in the regimental camps. But you should know that. Didn't you say you got your start performing for regiments?"

"I did indeed." He drew off his shirt, and she turned to take it, then froze, her eyes going wide as she saw his bare chest.

His breath quickened. The way she looked at him roused his blood, and that was perilous. Thankfully she realized she was staring, jerked his shirt from his outstretched hand, and turned to working out the bloodstain on it.

"How does a count come to be entertaining soldiers?" Her voice trembled.

It took him a second to get himself under control enough to register what she had said, but then he stifled a groan. That was the last thing he wanted to talk about with her, especially if he was to get her to trust him with her own secrets. "Do not tell your friend Hunforth, but I was one of the many lords left penniless by the war in Spain. I had to make my way somehow. So I learned a trade."

She laughed. "A trade? Is that what you call becoming the great Diego Javier Montalvo, Master of Mystery?"

"It is not what I was raised to do, so yes." This conversation had veered into dangerous territory. Time to change the subject. He would never get a better chance to find out what she knew of her own past. "I probably even entertained your father's regiment at some time. What regiment was he in?"

"Which father?" She peered closely at the stain, then sponged some more.

"They weren't in the same regiment?"

She frowned. "Actually, they were, but only for a while. Papa—the colonel—transferred to the Seventy-third later." She paused. "I'm not sure why. He doesn't like to talk about it. Anyway, he was my real father's superior officer in Gibraltar and then in Spain. That's why, when my father was dying, he asked the colonel to take care of me. My parents had no family."

Diego sucked in a breath. The sergeant must indeed have been the nurse's lover. But like others in the regiment, he and the nurse had died on the miserable campaign to and from La Coruña, leaving Lucy to the colonel.

Still, Diego doubted the colonel had adopted Lucy just because his subordinate asked it. Perhaps the colonel had been covering up the despicable way they had acquired their child. It would explain his changing regiments, so as not to have his collusion discovered when her Spanish relations searched for her. Don Carlos had said he only recently learned that the nurse's lover had been a soldier.

Only one thing did not fit: the nurse taking the name of Catalina. Why would she take such a risk? "Do you remember your parents?" he asked as she hung the damp shirt and cravat over a chair near the fire.

"No. Well, sometimes I get this . . . picture in my head of my mother. At least, I think it's my mother."

"What does she look like?"

"Very beautiful. Black hair, black eyes, olive skin. And a small mole right here." She touched her finger to her upper lip.

Diego frowned. The miniature had shown no mole on her mother's face. But it was only a miniature. Or Lucy might be remembering the nurse.

"I can't even be sure I'm really seeing *her*," Lucy went on, as if she'd read his mind. She walked back to the table. "I wish I knew more about them than the little Papa has told me." She stared down at the pot of makeup. "When I first came to the school, I envied the other girls so much. They had sisters and grandparents and uncles and cousins. I had only Papa. His parents died before the war, and he was their only child. He said my real parents had no family either, so it's always been just us. Until my stepmother, of course."

"Do you at least know your real parents' names?"

Picking up the small pot, she eyed him curiously. "Why all these questions?"

He managed a shrug. "Your mother was Spanish. How could I not be interested?"

"She was no one of consequence, or at least that's what Papa says. She was certainly no one of consequence compared with a count."

"A penniless count," he reminded her.

"Not penniless anymore, I should think, given your fame."

He stiffened, remembering how many women had flirted with him simply because they thought he must be rich. "Trust me, even famous conjurers make about as much money as actors."

Her gaze shot to him in surprise. "Then how can you afford Rockhurst?"

Hostias, he must watch his tongue. "I have investors. In Spain."

"Forgive me," she said with a blush. "I did not mean to pry."

"I do not mind. I am secure enough for now, I suppose."

"That's all that matters, anyway. As long as a person has enough to be comfortable, the rest is excess." Walking up to him, she opened the little pot and dipped her finger into it. "Mrs. Harris has taught us time and again that money can be a curse. I am often very happy not to be a great heiress like my friend Elinor. How awful to have men sniff around you just for your money! At least I know that anyone who marries *me* will marry for love."

Before he could voice his opinion about that unpredictable emotion, she murmured, "Hold still," and dabbed something on his lip.

"Ow!" He jerked back. "That burns like the devil."

"Do you want the press to notice your split lip or not?"

With a roll of his eyes, he acquiesced. The second dab did not hurt so much. Not his lip, anyway. But other parts of him started to ache, with her so near that he could smell violets and see the shadow between her lovely breasts and hear her breath quickening.

"There." Her eyes focused on his lip. "That ought to suffice." Her voice sounded as shaky as he felt.

"Thank you," he said through a throat gone tight with need.

"Thank *you* for saving me from Peter and his idiocy." Her fingers lingered over his lip to smooth and dab and drive him stark raving mad. "I'm sorry I ever dragged you into it. Truly, I am."

"You did not drag me into it," he said firmly. "I dragged myself. I provoked him into it, even before the performance. When he and I were alone, I told him to leave you be. I told him he had no right to toy with you." His voice grew choked. "But I should have left it at that and not made a fool of him in front of everyone."

"Don't you dare apologize for that." She flashed him a wry smile. "I'm just wicked enough to have enjoyed it."

"You are not remotely wicked," he corrected her. "And he deserved that and more, for not seeing what a jewel you are." He shook his head. "But I should have realized he would come after you for it. That is what bullies do—prey on those weaker than themselves. Your Peter is a bully of the worst kind, one who bullies women." Like the soldiers who had—

No, he could not bear to remember that right now, with the image of Lucy being mauled still fresh in his mind. "If he had hurt you, I would never have forgiven myself."

She touched her fingers to his lips. "But he didn't hurt me. You were there. And I cannot thank you enough."

He stared blindly at her, at the woman he could not have if he were to regain what had been stolen from his family. Her kindness cut him to the heart when he knew how he was deceiving her. Yet he was just devil enough to exult in the tenderness on her face, the gentle touch of her fingers on his lips.

He kissed her fingertips, then pressed a kiss lower, into her palm.

A look of uncertainty passed over her face as she dropped her hand from his mouth. "I-I should return to the others." She glanced away. "I'll see if I can distract anyone who's looking for you."

"Don't go yet," he rasped, looping his arm about her waist. "You still owe me a waltz." It was a mistake—he knew it was a mistake to hold her.

But he wanted her with him a while longer. He had been able to think of nothing but her since their kisses backstage.

"We can dance on the lawn with the others," she whispered, though she made no attempt to leave his embrace.

"And rouse the press's attention? Not wise, *mi dulzura*—not wise at all."

Hearing music filtering in from outside, he took her hand and began to waltz. After a second's hesitation, she followed his lead.

He told himself he would just dance with her. He would show her that not all men were animals like Hunforth, savaging a woman with brute force. He would hold her and smell her and nothing else.

Then she made the mistake of placing her hand on his bare waist and lifting her gaze to his again. He read the desire in her eyes, and he was lost. Eternally lost.

He had already broken the *marqués*'s rules about not touching her. What harm could there be in touching her more, as long as he did not ruin her? After he got a look at her thigh to confirm her identity, she would be out of his reach forever. She would belong to whatever man her grandfather picked for her.

Unless she was *not* the one he and Gaspar sought. Diego seized on that possibility with a vengeance. It had happened before, and not every piece of the puzzle of her background fit perfectly. If she was not the *marqués*'s granddaughter, he would be free to court her. What could it hurt to start now?

His conscience screamed that he knew better, that he had made a promise to the *marqués*, that even without the promise, he would be taking advantage of her as surely as Hunforth had tried to do. She deserved better, and he knew it.

But her succulent lips were inches from his, her body soft and yielding in his arms, and he could not help himself. "*Cariño*," he said hoarsely.

Then he kissed her.

Chapter Eleven

> *Dear Charlotte,*
>   *Impenetrable I may be, but surely you know by now that I have only your best interests at heart. Heed my second warning, and keep an eye out for your Master of Mystery. He still has not applied for a license, and his assistant is asking peculiar questions about the school and its staff. Be very careful with him.*
>
>   *Your concerned cousin,*
>   *Michael*

*E*ven before Diego's lips met hers, Lucy had been wavering in her resistance to his temptations. Now she was drowning in them, and she didn't care. She was in his arms again, and he was kissing her with such tenderness it made her heart hurt. How could she not kiss him back?

Do you really think a man like that has honorable intentions?

Probably not.

He'd asked about her parents, and a man of venerable Spanish rank would only ask such questions of a woman he courted. Unlike English gentlemen, he would find her mother's blood an advantage, too.

But she wouldn't place her hopes in that; she'd made that mistake before. And his emphasis on being a penniless count was probably meant to be a warning that he couldn't afford a wife.

Still, he did seem to care for her. He'd fought valiantly for her, had raised money to destroy his own aims, and had given some of his own hard-earned funds to that cause. More important, when he'd leaped to her defense, he hadn't blamed *her* but Peter. And himself. Surely that showed him to be a man of character.

She was tired of worrying about it. She'd tried hard to be good. She'd waited patiently for Peter to return from abroad, not even countenancing anyone else's attentions, and for what? For him to admit he loved her, yet it still didn't matter? For him to insult her and try to ruin her?

He still might, too. Nothing could stop Peter from telling people about the brawl later and blackening her name, as well as Diego's. People might even believe what Peter said—not only because he was an earl but also because of Diego's performance. Peter would use that. He clearly wasn't the gentleman she'd thought.

While Diego was far *more* of a gentleman than she'd thought. He'd been honest about his intentions from the beginning. And if she found her reputation ruined through no fault of her own, shouldn't she have some pleasure out of it? What was the point of being proper if everyone believed the worst about you anyway? Might as well be improper, it seemed to her.

As if reading her thoughts, Diego drew back. "I do not want you to think I am like Hunforth, willing to take advantage of a woman—"

"I'd never think that," she whispered, once more re-minded that Diego was a good man at heart. This time, she was the one to kiss *him*.

He pulled away abruptly. "Careful, *cariño*." He cast her a rueful smile and tapped one end of his lip. "Best to stay on this side."

Oh, dear, she'd forgotten about his injury. "I'm sorry."

"I do not mind a little pain for one of your kisses," he said huskily. "But if you start the bleeding again, your ef-forts will have been for naught."

She suspected her efforts would be for naught anyway, but she wasn't about to point that out. He would get all noble again and try to protect her. Right now, she didn't want nobility. She wanted *him*. "Then let me kiss it to make it better."

He arched an eyebrow. "I thought that was only some-thing mothers told their children to take their minds off their troubles."

"Let's find out, shall we?" she teased, stretching up to kiss his split lip. "Better?"

"Much." His dark eyes gleamed in the candlelight as he bent to nuzzle her cheek. "But now you will have to apply the makeup again."

"I will." She brushed her lips over his cheek. "Once we're done waltzing."

"Is that what you English call this?" He clasped her head in his hands for another magical kiss that stole the soul from her body. He dragged his mouth down her chin, then her throat. "I like the English version of waltzing."

"So do I." She clutched at his bare shoulders, then swept along them to memorize every curve and muscle.

It was her first time touching a man's naked torso, and

she meant to relish it. Her hands fanned down his well-wrought chest, her thumbs exploring his flat nipples.

He groaned low in his throat. "*Mi dulzura,* as much as I enjoy this . . . we should stop."

"Why?" she whispered. "Don't you like my hands on you?"

"Too much," he growled. "That is the problem."

"It doesn't sound like a problem to me," she said with deliberate coyness.

Diego searched her face. "What are you doing, Lucy?"

"Finding out if you are as amazing a lover as the papers say you are."

At the word "lover," heat flared in his face. "I refuse to ruin you. And I know that is not what you want, either."

"Perhaps it is." She lifted her chin, trying to look sophisticated and certain of her desires, though his words made her feel unsophisticated and uncertain. "Perhaps Peter is right, and I really am a hoyden."

He cupped her chin tenderly. "What you are is curious. And passionate. No matter what English propriety says, that is perfectly natural in a young woman. Why do you think we Spanish have such stern *dueñas?* Because we do not trust the young gentlemen *or* the young ladies when the heat has got hold of them."

"Mrs. Harris is my chaperone," she said defensively.

"And yet you are here alone with me."

"For all the good it does me." She pulled free of his arms, hurt by his clear rejection. Peter wanted her only for her body, and Diego didn't even want her for that. "Not only am I a reckless hoyden whom no honorable man would wish to marry, but I'm not even desirable enough to attract a man known for his dalliances."

"*Por Dios, mi dulzura,*" he said, catching her from be-hind to pull her against his chest. "You know I find you desirable."

"Do I?" Tears clogged her throat. "Peter would already have tried to . . . to touch me. But you . . . you probably think I am just a silly English fool. Compared to your . . . your Russian princesses and . . . o-opera singers, I am just—"

"Sh, sh, *cariño,*" he murmured against her ear, his hands roaming up and down her waist. "You are twice the woman of any of them."

"But not enough to t-tempt you."

Turning her in his arms, he pressed her hand to his chest. "Can you not feel that? My heart pounds like thun-der. I could not desire you any more than I do at this mo-ment."

"Then show me," she said softly. "Show me how you feel. I want to know what I've been avoiding all this time."

His face darkened, and he muttered a curse under his breath. "Very well. I will do as you wish. But I will not ruin you. Understand?"

"Not really."

He led her to the settee, sat down upon it, then pulled her onto his lap. "I am going to give you pleasure, *querida.* When I am done, you will still be an innocent." He flashed her a wry smile. "Or rather, you will still be chaste."

That relieved her, then intrigued her. A little thrill of ex-citement coursed along her spine. "But what about you?"

"Me?" he choked out. "I will be in hell. But it is a hell I can stomach. Ruining you is a hell I cannot."

Clearly, marrying her was also a hell he could not. She pushed down her hurt. He'd always told her what to expect from him. At least she'd have something to remember after he was gone.

His hand started raising her skirts.

"D-Diego? What are you doing?" She was not so innocent that she didn't know ruination began with a man lifting a woman's skirts.

"Dallying with you." He bent her back over his arm, then began to kiss his way to her breasts. "Drinking my fill. Or as much of it as I dare."

His hand left her skirts just long enough to drag her bodice and corset down so he could plunder her bare breast with his mouth. She arched up as an exquisite sensation shot through her, making her clutch at his head to hold him fast.

Meanwhile, his hand returned to her skirts, tugging and pulling until they were up around her thighs, exposing her drawers. With the deftness of long experience, he found the slit and slid his fingers inside to touch the part of her only she had dared to touch, the part that grew damp at night when she dreamed of him.

Having him touch her *there* gave new meaning to the term "sleight of hand." It was so astonishing that it made her sigh aloud and press herself against his fingers.

"You like that, do you, *querida?*" He rubbed the cleft with a stroke that made her gasp. He raised his head to stare at her with a slumberous glance. "You are so wet, so hot and wet. Will you let me taste your nectar?"

"M-my nectar?" Ohh, the dampness. He knew about that?

Of course he did. He had done this with many women.

Time enough to be jealous of them later. For now, he was hers.

"You can taste whatever you want," she whispered, wondering if he meant "taste" literally. Surely he would not . . .

But as he stretched her back to lie on the settee, then slid far enough down to stare at her private place with decided hunger, she realized he would. He actually intended to put his *lips* . . .

He did exactly that. Good Lord.

She shuddered deliciously at the amazing sensation of his mouth covering her *there*. It was . . . amazing. Downright inspiring. Even magical.

The sight of his dark head between her legs sent such excitement soaring through her that she could not tear her eyes from it. Did English men and women ever do this? Or was it just a Spanish custom?

No, the harem tales had mentioned it, too. But she and the other girls had decided it was too ridiculous to believe. What man would want to lick someone down there?

Clearly Diego would, for his tongue stroked her in shocking ways, lapping at her, toying with her. And it was every bit as talented as his hands, one of which still teased and fondled her breast. He roused her above, he roused her below, until she was so aroused that she ached with her need.

"Please . . . Diego . . . please," she begged, sensing that something more lay just beyond her reach.

"Patience, *mi dulzura*," he murmured against her flesh. "Close your eyes. Relax. It will come."

Closing her eyes would mean losing control, which made her nervous, especially when she saw him untie her drawers and slide them off. Yet when he returned to arousing her with his mouth, and she did close her eyes, the pleasure intensified to an almost unbearable degree.

Now one of his fingers was thrusting inside her, making

her arch up to meet it. And to meet his tongue, which continued its dance, until a most peculiar heat began in her toes, flashing higher, searing her blood, until it seemed to gather right at the spot his tongue was strafing.

She exploded. The most exquisite explosion of pleasure rocked her, making her utter a small cry as she clasped his head against her.

For a moment, she lay there relishing it. No one had ever told her about *this*. In the harem tales, a woman's pleasure, when there was any, was couched in lofty terms she hadn't understood.

She understood now.

And she understood something else, too. He had not been given the same pleasure. The harem tales had been quite clear about what constituted pleasure for a man.

That was confirmed when she opened her eyes to find him staring at her thighs with a look akin to desperation. Actually, staring at just one thigh. She could almost swear he was looking at her birthmark.

No, that was silly. It was barely light enough in here to see it.

"Diego," she whispered, and his gaze jerked to her face. He wore the guilty look of a man who'd just done something very wrong. It was rather endearing. "That was incredible." She sat up, covering herself with inexplicable modesty, given what she'd just been doing. "But can't I give *you* pleasure?"

"Lucy, I do not think—"

Remembering what she'd read, she reached for his breeches buttons. "Surely I could do *something*."

"God help me," he muttered. "I shall burn in hell for certain."

"Then we'll burn together," she said, amused by his attack of conscience. He could be so oddly prudish sometimes. "Show me what to do."

With a groan, he unbuttoned his breeches and his drawers in an almost feverish haste. Then he took her hand and led it inside both. "Touch me here, *querida*." He closed her fingers around his flesh. "If I am to burn, it might as well be for something serious."

Laughing, she let him show her how to tug on him, to fondle him. She couldn't believe how firm a man's privates grew. And how long. Why, it was longer than her hand, and grew longer still as she caressed him.

He threw his head back, his eyes sliding closed. "Ah, you are a witch. Yes, like that . . . stroke me like that. Firmly . . . yes . . ."

A noise outside the glass door to the terrace made her pause. Diego's eyes shot open. They both caught their breath as voices filtered in. They hadn't locked that door, and the lamp still burned, though the heavy curtains over the door would probably keep anyone from seeing inside.

Still . . . He drew her hand from beneath his drawers, buttoning them and his breeches swiftly.

"I have looked all over for her," Mrs. Harris told someone. "I can't imagine where she has gone."

"What about the magician?" a muffled voice responded. "Have you seen him?"

Lucy recognized Mr. Godwin's voice. Oh, dear. That was one person she most certainly did not want to learn what she and Diego were doing. Given his friendship with Mrs. Harris, she didn't think he would publish anything about her, but he would certainly vilify Diego in the press for dallying with her.

"I asked his assistant," Mrs. Harris replied. "He said he was certain the man had returned to Rockhurst. That he finds performing exhausting."

Lucy glanced to Diego, who shot her a rueful smile. Clearly Gaspar had no qualms about lying for his master. Leaving the settee, she slid her drawers on and edged closer to the door.

"I wouldn't trust that if I were you," Mr. Godwin went on.

"Charles, I do hope you are not implying that Lucy would ever—"

"Perhaps not, but Montalvo has a shady past and a reputation with pretty females. You have no idea what he is capable of."

"And you do? Oh, dear, what do you know? Why have you not said anything? I swear, if you knew he made a practice of ruining young women—"

"No, no," Mr. Godwin said, even as Diego sat up stiffly, his expression full of outrage. "Nothing like that."

"Then what?"

There was a long pause. Lucy held her breath. Diego sat there, his mouth set in a stony line.

"Actually," Mr. Godwin went on, "it's not what I've heard of him in the press. It's . . . well, you know I served on the Peninsula."

Diego tensed.

"Yes, what of it?" Mrs. Harris asked.

"I didn't recognize his name when I first heard it, but when I saw his performance, I realized I'd seen bits before."

Lucy relaxed. Diego had already told her he'd had his start performing for the regiments. That was nothing to be ashamed of.

"The thing is," Mr. Godwin went on, "the word around the regimental camps was that he was a thief and a cheat. You have to admit he's good with cards. I imagine he can deal from the bottom as well as any cardsharp."

I am not a cardsharp or a thief, he'd once said to her.

Her stomach sank. She glanced over to find his eyes fixed bleakly on her. He'd been lying that day on the river landing. She could see it in his face.

The blood rose in her as she remembered how pompously he'd said it, with that Continental air of the man of honor. It was the same way he said everything. Had his courtly behavior and impeccable manners been just a façade? And if so, what else had he lied about?

"You saw how much money he raised," Mrs. Harris remarked. "And how much of his own he contributed. I hardly think those the actions of a thief."

"You don't consider it odd that he would give money to a cause that, if successful, will prevent him from doing what he came here to do?"

Lucy held her breath for Mrs. Harris's answer, trying not to give in to the alarm rising in her chest.

"Perhaps he'd expected to have the money fall more evenly on *his* side."

Mr. Godwin snorted. "Come now, Charlotte, you're a clever woman. Why should he leave such a thing to chance? He still has not applied for a license, and he is only leasing the property from Pritchard. What if this is merely a scheme to get his hands on all of your friends' money? I wonder if the notes *he* donated are genuine—I'd have them checked by a bank, if I were you."

Diego leaped to his feet, his eyes alight with anger.

"His assistant doesn't know where he is," Mr. Godwin went on, "and Lucy is missing. And I heard from one of the footmen that Montalvo was last seen asking for Lucy in the duke's study. Which, by the way, is where you ladies were tallying the donations, is it not? No one has seen him or her since, if I am to understand you correctly."

He had been in the study after she'd left? Good Lord, what if he *had* switched out the money?

No, how could she believe that? He'd been nothing but honorable toward her.

Except when he was blackmailing her. Lying to her. What did she really know about him except what he'd told her?

When Diego started toward her with his mouth set in a grim line, she realized she had to do something before he reached her. She could not bear to be alone with him any longer. She had to sort out her conflicting thoughts and this new information. Hurrying to the door, she closed her hand about the handle.

"Lucy, wait, damn you," Diego hissed beneath his breath. "We have to talk."

She shook her head and opened the glass door just enough to let herself through. With her blood thundering in her ears and her mind still reeling from the doubts Mr. Godwin had raised, she stepped onto the terrace. "Mrs. Harris, you were looking for me?"

Pray God she was presentable; she'd had no time to check.

Mrs. Harris jumped and turned around, as did Mr. Godwin. "Lucy!" the schoolmistress exclaimed. "Where on earth have you been?"

Lucy gave an exaggerated yawn. "I'm sorry. It was all just too exhausting for me, and we did leave awfully early this morning. I went into the library, thinking to sit a moment alone in the quiet . . . and I fell asleep. Your voices roused me." That at least would cover anything questionable in her appearance. "Was there something you needed?"

Looking suspicious, Mr. Godwin stepped to the library door and opened it to glance inside. Lucy held her breath. *Please, God, don't let Diego ruin me. Let him have gone out the other door or hidden.*

"You shouldn't have left the lamp burning so high," he muttered as he walked inside, turned it down, then came out.

Only then did Lucy release a breath. "Yes, thank you."

Mrs. Harris looped her arm through Lucy's. "Come along then. We need to find Señor Montalvo. Mr. Godwin wants to ask him some questions."

"I think he went home," Lucy said vaguely.

Had she just made a narrow escape?

So he was a thief in his younger days, her mind said. *Has he done anything to make you distrust him since then?*

Aside from claiming he meant to build a pleasure garden when no one was sure he really did? If she took a good, hard look at his behavior—and things he'd said—these past few days, she had to admit there were several inconsistencies. There was the huge one of raising money to hurt his own cause. There was his sudden claim to be a count, which he'd only mentioned to annoy Peter.

There was his odd insistence on her being the one to show him the school. He'd scoffed at her suspicion that he'd only kissed her to try to soften her toward his aims, but what if his goal was even worse, a scheme to siphon money from the school's friends? To lull her into believing he was harmless before he closed the trap? A chill shook her.

You were the one to start this latest intimate encounter, her conscience reminded her. *He protested.*

Not for long, he hadn't. Besides, she wasn't the best judge of character, was she? Look at how she'd believed Peter. Perhaps she was making a cake of herself over Diego, too.

Only this was worse. He'd acted guilty when Mr. Godwin had spoken. Though it was hard to believe a man as famous as he could be a thief, he *was* an expert at creating illusions. And she seemed to be an expert at believing them.

Tears stung her eyes. She swiftly dashed them away, hoping Mrs. Harris wouldn't see.

But she couldn't stop her brain from going around and around, asking the same questions. Why had he made *her* his companion? What was his real plan for Rockhurst? Was he a count? Or a thief? What if everything tonight had been a lie?

There were too many unanswered questions about him, too many evasions. And she was too susceptible to him. She'd nearly *given* herself to him!

It was time she ended this dangerous association. At least until she found out what he was hiding.

Chapter Twelve

Dear Cousin,

    Very well, I'll concede that you are probably right about Pritchard, but I can't decide what to think about Señor Montalvo. He came to our Venetian breakfast and raised an enormous amount of money for our fund, but I also heard rumors about him that give me pause. These days, I cannot tell the good men from the villains.

        Your perplexed relation,
        Charlotte

Three days after the charity breakfast, Diego stood in what passed for a study in his gloomy temporary abode, a cup of coffee in one hand and a tersely written note wrapped around a sealed envelope in the other.

With a howl of rage, he hurled his cup at the fireplace, where it shattered. Gaspar exploded into the room seconds later. *"Qué demonios!"*

"Lucy will not even read my letters! She sends them back unread." He waved her note in the air. "And this time, she told me not to send more, or she would toss them in the fire. Stubborn female!" He glanced to Gaspar in desperation. "What does your friend the cook say about Lucy's refusal to see me?"

"That Miss Seton has been busy giving drawing lessons. Sally isn't privy to your Lucy's secrets, you know."

"She is not *my* Lucy," Diego snapped. If anything demonstrated that, it was their last encounter.

"Well," Gaspar said, "I suspect Miss Seton has caught on to my role in your household, because she's not saying much. Sally still talks to me, but the other servants aren't as forthcoming with their gossip as before."

Of course not. Thanks to that damnable Godwin, Lucy saw him once more as the suspicious magician, the villain, the devil who wished to ruin her beloved school. As, no doubt, did her employer.

It probably did not help that he had been fool enough to satisfy Lucy's curiosity about sensuality. And his own rampant need to see her, touch her, make her his, even if only imperfectly and temporarily.

He closed his eyes, seeing her lying beneath him, trusting, hopeful. He could still taste her—it tormented his nights. How could he have ignored who she was, letting his cock guide him? He should have known his lapse of judgment would come back to taunt him.

The minute he had seen her birthmark, he had known he was done for. Until then, he had prayed she would prove not to be the *marqués*'s granddaughter. Then she could be his, and he could still gain Arboleda.

That birthmark had mocked him. He could have Lucy, or he could have Arboleda. Not both.

Gaspar went to warm his hands by the low fire. "What happened at the breakfast between you and Lucy?"

"Nothing," Diego said tersely.

"You've said that for three days, but *something* must have happened. When last I saw her, she was smiling fondly at you. Now she won't even let you near."

He groaned. It was time he told Gaspar what he had discovered. He had been hoping that once Mrs. Harris learned that the money he had donated was genuine, Lucy would realize she had no cause to be wary; then he need not reveal to Gaspar that he had overstepped his bounds. And that he had lost her trust through a trick of Fate.

Diego had recognized disaster the moment he had seen Lucy's stricken expression as she heard about his past. She would not understand how a Spanish count could come to be a thief. She would assume he had lied about his upbringing, then wonder what other lies there were. And his not applying for a license for his pleasure garden or offering for the property made him look even more suspicious.

That was the trouble: he and Lucy had spent just enough time together for him to learn how she thought and what things troubled her. The thieving would most certainly trouble her, especially since that damned Godwin had not bothered to clarify that it had happened when Diego was barely thirteen.

Now she felt confused and wary of him. God only knew if she would ever let him near her again. Meanwhile, the days were passing, and Arboleda slipped farther from his grasp with every one.

Hostias, had she learned nothing of his character by now? How could she still think him dishonorable, especially given his restraint in the library?

She probably saw that as another way he had tried to manipulate her.

With a curse, he crumpled the note and tossed it to the floor.

"Perhaps we should give up," Gaspar said.

"I am not giving up," Diego muttered.

"Did you read what the papers said about your performance?" Gaspar asked. "They extolled your cleverness, pronounced you to be vastly entertaining, even hoped that you would consider performing here again."

Diego glared at Gaspar. "I am not touring England, if that is what you plan."

Bending to pick up the crumpled note, Gaspar shoved it into his pocket. "Actually, I . . . er . . . went to see Philip Astley in town yesterday."

Astley owned a London amphitheater used for public amusement, with daily shows of equestrian mastery, conjuring, and juggling. Gaspar and Diego had met him while touring. He was the one who had shown Diego how to perform the bullet catch.

Gaspar continued. "You know he always admired my work, and he was very impressed with what he has heard of yours. He said he could find a place for me with his staff. He needs someone to book the acts. And you—"

"I am not going to work for Philip Astley just because some big-bosomed English female is leading you about by your cock, convincing you that we could have a life here," Diego growled. "I would rather slit my throat than live in England."

"We cannot keep beating our heads against the wall. We still cannot confirm that Miss Seton is the *marqués's* granddaughter, and even if we do—"

"She *is* his granddaughter," Diego snapped.

"I know you think so, but—"

"Lucy *is* Doña Lucinda," Diego repeated. "I *confirmed* it. For a certainty."

It took a moment for the truth to hit the man. Then Gaspar groaned. "*Por Dios,* please say that you told her about her grandfather, which prompted her to show you the birthmark of her own free will."

The hopeful note in Gaspar's voice made Diego wince.

As soon as Gaspar saw that, a string of foul Spanish left his lips. "And *I'm* being led about by my cock? No wonder she won't speak to you. I told you that you should tumble a whore, but did you listen?" Gaspar paced the study as he ranted. "Oh, no, not the proud count." He jerked one gnarled hand in Diego's direction. "Now that the grandee of Villafranca thinks he's about to regain his estate, he's too good for whores. No, he must have the granddaughter of a *marqués* in his bed—"

"I did not take her to bed, you old fool. You know I would never deflower an innocent."

Gaspar eyed him skeptically. "But you saw the birthmark. And not because she showed it to you."

"That is not why she is angry with me." Diego refused to elaborate on what he had done with Lucy. Bad enough he had to reveal the part about the birthmark. But those moments between him and her had been too precious to sully by relating them to anyone, even Gaspar. "She is angry because she heard about my early days in the regiment, when I used to be a cardsharp."

"And a thief," Gaspar reminded him, never one to mince words.

After all, they had first met when Diego was lifting Gaspar's purse. He had never known why Gaspar had taken pity on him, why he had decided to reward Diego's dexterity rather than punish it. But Gaspar had offered Diego a choice: be handed over to the local authorities or become his assistant.

For that, Diego would always be grateful. If his thieving had gone on much longer, he would surely have ended up on the gallows. Desperate for money for his ailing mother, and relieved to have another way of gaining it, Diego had agreed to Gaspar's proposal.

He had gritted his teeth when Gaspar assigned him such humiliating women's work as cleaning chamber pots and sewing pockets in handkerchiefs. He had practiced the Chinese rings until his fingertips bled. He had endured painful chemical applications to harden his hands so he could carry fire for their candle act.

And he had learned every bit of knowledge he could from the master, until Gaspar could no longer conjure, and the master became the assistant.

Although Gaspar was crotchety, with a penchant for expensive wine and exotic food, the man had earned his retirement, and Diego meant to see that he got it.

"I can think of only one good solution to this dilemma," Diego said, having spent the entire night developing a plan.

"You sneak into the school and carry her off?" Gaspar quipped.

"That is the not-so-good solution. And it would be very difficult to sneak into a house full of women without raising an alarm."

A cloud descended on Gaspar's brow. "I was not serious. Kidnapping is not a choice. The *marqués* said nothing of kidnapping."

Diego gave him a hard stare. "He wanted her returned, whatever it took."

Gaspar stiffened. "If you kidnap an Englishwoman, the authorities will hunt you down and have you hanged."

"I doubt the colonel would risk involving the authorities, given the criminal nature of his own actions. Even if he did not steal her, he covered up the fact that someone else had."

When Gaspar looked confused, Diego realized he had not yet told the man everything he had learned from Lucy and Hunforth. He quickly explained his theories about how Doña Lucinda had come to be adopted by the colonel.

"But even so, I would rather not carry her off against her will," Diego went on. "Too messy. We need to persuade her to go willingly, and that means we must bring her to us. Fear for her precious school just might do it. Here is what I propose: I make an offer to buy Rockhurst."

"Have you gone mad? Don Carlos barely approved enough funds to cover expenses. How will you pay for this property, with alchemist's gold?"

"I am not planning to pay. Just verbally offer. While Pritchard's attorneys draw up papers, I will consult with the licensing magistrates about how much a license would cost. We will make sure everyone in Richmond hears of our actions. It will send the school into a frenzy."

"And you think it will send Lucy rushing over here to talk you out of it."

"After she and her employer exhaust other options. At the very least, it will acquit me of concocting a scheme to defraud."

Gaspar frowned. "Meanwhile, when you don't complete the offer, *Pritchard* will accuse you of fraud. Except that *he* can have you tossed into gaol."

"It is a risk," Diego said with a shrug. "But we can keep him running around in circles to meet our requirements for some time, and Lucy is too impetuous to hold out long. She will want to speak to me, if only to lecture me." A grim smile touched his lips. "She does enjoy lecturing me."

Gaspar still looked skeptical. "Now that we know she is heir to the fortune, why not just send her a letter informing her? She'll be begging to go to Spain."

Diego rolled his eyes. "Did you not hear me say she refuses my letters? Besides, when I reveal the truth, she will involve the colonel, and he will move heaven and earth to keep us from either taking her home or revealing his perfidy to the press."

"Why would Lucy jeopardize her fortune by telling him?"

"She does not care about money."

"Everyone cares about money," Gaspar scoffed, "even you."

"Not Lucy."

Mrs. Harris has taught us time and again that money can be a curse, she had said. *At least I know that anyone who marries me will marry for love.*

As if love were the most important thing in the world. That was as foreign an idea to him as English propriety. A man married for land, fortune, or family honor, sometimes all three. And if he gained an amiable partner in the bargain, that was icing on the cake.

But love? That was an illusion, nothing more. Attraction he understood, but no sane man married for attraction alone. Especially when the object of the attraction was a vexing Englishwoman with a deplorable habit of thinking the worst of a man, even when he had been on his best behavior.

He scowled. Not that he could marry Lucy. That was impossible.

She would not have him, anyway. She had decided he was the devil, and she was not about to change her opinion for anything so inconsequential as the facts.

Diego headed for the door. "I am going to see Pritchard. You head for town. Gossip about our impending purchase of Rockhurst wherever you dare. But one way or the other, coax our canary out of her cage. She has kept us staring through the bars long enough."

Two days later, Diego stood in an office foyer after sundown, trying not to look bored. He had been summoned by a ghoulish-looking solicitor named Baines, on behalf of a mysterious client who wished to invest in the pleasure garden.

Diego did not care about that, of course, and since Gaspar's inquiries had not revealed any connection between Baines and Pritchard, this had nothing to do with the supposed purchase. So it was a waste of his time.

Nonetheless, it would add to his show of purchasing the property. Since Lucy had not yet come around, that could be useful.

Still, it was odd that Baines insisted upon meeting at night. And when a clerk ushered Diego into a dark room, Diego went instantly on his guard.

Either the solicitor's white pallor came from a loathing of light, or something else was going on. Only one candle burned, at the very front of Baines's desk. The man's client sat back in the dark, and Diego could barely make out his figure.

He scowled. Like any magician, he had a healthy respect

for what light and shadow could conceal. And he did not like having such tricks used against him.

"Sit down, sir." Baines gestured to the chair directly in front of the candle.

Diego gauged the lines of sight. When seated, he would be unable to see either the man in the shadows or Baines. His years with the regiments had taught him that a wise man kept any potential enemy in sight. "I prefer to stand."

A panicky look spread over Baines's face, until his companion leaned forward to whisper something that made the solicitor relax. "My client says he understands your caution, but he must keep his identity private. If you wish to hear his proposal, you will have to take a seat."

Diego weighed his options, wishing he had thought to bring a pistol. But he had expected a straightforward discussion, where he pretended to be interested in the investor until he could make an excuse to leave.

Still, he understood some men's need for privacy. "Very well." He sat down. "I take it that your client wants to keep secret his investment in my project?"

"Actually, he does not wish to invest," Baines said. "He wishes to purchase the property after you have bought it from Mr. Pritchard."

Diego blinked. This grew more curious by the moment. "Why not just purchase it from Pritchard himself?"

"Mr. Pritchard will not sell to him. There is . . . bad blood between them."

Not terribly surprising, given that Pritchard was a loathsome worm, but still interesting.

"And why should I consider such a thing?" Diego asked.

"Because my client will pay you substantially more than you pay Pritchard."

Diego couldn't contain a laugh. "Does he know what Pritchard is asking?"

"Yes. And he knows that the property isn't worth near that."

His eyes narrowed. "Yet he is willing to pay *me* even more."

"My client has his reasons."

"And he will have to tell me what they are before I take his preposterous proposal seriously."

A long silence ensued, followed by more whispering. "He prefers to keep his reasons private."

"Very well." Diego rose. "Good day, gentlemen."

"Wait!" Baines rose, too. "You must at least hear us out. My client is willing to offer you several incentives just to consider his proposal."

Diego paused near the door. "I am not interested in changing my plans at this late date, gentlemen, but thank you for the offer."

"So you're determined to ruin Mrs. Harris's School for Young Ladies for the purposes of your project?"

The whispered question came from the man in the shadows, and the mention of the school stopped Diego in his tracks. Why would some anonymous investor care so much about what happened to a ladies' academy that he would be willing to lay out a fortune—

The answer hit him. Ah, yes, the secret benefactor. Gaspar had told Diego about Mrs. Harris's anonymous "Cousin Michael," who saw himself as champion of the school. Diego could use that, after determining the lay of the land.

Retracing his steps, he took his seat once more. "So, you are a friend to the school, are you, sir?"

The man in the shadows leaned back, and Baines resumed his role as intermediary. "My client is concerned about what effect your project might have on the whole of Richmond."

Diego sat back, tucking his thumbs in his waistband. "And just how concerned is he? I believe you mentioned incentives."

More whispering ensued. "He is willing to go as high as double the price that Pritchard requires."

"I am not interested in money."

"My client has another piece of property that you might find an acceptable trade, if that is what you prefer."

"I have found the property I want. Its location makes it worth its weight in gold to me. So your property does not interest me, either."

"Then what the bloody hell *does*, sir?" hissed the man in the shadows.

Diego hid a smile. "Only one thing. If you arrange it, I will gladly sell you the property when I buy it. And at Pritchard's price, too." He could easily keep *that* promise. "All I want is a private meeting with a teacher at the school."

Baines blinked. "What?"

"I want an hour alone with Lucinda Seton, unchaperoned. Nothing else."

As another furious bout of whispering ensued, he held his breath. He was taking a huge risk by laying his cards on the table. If "Cousin Michael" was as good a friend to the school as he had heard, the man might balk at involving Lucy, and Diego would merely have put everyone on guard.

But he could not imagine how they would be any more on guard against him than they were now.

After all the whispering, Baines's reply was amazingly simple. "Why?"

"I believe your client knows why, given his long correspondence with Mrs. Harris. A man does not become a woman's champion without having some feelings for her, does he?"

As his client muttered a curse under his breath, Baines managed a weak smile. "So you know about my client's . . . er . . . association with the school."

"I am assuming he is the infamous Cousin Michael, but I am perfectly happy to be corrected. As long as I have my requirement met."

A short burst of whispering followed.

"You wish to make Miss Seton an offer?" Baines asked hopefully.

"Not unless I can talk to her first," Diego evaded. He hated taking this tack, but he had only one chance to persuade Lucy to return with him to Spain. If he had to equivocate to get that chance, then equivocate he would.

"How do we know your purpose is honorable?" Baines asked. "How do we know that you don't mean to use that hour to assault her virtue?"

"If that was what I wanted," he said tersely, "I have had ample opportunities to do so before now. You may set up the terms of the meeting however you please. It can take place in the middle of the damned school with a ring of teachers and footmen and whoever else aims to protect her virtue standing within shouting distance. But I wish to speak to her alone. Understood?"

A long silence ensued, followed by a terse whisper from Cousin Michael.

Baines stood. "My client says we will see if we can arrange it. But not an hour. Half an hour."

Diego hesitated. It was not enough time, but he could work with it. He nodded.

"You will also be expected to sign papers beforehand regarding our private agreement about the purchase of Rockhurst. But assuming that Mrs. Harris and Miss Seton agree, you will have your meeting."

"Thank you," Diego said, bowing to his worthy opponent.

Now all he need do was figure out how best to use the meeting to his advantage.

Chapter Thirteen

❧

Dear Charlotte,

I understand why you are concerned about Montalvo's latest proposal, but you did not see his face when he spoke of Miss Seton. He seems quite smitten. Even you admitted she fell into the doldrums after the breakfast. Why not see how she feels about it before dismissing it? You will know how to ask her without her feeling forced. But if we can save the school while at the same time resolving her feelings for the man, how can that be bad?

Your servant always,
Michael

Lucy paced Mrs. Harris's office, her mind awhirl. She hadn't seen Diego in nearly a week, afraid to trust him, afraid to trust herself around him.

After the breakfast, she'd been terrified that she'd actually let herself be swept away by some blackguard. There were his lies and inconsistencies to bolster her fears, plus Mr. Godwin's claims.

Then the truth had started to emerge. He *had* made an offer to Mr. Pritchard. He *was* applying for the license. The money he'd donated *had* been genuine.

But he'd lied to her about his past. He still hadn't even *told* her about his past.

She clasped her hands at her waist to keep them from trembling. What did he intend to say today? Could he truly mean to give up his pursuit of Rockhurst just to see her? It seemed impossible, but why else had he made this secret bargain with Cousin Michael's solicitor?

He wanted to see her and was willing to give up his plans to do so. He cared that much? Or was she just falling prey to her weakness for handsome gentlemen?

"Lucy, for heaven's sake, sit down," Mrs. Harris said irritably. "He will not arrive any faster for your pacing, I assure you."

With a sigh, Lucy dropped into a chair, then just as quickly rose to pace again. "Forgive me, but it's the only thing that keeps me calm." She halted to stare at Mrs. Harris. "Why does he not come?"

"Because our agreement was that he arrive at noon, and it's only ten till."

"Oh. Of course."

"You don't have to do this," Mrs. Harris said. "We will find another way. With the funds we raised, we can offer Mr. Pritchard a substantial sum."

"Yes, but will he take it?"

Mrs. Harris forced a smile. "I don't see why not."

"And you don't see why he would, either."

"My cousin says—"

"And that's another thing," Lucy broke in. "Why did Diego even go to your cousin? How did he know where to find him, when all these years you've never located him yourself?"

Irritation shone in Mrs. Harris's face. "He *didn't* go to him. My cousin requested a meeting with Señor Montalvo through his solicitor." She began to drum her fingers on the desk. "I have always known that Mr. Baines works for Michael—his office receives my rents, which, as you know, belong to my cousin. Yet that blasted Michael will not arrange any meetings with *me*. He only comes out of hiding for foreign magicians who—"

She halted, her cheeks reddening. "Forgive me, my cousin and his reticence drive me mad. When he first offered me this property at such a low rent, he made me sign an agreement that I would not try to learn his identity through any means, or risk eviction. I have held to that because I dared not risk the consequences. I honestly thought he would relent in his condition after he knew me, but if anything, he is more firm. It is exceedingly annoying."

"I imagine it is." Despite her anxiety, Lucy found it vastly amusing how much Mrs. Harris changed when she spoke of her cousin. She became almost as flustered as Lucy did around Diego.

Mrs. Harris schooled her features into serenity. "In any case, no matter what part my cousin played in arranging this, you should not feel obligated to go through with it."

Lucy managed a smile. "If Diego—I mean, Señor Montalvo—is willing to strike a bargain with Cousin Michael, it can't hurt for me to talk to him, can it?"

"That depends." Her gaze searched Lucy's face. "Why have you avoided him until now?"

"I told you. I don't . . . I'm afraid . . ." She was afraid of falling in love with him. And given her questionable taste in men, she wasn't about to risk it without knowing him better. "The bank is absolutely certain that his donation was genuine?"

"You've asked that three times already. Yes, Señor Montalvo donated three hundred genuine pounds to our fund. That is not the action of a thief."

Lucy whirled to pace the other way. "But why did he do it? Why did he go to the breakfast in the first place, if not for the reasons Mr. Godwin gave? I can't help feeling he isn't telling the entire truth."

"You don't trust him."

"No . . . yes . . . I don't know. I would trust him more if I knew his reasons."

"What if he has no good reason? Men in love do strange things."

Lucy eyed the schoolmistress askance. "He's not in love with me."

Mrs. Harris smiled faintly. "Are you sure?"

"Yes." But he desired her, and she desired him, which also frightened her. "I'm quite sure."

"He as much as told Cousin Michael that he wanted to make an offer."

As much as told. That meant nothing. Diego was very good at evasion. Besides, he'd told *her* that his circumstances didn't permit him to marry. As far as she knew, that hadn't changed.

Mrs. Harris was probably only considering this because she thought Lucy and Diego were in love. The widow could be cynical, but she wasn't opposed to love. She knew Lucy lacked the dowry to tempt a serious fortune hunter, so she'd probably decided that Diego's motivations were romantic. Especially after seeing how Diego had humiliated Peter publicly. So if Lucy told Mrs. Harris flat out that Diego had no interest in marriage, Mrs. Harris would call a halt to the meeting.

And Diego would buy Rockhurst.

But that's not really why you're going through with this, is it?

She sighed. No. She had to know why he wanted to see her. It must be something important. It might even hold the key to his sometimes inexplicable behavior.

It wasn't as if he would misbehave, with Mrs. Harris just outside the door and footmen stationed at either end of the hall. She was perfectly safe here.

"Señor Montalvo has arrived," announced a servant from the doorway.

Lucy's heart flipped over. Safe? She was never safe around Diego. Good Lord, when just the sound of his name trebled her pulse, she was done for.

Buck up, or you won't last a minute with him, let alone a half-hour. You must keep your wits about you, she told her thundering heart.

Mrs. Harris cast her a quick glance. "Well? Shall we let him in?"

Not trusting her voice, Lucy nodded.

Diego entered the room, his gaze seeking out Lucy before it shot to Mrs. Harris and hardened. "I said the meeting had to be private."

"It will be." Mrs. Harris headed for the door, then paused to look back at Lucy. "I shall be just outside, my dear. All you need do is call."

"Thank you." Lucy marveled at how calm she sounded.

The door closed behind Mrs. Harris. They were alone.

Diego stared at her as if starved for the sight of her. The intensity of his look reminded her of their intimate moments in the Foxmoor library. That seemed ages ago, yet it gave her the same primitive thrill.

"You look very well," he said in that accented voice that never failed to make her shiver deliciously.

She'd dressed with particular care but doubted he was referring to her attire. "So do you."

He gave a harsh laugh. "Really? I do not look as if I have been dragged down a country lane by a cart horse a few hundred times?" He speared his hands through his hair, disordering it. "Because that is how I feel."

She could see the circles under his eyes, the haunted look in his features, the brittle glitter in his gaze. "What's this about, Diego?"

"First, I must know one thing." He strode to the desk, propped his hip against it, then pushed away to stalk back to her. "Did I do something wrong that evening at Foxmoor's?" His voice was a husky murmur. "When we were in the library and I was . . . touching you, did I hurt you or alarm you or . . ."

"No." She wiped her clammy hands on her skirts. It wasn't what he'd done but what she'd been willing to do that still alarmed her.

"Then why have you refused to see me?"

"Because I realized how little I really know you."

His features turned stony. "Because Godwin said I was a thief."

"That was part of it, but—"

"He did not lie, Lucy. I was indeed a thief, and a cardsharp."

That took her aback.

"It was only for a short while in my youth, before I became a magician." He set his shoulders back with a defensive air. "I had an ailing mother to support, so I stole. Until Gaspar caught me and offered me a position as his assistant."

"Gaspar! I thought he was *your* assistant."

"Not until recently. Anyway, I have not been a thief in some years. So if you thought this was an elaborate plan to rob you and your friends—"

"I know it wasn't," she said hastily.

His eyes narrowed. "But you have refused to see me."

"Because I realized you're still a stranger to me." What he'd said just now proved it. She hadn't known of his ailing mother or Gaspar's role in his life.

"Nonetheless, I must ask you to trust me. I have something important to tell you."

She braced herself for a great revelation about his past. "All right."

"First . . ." He strode toward the door. With a sudden motion that took her by surprise, he jerked it open. Mrs. Harris nearly fell in.

Scowling, he shut the door in Mrs. Harris's face before heading back to take Lucy by the arm. He drew her rather forcibly to the other end of the room. Then he reached into his pocket, drew out an object, and handed it to her. It was a miniature.

"Do you recognize the woman in that picture?" he murmured.

She stared down into features that seemed familiar but also not . . . that seemed precious but also foreign. It was surely the face from her hazy memories.

No, how could that be? "Wh-who is she?"

"Do you recognize her?" he repeated more firmly.

She lifted her gaze to him. "She looks like . . . that is, she resembles the woman I have often thought of as my mother. But how did you come by this?"

"It was given to me by your grandfather."

Her *grandfather?* "I don't have a grandfather. Even if I did, why would he give *you*—"

"I am not here to buy a pleasure garden, *cariño*," he said, his voice infinitely gentle. "I have no interest in Rockhurst and even less in your school. I certainly have no desire to live in England. I came here for one reason only—to find *you*."

She gaped at him, remembering some of the things that had worried her about him: how he'd insisted upon her being the one to bring him around the school, how he'd involved himself to an inordinate degree in her personal life, how he'd demanded this meeting today. "I-I don't understand."

"Your Spanish grandfather, the Marqués de Parama, asked me to come to England to find you."

She had family? No, Papa would have told her if she had. "Why would this *marqués* send *you?* Why not just come himself?"

"He is ill, and his doctors said he could not manage the voyage. I agreed to look for you in his place."

And for that, Diego had manufactured this entire scheme of the pleasure garden? For that, he had engineered everything that had happened in the past week?

Pain knotted in her throat. "So you've been lying to me all this time."

His expression turned fierce. "I had to be sure you were the person I sought. I did not want to upset your life unless I was sure."

"That's why you've been coaxing me into talking about things?" With a groan, she remembered his questions about La Coruña, about her parents' deaths.

She shook her head, unable to take it all in. "But the papers said you're here to buy Rockhurst. Mr. Pritchard still *believes* you're here to buy Rockhurst!"

"It was a ruse, *cariño*. That's all."

"You looked at other sites up north! Mrs. Harris said—"

"Gaspar and I have traveled throughout England, tracking down daughters of officers serving in Gibraltar who were the right age to be Doña Catalina's. I needed a reason for being in the country, and a pleasure garden seemed as plausible as any. I dared not raise the authorities' suspicions."

A sudden chill swept over her as everything he'd said sank in. "How did you know my mother's name was Catalina? I never told you that."

"For the same reason I know that you are the one we seek."

Family. She had family other than Papa. Could that really be?

"Why is the *marqués* looking for me after so many years? What does he want with me? Why didn't my parents ever tell Papa I had family? I don't understand."

"I know. And I cannot answer your questions now." His voice dropped low. "I must speak to you more privately. There are other things you need to hear. I have documents to show you. And information about Colonel Seton."

Fear gripped her. "What do you mean? What has this to do with Papa?"

"I cannot speak of it here; these walls have ears. And I do not trust your guardians."

"That's absurd."

"Is it? They arranged this meeting. They deemed saving their school more important than keeping you from me—a man you did not trust."

"No! *I* did that!"

"You should never have been given the choice. In Spain, you would have been kept from me, not sacrificed for the good of Mrs. Harris's school."

"This is not Spain. Besides, aren't you glad of that? You wouldn't even be talking to me now if we English were as strict as you Spanish."

"You are *not* English," he said with surprising virulence. "You are Spanish."

She tipped up her chin. "Half Spanish." When he didn't answer, she narrowed her eyes. "What are you not telling me?"

"A great deal. If you wish to hear it all, you must meet me tonight at Rockhurst. Alone. Without your untrustworthy guardians."

A frown knit her brow. "Diego, you know very well I cannot go to an unmarried man's house alone at night."

"Would you prefer to come this afternoon, when every eye is upon you?"

"No, of course not, but—"

"Do not be concerned about your virtue. Had I wanted to take it, *mi dulzura,* I would have done so when I had the chance three days ago."

A blush heated her cheeks. He had a point. She'd practically thrown herself at him in the duke's library.

"You need only worry about preserving your reputation," he went on, "which can be done if you slip away tonight after everyone is asleep. Pay me a visit at Rockhurst.

Gaspar will be there, too. We will be discreet, I assure you. But I must have more time and privacy for this discussion."

"How can you even be sure I'm the person you're looking for? Catalina is a common Spanish name. All you have is a few bits of information."

"And your birthmark. It is the confirmation of who you are." He drew out a piece of parchment inscribed with the signature of Don Carlos, Marqués de Parama, along with an elaborate wax seal that bore the imprint of an ornately decorated P. On the parchment was drawn a butterfly figure exactly like the one on her thigh.

The *marqués* knew of her birthmark? Her hands began to shake. That, more than anything, lent truth to Diego's tale. Only Papa knew of it . . . and her parents, of course.

It also explained why Diego had reacted so strongly when he'd seen it.

A fresh torrent of betrayal swept through her. Good Lord. *That* was why he had spent the past week kissing her and caressing her and—

"Why, you despicable, vile . . . unfeeling . . ." She burst into tears.

Chapter Fourteen

Dear Charlotte,
    *And another thing. Sometimes we must weigh
the good of the many against the good of the few.
But do not worry—if I hear anything to imply Miss
Seton is in danger from Señor Montalvo, I will send
him packing. Richmond's businessmen will not be
so eager to see his pleasure garden established in
their environs at the risk of his preying upon their
innocent daughters.*

                Your protective relation,
                Michael

Diego watched in horror as Lucy began to sob. What the devil? "*Cariño*, please," he said, reaching for her.

She swatted his hand. "Don't you dare! And don't you ever call me *cariño* again either! Everything you said to me was a lie!"

"Not everything," he said hoarsely. "I avoided lying as much as I could. But I could not tell you the truth until I was sure."

"So you kissed me . . . and c-caressed me until you . . . could g-get a chance t-to see my . . . b-birthmark."

"No!" *Dios mio,* he should have realized she would think he had dallied with her only as part of his mission.

Backing away from him, she cast him an accusing gaze. "How *could* you? All you had to do was ask to see it. Instead, you let me think you desired me."

"*Dios Santo,* Lucy, I *do* desire you. How could you believe otherwise?" With panic rising in his chest, he stalked her. "It was desire that made me do what I did, not any need to see your birthmark. You have to believe me!"

"How much of a fool do you think I am?" she whimpered, her pretty eyes clouded by tears.

"What happened between us in Foxmoor's library had nothing to do with this, I swear," he murmured, conscious of Mrs. Harris outside the door. "Surely you recall that I wanted to stop it. I was the one who said it was unwise."

"But you didn't stop, did you? Not until you had your cursed confirmation."

She whirled toward the door, but he snagged her about the waist from behind, yanking her up close to him. At once, she began to fight him.

"Yes, I got my confirmation," he bit out as he struggled to subdue her. "And in the process, I broke my promise to the *marqués.*"

His words must have penetrated, for she went still. "What promise?"

"That I would not touch you." Burying his face in her hair, he breathed in the heady scent, knowing it was forbidden to him and not caring. "That I would find you and do as I was asked and no more."

She said nothing, but at least she had stopped fighting him.

"Every time I kissed you," he went on hoarsely, "I broke

that promise. Every time I caressed you, I broke it again. It was foolish. It was wrong. I *know* that. And you have no idea how much I regret it."

Realizing that if he held her any longer, he would break down and do more things to regret later, he forced himself to release her.

As he stepped back, she whirled to face him, her eyes uncertain. "You didn't give me pleasure just to get your confirmation?"

"No." He had not wanted the confirmation. In his mad hunger for her, he had even hoped she would not prove to be Doña Lucinda after all.

But she was. And he could not tell her how it tore him in two. Not if both of them wanted to gain their birth-rights.

"No," he repeated more firmly. "Giving you pleasure was never part of the plan. The *marqués* would skin me alive if he knew how I touched you."

"Then why did you do it?"

Because you have bewitched me. Because when you are near, I want only to have you.

This cursed desire was a temporary madness. It would surely fade once he brought her to Spain and could return to his old life. It had to.

They could never be together, for the same reasons as before—his lack of money, his aims for Arboleda, his vow to Father, her future. Even if she felt something deeper than physical attraction, nothing could come of it. It was time to end this insanity between them, so he must play the villain with her. Again.

"I know I am not the first man to desire you, Lucy." He forced coldness into his voice. "It should not come as a surprise to you that I am no more immune to your charms than other men."

Hurt swamped her lovely face. "You were dallying with me. For your own enjoyment."

For his own torture, more like. "And yours. If you will recall, you *asked* me to dally with you that day in the library."

"Oh, yes," she said in a hollow voice. "I recall it very well. And I am paying now for letting my impetuous nature rule my actions."

He wanted to shake her, to tell her that her impetuous nature was what fascinated him. That he envied her for it. He had long ago lost the ability to be impetuous—except when it came to her.

"I behaved unwisely at the breakfast," he said, "but you must not let my actions affect your decision about whether to meet with me tonight. I can restrain my urges, as you well know, as long as you are not tempting me to do otherwise."

A knock came at the door. "Lucy, are you all right?"

Diego held his breath.

After a second, Lucy said, "I'm fine, Mrs. Harris. Perfectly well."

"Inform Señor Montalvo that he has five minutes left."

With a stubborn tilt to her chin, she turned to him. "Tell me the whole story now, and I will speak with you longer."

He shook his head. "Not here." Bowing to her, he added, "Keep the miniature—it should belong to you regardless. But I hope to see you this evening. If not, Gaspar and I will be gone tomorrow. And that will be the end of this."

"Gone!"

"I can no longer afford to tarry in England. I have to make a living, you know." He had to coax her out tonight.

This had already taken longer than Don Carlos had predicted. "I would appreciate it if you kept this between us until we can talk, but of course, you have to do what you must."

It took all his will to head for the door, to pretend he did not care.

"Diego," she called.

He kept going.

"Diego!" she cried. "Wait!"

He paused at the door to bow to her, then opened it and strode out. Mrs. Harris watched with unveiled curiosity as he walked off. He heard Lucy rush into the hall behind him.

He was taking an enormous risk. She could tell Mrs. Harris the truth about their encounter and bring a world of trouble down on his head.

But he did not think she would. Not the adventurous Lucy. Not the woman who hungered for information about her parents. He was counting on that hunger to coax her into going where he wanted.

And once he had her to himself tonight, he would do everything in his power to get her to accompany them home.

What if she does not agree to go? Gaspar had asked him earlier.

Then he would simply change tactics. Because one way or the other, Lucy *was* going to Spain with them. For her own good *and* his.

Long after midnight, Lucy picked her way through the cherry orchard, guided by the candlelit windows of Rockhurst. Behind her, the school was dark. Everyone had retired, but her regular life dragged her back like a river current. It might have had its disappointments, and she might not always have felt part of the society she moved within, but it was still all she knew.

What lay ahead was unknown, and she had the sneaking suspicion that once she stepped inside the dilapidated old manor, her life would change forever.

She paused in the middle of the grove. It was mad to be here. She ought to run back, forget about her supposed grandfather, let Diego leave. Then she could close the intriguing chapter of her life that he'd opened.

But she couldn't. She touched her hand to the miniature that lay inside her pocket. Ever since he'd shown it to her, she'd been unable to think of anything but the tantalizing idea of knowing who her family was at last.

She'd nearly confided in Mrs. Harris, but something had held her back. For one thing, the schoolmistress would probably prevent her from speaking to Diego again. Mrs. Harris would summon Papa, and they would close ranks around her.

And Lucy would forever lose the chance to learn the truth about her parents. She couldn't bring herself to do that.

She had another concern. Diego seemed to think he knew something sinister about Papa. Though she was sure Papa was honorable, Diego had no cause to think so. He might act on his suspicions, and with the power of a Spanish *marqués* behind him, he might make trouble for Papa. She couldn't risk it.

As she continued through the orchard, she prayed she wasn't making a mistake, especially given how her heart still ached at the loss of Diego. He had made it perfectly clear that he wouldn't allow their relationship to progress further. There'd been no talk of marriage, no talk of love. Only desire.

As she reached the grove's edge, a figure melted from the shadows near the house, startling her. "I was afraid you would not come." Diego tossed down a cigarillo, crushing it with his foot. "I have been watching for you a long while."

With the moon only half full, darkness cloaked his features, but the familiar thrum of his voice settled her nervousness. "I couldn't get away any sooner."

He held out his arm. "Let us go in. I have papers to show you. It is too cold to stand out here, anyway."

In for a penny, in for a pound. She took his arm. As they entered the manor, she realized she'd never been inside. When Mr. Pritchard had lived here, he had not welcomed visits from the residents of the school, and Señor Montalvo was his first tenant. Gazing about, she marveled that Diego could stand to live in such a dismal place. And where were his servants?

Apprehension prickled along her spine until she reminded herself he wasn't the wealthy man she'd imagined. Perhaps he couldn't afford servants to man the doors.

"Tell me something," she said as he led her into a small, dank parlor only marginally improved by the fire in the hearth. "Are you even really a count?"

His arm tensed beneath her hand. "Does it matter?" Releasing her, he stalked to a tea table, where sat a carafe and glasses. He poured red wine, then returned with the filled glasses.

"It matters to me." She accepted a glass from him. "I want to be able to separate the truth from the lies."

He stared her down. "As I said before, I told you as few lies as I could."

She sipped wine to take off the chill. "So you really are a count."

"Not that it matters, but yes. And a man of honor, too."

The proud tilt to his head and the haughty inflection of his voice answered the question more than his words. She could easily see this rigidly arrogant man in the role of count. "Then tell me about my supposed grandfather."

"There is nothing supposed about it," he snapped. "You are the only daughter of Don Carlos's daughter."

"Catalina Crawford, you mean."

Diego drank some wine, as if to fortify himself, then set his glass down. "There is no such person. The woman pretending to be Catalina Crawford was your nurse. And Sergeant Crawford was probably her lover. They stole you from your rightful parents."

"My rightful . . ." A sudden chill swept her. Surely he could not have said . . . no, he must be confused. "What do you mean?"

"Your real parents are not the Crawfords. The real Catalina and her husband, Don Álvaro, had a four-year-old daughter named Lucinda. The girl went missing from San Roque, along with her nurse, while visiting her grandfather." His gaze bored into her. "San Roque is across the Spanish border from Gibraltar. The woman you thought was your mother abducted you as she ran off with Sergeant Crawford, when the regiment left Gibraltar on transports headed for La Coruña."

For a moment, she could only stare at him in shock. Abducted? From *Spanish* parents? No, how could that be?

"That makes no sense. I remember the retreat to La

Coruña. I remember my mother's face." Jerking the miniature from her pocket, she waved it at him. "I remember this face from when were on the march! I remember—"

"You might remember her face," he said softly. "But it cannot be from the march. You were four, *mi dulzura*. Memories from that time become jumbled. Are you absolutely sure you remember her being with you in the mountain passes?"

She gulped more wine in a vain attempt to warm her chilled blood. It was so long ago. She remembered her mother . . . but she couldn't remember anything else. "But why would Sergeant Crawford's wife be named Catalina, too?"

"I suspect the nurse used her mistress's name to keep you quiet."

"Then why isn't it *her* face I remember?" This was insane. He had to see it! "And why would my nurse steal me, anyway?"

"According to the *marqués,* she was fond of you and angry at your mother. She must have taken you to spite her mistress or out of jealousy. Who knows why a woman like that steals a child?"

Panic rose in her. "And Sergeant Crawford just looked the other way as he gained two people to take care of? That's absurd. Besides, Papa would have known something of it. He was Sergeant Crawford's commanding officer. Papa would have been the one to give him permission to take us on the transports."

"Yes. He would have."

As what he was implying sank in, she felt sick. The wine glass slipped from her fingers, but Diego caught it before it fell. She wrapped her arms about her waist. "You're saying Papa had something to do with this." She shook her head violently. "No. He'd never . . . he's a good man. He couldn't—"

"Then why, when the *marqués* wrote to the regiments asking if there had ever been a child named Lucinda whose father served in the Forty-second, did they say they had no record of it?"

"Good Lord." One thing she knew for certain—Papa had served in the Forty-second, and she'd been his daughter when he did. "Perhaps they . . . they misunderstood. Perhaps it was a mistake."

"Or your 'Papa' convinced the authorities to keep quiet about it. He either participated in the abduction or covered it up afterward. He has certainly been doing so ever since."

Her stomach churned. This was far worse than finding out that Papa had hidden her grandfather from her.

No, she wouldn't believe it. She couldn't believe it. "Papa would never do anything so despicable. You don't know his character."

"I know he changed regiments shortly after legally adopting you. Why would he do so? Officers rarely change the regiment they have come up in."

She knew that to be true. "H-he never said why."

"Of course not. And what has he told you about the Crawfords? When you ask about them, what does he say?"

Very little. Papa always changed the subject.

Horror swept down her spine. "I don't think he knew them very well."

"Yet he adopted you when they died. He did not send you to an orphanage. He did not even give you to some other married couple. Instead, he—an unmarried soldier who, according to you, had no close friendship with your parents—adopted a four-year-old girl he barely knew.

Just like that. Carried you with him from battlefield to battlefield." Diego fixed her with a pitying stare. "Does that sound like something the average unmarried soldier would do? For no reason?"

"He *had* a reason! My real father asked him to on his deathbed."

"*Cariño,* be sensible." Diego reached for her, but she backed away. His face hardened. "Do you truly believe a man takes on the raising and education of a child simply because a dying man he hardly knows asks him to?"

As tears burned her eyes, she turned away to hide them. Could her whole life really have been a lie?

She'd always wondered about Papa's reticence in talking about her parents but had never questioned why he'd adopted her. He'd done it because her real father had asked it of him, simple as that. Like any child, she'd filled in the rest. Papa had thought she was adorable or had felt sorry for her or had been captivated by her childish smiles.

But Diego was right. Unmarried soldiers didn't adopt small children.

"The colonel had to have known of the abduction," Diego went on gently. "It would explain why he could not return you to your family in San Roque when Crawford and the nurse died. That would have meant facing the authorities, admitting his culpability. Instead, he adopted you and changed regiments to keep anyone from finding you."

It was a monstrous idea, that Papa had adopted her to hide a crime. "It can't be possible," she whispered. "I don't believe you."

"Then believe this." He picked up a letter that lay next to the carafe and handed it to her. "The *marqués* wrote it, in case I were ever to find you."

With trembling fingers, she took the sealed parchment. The wax bore the same P as the one on the picture of her birthmark that Diego had shown her earlier. Breaking open the seal, she unfolded the letter. It was dated February 3, and was written in English in the shaky script of an old man:

> My dear child,
>
> If you are reading this, then my emissary, Don Diego Javier Montalvo, has found you at last. I have been searching for years, but only recently did I gain information leading me to believe you had left on the regimental transports with my daughter's deceitful nurse.
>
> You are all I have left in this world. My daughter (your mother) and my son are both dead, and your grandmother went on to heaven just last year, always hopeful that she would see you one day.
>
> I cannot bear the thought of meeting her in heaven without having held you again in this life, my dear girl. I am very near death's door, and I will not rest easy in the next world if I cannot be reunited with you before I die. Please do me the honor of indulging an old man and accompany my emissary and his friend back to Spain.

Her gaze jumped to Diego. "He wants me to go to Spain?"

Diego nodded. "As soon as possible. His doctors told me he does not have much longer to live."

"Diego!" she protested. "I can't just run off to Spain with you!"

"Gaspar will be with us. He's off right now hiring a maid to attend and chaperone you for the trip. You have no reason to stay."

"I have a very good reason," she said stoutly. "I already have a life here."

"Really? Is that what you call this? Being at the beck and call of some schoolmistress?" His voice tightened. "Enduring savage attacks from men like Hunforth who cannot see your worth, who revile you for your passion and your boldness, the very things that will make you admired in Spanish society?"

She flinched at his painfully accurate assessment of how she sometimes felt.

"When I spoke to your Peter alone," he went on ruthlessly, "he called your mother a 'Spanish whore.' To these English *cretinos,* you are the daughter of a whore. You should show them you are no such thing."

Swallowing past the lump of hurt in her throat, she said, "They don't all see me that way. Peter, yes, because he's a fool, but not the rest."

He snorted, clearly skeptical. "Is that why a beautiful, desirable woman like you has not yet found a husband? Why you're working as a teacher here instead?"

"You don't understand. It's temporary, and anyway—"

"In Spain, you are heiress to a vast fortune. Your grandfather has houses in Cádiz and San Roque and Marbella. He can make you the center of Spanish society. You were born to that." He grabbed her hands. "You told me you yearned for family, for people of your own blood. Now you have a chance to have them, and if you do not go now, you will lose that chance. You will regret it forever if you do."

"But I don't even know if I can believe this *marqués*'s tale about me."

"He knew of your birthmark."

She couldn't deny that. "At the very least, I have to hear Papa's side of the story. I'm sure if I could only talk to him—"

"There is no time for that! Your grandfather is dying. Besides, that monster you call Papa has done nothing to earn such a consideration."

"Except raise me and love me!"

"He had no right to! Your parents should have been the ones to raise and love you. But like all English soldiers, he took what he wanted without a care for the consequences. He covered up the abduction and kept you from your family for his own selfish purposes. *That* is the man you wish to alert to your plans? If you tell him you want to visit your grandfather, do you really think he will let you go?"

She doubted it.

"Has he ever encouraged you to look for your Spanish relations, ever made an attempt to seek out your English relations on your so-called father's side?"

"He said I had none," she whispered.

"Of course he did."

"But I'm sure he could explain this."

"I am sure he could. And it would all be lies." Diego stared at her with a look of desperation. "I do not want to risk your 'Papa' trying to keep you from being reunited with your family. You said he is far away in Scotland. Even if I wanted to risk your contacting him, there is no time. Indeed, I have instructed the captain of our ship that we are to sail at dawn tomorrow."

She blinked. "At dawn! So soon?"

"I would hate to arrive in Spain only to find that your grandfather had died before your arrival. Wouldn't you?"

"All the same, I . . . I need time to think about this. I'm sorry, Diego, but I can't just go off to Spain with you without looking for other corroborating evidence. You'll have to wait until I can talk to Papa."

The color drained from his face. Then he drew himself up with a haughty air. "Very well. But before you go to meet him, I must arm you against his lies. I have something more compelling to show you, but you will have to wait here while I fetch it from upstairs."

"Why is it upstairs?" she asked suspiciously. He was giving up too easily.

He shrugged. "I could not be sure you would come alone tonight, and I could not risk having it seized by anyone, so it is locked away for safekeeping."

The glance he cast her was intense, imbued with dark meaning. "I feared I would have trouble in England finding another copy of this particular document. It is the announcement of your birth in the Spanish newspaper."

Chapter Fifteen

Dear Cousin,

Lucy does seem to have feelings for Señor Montalvo. That does not mean he has feelings for her. If he made an offer to her at their meeting, she did not reveal it to me. Either he did not offer, or she refused him. I will give her some time and then demand to know more of what happened. It alarms me how quiet and contemplative she has been this evening. Lucy is never *contemplative.*

Your anxious friend,
Charlotte

Diego tried not to let the shock on her face affect him. What he had said was a lie, but surely an innocent one. For her own good.

He could see it all slipping away—her chance to have a real family, his chance to fulfill his vow. And all because some English soldier had filled her head with lies from the day she was stolen.

"You actually have a newspaper clipping of my birth announcement?" she asked, her face ash-white.

He returned to where the half-empty wine glasses sat.

"Have more wine while I fetch it," he evaded, loathing himself for the subterfuge.

With his back shielding her view, he took a vial from his front pocket. He had hoped not to need this, but he could see no other way. And after caring for his mother years ago, he knew exactly how much laudanum would send Lucy to sleep. He tipped in a few drops, then added a healthy measure of wine. If she didn't drink it, he'd have to subdue her by force. He *really* did not wish to do that.

Forcing a smile, he turned to hand her the glass. "I will only be a moment."

Fighting the urge to see if she drank the wine, he walked upstairs to be sure everything had been carried down to the river landing. After waiting a few more moments, he went back down. Where the devil was Gaspar? He should have returned with the steam packet from London by now.

Grumbling that Diego hadn't allowed him enough time, Gaspar had left for the Surrey docks this afternoon to arrange for a maid to travel with them. He was also notifying Diego's friend Rafael, captain of the Spanish brig that had brought them to England, that they wished to leave in the morning. Diego had convinced Gaspar they must leave right away, before Lucy's father returned to London.

Everything else was settled. The servants had been paid off. Diego had arranged for a courier to deliver the three months' rent to Pritchard on the morrow, with a terse note that said they would not be purchasing Rockhurst after all. Only one thing was left—spiriting Lucy off.

With his conscience beating at him, Diego returned to find her slumped in the chair. It had been quicker than expected, and panic seized him as he raced to check her pulse. It was strong and steady, her breathing that of a deep sleep.

"So you drugged the girl, did you?" came Gaspar's voice from the doorway.

Diego jumped, then cursed. "You are late." He straightened to face his mentor. "Is everything in order? Are they loading the steam packet?"

"Yes." Gaspar stared at Lucy. "It's all arranged—the maid, the passage, everything. Rafael is readying the ship for your arrival even now."

"Go on to the packet, then." He still had to dispose of the dregs in Lucy's glass and set the room in order.

"I'm not going with you," Gaspar said.

Diego gaped at him. "What do you mean?"

Gaspar cast him an accusing glance. "I told myself you wouldn't stoop to this. That you would abide by her decision if she refused to go." He let out a harsh breath. "But in my heart, I knew you'd do anything to get Arboleda back."

Ignoring the savage stab of guilt, Diego said, "This concerns her, too. She has a right to know her family."

"I agree." He pointed to where Lucy's head lolled against the chair. "But not like this."

"Once she awakens, she will be glad I took matters into my own hands."

"You'd better hope you're right." Gaspar set his shoulders. "Because I won't be around to keep her from killing you if you aren't. I'm staying here."

"In *England?*"

"Unlike you, I have nothing against the English."

"And you will do what, work for Astley?" he snapped, angry that Gaspar would abandon him. "Sniff around your

English cook, who will no doubt spurn you once she discovers your part in this?"

Gaspar glared at him. "You arrogant ass. Do you never think of anything but yourself and your own pain?"

Diego recoiled as if slapped. "I am not doing this only for me," he said hoarsely.

"Yes, I forgot." Gaspar's face was black with anger. "I'm supposed to be grateful that you want to put me out to pasture. That you want to sentence me to moldering on the side of a remote mountain in León while you try to rebuild a life that hasn't been yours in sixteen years." Holding up his gnarled hands, he shook them at Diego. "These don't mean I can't still be useful. I have plenty of life left in me, damn you, no matter what you think."

Diego didn't know how to respond. All this time, he had assumed that Gaspar wanted the same things he did. "I only thought to make those years more comfortable for you."

"Did you ever ask me what *I* really wanted? I went along with it because I was fool enough to think that once you got here, you'd see the money to be made off the English. You'd forget your hatred and give up this fool dream of Arboleda. Instead, you've turned to kidnapping. Well, I draw the line at that."

Diego couldn't believe his ears. He and Gaspar had been together most of his life. Gaspar had been like his second father, and the man Diego most respected. "You intend to stop me?"

"No." Gaspar crossed his arms over his chest. "I intend to clean up the mess you leave behind. As I always do." He removed a folded sheet from his coat pocket. "It took me an hour, with my fingers the way they are, but I wrote a note in

Miss Seton's hand that says she ran away with you to be married. It's the only way they won't come after you. I copied her signature from that note she sent you, and I think I managed a fair approximation of her hand for the rest of it."

Diego stared at him, incredulous.

"I palmed Sally's key this afternoon. I'll use it to get in, leave the letter, pack a few of Miss Seton's things to make it seem as if she left willingly, and bring them to the landing. You can't have her traveling without extra clothes. After you're gone, I'll return here to wait for the letter to be discovered."

"Gaspar, I cannot let you take so large a risk."

"At least I'm not risking my conscience. Or your life. *You* were only too willing to sail off to Spain, leaving destruction in your wake. This way they won't accuse you—or me—of kidnapping, and they might go north looking for you, instead of catching you before you leave English waters. I'll play the innocent, say you sent me to London on a fool's errand and that I found this letter from you upon my return." Gaspar waved another folded sheet at him. "By now, I know *your* hand well enough to forge a note."

"And what if they don't believe you? What if they clap you in gaol?"

"They won't," Gaspar said with a trace of his old confidence as he shoved both notes into his pocket. "I've got Sally to vouch for me. Besides, everyone saw how you and Miss Seton behaved at the charity breakfast—it won't surprise them." His voice hardened. "Once the truth drifts back to England, I may have to do some fancy stepping, but—"

"I do not want you to take such chances for me, damn it!"

"Then don't do this!" Gaspar said fiercely. "I'll sneak Miss Seton back into the school somehow and put her in her bed. You can call on her tomorrow, make up a tale for what happened. You can wait until she is ready to travel to Spain. You can tour England or work for Astley. You can write the *marqués* and say you decided not to disrupt her life."

The idea chilled Diego's blood. "I have already disrupted her life. I must see this to the end, for her sake as well as mine."

Gaspar snorted. "I knew you would—you're as bloody stubborn as the English." He gestured toward Lucy. "Just don't pretend you're doing it for *her*. You're doing it because you're so eaten up by the past that you can't think of the future. None of this will wipe out what the English did to your family. Returning to Arboleda and honoring your foolish vow to your father won't assuage your pain. Only *you* can do that. And I begin to fear you will have to stoop very low indeed before you realize that."

Before Diego could answer, Gaspar added, "Go on with you. The packet boat is waiting, and I have to slip in and out of the school. I'll meet you at the landing with clothes for her. If I don't show up within the next twenty minutes, it means I've been found out, so don't tarry beyond that."

When Gaspar headed out, Diego felt a moment's panic. "*Hostias,* Gaspar, come back here! You cannot do this. It is too risky."

Gaspar paused only long enough to shoot Diego a quelling glance. "I am not yours to command, boy. Best remember that." Then he left.

Boy. The word stung. Remembering when Gaspar had called him *boy* as a matter of course, Diego felt a hot flush of shame rise in his cheeks.

It rapidly turned to anger. *Por Dios,* he was a grown man now. Let Gaspar rail at him if he must, but Diego's mind was set.

Hurrying to Lucy's side, he lifted her in his arms. With a purring sound, she pressed her face into his chest. A lump caught in his throat, but he choked it down. He was doing what was best for her, no matter what Gaspar claimed.

As he carried her out the rear entrance and headed for the landing, the light of the half-moon dappled her pretty cheeks and dusted her tresses with silver. A jolt of desire hit him so powerfully that he had to look away.

What a fool he had been to indulge himself with her a few nights ago. It had only sharpened his need for her, a need that was never to be satisfied. Thanks to his idiocy, he now had the added torment of knowing he could never hold her like this again, never kiss her . . . never have her in his bed.

Cursing under his breath, he brought her aboard the packet boat, already loaded with his belongings.

Though the crew eyed Lucy with curiosity, they asked no questions. He laid her in the bow, where he could put himself between her and them. They seemed decent enough, but they bore the usual rough look of sailors, making him glad of the pistol inside his coat.

Nervously, he waited for Gaspar to bring the clothes. Just as he was sure he would have to go on, Gaspar appeared out of the darkness and tossed a stuffed canvas bag onto the boat.

"Take good care of her," he told Diego, his face stony. Then he turned and headed back to the manor, never looking back.

A hint of dawn shone on the horizon by the time they reached the Surrey dock, for the going was more treacherous at night, forcing them to move slowly. Lucy stirred once or twice, but he'd given her enough laudanum to keep her sleeping for several hours, so thankfully she did not rouse fully.

Once at the dock, it was easy to find Rafael's brig, the only one flying a Spanish flag. It was not so easy to move Lucy aboard, since he had to hoist her over his shoulder to carry her up the rope ladder.

"What's wrong with her?" Rafael asked as Diego came on deck.

"I gave her laudanum." His friend knew the whole tale of why they were here, so he might as well know the rest. Better to have it out now. "She was not as willing to leave England as I expected."

Rafael feigned shock. "And you, my oh-so-honorable friend, abducted her?"

"If you do not want to risk having her aboard," Diego said as he shifted her to lie in his arms, "say so now, and be done with it. I have already suffered one lecture from Gaspar. I do not mean to suffer another from you."

"Lecture!" Rafael burst into laughter. "Have you forgotten what I've been doing the past two months while waiting for you? I took more risk running brandy across the channel than I will carrying one English lady to Spain."

"She is Spanish!" Diego hissed. "And her passport proves it." The *marqués* had used his connections to gain her one in her Spanish name.

"That settles *my* conscience well enough," Rafael said blithely.

The mention of conscience irritated Diego, since his was beginning to plague him. "*Por Dios,* just tell me which cabin you prepared for her."

"Mine, of course."

"Rafael—" he began, well aware of his friend's love of the ladies.

Rafael flashed him a cheeky grin. "I'm bunking with the first mate, *imbécil.* As are you." He strode alongside Diego with his usual devil-may-care air. "Though if she's as rich as you said, perhaps I should take advantage of having her aboard and court her before we reach Spain. Might as well throw my hat into the ring before the other gentlemen get wind of her."

It took all Diego's control not to tell Rafael exactly where he could shove his hat. "Did you happen to acquire a fortune and high rank while I was away?"

Rafael gave an exaggerated sigh. "Alas, no."

"Because without them, you will not meet her grandfather's requirements."

"Perhaps you are considering throwing *your* hat into the ring." Rafael cast Diego a searching glance. "As I recall, you are still the great Conde de León. And once you hand her over to the *marqués,* you will have property, too."

"Only if the lady reaches there unscathed, so do not get any ideas about changing that. Or we will both end up with nothing."

"Not me. It cost me far less to carry you here and back than I gained on the cargo—not to mention what I made with the smuggling." Laughing, Rafael led Diego belowdecks to the captain's cabin. "I'll have to take care not to stumble in here by accident one night when I'm drunk."

Even knowing his friend baited him on purpose, Diego frowned as Rafael opened the door. "Will I have to stand guard the whole voyage?"

"I think not. I am sure I can find other . . . entertainment." Rafael glanced inside to wink at someone there.

Diego spotted the buxom female awaiting them, her cheeks heavily rouged and her hair lying in loose ringlets about her shoulders. "*Qué demonios,* who is *she?*" he asked Rafael as he carried Lucy to the bed.

"The little heiress's maid, of course. Gaspar hired her."

Setting Lucy on the bed, Diego took another look at the pretty woman who stood watching them warily, clearly unable to understand their Spanish. A *maid* she most certainly was not. In any sense of the word.

"The next time I see that *cretino,*" Diego ground out, "I swear to God I will kill him."

Rafael laughed as he swept his gaze down the woman's lush body. "And I will thank him."

That was when Lucy woke up.

Chapter Sixteen

꧁꧂

Dear Cousin,

I awakened this morning feeling a vague unease,
though I cannot put my finger on what has caused
it. The school is quiet, there is no cause for alarm,
and yet I am worried. Do forgive my mood, but
I cannot shake the feeling that something has
changed. I believe I shall close this letter now and
go to breakfast. Being with the girls in the morning
never fails to settle my nerves.

Your pensive relation,
Charlotte

Lucy's eyelids lay like lead, and her tongue swelled thick
as cotton. The soft surface beneath her kept shifting. She
remembered drinking wine. Could that have made her feel
like this? No, she'd only had two glasses. She was almost
sure of it.

She struggled to open her eyes, but it was too hard.
Meanwhile, a murmur of voices filtered into her mind,
male voices speaking Spanish, some of which she understood. The voice she didn't recognize said something about
"setting sail."

Diego's voice answered, "Go on, man." Or that was what

she thought he said, anyway. It was hard to be sure with her mind so woolly.

Then Diego said in English, "Go fetch your new mistress some water, will you?"

A female voice answered. "I don't know where to find—"

"Ask someone," Diego said tersely. "And find her something to eat, too."

Eat? Who was the woman? What did he mean by "new mistress"? And why were all these other people in Diego's house in the middle of the night?

Forcing her eyes open, she caught sight of a swarthy-looking fellow walking out through the lowest doorway she'd ever seen in a house; he had to duck to pass through it.

She was certainly not in the parlor now.

No, it was a bedchamber, but smaller than what she'd expect at Rockhurst. And she could smell something. The sea? Yes, she was almost sure of it. Struggling to sit up, she looked for Diego, but he was distracted by a man dressed as a sailor carrying in a canvas bag. She glanced to her right, startled to see that the windows looked like portholes, and the room was swaying . . .

Good Lord. "Diego Montalvo, you scoundrel!" she cried as she threw her legs over the side of the bed. "We are on a ship!"

Motioning the sailor out the door, he turned toward her, his eyes wary. "Yes. We're on our way to Spain."

She gaped at him. "You . . . you *took* me? Without asking? Without being sure that I—" She broke off as the fullness of his perfidy dawned on her. Ships did not come so far up the Thames as the school, and it would have taken hours to reach the Surrey docks.

"You *drugged* me, you wretched devil! You must have put something in my wine!"

His face was like stone. "A little laudanum, that's all. I had no choice."

"No choice!" She leaped from the bed, then nearly fell from dizziness.

With a stricken expression, he rushed over and urged her to sit back on the bed. "Stay where you are, *cariño*. You must rest until the drug leaves your blood."

Batting his hands away in panic, she struggled to rise again, but the ship lurched, tossing her back onto the bed.

In an instant, she realized what that meant—the ship had set sail! "I am not going to rest, you . . . you kidnapper!"

She leaped up again, but this time Diego swept her up in his arms and sat down on the bed with her. "*Por Dios!* Calm down before you hurt yourself."

"Let go of me!" She struggled against the arms that wrapped her like steel bands. "I must speak to the captain before we get under way!"

"You cannot." Diego struggled to subdue her. "He is busy sailing the ship."

"I know! That's why I must see him *now,* curse you!" She elbowed him hard enough to make him release her.

But before she got more than a foot away, Diego yanked her back and threw her down onto the bed, then covered her body with the full weight of his. "Stop this madness!" He caught her wrists and pinioned them to the bed. "There is no point to it!"

"If I could just speak to the captain," she cried, fighting futilely against the large body weighing her down, "I know he would turn the ship around!"

Remorse flashed briefly over Diego's face, leaving only determination in its wake. "The captain is fully aware of the situation, and he is not stopping, for you or anyone else. So save your breath and your energy, *mi dulzura*."

"I am not your sweetness!" she spat, tears welling in her eyes. "I am not your *anything!*" He had drugged her, for pity's sake! And now he was dragging her to Spain against her will? "You have no right to do this!"

"Lucy, listen to me," he said in a voice of maddening calm. "I know you want to meet your family, and I mean to make sure that you do."

She stopped struggling and glared at him. "Get off me, you devil," she said through gritted teeth.

"This will be easier for all of us if you just relax, enjoy the voyage, and prepare yourself to meet—"

"Enjoy the voy—" With rage surging through her, she bucked against him, trying to throw him off.

But he held fast.

Her eyes narrowed to slits. "Get. Off. Me. Or I swear that when I do meet my grandfather—*if* I meet my grandfather—I shall tell him that you held me down on a bed to have your wicked way with me."

Diego paled. "You would not lie."

"Try me."

"Fine," he growled. "I will let you up. But only if you promise not to run on deck to bother the captain."

"Do *you* promise to bring him down here to talk to me?" she shot back. "So I can see if you're telling the truth about his part in this . . . this madness?"

Diego actually had the audacity to look offended. "I do not lie."

That enraged her further. "Oh, no? All that nonsense about the birth announcement? About abiding by my wishes? That was the truth?"

Diego flinched, then abruptly rolled off her. "Very well," he said, his face taut with anger. "I will bring the captain here. As soon as he can leave his post."

A woman who looked about eight years older than Lucy suddenly appeared in the doorway, carrying a tray and glancing anxiously from Diego to Lucy. "Beggin' yer pardon, milord, but I brought food and some tea for the little miss."

Aware of what she must look like sprawled on the bed, Lucy shot up to stare at the female with the flaming hair, wearing a low-cut gown and with lips so highly rouged Lucy was surprised they weren't on fire. "Who are you?"

"Your lady's maid," Diego bit out. "As I told you, you have a chaperone."

Lucy was completely taken aback. The woman looked as if she'd just emerged fresh from a tumble in the hay. Good Lord, this got worse by the moment!

This time, when Lucy stood to face Diego, she managed to stay on her feet. "You . . . you hired a . . . a ladybird to chaperone me?" She broke into hysterical laughter. "Oh, that's rich!"

Diego winced, but before he could open his mouth, the woman spoke.

"Now see here, miss," she said with a sniff as she hurried to the table to set down the tray, "I'm a respectable woman, I am. I worked at the Anchor Inn before that fellow Gaspar hired me, and I did a right proper job of dressing the ladies' hair." She paused. "When we had ladies, that is, which weren't that often. Mostly we got sailors, and a gentleman or two. And one time—"

"Perhaps you should tell Miss Seton your name," Diego cut in with a grimace that showed exactly what he thought of Gaspar's choice of lady's maid.

"Aye, you're right, sir." With an exaggerated curtsy, the woman shot Lucy a winsome smile. "Name's Janet, Miss Seton, but most people call me Nettie."

Lucy blinked. "You're Scottish?" Nettie was a common Scottish nickname.

Nettie beamed and thrust out her chin. "I am indeed. That's why the other fellow hired me. Said it might make you more comfortable to have one of your countrywomen about."

Remembering the rumors she'd heard about Gaspar sweet-talking the school's buxom cook, she arched an eyebrow. "*That's* why he hired you?"

Her sarcasm was lost on the woman. "Well, that and the fact that there ain't a true lady's maid to be had for miles 'round, and he was in a tearing hurry to find someone to attend you on this trip."

Nettie poured a cup of tea and brought it to Lucy, who refused it. With a shrug, Nettie drank it herself. "But I can do what they do—wash linens and iron yer clothes and take the spots out of muslin neat as you please. And I brought my paints, too, seeing as how you're a lady and you might want some fixing up." She edged nearer to examine Lucy's face. "You could do with a bit of rouge, duckie, you're that pale."

"If I'm pale, it's because of *him*!" Lucy stabbed one finger at Diego. She strode up to him, hands on her hips. "Where's your fellow kidnapper? I'd like to thank him for providing me with such an able servant." She could well imagine the extra duties Gaspar expected the tavern wench to perform for *him* on the voyage.

"Gaspar stayed behind."

Lucy eyed him skeptically. "Why?"

He looked surprisingly discomfited. "To make sure no one follows us."

That set her back on her feet. She hadn't even thought of how this might be seen at the school. Her stomach roiled so badly she had to sit down to quell her nausea. She was ruined. Ruined! And all because Diego wanted to . . . to . . . to what? Why on earth would he go to such lengths for the *marqués*?

Oh, she could well guess.

"How much is he paying you?" she whispered.

A flush rose in Diego's cheeks. "What do you mean?"

"My grandfather must have paid you to do this. Otherwise, why would you risk it? They've got to be looking for me now, and it won't take them long to guess who abducted me. And if they catch up to you, you'll hang."

"Actually, they think we eloped." Diego looked decidedly guilty as he threaded his fingers through his hair. "You left a note, courtesy of Gaspar's forgery skills. He stayed behind to make sure that anyone who considers pursuing you continues to think we eloped."

As a powerful wave of fury swept through her, she jumped to her feet, her fists clenched. "So not only have you ruined me, but you made it look as if I leaped willingly into my own ruination! And when I return to England without you, they'll say that's what I get for running off with a Spanish magician who clearly only wanted my virtue. Who tossed me aside when he was done with me!"

"No!" he cried. "Once you're in Spain—"

"I don't want to *go* to Spain!" She snatched the teacup from Nettie's hand and threw it at his head. He ducked, and the cup smashed harmlessly against the wall, but he wasn't so lucky when he straightened just in time to get a meat pie in the face.

If she hadn't been so furious, she would have laughed at the picture he made, with bits of pastry and beef and little green peas dripping from his brow and mouth and cheeks.

Her anger intensified when he merely took out a handkerchief and began to wipe off the mess with an expression of wounded dignity. "We will continue this discussion when you can be rational," he announced in that oh-so-haughty tone he used when he was being an idiot.

Ooh, if he thought she could ever be rational about *this* . . . With a cry of rage, she threw the plate at him. Unfortunately, it only hit the door as he slipped through.

When he had shut the door behind him, she threw herself at it, crying, "Come back here, you scoundrel! We are not done!" She grabbed the door handle and yanked it in a frenzy, but he'd locked it.

She beat on the door, tears finally rolling down her cheeks in a torrent of anger and betrayal and hurt. Diego had given her no choice. He'd wrenched her from her life *forever!* How could he?

For the next few moments, she was insensible of anything but her fury. She raged at Diego, then Gaspar, then the grandfather she hadn't yet met.

Once her anger played out, she collapsed in a heap of tears on the floor. Would she ever see Papa again? Or Mrs. Harris? Or Lady Kerr? Oh, how she wished that she hadn't carped at her stepmother the last time she'd seen her. She would give anything to have her here now, chiding her for anything she pleased.

That brought on more sobbing, until she was weeping so hard it made her ill. Wrapped in her misery, she jumped when a gentle hand touched her arm.

It was only Nettie. "There, there, miss. It can't be so bad as all that, can it?"

"You d-don't understand," she cried between sobs. "That . . . that devil k-kidnapped me!"

"Aye, I gathered that much. But you'll make yourself sick if you keep going on this way." Nettie drew her into her arms and rocked her, patting her back, murmuring soothing words, until Lucy's crying subsided at last.

After Lucy had gained control of herself, Nettie pulled out a surprisingly clean handkerchief and dabbed at Lucy's eyes and nose. "There now, all done, are we?"

Lucy gazed at her, desperation making her grab at anyone who might prove a friend. Despite the rouge and powder caking her face, Nettie had kindly features and a warm smile. Perhaps she might prove an ally.

Clasping the woman's hand, she fixed her with a pleading gaze. "I have to get off this ship before we leave England." She knew from experience that the journey down the Thames could take some time, and then the ship would skirt the coast of England for another few days. If she could just reach the banks of the river . . . "You have to help me get off the ship!"

Nettie's face fell. "I'm sorry, duckie—"

"If it's a matter of money, I promise my papa will pay you whatever you ask. He can give you three times what Diego is offering."

"It ain't a matter of money. We're too far away. What will you do, swim?"

Lucy swallowed. She didn't know how to swim. Nor

did she fancy leaping into the dark, swirling waters of the Thames.

Pushing herself up off the floor, she hurried to the port-hole, her stomach sinking to see that Nettie was right. The river was far wider than she remembered. "If we could get a boat . . . or perhaps someone to row us—"

Nettie came over to stand beside her at the porthole. "It won't work, miss. None of the sailors speaks English, 'cepting the captain, and he looks to be a good friend of Señor Montalvo. What will you do, lower the boat yerself? Row it to the bank? In *that* current? It can't be done, even if you had a mind to do it. And to be honest, I don't fancy drowning in the river."

Lucy gazed out at the bank that taunted her by being so far away. She might as well be in Spain already.

Pulling her from the porthole, Nettie led her to a chair and poured tea into another cup. "Besides, Señor Montalvo is just bringing you home to your rich grandfather, right? That Gaspar fellow said you're heiress to millions."

"I don't want the millions," she said petulantly, cringing as she realized she sounded like a spoiled child.

"Only them that already has money ever says a fool thing like that." Nettie added milk and sugar to the tea, then handed the cup to Lucy. "Drink some of this now. You'll feel better if you do. I always say a cup o' tea is all a body needs to feel right with the world."

To her surprise, Lucy found that between the tea and her good cry and Nettie's kindness, she did feel a little better. She was still furious with Diego, but the situation didn't seem quite so hopeless.

Nettie smiled her approval and dropped into the other chair. "I say you should meet this rich grandfather of yours.

Let him spend his money on you. Them Spanish ain't so bad, you know. We gets a few of 'em at the inn from time to time, and some of 'em are right handsome. That Cap'n Rafael, for example . . . now he's a fine specimen of mankind, he is. And your Señor Montalvo—"

"He's not *my* Señor Montalvo," Lucy snapped. "I'll throttle him before I let him near me again."

That was what hurt most—that after Diego's sweet words and attentions and the way he'd seemed to understand her better than almost anyone, he could do something as awful as this. She would never forgive him for it. Never!

"Throttling might seem a good idea right now, with your temper up and all," Nettie said, "but there's better ways to get what you want from a man. Give him a little of this . . ." She tossed her hair. "And a lot of *this* . . ." She thrust out her chest. "And you'd be surprised what concessions you can weasel out of him."

Lucy didn't know whether to laugh hysterically or burst into tears again. "Nettie, I thought you said you were a respectable woman."

"I am. Most of the time." Seeing Lucy's expression, she thrust out her chin. "I ain't no whore or nothing. I'm just . . . practical. If a man wants to buy me sumpthin', well, I might be inclined to be a bit nicer to him, if you know what I mean."

"If you think I will cozy up to Diego—"

"No, no, you're too respectable for that, as well you should be. But I saw how he looked at you. He ain't happy about rousing your temper, and you can use that. If you really want him to turn the ship around, ask him nicely. Flirt a little. Won't do you no harm."

Lucy sighed. If Diego had gone so far as to drug her and have notes forged, he wasn't going to change his mind because of a few smiles.

First, she had to find out why he was so bent on reuniting her with her grandfather. Then she'd know better what to do. If it was money he wanted, she might convince him that Papa would pay him more to take her back to England. If she returned soon enough, she might even escape ruination. Mrs. Harris would surely keep it quiet as long as she could.

Nettie walked over to open the canvas bag the sailor had carried in earlier. "They told me they brought clothes for you." To Lucy's shock, Nettie drew out one of her evening gowns and held it up with a sound of delight. "See here, duckie, this is right pretty, it is."

"How in the dickens did they get my clothes?" Lucy went to look inside the bag. Day gown, shift, drawers, petticoats. No nightgown, but she could always sleep in her shift. There was even a pair of slippers. And down at the very bottom . . .

She dug deep and came up with her sketch pad. She sighed. It did her little good with no charcoals, inks, or pencils.

Nettie thrust the day gown at her. "You should put this one on."

Lucy peered into the bag, but it was empty now. "I can't. It's missing the chemisette that goes inside it, and without that I'd be indecent."

"Exactly," Nettie said with a gleam in her eye. "A man'll do much for a woman wearing a gown like this."

Her eyes narrowing thoughtfully, Lucy took it. Diego *had* been quite susceptible to her in her low-cut evening gown. And if she wanted to get information from him . . .

It might work on the captain, as well. If Nettie was right, outrage would do her no good, since the man was a friend of Diego's. But if she could turn his head with flirtation, she might persuade him to turn the ship around.

It was worth a try. She had to do *something.* Because she wasn't about to be led off to Spain like a calf to the slaughter simply because the almighty Diego Montalvo had decided it.

It was nearly noon by the time Charlotte Harris rushed into the Duke of Foxmoor's house, praying he was home. She'd already sent Terence, her personal footman, to Charles Godwin's house, only to have him discover that Charles was in Bath for the week. Then she'd gone to Cousin Michael's solicitor, who had only promised to pass on the message, refusing even then to reveal her cousin's identity. Without the help of Michael or other friends of the school, she didn't know what she'd do about Lucy.

Charlotte cursed herself again for her own stupidity. How could she have let that blasted magician meet with the young woman alone yesterday? She would never forgive Cousin Michael for talking her into *that* foolishness. She was almost certain Señor Montalvo had taken the opportunity to persuade Lucy to run away with him. That would explain Lucy's quiet demeanor at dinner, her refusal to reveal what she'd discussed with the handsome conjurer.

Still, she would never have guessed that Lucy, of all people, would do such a thing. Elope with a virtual stranger? Had she lost her mind?

"Mrs. Harris!" exclaimed a voice as she was ushered into the drawing room. "How could Louisa's note have reached you so soon?"

It was the duke himself, thank heaven. And rising beside him were the Marquess of Stoneville and Tessa's Uncle Anthony, the Viscount Norcourt. Good—Anthony would help her, though she wasn't sure about the rakish Stoneville. Why they were all here, though, she couldn't fathom. And where was Louisa?

Then the duke's words registered. "What note?"

The men exchanged glances as the duke's expression grew grave. "There's been an accident."

"What kind of accident?"

"Not an accident," Anthony snapped. "Though I still can't believe that the bloody little fool killed herself."

"Who?" Charlotte asked, now shocked.

"Lady Kirkwood took her own life last night," Foxmoor explained. "Kirkwood and his housekeeper found her in the bath. She left a note mentioning her gambling debts."

Charlotte stood thunderstruck, Lucy's situation temporarily paling. Charlotte had always hoped Sarah might come to her senses one day. Now she would never get the chance.

"There will be a huge scandal," Lord Stoneville said bitterly. "Selfish little twit. Kirkwood is destroyed. We've been discussing how to handle the gossip."

Heaven help her. Charlotte hadn't even thought of that. Society would eat her alive. *Two* of her graduates embroiled in scandal! Though it was no better than she deserved; she'd failed both women. Staggering a little, she had to be helped to a chair.

"Are you all right?" Anthony asked, a rock as always.

"We have a desperate situation at the school, too, I'm afraid. That's why I came. I hadn't heard about Sarah yet. But Lucy has eloped with Señor Montalvo."

Anthony frowned. "Lucy? Tessa's friend Lucy?"

She nodded. "You saw how he was with her at the charity affair. He must have been . . . working on her even then."

"Are you sure she eloped and didn't just visit a friend?" Foxmoor asked.

"Of course I'm sure," Charlotte retorted. "She left a note. Besides, that servant of Señor Montalvo's is still at Rockhurst. He had a note from his master, too. It appears that they left in the middle of the night."

Anthony shook his head. "It doesn't seem like something Lucy would do. She was in love with that idiot Hunforth for years, according to Tessa. Then she turns about and runs off with a Spaniard?"

"That's *why* she ran off with the man," Charlotte said. "She was very vulnerable. He took advantage."

"We all agree on that," Foxmoor said grimly.

"You know, Mrs. Harris," Lord Stoneville said dryly, "you really need to start offering classes to your girls about how to avoid elopements. This makes what, three of your pupils now? There was that girl Amelia who ran off with the American soldier, and then Lady Venetia who ran off with a Scot—"

"Stoneville, you are not helping," Anthony put in as Charlotte paled.

The man was right. This was happening with appalling regularity. Honestly, though, she could hardly have stopped the first two. Although few people knew it, Amelia had actually been kidnapped from her father's town house by that horrible Lord Pomeroy, forcing Major Lucas to rescue her by marrying her.

And Venetia was no longer a student at the school when she decided to elope. Besides, she and Sir Lachlan had known each other for years. It hadn't been a shock to either family when they'd run off together. Or so Charlotte had been told, though she did wonder about the truth of that tale.

In Lucy's case, however, Charlotte had clearly been lax. She had let the young woman be stolen right off the premises of the school.

"I assume they went north to Gretna Green—" Foxmoor began.

"Why?" Lord Stoneville drawled. "Just as easy for him to whisk her off to Spain. That *is* where the man is from, isn't it?"

Charlotte's heart sank. She hadn't even considered that. She seized Anthony's hand. "I need your help. I know you're upset right now, what with Sarah's suicide, but I have to do something about Lucy. There's no time to waste."

"We'll help, too," the duke put in. When the others eyed him in surprise, he added, "Kirkwood will be tied up for hours with the inquest. We can be no good to him until it's done. Louisa is with his family. I don't know about you, but I need to keep busy until we can help Kirkwood."

"I would be most grateful," Charlotte said.

"Here's what we'll do," the duke said, taking charge of the situation. "Anthony, go back with Mrs. Harris to the school. See if Tessa can shed any light on this. Perhaps Lucy confided in her."

"I already spoke to Tessa," Charlotte put in.

"Yes, but she might be more willing to tell the truth to her uncle," Foxmoor pointed out. "I'll go to the docks to see if I can discover whether any ships bound for Spain lifted anchor last night."

"Someone has to fetch Colonel Seton," Charlotte said. "He's still in Edinburgh."

"I'll do it," Lord Stoneville said.

The other three gaped at him.

"What?" he said. "I've got the fastest rig of any of you."

"Yes, but why would you—" Anthony began.

"For God's sake," Lord Stoneville said, "despite my title, I'm not made of stone. I'll stop at Gretna Green, and if I don't find them there, I'll go on to Edinburgh."

"Thank you, Lord Stoneville," Charlotte said. "I am very grateful for your help, no matter what the reason."

The marquess cast her a rakish smile. "Just how grateful might you be, Mrs. Harris?"

As she gaped at him, Anthony scowled. "Stop that, you blasted whoremonger. Can't you see this is no time for flirtation?"

"I was just asking," Lord Stoneville said with a shrug.

Charlotte tried not to show her consternation. She'd heard much about the marquess, one of society's most outrageous rakehells, and did not want to find herself owing him any favor of *that* kind.

"Pay him no mind," Foxmoor put in irritably. "He thinks every woman is fair game. But I assure you, madam, we will play your knights errant in this. After you helped three of us find our wives, Kirkwood included, we can do no less."

"Thank you, sir." She let out a pained sigh. "Though after what has happened today, I doubt Lord Kirkwood will be grateful to me. His family will have a difficult scandal to weather now."

"You can't blame yourself for that," Anthony said kindly. "Sarah brought her troubles upon herself." He offered her his hand to help her rise. "Come, then, let's go talk to Tessa. With luck, we'll catch up to them before they get too far, and we'll nip this thing in the bud before it turns into a raging scandal, too."

Charlotte prayed he was right. She would hate to see the school destroyed by this onslaught of troubles. And if any harm came to Lucy, she would never forgive herself.

Chapter Seventeen

❧

Dear Cousin,

I told you of the elopement, but the news grows worse by the day. We now believe it was <u>not</u> an elopement. Tessa is certain that Lucy did not write the note. I pray she is wrong, but I begin to fear the worst. I will know more as soon as I hear from Lord Stoneville, who has gone north to fetch the colonel.

Your alarmed relation,
Charlotte

Two hours passed before Diego headed belowdecks with Rafael in tow. He had to put a swift end to Lucy's foolish ideas about returning, and showing her that Rafael was firmly behind him ought to do it.

He still could not believe how she had reacted upon waking. He had expected some anger over his handling of the matter; he had not expected her to turn into a raging virago.

He had not expected heartbreaking sobs.

Dios mio, why had he tortured himself by listening to her rage at him through the door? But he had been too shaken to leave. Never had he imagined she would go on so. Never had he imagined her crying herself sick. It had taken every ounce of his will not to go in, sweep her up in his arms, and promise to do whatever she wished. Even now, he was tempted.

But that was madness. He had taken this step for a reason, and once she could consider it rationally, she would see he was right. He was offering her what she said she wanted—the chance to know her family. He was opening up a world of the highest society to her, a status she could never attain in England. He was offering escape from the villainous English colonel who had helped to steal her.

He set his shoulders grimly. He did not regret what he had done. And once she was calm, she would not regret it, either.

Outside the cabin, he paused, alarmed by the mysterious silence. Taking out the key, he said to Rafael in a low voice, "I should warn you, she is very angry. I have no idea what we will find, besides pieces of the crockery she hurled at me as I left. She went a little wild when she realized where the ship was headed. She could have done anything to your cabin after I went on deck—you might find your mattress torn to ribbons."

"Broken crockery? Torn mattresses? Ah, Diego, you do have a way with women," Rafael said dryly.

Not this woman. This woman tied him in knots—when she wasn't tempting him into madness. "I will reimburse you for any damage."

"Open the door, for God's sake," Rafael said with a laugh. "Let me see this wild woman for myself."

With a nod, Diego unlocked the door and opened it wide.

Then he stood gaping at the scene before him. The broken dishes and remnants of meat pie were gone, and

Lucy and Nettie sat at the table drinking tea as they played cards. Diego marvelled at the change in Lucy's demeanor. When had she gone from enraged spitfire to placid tea-drinking female?

She looked different, too. For one thing, her hair fell unfettered to her waist. And she had changed her gown.

When she stood to face him, he nearly choked on his tongue. From the side, the gown looked perfectly respectable, but as she headed toward him, he could see it lacked something essential. Like half the bodice.

The two parts of the wrap gown crossed at a point well below decency, revealing the top of her stays and the lacy border of her shift. He could swear he had seen her in this gown before, but something had covered her exposed undergarments and the upper swells of her lovely breasts, which drew his gaze like a pair of beacons.

God preserve his soul. And was that rouge on her cheeks? She looked like a more ravishing version of Nettie. *That* did not bode well.

"It's about time you returned." Lucy sashayed up to him, hips swinging. "Nettie and I were getting very bored."

Lucy did not sashay, and she did not get bored. She barely flirted. Some part of his mind registered that. But mostly he stood gawking at her, unable to breathe, unable to tear his eyes from the vision of loveliness that was Lucy with her hair down and her bosom half exposed. All he would have to do was slide his hand into the gown, and he could be fondling her breast.

"Where's the rest of your clothes?" he ground out.

"The chemisette, you mean?" She shrugged. "It wasn't in the bag. I had to make do." She gave a pretty pout. "Why? Don't you like it this way?"

Like it! He wanted to rip it open, toss her down on the bed, and take her like a ravening beast. *Por Dios!* How would he survive the voyage if she dressed like that the whole time?

This was all Gaspar's fault, for hiring that damnable tavern wench to attend her. Lucy would never have considered such attire without Nettie's encouragement. And when had they become such fast friends, anyway?

"*I* like it," Rafael said in his seducer's voice. Diego looked over to find his friend scouring Lucy's body with lascivious interest. "Diego, when you said she was a wild woman, you didn't say she was a . . . *wild* woman."

Diego barely restrained the urge to toss Rafael out the nearest porthole. Especially after Lucy smiled coquettishly and offered the man her hand. "You must be the captain. We really do need to talk."

As Rafael took her hand and pressed a lingering kiss to it, a red haze formed in Diego's vision. "Enough of that," he warned in Spanish. "Let go of her before I hang you from the nearest yardarm by your ballocks."

With a smirk for Diego's benefit, Rafael released her hand. "I'm happy to talk to *you*, Miss Seton, whenever you please. Perhaps you should join me for dinner. You're already in my cabin, after all."

"You gave up your cabin for *me*?" Lucy pressed her hand to her flagrantly exposed bosom, making both pairs of male eyes swing right to it. "Oh, how sweet. But I don't want to put you out. To be truthful, I'd rather remain in England. So if you could just weigh anchor while we're still on the Thames, I'll hail a passing waterman and be out of your hair before we even reach the coast."

Even Rafael wasn't fool enough to fall for *that*. "I wouldn't dream of keeping you from your relations, señorita. Besides, I've already delayed my journey too long. I'm eager to be home again with my cargo."

Lucy's smile grew steely. "And what if I offered you a substantial financial compensation?" She jerked her head toward Diego. "More than *he* offered. My papa has a number of friends who would be happy to reward you for my safe return." Her eyes glittered. "Otherwise, the next time you come this way for a cargo, you might find yourself delayed in an English gaol."

Diego stifled his smile. Rafael took to threats about as well as *he* did.

"You were wrong, Diego," Rafael said in a silky voice that his men knew to beware. "She's not wild; she's reckless. And on *my* ship, recklessness is generally rewarded with a stay in the hold and rations of bread and water."

When Lucy paled, Diego stepped between them. "You made your point, Rafael. We will not keep you."

Lucy darted around Diego to clasp Rafael's arm. "Please, Captain, is there nothing I can say or do to persuade you to return me to my family?"

Rafael frowned at her. Then his eyes trailed downward to her exposed bosom, and a wolfish expression darkened his face. "There might be one thing—"

"Out!" Diego shoved his friend. "Now! Lucy and I need a word."

With a chuckle, Rafael left the cabin, his good humor restored.

Diego's had vanished entirely.

Lucy sniffed. "I see that your friend is just as willing to take advantage of a woman as you are, Señor Montalvo."

Her return to calling him Señor Montalvo was the last straw.

"Nettie," he bit out, jerking his head toward the door, "go fetch more food for your mistress, will you?"

With a bob of her head, Nettie left.

"Some chaperone *she* is," Lucy said.

"She is here for appearance's sake only. And she knows who pays her salary." Diego stalked toward Lucy with grim intent. "Listen to me, *cariño*, and listen well. We are going to Spain. You are going to be reunited with your family, and I will make sure you reach there unharmed if I have to lock you up in this cabin the entire trip to do it!"

As she backed away, he cornered her, taking some satisfaction from the sudden flare of alarm on her face. "So I suggest you be careful about flaunting your feminine assets to all and sundry. Aside from the fact that Rafael would bed you if you gave him the slightest encouragement, there are thirty men on this ship who wouldn't require encouragement. And I cannot fight them all off."

She crossed her arms over her chest like a woman determined to brazen it out. "Why should you care if I take a lover or two?" she snapped, eyes blazing at him. "Just because my grandfather said *you* weren't to lay a hand on me doesn't mean no one can. And how would he know, anyway?"

The word "lover" sent a shaft of jealous fury through him so powerful that he forgot to be cautious. "He might not, but your future husband would. And your grandfather will skin me alive if you embarrass him by losing your innocence out of anger at *me*."

Her mouth dropped open. "H-husband? That's what this is about? The *marqués* wants to marry me off to someone?" Hurt spread over her features. "And you . . . you agreed to offer me up like some sacrificial lamb?"

Hostias, him and his quick tongue. She was making him insane. "It is not what you think. He has not arranged a marriage. But he does hope to see you married soon. He wants to bring you out in Spanish society, so you can find a rich and titled husband deserving of you. He needs an heir, after all."

"An heir." She swallowed, her expression crumbling. "I knew there was a reason he was suddenly so interested in me after years of silence."

"He was not 'suddenly' interested," he said tersely. "He did not know about the regiment's connection to your mother's nurse until recently."

"Right around the time his son died. How very convenient. So since he now has no other chance for an heir, he wants *me* to produce one."

Her remark struck him hard. He had been too caught up in the idea that he would be reuniting her with her family and regaining Arboleda to consider how much the death of the *marqués's* son might be connected to all this. Until now.

Diego could not believe the *marqués* had such calculating motives. He was dying, for God's sake. One wanted one's family near at such a time. "That is not the reason he wants you back. You are his only granddaughter."

"And thus the only one who can produce his heir." A troubled frown appeared on her brow. "That's why he didn't want you to touch me. He has to ensure the purity of his line."

"That is not the point."

"That is the whole point, isn't it? If I tumble into his emissary's bed, I am ruined for whomever he chooses to sire his precious heir." She stared at him, her eyes shimmering with tears. "Tell me something, Diego. Why didn't you volunteer for that part of the scheme, too? You're titled and Spanish. Or are you just not interested in acquiring my millions?"

He glared at her, furious that she believed he would marry her for her money. "If you think the *marqués* would consider a penniless and landless count as an appropriate suitor for you, you are more naive than I thought."

"Oh, right." Her lower lip trembled. "You would be considered a fortune hunter."

"He chose me to bring you back precisely because he knew I was a man of honor," Diego clipped out. "He knew I would not betray his trust."

"Odd, then, that you've already done so by 'touching' me several times."

Diego felt heat rise in his cheeks. She *would* remind him of that. "I suppose you mean to tell him that, too. Since you seem eager to punish me for trying to reunite you with your family."

"Perhaps I should just lie and tell him that you took my innocence. Then I wouldn't have to worry about being sold off to some stranger in marriage."

His temper got the better of him at the thought of his honor being impugned. "Even if he believed you, I would demand proof, which you cannot give."

She paled. "You mean you'd have some doctor confirm my chastity."

Dios mio, that would be appalling. "No, I didn't mean—"

"You would go that far to gain whatever reward he is offering you for bringing me to Spain? He *is* offering you a reward, isn't he?" When he winced, she scowled. "How much is he paying you to procure the prospective mother of his precious heir?"

"Damn it, Lucy—"

"How much?" she demanded.

"It is not about money."

"Mrs. Harris says it is always about money." Her voice shook. "I only wish I had paid better attention."

Too late, Diego remembered that Hunforth had chosen to marry someone else solely because Lucy's dowry wasn't large enough. "I did this for you, too," he said fiercely. "Because I know what it is like to lose your parents at a young age, to be without a family, without anyone who cares—"

"How *much* is he paying you?" she repeated, swiping at tears. "After all you've done, I think I deserve to know at least that."

Her tears nearly undid him. Damn it to hell. How had she managed to twist this into something sordid, when all he wanted was what was best for her?

"He is giving me my family estate, Arboleda," he said dully. "He purchased it years after my mother sold it to pay our creditors. Even if I could afford to buy it, he has refused to sell to me. Unless I do this. Then it is mine. Free and clear."

"An entire estate." She sucked in a harsh breath. "I see. I would never have guessed I was worth so much." Her look of betrayal cut him to the bone.

Turning away, she went to stare out a porthole. "Now I understand why the captain wasn't interested in my offer of financial compensation. Anything of that magnitude would beggar Papa. My dowry is only a thousand pounds."

"Lucy—"

"Thank you for clarifying things, Señor Montalvo," she said coldly. "If you don't mind, I wish to be alone now."

Mind? He minded a great deal. He hated her calling him Señor Montalvo. He despised making her cry. Most of all, he detested being at odds with her, when he wanted nothing more than to drag her into his arms, kiss the hurt from that lovely face, and claim her for his own.

But he had no right to that. She did not yet even know the full measure of what she was, *who* she was. Once her grandfather introduced her into society, she would see how much her new family had to offer and how little he did. Especially if he could not fulfill his vow, which would happen if he attempted to marry her. Without Arboleda, he was not worthy of her.

So he left.

From now on, he would have to keep a polite distance and treat her as he might treat any woman of her advanced station and prospects. Anything else would tempt him to do the unthinkable.

And that was not acceptable.

Chapter Eighteen

Dear Charlotte,

  I received your messages about Miss Seton. Do
not blame yourself. I alone am at fault. I should
have realized what Montalvo intended, but I truly
thought he meant to make a respectable offer of
marriage. Is it possible it was <u>Miss Seton's</u> idea
to elope? Perhaps she feared her father would not
approve of a Spanish son-in-law.

                              Your guilty cousin,
                              Michael

For the next few days, Lucy wandered the ship in a fog,
grateful that Diego hadn't followed through with his threat
to lock her in the cabin. She'd been given the freedom to
come and go as she pleased.

Diego avoided her, no small feat on a ship, and she was
grateful for that, too. Because every time she saw him, hurt
and anger roared up inside her again until she thought she
might choke on it. He was being paid to deliver her to her
grandfather like a trussed-up goose. How could he? She'd
thought him a decent man, for all his flirtations. He'd
claimed to be honorable.

But he wasn't. He was exactly the scoundrel she'd taken him for initially. The sooner she accepted that, the better.

Unfortunately, she kept remembering how he'd leaped to her defense with Peter, how his attentions had made her the toast of society for one afternoon . . . how he'd held her and kissed her and murmured endearments that still made her shiver to remember them. Even after he'd told her about her grandfather, he'd professed to desire her.

It was the desire that confused her. Clearly, he'd gone against every promise he'd made to the *marqués* just to kiss her and give her pleasure. That proved either he was a reckless fool—and she knew he wasn't that—or he really did desire her.

But if he cared for her, why do this mad thing? Was it just about his estate? He'd said no, but how could she believe him?

And what had he meant when he said he'd lost his parents at a young age? Why had his mother sold the estate? It was only the second time he'd mentioned his parents. He had said very little about his past until now.

How had a count been forced to turn to stealing in a regimental camp? Hadn't he possessed other family? Or was he like her, an orphan?

He knew more about her than almost anyone, yet she did not know *him* at all. Certainly not well enough to know why he'd risked so much to carry her off to meet her grandfather. Aside from his ruse about the pleasure garden, he'd never seemed that interested in acquiring property.

Then there was the mysterious *marqués*, who wanted to marry her off to someone so she could beget his heir. Diego had dismissed the idea of her grandfather wanting her only for such a reason. She snorted. And he called *her* naive?

Still, he seemed to think her grandfather was eager to meet her. Now that she'd had time to consider everything, she needed some matters clarified—not only about her background and her grandfather but also about his bargain with Diego. Unfortunately, only one person could fill in the missing pieces. She would have to talk to Diego.

It took her a while to find him, leaning against the quarterdeck wall out of the wind and smoking a cigarillo, his look pensive as he stared at the churning ocean. With his longish hair tousled by the breeze and his olive skin, he looked like a Barbary pirate contemplating his next prize. The Pirate Count. It sounded like one of those adventure novels she used to love to read.

Steeling herself against his good looks, she walked up to him. "I have some questions for you."

Though a muscle flicked in his jaw, he merely continued to smoke.

"I want to know what evidence my grandfather offered to prove that I was stolen from his daughter and son-in-law."

A frown touched his brow. He snuffed the cigarillo out against the wall, then looked at her for the first time in days. "I already told you—the birthmark."

"Why didn't he show you my birth in the parish register? It must be there."

Diego tensed. "He could not. I asked for a meeting to discuss my purchasing Arboleda, and he agreed to meet me in Cádiz, where he was taking the waters for his illness. That is where he asked for my help in getting you back. The register was in San Roque, where you were born.

There was no time to return there to look at a document that would not aid in finding you."

"So you made this trip only on the strength of what he told you? You never went to San Roque to determine if his tale about my abduction was true?"

"Why should I? He is a *marqués*, a highly respected man."

"And he owned the estate you wanted. That was all you needed to know."

His eyes darkened as he shoved away from the wall. "Why would he invent a granddaughter? Besides, he could not have known about your birthmark if you weren't his granddaughter."

She dragged in a breath. "I've been thinking about everything you told me, and there are other possibilities for what happened. Perhaps my *mother* ran away with her lover, taking me with her."

"Then why would your grandfather say otherwise?" Diego snapped.

"Out of embarrassment? Fear of scandal?"

"So you speculate that you were only stolen from *one* parent. That it was only Don Álvaro who lost his daughter."

She glanced away. She hadn't thought that far. "I-I suppose."

"And does that make the matter any better in your eyes? Would you rather Sergeant Crawford be an adulterer than a kidnapper?"

"No, of course not."

"I swear," he said coldly, "I do not understand you. I have never seen anyone fight so hard against gaining a fortune."

"I told you, money doesn't mean much to me."

"That is because you have never had to do without it. You were adopted by an English officer and given the advantages that his rank could provide. What do you know about having to scrabble for every morsel?"

Leaning one arm against a mast, he searched her face. "There was a time when I would have given anything for half a stale crust of an empanada, yet you look down your pretty nose at me because I agreed to take property for finding you. You have a chance to gain what I have struggled my entire life to regain—"

"And all I have to do is marry a stranger to produce an heir for my grandfather," she said coolly.

He stared bleakly at her. Then he drew himself up, every inch the haughty grandee. "You do not have to marry anyone if you do not wish. We Spaniards are not barbarians, you know." His eyes glittered at her. "If I were you, I would make good use of the great fortune at my disposal. But if you choose not to, it is not my concern. I will still do my part in delivering you to your grandfather. And yes, I will take Arboleda for it."

"Why is property so important to you? You're a famous conjurer, and—"

"I cannot talk about this with you." He started to walk past her.

She blocked his path. "Why not?"

He cast her a glance that chilled her blood. "Because it will not change anything. My mind is made up."

As he stalked off, his shoulders hunched against the wind and his back rigid, she felt the urge to run after him and push him over the side. She'd thought the man cared about her? She must have been insane! He was determined to hand her over to her grandfather, no matter what *she* thought about the matter. He acted as if she should be grateful for it, too!

Well, she would show him. It was time she had a say in this plan. He had some notion that her grandfather wouldn't force her into marriage, even though the man had already demonstrated what he wanted from her by placing conditions on Diego's behavior toward her.

Fine. She would use those conditions to her advantage. Her grandfather demanded a chaste granddaughter, did he? Well, there was only one way to thwart that: make herself *un*chaste. Once her virtue was gone, she would have the upper hand. She wouldn't have to fear anyone forcing her into marriage.

That meant she needed a man to take her innocence. And as angry as she was at him, Diego was the only man she could consider to do it.

Between his determination to avoid her and his skewed ideas about honor, he wouldn't just fall into her arms. She'd have to give him no choice.

A smile lit her lips. She could be as devious as he. For all his coldness, she was sure he still desired her. She hadn't missed the heat flaring in his gaze when she'd worn half a gown in the cabin a few days ago. There was a reason he'd been avoiding her, after all.

Not anymore. She'd see to that.

A thrill coursed through her at the thought of sharing Diego's bed, and she frowned. Careful, or she'd find herself falling in love with the cursed man. Diego had made it perfectly clear he had no interest in her beyond her usefulness to him; she must be just as ruthless. This was only about thwarting her grandfather, nothing more.

238 Sabrina Jeffries

This would not be lovemaking; it was simply eliminating a pesky inconvenience.

She would need help, and she knew exactly the person for that.

She found Nettie chatting with the ship's cook. "Nettie," she said, drawing the woman aside, "I need your particular skills."

"To do what?"

"Help me seduce a reluctant man."

Nettie smiled broadly. "Oh, duckie, that's the easiest thing in the world. There ain't no such thing as a reluctant man."

"I'm not so sure about that," she said, thinking of Diego's iron will. "Anyway, it's not so much the seduction part that I need help with but something else entirely. If you're willing, here is what I was thinking . . ."

Shortly before ten that night, Diego followed Nettie down the narrow companionway stairs, trying not to panic. The idea of Lucy suffering a "violent illness," as Nettie had called it, twisted his gut into a knot.

Now he wished he had not been so cold toward her earlier. But she had provoked his temper by raising questions about the *marqués*'s motives, implying that Diego had not examined the situation thoroughly. She had made him wonder what he had not thought to wonder before, which irritated him exceedingly.

"Are you sure she's not just seasick?" he asked, his heart in his throat.

"T'ain't that," Nettie said, "or she wouldn't have a fever. If you ask me, she took a chill from wandering that deck too much in the cold. Didn't your man think to put a cloak in that bag? The poor thing is shivering so."

"God preserve my soul," he said hoarsely as they reached the lower deck. If something happened to Lucy, he did not know how he would bear it.

Nettie opened the door, and he rushed in to find the cabin dark as pitch. The lantern light in the companion-way barely penetrated inside.

Even that was snuffed out when the door suddenly closed. "Damn it, Nettie, first light the lantern in here," he growled.

As if in answer, the lantern next to the door sprang to life, spreading light over the cabin. And the empty bed.

"*Qué demonios*—" he began as he turned to Nettie . . . and found Lucy instead.

He rushed to her in alarm. "You should not be out of bed, *querida!*"

"Why not?" she asked as she glided from the lantern toward the bed.

Barefoot, with her hair down, wearing only her chemise, she was a wanton goddess limned in golden light.

She did not look particularly ill. And as she passed the lantern, the light shone through the transparent fabric to silhouette her delectable body.

His breath caught at the luscious sight. "Lucy?" he choked out. "Nettie said you had a fever."

She halted beside the bed. "Nettie lied. I merely wanted to be alone with you. To talk. Among . . . other things." She sat down on the mattress with a seductive smile that gave no doubt what other things she meant.

As the blood rushed to his head—both heads—he struggled to keep control. Damn Nettie for maneuvering this. The last thing he needed was to be alone with Lucy when she was playing the seductress.

"I do not know what you think to accomplish with this little game," he said, "but I want no part of it."

He strode to the door and grabbed the handle, but it was locked. How could that be?

"Nettie, you foolish wench, open this door at once!"

"That will do you no good," Lucy said from behind him.

Tamping down the urges her silky voice brought roaring to the surface, he pounded on the door. "Damn you, Nettie, I will not pay you a penny of the twenty pounds Gaspar offered unless you open this door right now!"

"Funny thing about that," Lucy said smoothly. "I decided to heed your excellent advice about making good use of my new fortune. My first purchase was Nettie's services. She works for *me* now, since I have promised her quite a raise in pay once we reach Spain."

As he whirled on Lucy, she added smoothly, "Also, she doesn't *have* the key." She dangled it on a string from one slender finger, her eyes gleaming. "*I* do." Bending over, she pushed it under the bed, where it slid to the wall. "Or I did."

She straightened, giving him a glimpse of the full breasts loose inside her chemise, and his cock shot instantly to attention.

Dios Santo! This grew worse by the moment. "How did you get the key?"

"Nettie procured it from the captain. Not directly, of course. She had to steal it. But apparently he's not nearly as high and mighty as you when it comes to enjoying life's pleasures."

"Fortunately, I am not so easy to manipulate," he ground out.

"Who said anything about manipulation? This is blackmail." Lucy untied her chemise with languid motions that turned his blood to fire. "You know what blackmail is. You used it on *me* to gain my company at the school." Her voice turned steely. "And I learned the lesson you taught me very, very well."

With a shaky laugh, he crossed his arms over his chest. "Just how do you mean to blackmail me, *cariño*? And what do you plan to gain from it?"

"It's simple, really." She kicked her legs back and forth, looking for all the world like a little girl.

Except for the scant clothing. And the luscious cascade of hair. And the body he fiercely wanted to ravage.

He swallowed. Hard.

"I don't want to marry a stranger," she went on, "and if I arrive in Spain with my virtue intact, that's almost certain to happen."

"I told you, your grandfather will not force you into anything."

"I don't think nearly as well of men of rank as you do. They've done little to make me trust them."

He cursed under his breath. She was not just speaking of Hunforth, was she?

"Grandfather or no," she continued, "the *marqués* appears to have one aim, and that is to get his heir. I'm not ready to oblige him in that respect. So I plan to get rid of my virtue before we reach Spain. And I plan to do it with you."

That roused images in his fevered brain which would have sent a weaker man crawling over broken glass to bed her. But he was not such a man. "You mean to make sure I lose my chance at regaining my estate. Is that it? You think to revenge yourself against me and your grandfather in one fell swoop by beguiling me into your bed? Ending my hopes for the future at the same time you end his?"

"No," she said coolly. "This isn't about revenge. Don't worry, you'll get your precious property. *If* you do as I say."

That flummoxed him. "What do you mean?"

She rose from the bed to pad toward him, a cat toying with its prey. "If you share my bed, I'll make sure my grandfather never finds out. I can always blame my loss of innocence on Peter, assuming that my chastity proves as important to my grandfather as I suspect. But if you *don't* share my bed, I'll tell him about all the times you kissed me and touched me . . . all the *places* you touched me. And you will never regain your estate."

He froze as she circled him, her sweet violet scent engulfing his senses. "He will not care about that as long as I have not ruined you," he lied.

"Oh, I will arrive ruined," she said silkily. Halting behind him, she whispered in his ear, "If not by you, then by the captain or one of his men."

In a fury, he turned to seize her by the shoulders. "The hell you will!" He wanted to shake her until her teeth rattled. "I will lock you up before I—"

Hostias. She'd made that difficult by stealing the key.

She stared at him with a taunting smile, a vixen sure of her power. "If you force me to turn elsewhere, I'll make sure you get blamed for it. All the punishment and none of the pleasure. As you said when you blackmailed *me,* the choice is yours."

"Not much of a choice," he ground out.

"That's why it's called blackmail." She began to untie his cravat. "Besides, you and my grandfather are giving *me* no choice. I don't see why I should give you any."

He caught her hands, gripping them to keep from putting his own hands where they did not belong. "You think you have won, don't you?"

She gazed at him, clear-eyed. "Yes."

"You are a scheming little witch," he hissed.

A smile touched her lips. "Yes."

Torn between anger and admiration at her clever plan, he yanked her against him roughly, his arm manacling her waist. Though she gasped, she met his furious stare with eyes that shone luminous and triumphant in the lantern light.

Surely she was bluffing about giving herself to another. But did he dare risk it? And why was he fighting, anyway? She offered what he'd been waiting for: the chance to kiss her, caress her, make love to her without repercussions.

Yet that terrified him. Once he had her in his bed, he might never want to let her out.

"Well?" She managed to imbue that one word with a wealth of meaning. "What's it to be, Master of Mystery?" She stretched up on tiptoe to nip his ear, sending a jolt of desire flashing down his spine to stiffen his cock.

He gripped her head in his hands. "You will regret this later," he growled.

"I doubt that very much," she whispered with a mesmerizing smile. Then she kissed him, a sweetly innocent kiss that pushed him over the edge into madness.

In a frenzy, he took her mouth, devouring it, plundering it, dizzy from the pleasure of it after being deprived of it for days. She was his for tonight, *his*, damn it, and he meant to brand her as his for all eternity.

As he reveled in how eagerly she met his kisses, he swept his hands down to fondle her breasts, which might as well have been naked for all the protection her chemise afforded. Which he wanted naked *now*.

He tore his lips free. "So you wish to lose your innocence to the devil?"

"It's not a matter of wishing, is it?" she said stiffly. "It's either that or lose it to a husband who's been picked for me, and I refuse to do the latter."

Annoyed by her persistence in believing the worst of her grandfather, he left her to go sit on the bed. When she started to follow, he said, "No, stay there."

A perplexed look crossed her face. "I thought—"

He tugged off his boots. "You thought you would take charge. You thought you would lead me about by my *cojones*." Tearing off his cravat, he threw it aside. "We will do this my way or not at all. Which is it to be?"

"I don't see why you care *how* it's done as long as you get to do it," she said.

That ignited his temper anew. While he sat aching for her, she meant to go about losing her chastity like a general leading a campaign. She probably expected him to play the rutting pig and take her with blithe unconcern, so she could dismiss him once it was over, the way she'd dismissed him that night in the duke's library.

Well, his little seductress was in for a surprise. He meant to make her realize the enormity of her decision, be fully aware of what she chose. As aware as *he* was.

"The 'how' matters a great deal." He peeled off his coat and waistcoat, then tossed them aside. "So, do we do it my way? Or not at all?" He prayed she would not call his bluff. Although he did not want her playing the sacrificial virgin in his bed, neither would he permit her to turn to one of the others.

She lifted her chin, offering him a maddening glimpse of her lovely throat. "That depends. What *is* your way? What do you want me to do?"

"You can start by doing more than teasing me with glimpses of your body." He leaned back on his elbows to scour every inch of her. "Take off your chemise, *querida*. I wish to see what I will be selling my honor for."

Chapter Nineteen

Dear Cousin,

One piece of interesting information has come out of our discussions with Señor Montalvo's assistant, Gaspar. It appears that Diego Montalvo is a Spanish count! So . . . perhaps it really <u>was</u> an elopement. We begin to believe they traveled by sea, possibly to Scotland though more likely to Spain. A neighbor saw people boarding a steam packet in the wee hours of the morning on the day in question but was not close enough to confirm it as them.

Your concerned friend,
Charlotte

*H*onor, hah! Lucy scowled at him. As if the scoundrel had any honor, trying to dictate the terms of this seduction.

And what did he mean by expecting her to disrobe for him? Nettie had said men never bothered to do that with tarts—they just moved the clothes enough to get to whatever they wanted. Undressing entirely while he watched was far more intimate than she'd anticipated.

"Take it off, *cariño.*" His commanding voice sent a delicious warmth pooling in her belly. The dim light left his face in shadow, but his eyes glinted hungry, hard, and eager as they devoured her. She found that terribly exciting.

"But I'm naked underneath," she protested weakly.

"Did you not expect me to see you naked?"

She had hoped he wouldn't. "I thought you would . . . you know . . . do what you did at the Foxmoors'. Lift my skirts—"

"And take you like a savage, so you can keep hating me once we are done?"

Annoyed by how close he came to the mark, she crossed her arms over her chest. "Something like that."

"Abandon that idea right now." Keeping his brooding gaze fixed on her, he rose to circle her as she'd circled him earlier. "If I must play the stud horse to your mare, I shall enjoy it. And make *you* enjoy it as well. I will pleasure you until you beg for more, even if it takes me all night."

"All night! But . . . but . . . Nettie will want to sleep here!"

"I doubt your fellow conspirator will have trouble finding a comfortable berth." He came up behind her to wrap his hand in her unbound hair.

"Diego, we cannot—"

"It is the only way I will agree to your scheme." He tugged her head back just enough so his mouth could plunder the skin of her throat.

A dangerous thrill coursed through her that shook her to her toes. Lord help her, how could she survive a whole night of such tender caresses?

This was supposed to be swift, impersonal. That's why she'd worn only her shift—to inflame him into dispensing with preliminaries. She'd thought he'd just lift the hem, do his part, and be done. No long seduction full of tempting kisses and sweet words.

This was *so* like Diego.

He released her hair without moving his lips from her neck. "I intend to take my time with you," he said darkly, throwing her plans into confusion. "I will taste and touch every part of you—as often as I wish, as thoroughly as I wish."

A thrill shot through her that wouldn't be denied.

He laid his hand on her waist and slid it down her hips in an intimate caress that made her gasp. "You will not hide yourself from me tonight, *mi dulzura*. So if it is a quick deflowering you want, best to abandon that scheme right now."

The dratted devil thought to cow her into giving up her plans by threatening to make his seduction last all night. Well, that wouldn't work.

"I am sure Rafael would still welcome me in his bed," she countered.

His hand stiffened on her behind. "Go ahead, if that is what you want. He will be happy to rid you of your virtue in whatever manner you dictate. He is not as particular in his bed partners as I am."

She tensed. Would he really give her up to Rafael? She didn't think so, but she couldn't be sure. "You know I don't want Rafael," she rasped, relinquishing even that weapon.

"And I don't want to make love to a martyr." He moved in front of her, far enough away to see all of her, close enough to touch her if he wished. "These are my conditions. Do you accept them?"

"Fine. We'll do it your way." She couldn't bear anyone else taking her innocence.

She would simply use Nettie's tricks for inflaming a man's passions. Nettie had said men generally couldn't manage more than one encounter a night, so all Lucy had to do was goad him into a quick seduction, and she'd be done.

His smile was positively feral. "Then pray remove your chemise. Now."

A shuddering breath left her lips as she drew her shift over her head. Before she released it, she clutched it to her bosom. "What about you? Aren't you going to take off your clothes?"

"Not yet." He reached out to tug the shift from her trembling hands. Fire flared high in his face as his gaze scorched the full length of her body, sparing no part. "*Válgame Dios,* you are even more lovely than I imagined," he said hoarsely.

She drank his adoring words like a sailor gulping down fresh water after months at sea. How she wished he didn't excel at compliments. Every time he said something like that, she wanted to throw herself at him.

He swept the back of his hand down her breasts, leaving her weak in the knees. "Do you know how often I have wished to see you in all your perfect glory?" He grazed her nipples with his knuckles, rousing them to aching points. "You have given me many sleepless nights, *querida.* Too many."

It salved her wounded pride that he'd thought of her as much as she'd thought of him. He slid his hand lower to caress her belly. When he covered her *down there* with his hand, she couldn't suppress a moan. But when he delved between her slick folds with a long, teasing stroke of his finger, she caught his hand. She felt too exposed, too aware of her nakedness like this.

"Please, Diego, take off your clothes, too."

He stared at her with slumberous eyes. "Why don't *you* take them off me?"

She sucked in a harsh breath. The man was diabolical. The very idea of performing such an intimate act for him made her feel more like a wife than a shameless wanton.

But he didn't want a wife, God rot him. Why keep acting as if he did? He was supposed to tear off his clothes, throw her down on the bed, and ravish her like a fiend. Not make love to her with the tenderness of a husband. Not make her heart ache for his touch, his voice . . . his love.

No, she did not want his love. She couldn't, *mustn't* yearn for it. Not when he meant to hand her over to her grandfather at the end of this trip.

She would have to hurry this seduction along. And that meant breaking his iron control.

Sidling up to him, she went straight for his trouser buttons. With his thickened male flesh stretching the fabric to the breaking point, she had to struggle to release them, which reminded her of how he'd wanted her to touch him that day at the breakfast. She did so now, her hands stroking along the ridge of his arousal with each button she undid.

He groaned. "Why didn't you start with the shirt?" he gritted out.

"Because this is the part that interests me," she murmured.

She had his trousers and his drawers unfastened in seconds and his flesh freed of the fabric even more quickly. As it sprang out like some impudent hound sniffing the air, she froze.

It was long. Thick. Much more imposing than she'd expected.

Good Lord in heaven. The harem tales had spoken of "swords" and "rods" and "lances," and she'd assumed such terms were gross exaggerations. But they weren't far off the mark.

As she stared, his flesh grew even larger. Wondering at that, she reached out to touch it, but he caught her hand.

"Don't," he said in a voice thick with desire. "Or your scheme will be spoiled before it's begun."

She blinked at him, not sure what he meant. She only knew that he didn't want her to touch him. Which, of course, meant that she had to do so.

She slid her free hand to his back, ostensibly to pull his shirttails out of his waistband but really so she could slide her hand beneath his loosened trousers and drawers to caress his behind as he'd caressed hers.

"I see what you are about." He grabbed that hand, too. "You think to make me insane with need . . . and get your quick tumble, after all. It will not work."

Lifting her mouth to suck his whiskered neck, she deliberately rubbed her breasts against his shirt-clad chest. "It's already working," she teased, then tongued his throat.

He tried to move back, but that slackened his grip on her wrists, allowing her to pull both hands free. Instantly, she returned to stroking his shaft with one hand while she took his hand in the other to press it to her breast.

He gave up. With a growled oath, he lifted her bodily and tossed her onto the bed, pausing only long enough to shove off his trousers and drawers before stretching out atop her, covering her with his body.

"Hunforth was right." His eyes blazed at her as he spread her thighs apart so he could kneel between them. "You really *are* a reckless hoyden."

She might have been insulted if she hadn't been trying to be one. "I do my best," she said with a triumphant smile.

She tore off his shirt, eager to see the fine chest she remembered from the duke's library. As she smoothed her hands over the wide expanse of muscle and sinew and bone, he retaliated by sliding his hand between her legs to fondle her, roughly, thoroughly, possessively.

"This is not over, you know," he vowed as he dipped his mouth to tongue her nipple erect, then suck it so exquisitely that she arched up for more. "I still intend to make you beg. Later."

"We'll . . . see," she gasped, his motions below and above rousing her blood to a fever pitch.

"We will indeed. The night is young."

She blinked. Could she have misunderstood Nettie about men only being able to make love once? Good Lord, what if . . .

He drove out that thought by slipping something larger than his fingers inside her. And it was every bit as uncomfortable as she'd heard.

This was the part she'd dreaded. With horror and fascination she'd listened to tales of what it was like to lose one's innocence. She'd told herself lovemaking mustn't be too awful, or women wouldn't allow men to keep doing it, yet the idea of a man driving his thing into you hard enough to produce pain and blood sounded distinctly unpleasant.

Yet as he inched inside her, it did not *feel* unpleasant. Uncomfortable, perhaps. Intimate, certainly. But not entirely unpleasant.

It was embarrassing, however—and she couldn't look at him while he entered her, couldn't do anything but lie stiff beneath him.

"Relax," he murmured against her ear. "It will go easier for you."

"How do you know?" she said skeptically. "You're not the one having a Maypole thrust inside your tender parts."

He uttered a choked laugh, then kissed her long and deep, distracting her from what he was doing below.

Within seconds, she realized it was indeed better. Having him inside her warmed her in ways she hadn't expected, in *places* she hadn't expected.

He froze, as if coming up against something, and drew back to stare at her. "Are you sure about this, *querida?*" he asked softly, poised over her like a panther on the verge of pouncing.

This was it. The moment when she would lose her innocence. She swallowed her trepidation. "Yes. I'm sure."

But she wasn't at all sure. He gave a sudden fierce push. The tearing pain proved fleeting. But now he was planted inside her so intimately that she couldn't escape him . . . or the reality of what she'd done.

She'd thought that a swift loss of her innocence would keep her from yearning for him too much. She'd been wrong. Diego was brushing her cheek with tender kisses, murmuring soothing words, asking if she was all right. She nodded, but she wasn't all right in the least. He was around her, above her, encompassing her with his delicious smell and his enticing body and his sweet endearments that made her want . . . and want some more.

When he thoughtfully paused to let her adjust to him inside her, it brought tears to her eyes. She turned away to hide them.

Misunderstanding her sudden shyness, he began to caress her below. "Ah, *cariño*, it will get better, I swear." He branded her neck with kisses, his mustache tickling her. "For me, it is . . . indescribable. You are as warm as the Galician sun. I could lie here inside you forever."

"Forever?" she choked out.

He pulled back to give her a haunted smile. "Well . . . at least all night," he amended, his beautiful black hair falling over his damp brow.

Lifting himself a little, he began to move again. He slid in and out, his expression intent, his eyes eating her up as if staking his claim, though she knew he did not want any claims put on *him*.

Determined to mark him as hers, she looped her arms about his neck and dragged him down for her kiss, pressing her breasts up against him, letting her body envelop him as he'd enveloped her. He would never forget this night—not if she could help it.

His breathing grew labored. His kiss grew savage, his thrusts deeper. When he tore his mouth from hers to pant, she used her lips and hands to fondle every inch of him, wresting a guttural groan from low in his throat.

"*Mi dulzura . . .*" he said hoarsely. "Ah, *mi querida . . .*" Fluid Spanish flowed from his lips, words she only half understood.

She could have sworn he said, "You are mine now, mine and mine alone." But that wasn't possible. Still, the thought heated her blood, adding to the heat he roused with his hand between her legs, stroking and rubbing and turning her wild.

Then he pulled her leg up to settle her more firmly against him, and she went insane. The thrum that had begun low in her belly grew into an insistent pulsing, vibrating through her, making her see spots behind her eyes.

"Vixen," he accused as he pounded into her. "Beguiling witch . . . must you take . . . my soul . . . too?"

"Yes." He'd taken hers; why shouldn't she take his? "Yes . . . yes . . ." she repeated, the vibration growing to a roar inside her head.

Suddenly, the spots exploded into a wild array of light and color, so brilliant and intense she thought she might swoon.

"Yes!" she cried, straining against him.

He gave a hard thrust that drove him in to the hilt. Then, with a hoarse cry, he shuddered violently against her.

For a moment, they remained frozen, so intimately joined she could feel the spasms as he spilled himself inside her.

And in that moment of exquisite pleasure, she knew how grossly she'd erred. Foolish, foolish girl. She could never protect her heart from *him*.

She might have won the skirmish, but he'd won the war. And now she would reap the bitter fruit of her defeat.

Chapter Twenty

❦

Dear Charlotte,

   I took the liberty of having Mr. Baines speak to
Mr. Pritchard about his tenant, only to find that he
was as oblivious to the Spaniard's true purpose as
any of us. What does the colonel say? Has he arrived
in London yet?

                              Your concerned cousin,
                              Michael

*L*ucy awoke hours later to the most blissful sense of contentment she'd ever felt. She lay there with her eyes closed, savoring the feeling of being a woman.

Of having a lover. A lusty, amazing lover. She felt well and truly used, slightly sore, but sated and happy.

Nettie had been wrong—a man could indeed take a woman more than once in a night. The second time had been an hour after her deflowering. It had started with him washing her, so gently it had made her want to cry.

But soon his ministrations had become something else—kisses, caresses, wild and heady temptations. She'd never dreamed a man could be so passionate. He'd brought her to release over and over until he'd had her begging, just as he'd promised. Begging to feel him inside her. Begging to see him lose his restraint again. And when at last he did, it gave her as much of a thrill as before.

She ought to be appalled by her shameless behavior. Why wasn't she? Because it was Diego, who'd taken her innocence with the tender care of a husband.

She sighed. This might be their only night together. Sobered by that thought, she opened her eyes and turned toward him to memorize the face that had become so dear.

The bed was empty. She sat up in a panic, only to be arrested by the sight of Diego in drawers and trousers, standing at the table with his head bent as he examined something in the light of the oil lantern.

Her sketch pad.

"Find anything of interest?" she asked.

He started but didn't look at her. "This drawing you did of me is very good. You are quite talented."

"It's not finished, actually." Heartened by his praise, she pulled the sheet up to tuck beneath her arms. "I had no time to add the final touches when I was in England, and now I can't. No pens or ink or charcoal."

"Ah, I shall have to remedy that." He turned toward the bed, then dragged in a sharp breath, his gaze growing hungry as he took in the sight of her.

Oh, but didn't he look luscious without a shirt, all sculpted muscle dusted with dark hair? Her gaze skated down to where his trousers began to bulge, and she smiled, feeling the full power of being a woman he desired.

She let the sheet slip enough to bare one breast. "Come back to bed, Diego. It's still early."

With a low curse, he tore his gaze from her and went to put on his shirt. "Not that early, *cariño*. The watch changed an hour ago. Before long, Rafael and the first mate will be stirring, and I would rather they not find me gone from the cabin." He fastened his shirt buttons. "We must preserve your reputation as best we can until we reach Spain and can be married."

"Married!" Her heart soared. "But you said . . . I thought . . ."

"I took your innocence. I am not so dishonorable as to leave you ruined."

The emotionless statement stopped her heart in midsoar. "But what about your property? You said my grandfather won't give it to you if we marry."

"It does not matter."

He said it so curtly that she knew it mattered very much. "But Diego—"

"I am not like Hunforth," he ground out as he picked up his cravat and tied it about his neck. "Taking a woman's innocence levies certain obligations on any decent man—and I always honor my obligations."

Her temper flared. She didn't want to be his obligation. "*I* seduced *you*. Don't make it sound as if you ravished me against my will."

"Did I not?" He turned to look at her, his expression softening. "Come now, *querida*, I could have left whenever I wished. All I had to do was ignore your lovely body, crawl under the bed, and find the key. Which, by the way, I just did." He held it up. "Your pretty tactics would not have kept me here long if I had not chosen to stay."

"You didn't choose to stay." Guilt gnawed at her for how she'd convinced him. "You did it because I threatened to give myself to another and blame my lack of chastity on you."

He arched one eyebrow. "I called your bluff, remember? You did not leave to go to anyone else's bed. And if you had tried, I would have locked you up for the rest of the voyage. I would not have let another man have you."

"Why?" she whispered.

"For the same reason I first kissed you—because I wanted you in my bed. I wanted to ravish you from the moment I saw you in that orchard." He looked almost angry, as if the words were torn from him. "I want to ravish you now." He took a step toward her, halted, then pivoted away to finish dressing. "But that must wait until we marry."

Silently, she watched him sit to pull on his boots. She should be glad, ecstatic, that he'd decided to marry her. It made everything easier. So why couldn't she shake the feeling he did it against his will?

It wasn't just his refusal to speak of love. After all, she hadn't mentioned love to *him*. But that word "obligation" rang in her ears. He'd fought so hard to fulfill his promise to the *marqués* and gain his property, yet now he was ready to abandon it? Simply because he'd taken her innocence?

"Diego, I . . . I didn't expect you to marry me when I set out to seduce you."

"I realize that."

"I just didn't want to end up forced into marriage with some stranger."

"Yes," he said tightly. "You explained that perfectly well last night."

"I certainly didn't want you to give up this property you seem to—"

"Arboleda! It has a name!" He whipped his head around to glare at her. "And it is not just any piece of property. It is . . ." He trailed off as he saw her wounded expression. "It does not matter. What is done is done."

A hollow hurt settled in her chest. After last night, she wanted nothing more than to marry him, but not like this, with him stiff and formal and unhappy.

He rose to walk to the door. "When we reach Spain, I will take you to your grandfather and ask for permission to marry you. I owe him that courtesy, at least. If he refuses, we will elope. But one way or the other, we *will* be married."

When he unlocked the door, she leaped from the bed, dragging the sheet with her. "Wait, Diego—"

"Get some rest," he ordered. "I will send Nettie to attend you."

Then he left.

She stood gaping at the door. He'd just announced in his high-handed manner that they were to be married, and he actually expected her to *rest*?

That was impossible now. She stared at her sketch pad with her heart in her throat. She hadn't looked at the sketch since the day she'd drawn it. Now she could see that it was a terrible likeness. She'd done it when she'd thought him quite the devil, and she'd made his eyes far too cold, his mouth too cruel.

While the Diego she had come to know . . .

A sob caught in her throat. Too late she realized just how honorable he was, willing to give up everything to preserve her reputation. He didn't love her; she wasn't even sure he *liked* her beyond the bedchamber. Yet he meant to marry her?

When the door swung open, she whirled toward it, praying Diego had returned. But it was only Nettie.

The servant closed the door with a knowing glance. "Well? Did it work? Did he end up in your bed?"

"Look at how I'm dressed," Lucy said irritably. "What do *you* think?"

Nettie chuckled as she picked up Lucy's shift. "Was it everything you hoped?"

Lucy blushed. "Was your night with Rafael everything *you* hoped?"

With a dreamy smile, Nettie clutched the shift to her chest. "Oh, miss. You have no idea."

"Trust me, I have a very good idea. And there's your answer."

Nettie laughed. "I told you them Spanish men ain't so bad."

What an understatement. "Did Rafael guess what I was up to?"

"Not at first." Nettie straightened the room. "But when his friend didn't return last night, he got a good idea. Didn't seem too happy about it, neither. I thought p'raps he fancied you for himself, but he said no. Said his friend was fool enough to do the right thing by you, and that would mean trouble."

Because Diego wouldn't get his estate?

Lucy frowned. Surely he made an adequate living as a magician. His dress indicated a certain level of comfort, and he didn't live as if money were his main concern. He didn't cater to the whims of his rich patrons. Then there'd been the huge sum he'd given to charity at the breakfast.

Perhaps she should find out how financially secure he really was. And why Arboleda was so important to him. If his family was dead, why did he care?

He probably wouldn't tell her, but his friend might.

"Has the captain arisen yet?"

"Aye. He was waiting for Don Diego when I left."

Hearing Diego's name said with the Spanish honorific gave her a jolt. She often forgot he was a count, but the others clearly did not. With them, his position went far beyond his fame as a performer.

Was that why he clung to his honor? Some men of rank took very seriously the responsibilities of their station. The *obligations.*

Oh, how she despised being simply an obligation to him. "I have to talk to the captain alone. Do you think he and Diego will be together long?"

Nettie laughed. "After the night you had? I doubt it. Don Diego will wish to sleep, and Rafael usually goes to the wardroom early for breakfast."

"Good. Help me dress. Quickly."

A short while later, she headed for the wardroom. She entered to find Rafael alone, hunched over his plate of fried bread and cured sausage.

"If you're looking for Diego, I'd leave him be. He's in a devil of a temper," he said.

"Actually, I was looking for you."

He eyed her with suspicion. "Why?"

She took a seat across the table, not sure how to begin. "I gather that you know . . . that you've guessed—"

"That you and Diego spent last night doing the blanket hornpipe?"

When she caught his meaning, she blushed. "He told you."

"Diego? The man who threatened to hang me from the nearest yardarm by my *cojones* just for kissing your hand? No, he didn't have to tell me. He announced he was marrying you. That was enough. The only way he'd give up on regaining Arboleda is if he'd done something foolish."

She fought to appear calm. "Is the property worth so much, then?"

"In money? Now? Hardly. After the way the soldiers ravaged it—"

"What soldiers?" Sudden trepidation gripped her. "Where exactly is Diego from in León?"

His eyes narrowed. "You don't know?"

She shook her head. "He never talks about himself to me. I didn't even know he had an estate until this journey."

Rafael's expression softened. "Ah, that explains it. I did wonder how you could be so cruel as to tempt him into losing everything for one night of pleasure."

"What makes you think *I* tempted *him*?" she said, momentarily nonplussed.

"Because Señor Honorable wouldn't bed you without extreme provocation. He's spent most of his life trying to get Arboleda back, and he wouldn't throw it away easily."

"Why is it so important? What happened with the soldiers? Please tell me. I have to know more before I begin a future with him. Perhaps you could start by explaining how you met?"

"In the regiments." Leaning back, Rafael regarded her consideringly, then let out a long breath. "I'm the bastard of an English soldier and a Spanish camp follower. Diego and I have been friends since he was thirteen and I fifteen. What little I know about his life before that he told me, or I gleaned from Gaspar and Diego's mother."

"You knew her?"

"Briefly. She died of a liver disease shortly after I met her. According to Diego, she was never the same after what happened to his family at Villafranca."

Shock gripped her. "Diego is from Villafranca?"

"You've heard of it."

Oh, yes. Thanks to her reading, she knew more than she wanted about the horrors that had happened there. During the harum-scarum retreat through the mountains of northwest Spain to La Coruña, with the French nipping at their heels and their food stores depleted, the English soldiers had swarmed Villafranca like locusts. Maddened by hunger and cold, the worst of them had broken into Spanish storerooms, guzzling the wine, robbing and even murdering any civilian who tried to stop them.

By the time the officers had reeled them in, the local Spanish populace had dubbed their "allies" *malditos ladrones*, "damned robbers." And the French, who'd stormed through next, had finished off any Englishmen lying drunken in the streets, while behaving equally badly to the locals. Villafranca was left shattered, nearly razed to the ground.

"You *have* heard of it," Rafael said as he watched the play of emotions on her face. "Or even remember it. You and your supposed parents were there, right?"

"Yes, but I wasn't yet five. All I remember is the cold and hunger. But years later, while trying to learn more about my parents, I read what occurred on the march." She shook her head. "I had no idea Diego had lived there."

"Arboleda borders the road to La Coruña. His parents used to own a vineyard that produced some of the region's best wine. The estate had been in his family for generations . . . until the soldiers came through."

Her stomach knotted. *This* was why he'd become a thief in the regiments. "The English soldiers?"

"They were the first," Rafael said coldly. "They ravaged his family's wine stores. I gather that Diego's father tried to reason with them, assuming that Spain's allies would treat him and his family with respect. But drunken, starving men are no respecters of persons. They ignored him, bullying Diego and his mother, though Diego says little of that. All I know is by the time the soldiers stumbled on, the family was left with nothing to survive the winter or take to market."

"Good Lord," she whispered.

"The French arrived a day later," Rafael said bitterly. "Diego's father was so angry he met them with a blunderbuss. They shot him for it."

"They shot him!" she cried. "The monsters!"

"Yes, and they set fire to the vineyards. As he lay dying in Diego's arms, he made Diego promise to take care of his mother and keep Arboleda alive. The place had been in the Montalvo family for generations; it was everything to the old man, and he'd raised Diego to feel the same. Unfortunately, there was little left to preserve once the solders got done."

Stunned by the litany of crimes committed against Diego and his parents, Lucy stared at Rafael, appalled. To have his father die in his arms, to watch his inheritance destroyed. He'd have been only twelve, too young to fight but old enough to remember. The thought made her ill.

"But if the French killed his father, why does he rail so against *my* countrymen?"

"His family expected mistreatment from the French, but not from the English, their 'saviors.' Diego is convinced his father would never have foolishly confronted the French if not for what the English had done. He still doesn't like either side. You may not realize this, but he's never performed in France or in England."

Until he'd come after her. Tears welled in Lucy's eyes. "But he performed for the English regiments. For years."

"He didn't start out there. He and his mother tried to run the estate, but without the vineyard, it was impossible. Diego was too young and his mother too devastated to recoup their losses." Rafael drank some coffee. "His father's creditors took advantage of Diego's youth to make demands he couldn't meet, and he and his mother couldn't satisfy the debts. They had no choice but to sell Arboleda."

"To the *marqués?*"

"He's the most recent owner. It changed hands often before him, but no one managed to revive the vineyards sufficiently to make a go of it." Rafael planted his elbows on the table. "Anyway, after the estate was sold, Diego took his mother to live with a poor relation in Oporto. The regiments had returned there, so he became a camp follower, determined to wrest from them everything they'd taken from him and his family. He began stealing and cardsharping, partly out of anger, partly to pay for his mother's medical treatments."

"No one caught him?"

"Eventually, yes. Fortunately, it was Gaspar. He told Diego he could either learn to be a magician's assistant or be handed over to the authorities. Gaspar was no fool. He recognized Diego's dexterity and amazing skills at cards even then. And I suspect the man knew he couldn't continue his profession much longer without someone younger to help him."

Rafael gave her a wry smile. "He pointed out to Diego that there were more legitimate ways to fleece the English. I think it pleased Diego to make fools of the English soldiers at his performances, though he never let on he was mocking them behind their backs."

She remembered only too well how Diego had humiliated Peter. He must have done that before, with other men he'd held in contempt. That was why he'd been so masterful at it. "He really despises the English, doesn't he?"

"Not all the English. Just their soldiers."

That explained why he was so ready to believe the worst of Papa. Why he'd thought he was doing her a great favor by abducting her.

It also explained why he'd been willing to come to England—to save her.

She stared down at her hands. Not just to save her. He'd come to regain Arboleda, willing to steal her to accomplish it. Even though it might hurt his future as a performer.

"I take it that fulfilling his promise to his father means more to him than even his profession," she whispered. "Despite his fame and great talent—"

"Haven't you realized how little he values that? He considers himself an entertaining trickster, a man of no worth and honor. He doesn't care that he can hold an audience of five hundred rapt in the palm of his hand." Rafael shook his head. "Why should he? His damned father drummed into him that he must continue the traditions of generations of Montalvos. He believes he failed his family by not holding on to Arboleda in the first place."

"But he was only twelve! He expects too much of himself."

"I know that, and you know that. He doesn't. The hope of regaining Arboleda has been the impetus behind his success. If that's taken from him . . ."

"It mustn't be!" she said stoutly. "He should wait until he gains the estate from the *marqués* and *then* marry me. I wouldn't care."

"No, but that also wouldn't help. Arboleda is in a shambles. He'll have to revive the vineyard, then regain a market for the wine. If a man as powerful as the *marqués* decides to oppose Diego—because, say, Diego married his granddaughter behind his back—the project will come to naught. Diego has saved some money but not enough to combat the active resistance of your grandfather."

Every word slammed a stake through her heart. "But Diego told me that the *marqués* was on the verge of death. Can't he just wait him out?"

"Men have been known to outlast legions while on 'the verge of death,' and if I know him, Don Carlos will hang on just to spite Diego."

That made her even more loath to meet the man. "You know my grandfather?"

"I've had dealings with him." His eyes narrowed. "Don't be fooled by his advanced age and courtly manner. Don Carlos is shrewd and ruthless. When Diego first approached him, hoping to negotiate a sale on credit, Don Carlos realized that my friend was perfect for fetching you back to Spain. Diego possessed a thorough command of English, the resolve and motivation to complete the task, and, most of all, an honorable character."

"Yes, it was very honorable of Diego to abduct me," she said dryly.

"That was a necessary part of completing the task. Don Carlos won't mind that. But when he learns that Diego means to marry you, he'll be livid. He wants something more than a poor magician with a run-down estate for his precious, long-lost granddaughter, and if Diego marries you in spite of him, he'll retaliate by destroying all Diego's plans and dreams for Arboleda."

"And then Diego will resent *me* for it. Or worse." Her heart ached at the awful choices before her. "Not only will he lose his estate, but he'll lose it because of an English-woman. It'll be like enduring the soldiers all over again."

"Nonsense," Rafael said kindly. "He thinks of you as Spanish, not English."

She smiled sadly. "Only because he ignores the raised-by-the-English part. But he won't ignore it for long. I still act and think like the English. I represent everything he de-spises. Add the fact that I've forced him into breaking his vow to his father, and our marriage is doomed. Eventually he'll come to hate me." Especially since he didn't consider himself in love with her.

His brow furrowing, Rafael sat back. "What do you mean to do?"

"Tell him I can't marry him, of course." She tipped up her chin. "I already had a plan in place to preserve Diego's aims before he came up with this hare-brained idea. I'll simply return to it."

"If he lets you."

"I'll leave him no choice. He's not the only one with pride. I want a husband who cares for me, not one who simply has foolish notions about defending my honor." She shot Rafael a beseeching glance. "And you mustn't tell him what you revealed, or he'll guess what I'm doing. Then it'll all be for naught."

Looking uneasy, Rafael didn't answer.

She leaned forward to grab his hands. "Promise me you'll keep my secrets, Rafael. You mustn't let him know any of this—"

"Any of what?" said a terse voice from the door.

Her heart sinking, Lucy released Rafael's hands and sat back, imploring him with her eyes to keep silent.

"Damn it, Rafael," Diego demanded, "what are you two plotting?"

Rafael's jaw stiffened, and she held her breath. But just as Lucy's stomach twisted into a knot, he met Diego's gaze. "You'll have to ask Miss Seton."

Relief flooded Lucy . . . until she saw the fury in Diego's expression. Now there would be hell to pay.

"What were you discussing, Lucy?" Diego demanded.

She stood. "Let's talk in private, shall we?" She swept past him to the door, her mind racing.

He followed her, but they'd gone only a few feet down the companionway when he pushed her inside a small cabin. When she saw the three hammocks, she realized that this cramped space was where he'd been staying.

That was all she registered before he shut the door and shoved her against it, bracketing her shoulders with his hands.

"What is it that you don't want Rafael to tell me?" he gritted out as he loomed close. "And why the devil did it require your holding his hands?"

That was why he was angry? He'd seen her grab Rafael's hands?

As she stared at him, speechless, his eyes darkened. "Perhaps I should remind you who you belong to now," he growled.

Then he kissed her roughly, angrily, his body hard and unyielding against hers. His hands swept over her with proprietary intimacy, and for a moment, she responded, caught up in the sweet fury of his jealousy. Perhaps he did care. Perhaps more than just honor prompted his proposal.

No, his pride was only wounded. He was angry at the situation and taking it out on her, which he would continue to do if she let this madness go on.

She dragged her mouth from his. "It wasn't *you* I was begging Rafael not to tell," she lied, thinking quickly. "It was my grandfather. Since you clearly didn't hide from Rafael what you and I did together last night, I was asking him to keep it quiet."

Diego blinked. "What point is there to that, if we're going to marry?"

She drew in a ragged breath. Time to do what would surely wound his pride, if nothing else.

But she had pride, too. Too much to marry a man who only wanted her in his bed. She forced her chin up, forced defiance into her face. "You didn't give me the chance this morning to respond to your charming proposal of marriage. If you had, you would have heard me refuse you."

A look of pure astonishment crossed his face. "What do you mean?"

"Just what I said. I do not wish to marry you."

Chapter Twenty-one

Dear Cousin,

    We expect the colonel any day now, and we hope he will have answers, for he knows his daughter's mind best. Still, I beg you to learn everything you can about Señor Montalvo's character beyond what we already know. If he proves a scoundrel, then she is ruined for certain.

                      Your anxious relation,
                      Charlotte

*D*iego's first reaction to Lucy's insane pronouncement was a blend of relief and disappointment, followed swiftly by outrage.

He stared at her impassive expression, sure that he had misheard her. "You do not have a choice. You must marry me."

She crossed her arms over her chest. "Why? Because you say so?"

"Because I have taken your innocence!"

"No one need know that. You don't wish to marry me, after all, and I certainly don't wish to marry you. So why should we?"

I certainly don't wish to marry you.

That stopped him cold. After he had spent the last few hours simmering with anger over what he had thrown away for one tempestuous night with her, *she* had the audacity to refuse *him?*

He shoved away from her. "I never said I did not wish to marry you."

"But it was painfully clear." When he opened his mouth to protest, she added, "And I understand, believe me. We both know that a marriage between us would never work."

"Why is that?" he snapped.

"Because, for one thing, you don't love me."

Though that assertion sparked his temper, he could not deny it. All right, so he desired her past all reason, and he liked her a great deal. But he was not fool enough to confound that with an imaginary emotion drummed up by poets. "I do not believe in love," he said, though the words rang a little hollow. "Love is an illusion."

A hint of pain flickered in her eyes, gone so swiftly he was sure he had imagined it. "And it so happens that I do," she said lightly. "So a marriage between us wouldn't work."

"Are you saying that *you* love *me?*" he asked.

She strolled over to the hammock, keeping her back to him. "I'm saying I only seduced you to give myself choices. I'm not about to relinquish them just because you have some notions about your honor."

His blood pounded in his ears. Did she not recognize the sacrifice he made on her behalf? He had expected her to be pleased, even grateful, for his willingness to give up everything he had worked for in order to behave honorably. Certainly he had expected her to be more enthusiastic about the prospect.

Could she really have felt *nothing* for him when they

made love? What had happened to his sweet Lucy, who gave herself to him so freely and ardently?

Or had that just been an illusion? She *had* set out very cold-bloodedly to seduce him. She had tried to make it swift and easy. Even at the time, he had thought it was because she was preserving her anger at him.

Perhaps he had been right. Perhaps when he had kidnapped her, he had killed any small affection she had felt for him in England. This might be her way of revenging herself on him. Could that have been her plan all along, to have him so desperate for her in his bed that he threw away everything? Then renege on her promise to keep the truth from the *marqués?*

It did not seem possible. But he had to know.

"What do you intend to tell your grandfather?" he asked.

She whirled to face him, her expression showing her surprise. "The same thing I planned to tell him before—that I lost my innocence to Peter. Why? Did you think I would tell him the truth?"

Belatedly, he realized how insulting that must sound. "I . . . that is—"

"You did!" Her pretty eyes filled with hurt. "You think I'm doing this out of spite. That I mean to ignore my end of our bargain."

He reached for her, but she stepped away, and he dropped his hands to his sides. "I am merely trying to understand. I am willing to marry you, so I do not see why—"

"I should refuse your immensely flattering offer?" she said dryly. "Just be glad that I am. You'll have your estate, and I'll still have my freedom."

Her freedom—damn her to hell for that. His only consolation in all this had been that he would have Lucy as his own. But she clearly did not want to *be* his own. "So last night really was only about ruining yourself to keep from being forced into marriage by your grandfather."

"Of course. Not that I didn't enjoy it immensely. You're very talented, Diego, in bed and out."

"Just not talented enough to be your husband." He sounded like a sulky, smitten idiot, but he could not help it. He had finally resigned himself to being her husband, and she did not even care. It rubbed him raw.

With a heavy breath, she turned her back to him again to toy with the hammock strings. "If circumstances were different . . ."

His eyes narrowed. What circumstances?

He observed the stiffness of her back, the way she would not look at him. Could he be reading this entirely wrong? Could she finally have realized how much Arboleda meant to him and be trying to make sure he did not lose it? Might Rafael even have told her how important it was?

No, Rafael would not interfere. And yet . . .

Coming up behind her, he drew her around to face him. He had to see her face, had to determine if she meant her words. She shot him a questioning glance, but not before he briefly saw unhappiness in her eyes.

Or was it just his wounded pride making him think it?

Her vacillation drove him mad. If it *was* vacillation. "What has changed since I left your cabin?" he demanded. "When I mentioned marriage earlier, you seemed pleased by the idea."

"I wasn't so much pleased as stunned," she shot back. "You didn't exactly give me time to discuss it with you. And after you left, I had plenty of time to think. If you lose your estate because we marry, how will you support us?"

That sparked his temper. "I am not poor, Lucy," he clipped out. "I am not rich, but I am certainly capable of supporting a wife."

"For as long as your act is popular and successful, yes." She tipped up her chin. "But a handsome unmarried performer will always attract the female portion of the population, while a married one—"

"Will attract the portion of the population who wants to be surprised by his act," he bit out, unaccountably annoyed by her assumption that he would only be successful as long as he was free to charm the ladies.

Never mind that he had often complained to Gaspar that the women only came to see him in hopes of a flirtation. "I am good at what I do, damn it. My career will not end simply because I marry."

"Even assuming that you're right," she went on, blithely battering his pride with every word, "I'd have to travel with you, living in hotels, unable to settle anywhere, unless I wish to be without you for months on end."

It was the same thing he had told himself when deciding that he could not have her. But that made it no less galling to hear *her* say it. "You grew up traveling with the regiments, did you not?" he snapped. "I should think it would be the sort of life you know well. And we would at least be traveling more comfortably."

"Travel is travel," she said lightly. "If you'll recall, my fa- . . . the colonel sent me away to school at twelve. Clearly, even he didn't think it a good situation for a woman."

Diego had always claimed that the life of a traveling conjurer was no life for a wife and children. So why could he not accept that same claim from her?

Because he still desired her.

It made no sense. Last night should have quenched his obsessive need to touch her, kiss her, make love to her. Her coldly practical assessment of his acceptability as a husband should certainly have squelched any further longing to possess her.

It had not.

Sliding his hand about her waist, he drew her close. Undaunted by her sudden look of panic or the fact that she turned her head aside when he bent toward her mouth, he brushed kisses to her brow, her cheek, her ear. "But we would have *this*." He nuzzled the pale, fine skin of her neck. "We would have our nights."

"That isn't enough," she choked out. "Not for me."

She slipped from his arms and hurried to the door, but he caught up with her, hauling her back against his chest. "*Dios mio, querida,* do not do this. We could make it work."

"Why should we?" she asked, her voice oddly breathless. "You said you wanted me to meet my grandfather, to see what sort of life he could offer me, and now I'm willing to do that. Unless you can give me a good reason for doing otherwise, it seems sensible to do as I originally planned."

What reason could he give? It *was* sensible. Not marrying her would allow him to bring his plans to fruition. Indeed, marriage would bring only disadvantages to them both. And if the passion he felt was not enough for her . . .

As he hesitated, she stiffened. "Let me go, Diego. It is better this way."

Reluctantly, he released her. He had bungled this, but he was not sure how. Perhaps if he had sworn his undying love—

He scowled. He would be damned if he spouted such nonsense just to have her in his bed. He still could not promise her any kind of life. In a few years perhaps, once Arboleda was restored and he had money and position, but not at present. By then, though, she would quite likely be some other man's wife.

The thought opened a fathomless desolation in his chest that he forced himself to ignore. She was giving him what he wanted. He had to be wise and grab it with both hands.

She started to open the door, then paused, still not looking at him. "I think it best that we be careful how we act around each other from now on. We must show a front of perfect propriety. If Rafael guessed that we shared a bed, the others might, too, and that would ruin both our aims."

A cold chill swept him. "Rafael guessed because I told him I meant to marry you, *cariño.*"

Her gaze shot to him in alarm. "You mustn't call me that. Or any other endearments. We must be Miss Seton and Don Diego from now on. Understood?"

Dios Santo, the woman knew how to prick a man's pride. Yet she was right. If they did not mean to marry, they must behave as strangers or lose everything. He managed a terse nod.

"Thank you," she murmured.

But as she reached for the door handle again, he cried, "Wait!"

She eyed him warily. "What is it?"

He did not know. He just could not stand the thought of never having her in his arms again. "You said you enjoyed what we did last night. There is no reason we cannot . . ." Though her face grew stony, he bumbled on. "That is, I am sure Rafael would be willing to keep Nettie busy at night if we should wish to—"

"Dally?" she finished, her face impassive.

"Pleasure each other," he countered. "We will not reach Spain for at least another two weeks, possibly three. Why not make the best of it?"

"Because I am not a whore," she snapped. "There will be no private enjoyments."

She left, letting the door bang shut behind her.

He stood there a long moment, staring blindly at the door. Too late, he saw how insulting his suggestion must have sounded. He had never liked being wanted only for his fame. She would hate being wanted only for her body.

Except that it was *not* only her body he wanted her for, damn it! He enjoyed her company. He liked how she threw herself with great fervor into whatever she did. He admired her caring treatment of her young pupils and her loyalty to those she loved—her "Papa" and Mrs. Harris and a whole school full of women. The idea of becoming a formal stranger with her did not sit well.

But the alternative was to beg, to turn into some blithering idiot whose desires controlled him. He had already done that far too much.

The door swung open, and Rafael stepped into the room, then halted, clearly taken by surprise. "I thought you were with Miss Seton."

"I was. She just left. It seems she does not wish to marry me."

"I see." His friend did not look surprised. "But then you didn't really wish to marry her, did you?"

Diego glared at him. "Is that what she told you?"

"That is what *you* told me, with every action and word. You came into the cabin angry this morning, stomping about, announcing in your rigid and bloodless manner that you had to marry Miss Seton. I didn't have to tell your little captive anything. If you behaved like that with her when you proposed marriage, she would have noticed your obvious lack of enthusiasm."

He winced. Was that how she had seen his offer? As a duty? He supposed he had presented it that way. But what had she expected, that he would profess himself thrilled by the prospect of losing Arboleda? Merely for the pleasures she might offer?

That isn't enough, she'd said.

She was right. And she had not sounded thrilled by the prospect of being dragged from pillar to post as his wife, either. He drew himself up stiffly.

Rafael shrugged. "I wouldn't complain if I were you. You made a narrow escape." He cast Diego a considering glance. "It's not every day that a man receives the gift of a woman's innocence without having to suffer any obligation. How lucky is that?"

"True," Diego said tightly.

So why did he not feel particularly lucky?

Colonel Hugh Seton blazed into the school like a one-man regiment. Charlotte could hear him coming even before he reached her office. She hurried out to meet him and his wife, Maggie, who happened to be one of Charlotte's good friends.

"Where is this scoundrel Gaspar who had a hand in this disaster?" the colonel demanded. "I must speak to him at once."

"I hardly think he would have remained in England if he had been part of it." Charlotte assured the colonel. "But I will have him fetched so you can question him yourself." Passing the order to a footman, she led the Setons into her office. "While we wait, you should look at this letter Lucy left behind."

When she handed the colonel the missive, he gave it only a cursory glance. "My girl didn't write this," he said stoutly.

"Are you sure? I compared it to her other work—"

"Do you think I don't know my daughter's hand?" he roared. "She didn't write it, I tell you!"

"Hugh, dear, you must calm yourself," Maggie murmured. "Nothing can be accomplished if you have an apoplexy."

"Aye, aye, ye're right about that." He shot Charlotte a worried glance. "Do you happen to know what part of Spain this Montalvo fellow is from?"

"I believe Gaspar said he was from the northeast."

"Thank God," the colonel said, looking a little relieved.

"Why?"

"It seems quite the coincidence that Montalvo is Spanish, when I was informed by the War Office six months ago that Lucy's Spanish grandfather has been trying to find her. But Lucy's mother was from a town near Gibraltar, on the opposite end of Spain from where Montalvo is from."

A sudden shiver snaked down Charlotte's spine. "Oh, dear."

"What?" he asked, his relief vanishing.

"The ship that we think they left on was embarked for San Roque. That is not far from Gibraltar, is it?"

The color drained from the colonel's face. He sat down heavily in the nearest chair. "Damn that bastard. All these years, her grandfather has not given her a thought. And now . . ."

As he trailed off, Maggie stared at him. "You told me Lucy had no living relations. And I know she always believed it to be true."

He stared blindly ahead. "I had a reason for keeping it from both of you. Not that it matters now." He lifted his gaze to Maggie. "If that devil Don Carlos has somehow lured her to Spain, it cannot be for anything good. I have to go there. I have to save her."

"From what?" snapped a voice from the doorway. They all turned to see Gaspar standing in the doorway, his face dark with anger. "From finally knowing her family? You stole her from her parents, yet you condemn her true relations?"

Jumping to his feet, the colonel drew himself up to his full height, every bit the British officer. "I assume that you're Montalvo's servant, who supposedly had no hand in this."

"I didn't. The . . . elopement was all Diego's idea." Gaspar crossed his arms over his chest. "But much as I wish he'd chosen a less dramatic method of doing right by Miss Seton, I know he believes he's acting on her behalf. Certainly it's time she knew the truth about her parentage."

The colonel marched up to him, his eyes a livid blue. "And what the bloody devil do you think *that* is, ye damned insolent bastard?"

Unbowed, Gaspar jerked his head toward Charlotte and Maggie. "Are you sure you want them to hear?"

"I've done nothing wrong to hide from them," the colonel growled. "Except protect my daughter from those who might prey on her."

"Like her own grandfather, you mean?" Gaspar said.

"Aye. He had his chance to keep Catalina and my daughter. He gave that up when he let them leave Gibraltar with Tom Crawford. Once the *marqués* told Catalina she was dead to him for marrying an English soldier, he lost his chance to be anything to her. Or to his granddaughter."

Gaspar looked taken aback. "What the devil are you talking about? The woman you're calling Catalina was Lucy's nurse. She stole Lucy from the real Catalina and her Spanish husband, to run off with Crawford. You had to have known that."

"The real Catalina and her Spanish husband?" The colonel gave a harsh laugh. "Is that what that bloody arse Don Carlos told you?" A scowl knit his brow. "Oh, God, is that what your master told Lucy to get her to leave with him?"

A sobering apprehension swept over Gaspar's face. "*Dios mio,*" he said hoarsely. "Are you saying . . . do you mean to tell me—"

"The man is a liar and a scoundrel, and so is your master if he's aiding him." Colonel Seton headed for the door. "I've no time for this. I'm going after my daughter. They can't have gained too many days on us, since Lord Stoneville procured us passage here from Edinburgh on one of his ships."

"Still, it might take a while to get a berth to Spain, Colonel," Charlotte put in. After her brief marriage to a regimental officer, she was only too aware how difficult travel between countries could be. "And you will need documents to enter the country."

"Stoneville is seeing to that passage as well, since I'd already anticipated I might need to go to Spain. And his friend, the duke, is taking care of the documents."

"Hugh Seton, you scoundrel!" Maggie cried in a hurt voice. "You'd already anticipated a trip to Spain and said nothing of it to me? Indeed, it appears you've said very little to me about your life before you adopted Lucy."

The colonel lost some of his fire and vigor. "Maggie, my love, I'm sorry you had to hear of this in such a fashion. There are other things, too, I should have told you—"

"Then why didn't you?"

A flush spread over his cheeks. "Some of it I am not . . . proud of. And since I know I'm not entirely the sort of man you wanted to marry—"

"You big lummox!" Maggie's voice was choked as she stalked up to him. "Haven't you figured out by now that I love you just as you are? Nothing you could ever say would make me stop loving you. And if you think I'll let you trot off to Spain after Lucy without me, you have another think coming."

"It will be a rough voyage, love." He grabbed her hands. "And I don't know what we'll find."

"I don't care! She's my daughter, too. I'm going with you, and that's that."

After a brief hesitation, he nodded, tucking her hand in the crook of his arm.

"I wish to go with you as well," Gaspar put in. "The Spanish will be more likely to allow you into the country if a Spaniard is with you to plead your case."

The colonel paused to give him a cool appraisal. "If you come, I'll expect you to tell me everything you know about Don Carlos and his plans. And everything I need to know to stop your master from furthering them."

"I realize that."

"Come along, then. I can use your help with the Marqués de Parama. He won't get away with stealing my daughter."

Chapter Twenty-two

Dear Charlotte,
    I can learn nothing of Señor Montalvo's past, but I do not have the same access to foreign affairs as I do to London gossip. If I were to believe the papers, then he is at once brilliant and foolish, generous and despicable, a great man and a small one. Which is why I never rely solely on the press for information.

                    Your cousin,
                    Michael

The day after her discussion with Diego, Lucy stood with Nettie at the rail on deck, staring pensively out to sea. "I don't understand men."

"What is there to understand?" Nettie said. "If you feed 'em regular-like and give 'em a bit of 'sugar' now and then, they're easy enough. And if they don't behave, you just toss 'em out on their arses. That's what I always say."

Lucy smiled despite her misery.

"Ah, it's good to see you smile, duckie." Nettie patted her hand. "You can't be going on so over that Don Diego. Give one man too much hold on your feelings, and you're headed for trouble, you are."

"Then I'm headed for trouble."

In the heat of her disappointment yesterday, Lucy had told Nettie everything. She'd expected Nettie to call her a fool for not accepting Diego's marriage proposal, but the tavern maid had surprised her by taking Lucy's side.

If a man can't at least pretend to be in love with a woman long enough to propose all proper-like, she'd said, *he'll never last a whole lifetime with her.*

That was what she loved about Nettie—her practical approach to life. It was a shame she couldn't be so practical herself, at least when it came to Diego. She didn't want him to *pretend* to care about her. That wouldn't be nearly enough.

Lucy turned her face to the wind. "I still can't believe he had the gall to suggest that we should remain lovers for the next few weeks."

"I still can't believe you said no."

"Nettie!"

The woman shrugged. "Sometimes the way to a man's heart is through his tallywhacker."

"His *what?*"

"You know." Nettie made a vaguely obscene motion. "Ain't you never heard a man's privates called that?"

Lucy choked down a gasp. "Nettie, I have never heard any woman call a man's privates anything whatsoever, much less a tallywhacker."

"You fine ladies lead boring lives, seems to me," Nettie said with a shake of her head. "Though I can see as how it wouldn't be proper for a respectable female like you to have him leapin' under your sheets every night, if he don't mean to marry you."

"Not in the least proper," Lucy said firmly.

"But more fun."

Lucy burst into laughter. "You're very wicked, do you know that?"

"Aye. That's why you hired me away from Don Diego." Suddenly she leaned close to murmur, "Speak of the devil. He's coming toward us."

As Nettie began to sidle away, Lucy shot her a quelling glance. "Don't you dare leave me alone with—"

Too late. Nettie had disappeared around the fo'c'sle, and Lucy could see Diego approaching from the corner of her eye.

Jerking her gaze to the ocean, Lucy tried futilely to summon up her righteous indignation. But it was no use. After spending yesterday apart from him, her tender feelings remained as hardy and inconvenient as dandelions, blooming ever hopeful when he halted beside her.

Until the chill in his manner wilted them. "I came by the cabin yesterday evening," Diego said stiffly. "But Nettie told me you were sleeping."

"Yes, I retired early." Though she'd only tossed and turned. She kept remembering the last time she'd lain in that bed—and with whom.

He cleared his throat. "In any case, I thought you might like something to keep your boredom at bay for the remainder of our trip."

He extended a box of charcoals. "You said you had no implements for drawing, so I hunted through the crew until I found a sailor with an artistic bent. Fortunately, he was willing to sell me these."

She took the box, her heart leaping into her throat. "Thank you." She struggled to hide just how much the small gesture meant to her. "It is most kind of you, Die— Don Diego."

A scowl knit his brow. "*Por Dios,* you did not speak to me as if I were a count even before we were intimate. I do not see why you must do so now."

"I want to get accustomed to it before I meet my grandfather." She was terrified she would give away how much Diego meant to her. What good would refusing him do if he ended up losing everything he'd fought for anyway?

She managed a smile. "Haven't you learned I'm not good at governing my tongue? If I slip up and call you Diego, he might guess the worst."

"Yes, and we dare not risk *that.*" His voice was snide, but his eyes seemed to eat her up. "It would be the end to your precious freedom."

"And yours," she pointed out, annoyed. She was doing this for him, after all.

Of course, he didn't know that. Must *never* know that. So how could she blame him for his anger? She'd deliberately pricked his pride and put an end to his half-hearted decision to marry her.

Yet it still hurt that he'd acquiesced, that he'd wanted her for nothing more than a bed partner. That would always hurt. After their night together, she couldn't imagine herself marrying any other man.

Apparently, he had no such problem. He seemed perfectly content to hand her over to her grandfather.

"Thank you again for the charcoal, sir. Now, if you'll excuse me, I promised Nettie I'd show her how to play piquet."

She fled, managing to suppress her tears until she was in the companionway stairs. Bother it all, she had to stop this! Nettie was right—she had to stop mooning over a man who only wanted her to shore up his honor. She couldn't let him ruin his future because of some injury to his pride. She couldn't do that to the man she loved.

Loved?

The truth walloped her as suddenly as the swinging boom of a sail, making her halt in the stairwell.

Good Lord—she loved him. With all her heart.

Oh, no, how could she have gone and fallen in love *again?* And this time with a man twice as wonderful—and twice as inaccessible—as Peter. Although, honestly, Peter had been a mere infatuation, the foolish object of her girlish fancies.

Diego, on the other hand . . . How brave he must have been to endure what the soldiers had done to his family. How strong to have tried, even futilely, to save his family's estate. And at twelve, for a boy of such privilege to be forced to learn a new way of life and yet succeed! It showed astonishing determination.

That same determination had driven him to find her and steal her. That same determination would serve him well in his plan to restore his family's estate, to redeem their name. She might be Spanish only by blood, but she knew enough of the people to know how much honor mattered.

It certainly mattered more than some foolish Englishwoman's hopeless love for a man who could not love her back.

Tears stinging her eyes again, she hurried down to the cabin before she could run back on deck and beg him to marry her, no matter how little he wanted it. She had to get control of this mad need for him, before he guessed she wasn't as immune to him as he thought. Before they ended up right back where they had started.

As she hurried into the cabin, Nettie glanced up. "Are you all right?"

She sighed, tired of examining the state of her heart. She'd have to learn to stay away from men. They were not good for a woman's constitution.

"I'm fine," Lucy lied. "Nothing that a brisk game of piquet won't cure."

But over the next week, after becoming insanely proficient at piquet, Lucy found herself far from cured. Apparently, playing piquet did absolutely nothing to assuage the pains of the lovesick.

Diego was no help, either. At first, he spent his time on deck, smoking cigarillos and glaring at her whenever she entered his sight. Then one day, after she mentioned to Rafael that she wished to improve her Spanish, Diego brought her a Spanish dictionary.

"Here," he said without preamble, dropping it onto the table in the wardroom where she and Nettie were finishing supper. "Tomorrow morning, you and I begin lessons. Living in your grandfather's household will be hard enough without the added difficulties of needing him to translate all the time."

She blinked at him. Diego meant to teach her himself? Because he worried about her alone in her grandfather's household? That was enough to give a woman the wrong idea. And Lord knew she already had plenty of wrong ideas about Diego.

"One more thing." He glanced at Nettie. "Your maid needs suitable clothes."

Nettie blinked. "Here now, ain't nothing wrong with my gown. This is what all the tavern maids wear."

When a pained expression crossed Diego's face, Lucy

bit back a smile. "That's the problem, Nettie. Don Diego doesn't want anyone guessing that he hired my 'chaperone' from a tavern. It might not sit well with my rich relations."

"Just make her something more appropriate, will you?" Diego snapped.

Make her something? Lucy laughed. "Shall I weave it from seaweed, sir?" she said, unable to resist teasing him.

"I thought you were taught to sew," he shot back. "Or do they not include that instruction in your English schools, along with those lessons in propriety?"

"We're taught to do needlework, yes. But sewing of gowns is generally left to seamstresses."

"I can make a gown," Nettie put in, surprising Lucy. "But I'll need cloth."

"I will see that Rafael gives you some. He must have something among the goods in his hold." He shot Lucy a furtive glance. "He might have something for you, too, although I imagine your grandfather will wish to provide you with gowns himself."

Lucy merely nodded as he stalked off. She didn't intend to stay in San Roque long enough to make good use of those gowns. As soon as they landed, she'd have Nettie post a letter to Papa to tell him to come fetch her. Even if Diego was right about Papa's role in taking her from her real parents, he deserved the chance to explain himself. She couldn't have him worrying himself sick over her back in England.

Of course, after Papa came for her, she'd have to return to England and face her ruin. That wasn't an appealing prospect, even with her family standing by her. But neither was the idea of marrying a Spanish grandee of her grand-father's choosing.

That was why she would accept Diego's Spanish lessons gladly. She didn't know how long she might have to live in her grandfather's household, and the thought of being helpless because she couldn't speak the language worried her even more than the prospect of being in Diego's company daily.

In the days that followed, she was surprised to find more of her Spanish coming back to her. It helped that Diego only spoke to her in Spanish, though she took care to keep their topics of conversation innocuous.

That proved easier than expected, since she had much to learn about Spain. She was discovering that living in the country as a foreigner would differ vastly from living there as a native. In the regiments, she'd been cocooned in English habits and manners. That wouldn't be the case now.

Fortunately, Diego understood that even better than she. And since he seemed equally eager to avoid any subject that might tempt them into their former intimacy, her lessons proceeded without incident.

Until one evening after they'd been traveling down the coast of Spain for several days. At dinner, Rafael informed them that the ship would pass through the Straits of Gibraltar during the night. He expected to weigh anchor in Algeciras Bay by the next morning.

His announcement hit Lucy like a roaring typhoon. She'd grown accustomed to the lazy pattern of life at sea— morning lessons with Diego, afternoons spent drawing or sewing with Nettie, evening dinners listening to Diego and Rafael regale the company with tales of their exploits in the regimental camps. If not for the painful fact that she'd fallen more deeply in love with Diego each day, the time had been almost magical. Now it was coming to an end.

As soon as dinner was over, she hurried to the bow, the only place on deck where she could be relatively private. She'd taken to coming here whenever she felt low, sitting sandwiched between the fo'c'sle wall and the capstan as she watched the ship plunge through the waves.

She was so sunk in her misery that when Diego appeared suddenly before her, she uttered a cry.

"What is it?" he asked as he dropped down beside her, his face tight with alarm. "What is wrong?"

He could ask that? When tomorrow they would part forever? The thought was almost more than she could bear.

But he was taking it in stride, so she must, too. She'd done well so far, never once hinting at what she knew of his past. Now she merely had to survive until she reached her grandfather's.

"You startled me, that's all," she said.

"That is not what I meant. Why did you leave the wardroom in such a rush?"

"No reason," she choked out.

"No?" he said skeptically, lifting his hand to rub a tear from her cheek.

She hadn't even realized she was crying.

It was the first time he'd touched her since their night together, and it was all she could do not to lean into his caress. But that would be dangerous. Especially when he wore an expression of such grave concern.

"Lucy," he went on, "is it possible that you . . . is there a chance that you . . ."

"That I what?" She held her breath, praying he would say what she wanted to hear. That he hoped she would change her mind and marry him. That he wanted her to love him. That he loved her.

"Is there any chance that you are with child?"

Her heart sank. What a fool she was. He didn't believe in love, remember?

"There's no chance," she assured him, putting the last nail into the coffin of her hopes for any future with Diego.

If he'd given her a child, he would almost certainly have renewed his proposal of marriage, and she would have accepted it, too. It was one thing to release a man from his obligations out of love for him. It was quite another to punish a child for its parents' mistakes by depriving it of a father.

Oddly, Diego didn't look as relieved to hear her answer as she'd expected. "Are you sure?"

"I'm sure." She ducked her head, her face flaming. "My courses came and went last week."

He tipped up her chin, his hand infinitely gentle. "Then why are you crying?"

With him touching her, her mind was a complete blank. "It's nothing."

A sudden gleam entered his eyes. "Perhaps you are in pain from having *this* in your ear." He reached up and came back with an orange.

She eyed him askance. "No, that is definitely not the problem."

"Then it's the one in the other ear." Dropping the first orange in her lap, he repeated the trick on the other side.

She couldn't help it. She laughed.

"I can do this all night, you know," he teased.

"You have that many oranges tucked inside your sleeves?" she said archly.

"Oranges. Walnuts. We had quite a supply at dinner, if

you recall, since Rafael broke out the rest of the stores now that we are nearly there."

That brought her misery back again. "Yes," she said tightly.

His smile faded. "Come, Lucy, tell me what is wrong," he coaxed. "Or you will force me to turn you into a fruit basket until you do."

Diego could be so persistent, God rot him. She seized on the only reason she could think of. "I'm nervous about meeting my grandfather."

His face cleared. "Ah. Do not make yourself anxious over *that*. The man will be beside himself with joy to have you returned to him."

"At first, perhaps. But what if he hates me? Or is disappointed in me?"

"You mean because you are no longer chaste?"

She blinked at him. That hadn't even occurred to her. "Actually, no. Besides, I've decided not to tell him until I see how things go. Now that I've found the family I lost, I should make an effort to get to know them before I do anything drastic, don't you think?"

Inexplicably, his face turned stony. "You understand what that means. He will begin introducing you to eligible men of his acquaintance."

"I realize that." She opted for nonchalance. "Who knows? I might actually meet a fellow I wish to marry. Of course, I'll have to pretend to be an innocent, since that's the only way a decent man would have me now."

"That is not true," he protested. "No man worth his salt would give you up for something as paltry as that."

His remark startled her. *You did,* she wanted to say.

But it hadn't been for that reason. Unfortunately, he'd done it for a more important one. She could still hear Rafael's voice: *The hope of regaining Arboleda has been the impetus behind his success.* And how could a man with Diego's pride break the solemn vow he'd made to his father? How could the woman who loved him let him?

"All the same," she murmured, "it would probably be best to maintain the illusion of my innocence as long as I can. After all, I don't know my grandfather. He may prove a draconian sort."

"If he does," Diego said fiercely, "then Rafael and I will pack you off on this ship and head back to London."

She shot him a surprised glance. "Don't be silly. If you did such a thing, you'd have to give up your estate."

"I will not let him hurt you, Lucy." He seized her hands, gripping them tightly. "I did not bring you all this way just to see you harmed. If anything about your situation alarms you in the weeks ahead, you must get word to me. I will come to you at once, I swear."

Her breath caught. The feel of his hands against hers sent fire through her veins, and the way he was looking at her, as if he meant to kiss her . . .

Oh, no—that was exactly what he intended. He was lowering his head, his eyes smoldering in that way that made her heart flip over.

She ought to stop him. Even if this spot on the deck was hidden from sight of the sailors, someone *might* go up in the rigging and *might* see them. And she just *might* very well lose her heart.

Yet she lifted her mouth to meet his.

The kiss began softly, as if he feared startling her into bolting. His lips played over hers, tasting, savoring. She leaned into him and placed her hand on his chest, reveling in the quickening beat of his heart.

Then the kiss changed, became a hot, exhilarating se-duction of her mouth. With a heartfelt groan, he slid his hand behind her neck while he ravished and plundered, like a pirate laying claim to a captive. His other hand drifted to her breast, and his wicked, glorious mouth burned wild and heady kisses down her throat.

"*Mi dulzura,*" he murmured. "Spend tonight with me. Please. Let us be together just once more."

The words hit her like ice water, reminding her that for all his sweet words and sweeter caresses, he valued his duty more than her.

She wriggled free of his arms, fighting to quell the thundering of her pulse. "We were fortunate enough not to conceive a child the last time we spent the night together. Do you really wish to tempt Fate twice?"

A look of desperation came over his face. "There are ways to prevent—"

"It doesn't matter." She pushed herself to a stand, letting the oranges drop to the deck. "I can't do it. I just can't."

It took all her will to leave. But she knew if she gave in to the siren call tonight, she would be begging him in the morning to give everything up for her. And regretting it later.

Diego watched her go with a pain as deep as the ocean that surrounded them. Somewhere in the recesses of his besotted brain, he knew he should not have asked her to share his bed tonight. He and Lucy had found a sort of friendship in these last weeks, and now he had wrecked it in one unguarded moment.

Yet he could not seem to help himself. Without her, he felt ill, like a sailor deprived of lemons to stave off the scurvy. In the past two weeks, he had vacillated between relief that he would be able to go on with his plans and regret that he could not have her. The regret overtook the relief more every day.

Their daily lessons had been bad enough, with him forced to sit beside her and ignore the sheen of sun on her hair or her soft smile of delight when she mastered a new conjugation. But tonight brought a double jolt of torment. First, the news that there was no chance of a child to force her back into his arms. Second, the unexpected agony of hearing her speak matter-of-factly about other men courting her.

He smashed an orange beneath his hand. *Dios mio,* how could he bear that? Until now, he had consoled himself that at least she would not be marrying any other man. She would tell the *marqués* of her lost innocence, and Don Carlos would give up on trying to arrange a fine marriage for her.

Diego had even toyed with dreams of coming after her once Arboleda was well established as a working vineyard. Thanks to the lovemaking that had ruined her, she would still be free, whether in England or Spain, and he would be able to offer marriage without breaking his vow to his father.

What a selfish beast he was. He wanted her pining for him, waiting for him, while he did as he pleased. He had no right to that.

It took him several moments to gain enough control over his willful body to be presentable, but he lingered above deck a while longer, smoking a cigarillo. This was not supposed to be so difficult. He had what he wanted, and she would soon have more than she had ever dreamed of.

Who knows? I might actually meet a fellow I wish to marry.

He scowled into the moonlight. She would belong to some other man. The very idea ate him up inside.

"I thought I'd find you here," Rafael said, coming up beside him. "Couldn't resist running after her, could you?"

Diego flicked some ash. "What do you want?"

"Was Miss Seton all right?"

"She was nervous about meeting her grandfather, that is all."

"She should be. He's a powerful man used to getting what he wants. And if I am to understand the situation correctly, he wants an heir."

Ignoring the chill that chased down his spine, Diego dropped the cigarillo and ground it out with his boot. "I know the *marqués,* too, and I know his reputation for ruthlessness. But this is the granddaughter who was stolen from him. He will not force her into anything."

"Are you sure?"

"I am sure."

But he was not sure at all. He was not sure of anything anymore.

Except for one thing: he could no longer just take his property and leave town. Perhaps he was being overcautious, and almost certainly, he was a fool to prolong his torment.

But he did not care. He would stay around as long as he must to be certain that Lucy was all right. Even if it tortured him to do so.

Chapter Twenty-three

◦◦◦◦◦

Dear Cousin,

Though Lucy's fate still weighs heavily on my mind, I have a new concern. Mr. Pritchard is actively seeking a tenant for Rockhurst, and some of his choices would make inappropriate neighbors for a girls' school. Yesterday, a gentleman who wishes to convert it into a cricket ground surveyed Rockhurst. Today, Mr. Pritchard took around a man who runs a prison. Has the man no conscience? Does he not care what this will do to us?

Your concerned relation,
Charlotte

Although Rafael's ship weighed anchor in the pristine waters of Algeciras Bay the next morning, it took several hours for the passengers to be cleared for entry into Spain. While Diego arranged for a message to be sent to Lucy's grandfather announcing their arrival, Lucy spent the time gazing over vistas that took her breath away.

On one end of the bay lay the city of Algeciras, its whitewashed buildings glistening in the brilliant May sun. An impressive sweep of shore followed, dotted by villages with fishing boats crowded up to the docks. Next came a larger town that Rafael informed her was San Roque, their destination, built on a hill with a backdrop of mountains. After San Roque came other small villages, then the border between Spain and the English city of Gibraltar. The mighty rock itself perched at the very tip of the isthmus. It dominated the landscape as powerfully as the massive Salisbury Crags dominated Edinburgh, her home.

Her home most recently, that was. Only after Papa had retired from the army had she even really had a home. The thought of how he must be worrying gnawed at her, but her worry was tempered with growing distrust. Could he have known the truth about her lineage from the start? And if so, how could he have kept it from her?

Unless he'd worried about this very thing—that she might run off to Spain to meet her relations without him. But he surely knew her better than that. Even now, unease squirmed in her belly at the thought of meeting her rich and powerful grandfather. The man might very well hold her future in his hands. Lord knew he held Diego's, and after what Rafael had said, she wasn't sure she even *wanted* to meet him.

Nor did her consternation dim after they left the ship. Her hands grew clammy as the carriage carrying her, Nettie, and Diego climbed the narrow cobblestoned streets. Diego explained that when the British and Dutch had conquered Gibraltar more than a hundred years before, most of the Spanish inhabitants had left to found San Roque a short distance away. Her grandfather's grandfather had been one of them.

It was hard to believe that this alien, gorgeous place was her heritage, with its houses piled up on the hill like delicate sugar cubes adorned by ironwork and copious flowers at every entrance and window. It was almost too much to take in. Even the sweet smell of jasmine and the drifting clacking of castañets coming from what looked like a dance hall overwhelmed her.

By the time they pulled up before a lavish mansion of Moorish architecture, she felt bludgeoned by unfamiliar colors, smells, and sounds. The Spain she'd known as a girl was the rough terrain of the interior, not this orgy of sensations.

And this impressive edifice, with its exquisite mosaics, marble pillars, and tiled roofs, was to be her home for a while? It seemed incomprehensible.

"Now ain't that grand!" Nettie exclaimed as she gaped out the window. "That's right near to being the finest house I ever did see."

The finest and the most intimidating. "I take it you're still content to be my servant, instead of rushing back to England with Rafael?"

"I ain't leaving you with your grandfather and no friend to turn to," Nettie retorted.

"She *has* a friend to turn to," Diego bit out.

"You?" Nettie snorted. "You're trotting off to your estate in the north of Spain."

"Not right away." When Lucy's gaze shot to him, he gave her a long, level look. "Arboleda has sat idle this long; it can wait a while longer. I mean to stay in San Roque as long as necessary to be sure you are comfortable. And happy."

Happy? She wasn't sure that was possible without *him*. "I thought that Rafael was carrying you north when he left here," she said, wondering at this new development.

He shrugged. "Rafael will be here a week or more, unloading his cargo and picking up his new one. If necessary,

I will move into a *pensión* and delay my trip until the next time he docks here."

He would do that for her? She was debating whether to ask why, when the double entrance doors of her grandfather's abode burst open, and an elderly man was helped out onto the marble porch by a wiry attendant.

"Is that her?" the older man's querulous voice demanded in Spanish. He tapped his cane with impatience. "Don Diego?"

As a groom scurried to put down the carriage step, Diego shot her a reassuring glance, then opened the door and leaped out. He bowed deeply to the man before turning to help Lucy disembark.

"Don Carlos," he said in English, "may I present Doña Lucinda. Your granddaughter."

As she alighted, Diego's hand left her. She felt naked and exposed before the sharp-eyed *marqués,* who scanned her as if assessing her worthiness to be his descendant.

Just as she thought this might have been a huge mistake, that she should have refused even to leave the ship, he clutched the head of his cane in both hands and began to cry.

What should she do? Perhaps he wouldn't want her to notice the tears. Perhaps it would embarrass him if she tried to comfort him. A glance at Diego gave her no help, for he looked equally discomfited.

This was the "shrewd and ruthless" man Rafael had warned her against? This broken-down fellow with heavily pomaded white hair?

After an awkward moment, the *marqués* raised a shaky hand to brush away his tears. "Forgive me, child," he croaked out in heavily accented English. "I am an old man.

How do you say it in English? We wear our hearts in our sleeves."

Stifling a smile, Lucy curtsied, not sure how a Spanish woman should respond to her stranger of a grandfather. "It is an honor to meet you, sir."

At her formal tone, he frowned and gestured her forward with an imperious hand. "Come, come, girl. Have you no kiss for your poor old grandpapa?"

She approached him nervously. He was stooped so far down over his cane that she had to bend to press her kiss to his papery cheek. How old *was* he, anyway? She hadn't expected him to be this old.

When she started to move back, he clutched her arm. "Let me look at you up close," he said. "My eyes aren't as good as they once were."

He peered up at her face, a smile growing on his lips. "You're the very picture of your mother," he went on. "The very picture."

His eyes were definitely not in good shape. "Forgive me, sir," she said in Spanish to be sure he understood her, "but I don't think I look anything like her, judging from *this*." She showed him the miniature she'd kept close all this time.

He blinked, though she couldn't tell which surprised him more, the fact that she would gainsay him or the fact that she spoke Spanish.

Then he set his shoulders stubbornly. "That likeness isn't the best," he replied in rapid Spanish she had to concentrate to understand. "Take my word for it, you're more like her than any picture can convey. Come, I'll show you." He broadened his gaze to include Nettie and Diego. "All of you, come."

With his talonlike fingers digging into her arm, he

urged her toward the open door. His attendant tried to take his other arm, but Don Carlos waved him off. "My granddaughter will help me. Won't you, child?"

"Of course, *Abuelo*," she said, not sure whether to be flattered or terrified by his clear eagerness to have her about.

Now she understood what Diego had been trying to tell her. The *marqués* had been deprived of his grandchild through no fault of his own. What must that have been like? And how much harder must it have been for her parents to have their child stolen?

With him leaning heavily on her arm as he led the way at an excruciatingly slow pace, Lucy had plenty of time to gaze around her. Lord help her. The place was a palace. They walked down a gallery that circled a courtyard large enough to hold Papa's modest town house. It sported an elaborate fountain, not to mention potted fruit trees. Brilliantly colored mosaics punctuated the creamy walls, and costly Oriental rugs littered the rooms floored with tiles of intricate designs.

As they passed through various chambers, her grandfather pointed out paintings by Rembrandt and Velázquez, Chinese vases and native ceramics, things she'd only seen in the Duke of Foxmoor's house heretofore.

"This will all be yours one day, my girl," he said as they crept along.

For a moment, she actually thought that giving up everything in England might be worth a lifetime among such beauties. Then she remembered the possible price—a husband not of her choosing. A husband who was not Diego.

Not that Diego was a possibility anymore, if he ever had been. The farther they advanced through luxurious rooms, the grimmer he looked, and she understood why. Despite his rank and fame, Diego's situation couldn't begin to compare to her grandfather's.

She really *was* a fine heiress, and her grandfather would probably consider Diego little better than a fortune hunter. If he considered him at all. And Diego's pride would never allow him to tolerate that.

They climbed the stairs to a second gallery, then entered a well-appointed parlor. "This apartment is yours, my dear," her grandfather said. "There's a dressing room, a bedchamber, and a balcony overlooking the bay. The apartment used to be your mother's."

A lump caught in Lucy's throat. Her mother's room. Had she stood in this very spot as a young woman, dreaming and planning for her future?

"And this, my dear, is the likeness of your mother I was telling you about," the *marqués* said, gesturing behind her.

She turned to find a large portrait that took up half of one wall. The lump in her throat thickened. Her mother. Yes, Lucy recognized her. This particular image showed her beauty mark, and the tilt of her head was painfully familiar.

With tears in her eyes, Lucy approached the painting.

"I commissioned it on the occasion of her betrothal," her grandfather said.

"To my father?" Lucy said, then realized how stupid that sounded. Of course, it was to her father. Who else would it be?

Her grandfather took a moment to answer, but when she turned to him, he smiled. "Yes, of course, Don Álvaro."

"Is there a painting of him as well?" It began to bother her that while she had a clear image of her mother, there was no corresponding image of her Spanish father.

Then again, he probably hadn't been active in her life. Many aristocratic fathers left child rearing to their wives and servants.

"No," Don Carlos said abruptly. "He was much too busy to sit for an artist."

She glanced back at the portrait. Her mother didn't look nearly as happy as a woman should on her betrothal. "Was her marriage arranged?"

"I know that the English no longer subscribe to such things, but we Spanish still find arranged marriages useful."

What an evasive answer. Had he meant it to be a caution for her? Or a mere statement of fact?

Before she could probe further, he tapped his cane. "You and Don Diego must be famished. My cook has prepared a feast in celebration of your arrival. Your maid can unpack your bags while we dine." He held out a shaky hand. "Come, I have a friend joining us for *el almuerzo*."

As she took her grandfather's hand, she shot Diego a panicky look. Did "friend" mean just that, or was Don Carlos already plotting her marriage?

But Diego wouldn't even look at her, staring stonily ahead as he followed them. They entered the dining room to find a slender man awaiting them, his hands clasped behind his back as he strolled the room with the unruffled manner of an aristocrat who had nothing better to do than wait for his dinner.

"Ah, Don Felipe, my granddaughter is here at last!" Don Carlos cried.

As the "friend" turned to meet them, he looked her over most rudely. With a defiant tilt to her chin, she returned the favor.

Appearing to be in his late twenties, he didn't look much different from an Englishman, especially when compared to the swarthier Diego. The soft-featured gentleman's profusion of black curls, extravagant silk attire, and jeweled rings made him the very image of a rich and indolent grandee.

"This, my dear girl," Grandfather said, "is the grandson of my dearest friend, who recently passed away. This is Don Felipe, Duque de Málaga."

A duke? She doubted he was here merely as a friend to her grandfather; he was much too young. And judging from his smug acknowledgment of his introduction, he was much too full of himself to tolerate an old man's company for long.

Forcing a polite smile, she curtsied. "I'm honored to meet you," she said in Spanish, since her grandfather had spoken only Spanish to him, making her uncertain if he knew English.

"As am I, señorita." He bowed, putting his eyes right at the level of her bosom, where they stayed for a full five seconds before he straightened.

Lord, he was worse than Rafael.

She glanced over at Diego, whose tempestuous gaze was locked on the duke. He looked as if he'd like to throttle the fellow with his bare hands. Oh, dear. Why did he have to show his jealousy *now*? She could only pray her grandfather didn't notice.

Fortunately, Don Carlos chose that moment to introduce the two men, and Diego managed to regain his control. But though he smoothed his expression into bored indifference, his eyes still glittered with an unholy light.

They took their seats at the table, with her on one side

of her grandfather and the duke on the other. Diego was put next to the duke, almost as an afterthought.

A dizzying array of courses followed—a cold tomato soup, fried balls of potatoes and ham, and various stews of meat and beans, all accompanied by different wines, of which the duke liberally imbibed.

Lucy tasted everything but got little chance to actually eat, since Don Carlos began interrogating her as soon as the meal began. Had she lived as an orphan, or had someone taken her in? How had she been educated, and where? How long had she traveled with the regiments? Had she been presented yet to the English court? When Don Carlos actually asked how many suitors she'd had and who they'd been, Diego thankfully came to her rescue.

"Don Felipe," he asked, interrupting the duke in the middle of his fourth glass of wine, "do you live in San Roque?"

"During the spring, yes," the duke said with a languid flick of his hand. "But once it grows too hot, I decamp to my castle in the Sierra Nevada. In autumn, of course, I prefer my villa in Seville. Or the one in Madrid. It depends on my mood."

"My, my," Lucy said in English, wondering if Lord Pompous had acquired as many languages as he had houses. "I prefer a less complicated system for indulging my moods. Maintaining so many homes would tax my organizational capabilities."

The duke eyed her blankly, though her grandfather scowled. Arching a brow at Lucy, Diego swiftly translated.

Once Don Felipe grasped her meaning, he looked appalled. "I do have servants, Doña Lucinda. I have no need to stoop to maintaining my properties myself." He cast her a meaningful glance. "And neither shall my wife."

A mischievous impulse seized her. "So you're married, are you?" she said blithely. "I should love to meet her sometime."

Diego's lips twitched, and he became suddenly fascinated with his roast pork.

"You misunderstand me," the duke replied smoothly, obtuse as a slug. "I speak of my future wife." He flashed her a knowing smile, then dropped his gaze to her bosom again. This time he fixed it there so long she had to bring her napkin to her mouth to break his gaze.

Her grandfather didn't seem to notice. "The duke is considered one of the most eligible bachelors in southern Spain, my dear," he offered.

"How nice for him," she muttered in English. "And apparently I am considered a horse up for auction."

"Eh?" her hard-of-hearing grandfather asked.

A strangled cough escaped Diego, drawing everyone's attention. He knocked his chest with his fist. "Fish bone," he explained. "Beg pardon."

Thankfully, her grandfather was further distracted when a new and strange-looking dish was set before him. "Ah, the *pulpo* is here. Excellent!" He spooned what looked like thin scallops onto Lucy's plate. "You must have some, my dear. My cook has the best *pulpo* in town."

For the first time since they'd begun dinner, he spoke directly to Diego. "What is the English word for *pulpo*, Don Diego?"

"Octopus," Diego translated.

Her grandfather slid a tentacle onto her plate.

She'd eaten many things, but tentacles weren't among

them. She stared at its array of suckers, sure that she had gone quite pale.

"I do not believe the English eat octopus," Diego told her grandfather as he watched her with gleaming eyes.

The devil was enjoying this, wasn't he?

His amusement got her dander up. Stabbing a tentacle, she lifted it to her mouth. "You forget, sir, I was raised a Scot. We eat haggis."

She popped it into her mouth and chewed. Lord, it was vile. The flavor was decent, but the flesh was rubbery, and she could feel the suckers in her mouth. She reached for her wine, swallowing a healthy gulp to wash the tentacle down.

Clearly struggling not to laugh, Diego served himself a generous portion. "Isn't haggis the dish of sheep's entrails stuffed into a sheep's stomach?"

"You've had haggis?" she said, surprised.

"I smelled it while I was in Edinburgh looking for you." He made a face. "That was enough. I prefer the Scots' whisky to their cuisine."

"Englishmen feel the same," she replied. "I enjoy haggis myself, but even I dislike oatcakes. The good ones are tasteless, and the bad ones are so hard you could probably fire them out of your pistol in your act."

"I believe I shall stick to bullets." Diego smiled. "More accurate."

"But not nearly as Scottish," she said.

They both laughed. She happened to glance over at her grandfather, who wasn't laughing. He was watching them, his mouth a thin line.

Uh-oh. Dropping her gaze to her plate, she said, "The octopus is quite good, Grandfather. Is it a local specialty?"

Instead of answering, he scraped back his chair and stood abruptly, startling not only her but the duke, who'd been too busy enjoying the new wine brought with the *pulpo* to notice the undercurrents at the table.

"Don Diego, we have business to discuss, I believe," her grandfather clipped out. "Come, let us take care of it now."

Diego nodded tersely as he rose, too.

Don Carlos patted her arm. "Enjoy your meal, dear girl. I'll return shortly. In the meantime, I'm sure Don Felipe will be happy to keep you company."

No doubt, judging from the pointed look the duke cast her bosom as the other two men left. Lord, she could only imagine what would happen if she wore an evening gown around him. Between his love of wine and his love of bosoms, Don Felipe would probably plop his head into her bodice and keep it there.

Clearly, she had to rethink hiding her loss of chastity. If Don Carlos had his way, she would soon be trussed up and presented to the duke on a platter. And she'd rather eat tentacles morning, noon, and night than marry a man like Don Felipe.

Half an hour later, after he'd regaled her with tales designed to show the great honor he paid her by deigning to court her, her opinion had only solidified. And that was *before* he began a parry and thrust with his feet against hers under the table that she assumed he meant to be seductive but she found most annoying.

She was about to stamp her foot on his instep when Diego and her grandfather returned. Grateful for the reprieve, she smiled up at them both.

Don Carlos looked a trifle too self-satisfied. And Diego looked grim as he approached her chair, then bowed.

"I fear I must take my leave now, Doña Lucinda," he said tightly.

She leaped to her feet. "But you haven't finished your dinner!"

"Don Diego has a number of important business affairs to settle, my dear," her grandfather said firmly.

Her heart twisted. Was the moment here so soon? She held out her hand to Diego. "Then I must thank you for tarrying as long as you have."

He ignored her hand, though frustration showed in his eyes. "You owe me no thanks, my lady." He gazed at her face as if trying to memorize her features. "It has been an honor to serve you," he said softly.

That sounded so final. She could scarcely keep her expression impassive. "Tell me, sir, did you receive everything you hoped for?"

She had to know *that*. If Don Carlos had refused to honor his bargain with Diego, she'd drag Diego to the nearest altar herself.

His eyes locked with hers. "Everything that your grandfather promised me. That will have to be enough."

With those enigmatic words, he bowed again and left.

She stood there a moment, desolate. Then she caught her grandfather watching her. He must never guess what had happened between her and Diego. Never.

"Well, that's done," she said with false brightness as the duke leaped up and came around the table to pull out her chair for her.

Now all she had to figure out was how to live the rest of her life missing a piece of her heart.

Chapter Twenty-four

Dear Charlotte,
    You should assume that Mr. Pritchard has no
one's best interests at heart but his own. I shall try
to counter his tactics, but unfortunately he has a
right to do as he pleases with his own property.
Perhaps it is time you consider finding another,
better place to locate the school. I fear this situation
will only worsen in time.

                            Your concerned cousin,
                            Michael

$\mathcal{H}$e had Arboleda at last.

With the deed tucked safely inside his coat pocket, Diego strode down the steps outside Don Carlos's impressive mansion. Yet instead of crowing over his success, he could only seethe over his last sight of the group at the table. That dandified duke was holding out Lucy's chair, staring into her bosom with such a leer that it had taken all Diego's will not to lay the man out.

Damn Don Carlos! During their brief interview in the man's study, the *marqués* had informed him that he would be pleased to give Arboleda to Diego in exchange for his successfully bringing Doña Lucinda home. But with one condition—Diego must agree never to go near her again.

The *marqués* was no fool. He had noticed how comfortable they had been with each other at dinner. He had voiced great concern about the apparent "infatuation" for Diego that Lucy seemed to have developed during their journey.

He did not blame Diego, he'd said.

It had to be nipped in the bud, he'd said.

The Duque de Málaga was very interested in her, he'd said. And it would be a brilliant match.

Between that overblown drunk and Lucy? The very idea made Diego want to pound the man into a bloody pulp.

His only consolation was that Lucy had not seemed pleased by the duke. But how long would it be before her grandfather found a fellow who *did* please her?

He gritted his teeth. He could not dwell on that. She was no longer his concern.

Over the next four days, as he formed connections with local wine merchants and arranged to visit a local vineyard, he repeated that litany to himself. It was the only way he could endure seeing Lucy being squired about town by the Dandy Duke, with Nettie playing her *dueña*.

Why was Lucy putting up with him, anyway? Had she warmed to the man? Could she possibly be attracted to his riches and grand connections?

No, he could not believe it. Either she was simply indulging her ailing grandfather, or the *marqués* had used unsavory tactics to encourage the match.

That thought kept Diego up nights. As did the knowledge he had gleaned from asking about the duke in town. Apparently, not only was the idiot a self-important grandee, but he also liked his *coñac* a little too much. There were tales of the havoc he had wreaked on local businesses when he was in his cups.

Dios Santo, he had not brought Lucy here just to deliver her to a dissolute devil. And why did she continue to let the duke escort her about town? Why did she not tell her grandfather that she was no longer chaste? That would put a swift end to the duke's interest.

By his fifth evening in town, Diego could not bear it anymore. Ignoring the fact that he was acting like a besotted fool, that he might make a powerful enemy if the *marqués* learned of his interference, he decided to follow the duke once he left the *marqués's* abode.

Don Felipe headed straight for a nearby *taberna.* Diego headed inside after him. He would just talk to the man and see what his intentions were. No harm in that, right?

The duke sat drinking at the bar, while half the tavern maids vied for his attention and the other half gossiped about him.

Acting as if they were old friends, Diego sat down next to him and clapped him on the back. "I thought that was you, Don Felipe. Let me buy you a drink."

Don Felipe glanced at him through bleary eyes that made it clear he'd started drinking long before he'd left the *marqués's.* "Don Diego, isn't it? That fellow who found the *marqués's* granddaughter?"

"That's the one." Tossing some *pesetas* onto the counter, Diego ordered two brandies.

"Surprised to see you still here in town." Don Felipe drained the rest of his *coñac.* "Don Carlos said your wife was eager to return to the north."

His *wife?*

"It was kind of her to chaperone Doña Lucinda on the trip," the duke went on, "but surely she's ready to go home by now."

Diego scowled. Apparently, the *marqués* had been nervous about how the duke might view the long voyage with Lucy and had invented a lovely tale to keep Don Felipe happy. Devious old wretch. "As it happens, my business is keeping me in town longer than I had expected."

"Ah. Planning another conjuring performance, are you?"

"You could say that." Conjuring Lucy right out of the duke's grasping arms. She deserved better than this sot.

Actually, Diego *had* been approached by several gentlemen eager to finance tours in Spain. One had even suggested that they partner to open a pleasure garden in Cádiz. Lucy would have appreciated the irony of that.

"I understand congratulations are in order," he told the duke. "Don Carlos said that you and his granddaughter are as good as betrothed."

"Well, she's being stubborn, but I'm sure the *marqués* will bring her 'round." Don Felipe sipped the fresh glass of *coñac* set before him. "He's eager to have me for a son-in-law, you know."

"And I'm sure you could use the nice inheritance she'll bring." When the duke scowled at him for his presumption, Diego reined in his temper. "With all those properties to maintain, one must be practical."

Apparently that mollified Don Felipe. "True, true. And she is quite pretty to look at. Though a bit too outspoken for my taste."

Diego wished she were a lot *more* outspoken. At least, about protesting any interest in the duke. He took a long swallow of brandy.

"I suppose that couldn't be helped," the duke went on, "given her background. From what my aunt says, her mother had quite a defiant streak herself. She would have had to, running off with an English soldier the way she did."

Diego froze with his glass of *coñac* in midair. "What are you talking about?"

"Doña Catalina. She eloped with some fellow from the Forty-second Regiment."

"No, no, you are wrong." He *had* to be wrong. Otherwise, Diego had done all this for . . . *Por Dios*, it was not possible! "Her father was Spanish. The *marqués* told me that most specifically."

"He tried to pass that tale off on you, too, did he?" Don Felipe downed more brandy. "He's been saying that for years, to prevent a scandal—that Doña Catalina married Don Álvaro in a remote part of Spain, that they died of grief after their daughter was stolen from them. Doña Catalina was indeed engaged to such a fellow, but it never came to anything." He shook his head. "Ah, well, I suppose Don Carlos didn't want you to slip up and tell the girl. He said he'd just as soon she didn't know. Didn't want to ruin her rosy image of her parents."

Anger roared in Diego's veins. No, *that* was not why Don Carlos had lied. He had lied so he could manipulate Diego into doing what he wanted. He must have guessed that the best way to get Diego to help him was to play on Diego's hatred of the English. Offering Arboleda might not have been enough to overcome Diego's scruples, and he had probably realized that Diego would do anything to rescue some poor victim of an abduction by an English devil.

Like a fool, he had played right into the man's hands. He had been stupid enough to believe a fabrication created for the *marqués*'s selfish purpose—to regain his granddaughter and have her produce his heir without involving her legal guardian.

"Of course," the duke went on, his words slightly slurred, "I have more at stake than you in the matter. So after my aunt told me that Doña Catalina had run off with a soldier, I demanded that Don Carlos tell me the real story."

"How did your aunt know of it?" Diego asked, grasping at straws to assuage his guilt. Perhaps she had merely heard some idle gossip.

With a laugh, the duke downed the rest of his brandy, then motioned for another. "Apparently, quite a few knew. Once Doña Catalina married her sergeant, she lived in Gibraltar at the garrison. Doña Lucinda spent her first four years there, though I doubt she remembers. Occasionally, people from San Roque would see Doña Catalina with her husband and daughter. Of course, no one said anything to Don Carlos—they wouldn't have embarrassed the old man—but he must have known she was there. He'd disowned her by then, but he knew."

Diego clenched his fist around his glass. What kind of father cut his daughter out of his life just for marrying badly? "What about Doña Lucinda's grandmother? Did she not have a say in the matter?"

"Are you mad? That woman always did whatever Don Carlos commanded. I think after the regiment left she began to regret it, but she devoted herself to making sure her son made a good marriage. A pity that his wife proved barren."

His mind reeling, Diego could only sit there running through everything he had believed, everything he had thought. The facts made so much more sense now. Aside from the still-peculiar one that Colonel Seton had chosen to adopt Lucy after her parents died, this explained why the "nurse" had been named Catalina. Because she *had been* Catalina.

It also explained why the *marqués* had not begun searching for his long-lost granddaughter sooner. It was just as Lucy had speculated. The *marqués* had waited until he had lost his son and needed an heir. Only then had he tricked Diego into retrieving her.

Diego winced. No, he had only himself to blame for that. If he had delayed the trip in order to come here from Cádiz and ask a few questions, he would have uncovered the real tale. But he had been so consumed by outrage over the *marqués*'s tale of an abducted Spanish girl, so blinded by his own hatred of English soldiers, that he had not bothered to be cautious. And the *marqués*'s very real illness had added to his sense of urgency.

He downed his brandy and ordered another. He had to tell Lucy the truth.

His stomach sank. *Dios Santo,* she would hate him for it, and rightfully so.

"Of course, it is not a pity for *me,*" the duke went on, oblivious to Diego's torment.

Diego had to search his memory for what the damnable man was talking about. Ah, yes. The barren wife of Don Carlos's late son.

"Now that the son is out of the running," Don Felipe continued, "I get to step in and provide the *marqués* with an heir." He smirked at Diego. "I believe that is something I will enjoy."

Not nearly as much as Diego would enjoy smashing the man's face against the bar. "You are not perturbed by her dubious family background?" he gritted out.

The duke shrugged, swaying a little on his stool. "Her fortune makes it worth it." His words were seriously slurred. "All those lovely properties, you know. Got to keep 'em up somehow."

"What if she refuses to marry you?" Diego asked as the barkeep placed another *coñac* before him. "What if her grandfather cannot convince her?"

Don Felipe rolled his eyes. "The *marqués says* that it's her choice. Bloody old man is turning into a sentimental fool now that he's got his granddaughter back." He tapped his forehead. "But I have got a plan, you see."

Diego carefully blanked his expression. "Do you?" he said encouragingly.

Clutching his brandy glass, the duke looked around as if expecting spies to be lurking in the busy *taberna*. Then he leaned close. "All I have to do is seduce her. She'll be only too eager for marriage then."

Or Diego could break the brandy glass over the man's head and slit his throat with the shards. "She may not be that easy to seduce. The British have strict rules of conduct. And her maid is a fierce protector of her." When she was not helping Lucy get herself ruined. Diego scowled.

"Doesn't matter." Don Felipe patted his breast pocket. "I have a key."

Diego blinked, not following. "To what?"

"To the kitchen door of the *marqués's* house."

Horror seeped into Diego's bones. "The *marqués* gave that to you?"

"No, he's much too old-fashioned to approve of seduction. I bribed a servant. Had a copy made. Easy as that." He attempted to snap his fingers and nearly fell over. "Not my first choice but good enough. Imagine how the old man will react to finding me in her bed. Won't have a choice then." He winked at Diego. "Neither of them will."

For a moment, Diego could only stare at the man, his mind inventing several creative tortures for the lecherous duke. But he had to be smart about this. Lucy's well-being depended on it.

"Sounds like a plan that will work," he said, forcing nonchalance into his voice. "Good luck with it. I must go now; my . . . er . . . wife is expecting me."

As he rose, he bumped the duke, then apologized profusely, making a great show of dusting off his coat. When Diego left the *taberna,* he had the key in his own hand.

Try to seduce Lucy, would he? Try to take her by force?

Diego would see the man dead first. Or better yet, he would marry Lucy out from under the duke's nose.

He stopped short in the street. Yes—that was the answer. She would *have* to accept Diego's proposal now. How else could he protect her from the machinations of her grandfather and the duke?

Of course, when she heard of how reckless he had been to trust Don Carlos, she would be furious. It would not exactly persuade her to trust him further.

Fine. First, he would get her out of the *marqués*'s house and back on Rafael's ship. Then, once he had persuaded her to marry him, he would tell her about her grandfather.

And make an enemy of Don Carlos in the process.

He considered that a moment. If Don Carlos chose to oppose him, he might never be able to gain a market for his wine, even if he could revive the vineyards. He might lose any hope of ever restoring Arboleda.

But it did not matter. He had wronged Lucy. He had ruined her, and now she was in trouble. There was only one way to make that right. And this time, he would brook no refusal.

Chapter Twenty-five

⟨≈⟩

Dear Cousin,
  Move the school? It has taken me years to adapt
this building to my purposes. How could you even
think it? Or perhaps you have another reason
for your appalling suggestion. Perhaps you are
reconsidering our paltry rent. You could gain much
higher rents these days. Perhaps you grow tired of
carrying your "cousin."

              Yours sincerely,
              An outraged Charlotte

"You're awful quiet tonight," Nettie said as she brushed out Lucy's hair.

To Lucy's surprise, Nettie had stepped into the role of lady's maid with aplomb. Grandfather hadn't even guessed she'd ever been anything else. For Lucy, she was also a rock to cling to, and Lord knew she needed one these days.

"You miss Don Diego sumphin' fierce, don't you?" Nettie asked, correctly assessing her mood as usual.

"Of course I miss him." Sometimes she felt as if her heart had been excised from her chest, leaving only the hollow shell of her ribs.

"If you really missed him, you would fight for him," Nettie said.

"How? He has duties, obligations. I can't ask him to put them aside for me."

"You never gave him the choice."

"Because I knew he would do it only to satisfy his honor."

Nettie snorted. "A man don't hang around pining for a woman just for honor."

"Diego would. You don't know him."

"Neither do you, if you think those looks he gives you mean nothing."

Lucy set her lips in a line. "I don't want to talk about this."

Nettie brushed harder. "So you're going to marry that ass of a duke?"

"No! I don't even like him."

"Well, thank God for that. You been going 'round with him so much I thought you were considering it."

"I told you, Grandfather said that if I spent a week with the duke and still didn't like him, I needn't marry him. Indulging his request is the least I could do, considering how much my poor *abuelo* suffered all those years, not knowing where I was." And given how her grandfather had acted about her and Diego, she dared not tell him she was unchaste. He would assume it was Diego, no matter what she said.

"I notice you been dropping that Spanish into your speech more and more," Nettie said. "And you and the *marqués* have got right chummy."

Lucy smiled at Nettie's sour expression in the mirror. "I know you don't like him much. I know you think he should have searched for me sooner, and so do I. But he's my only connection to my real family. And he dotes on me."

It was rather sweet. It reminded her of how Papa had doted on her before he'd married.

She swallowed. She missed Papa, too, in spite of everything. "That's enough hair brushing, Nettie. I'm tired. I believe I'll retire."

"I'll be off to the kitchen then." Nettie grinned. "Your grandfather's handsome cook has been eyeing me for the past three days. Might just see what he's got on his mind."

As she sashayed from the room, Lucy shook her head. The woman really was an incorrigible flirt.

Lucy went to find her sketch pad. Gazing at her drawing of Diego was the only thing that settled her enough to sleep. She'd altered it on the trip to make it a better likeness, and now she wished she'd had him sit for others. But then she'd have had to explain why she wanted them, and that would have meant revealing her feelings.

The door opened behind her, and she shut the sketch pad swiftly, not wanting Nettie to see her pathetic nighttime habit. But when she turned, it wasn't Nettie standing inside her door. It was Diego.

Lucy froze. Good Lord, had she dragged him out of the sketch and into flesh and blood? Or was she simply so obsessed that she imagined him everywhere?

Then he came toward her, and she knew he was real. "Diego! Are you insane? What are you doing here? If my grandfather finds you—"

"I can handle your grandfather." He devoured her with his eyes. Then he seemed to catch himself and turned to scanning the room. "We must leave—now. Rafael says he can be ready to sail at dawn. But we have to escape while the household is still asleep, and the duke hasn't yet discovered that I took his key." He strode to her closet and began tossing clothes into a pile on the bed.

"The duke? His key? You're making no sense." She was torn between throwing her arms around Diego to lock him to her forever and tossing him out before someone caught him here. "What has the duke to do with this?"

He held up a key. "I stole this from the duke. He had a copy made of the key to the house so he could sneak in and 'seduce' you—though I greatly suspect he was not terribly concerned about your opinion in the matter." He paused, his brow knitting. "You didn't want him, did you?"

"Don't be ridiculous."

His face cleared. "That is why I am here. He wants your fortune, and he means to get it at any cost. I mean to prevent him."

"By spiriting me back to England?" she said tartly.

"By marrying you. That will put an end to this nonsense once and for all." He tossed a gown at her. "Now, get dressed."

"What? No! You can't just march in here and announce that you're marrying me!" Even if it did thrill her to her very soul. She tossed down the gown. "Besides, I'm just now getting to know my grandfather. I'm not ready to leave." Nor was she about to get back on a ship when Papa would soon be on his way here, assuming he'd received the letter Nettie had posted.

"You do not understand." He strode up to grab her by the shoulders. "That ass Don Felipe will not stop pursuing you merely because you refuse him—or even because your grandfather does. He will take you by force if he has to."

"But you have his key now."

"And he will have another made. There is only one way to solve this, Lucy. I will marry you. I will not be responsible for your disastrous marriage to that ass."

Once again, he was only considering marriage to her because it offended his sense of honor. "I can take care of this myself."

Anger flared in his face. "Some things a man has to do."

Has to do? Must she always be an obligation to him? "Yes, and my grandfather will be the one to do it. I will tell him—"

"You will tell him nothing!" Diego looked as if he wanted to toss her over his shoulder and carry her off, an intriguing notion, even if rather problematic. "For all I know, he has engineered this!"

"I doubt that."

"I will not risk it."

"Diego—"

"You are coming with me."

"But you have to give me at least a chance to—"

"Damn it, Lucy, I will not watch yet another woman dear to me destroyed because a man takes her by force! Not now that I am old enough to stop it!"

She gaped at him, something Rafael had said about the soldiers in Villafranca niggling at the back of her mind. *They ignored him, bullying Diego and his mother, though Diego says little of that.*

A cold chill raced down her back. "Oh, my Lord. Your mother was the one taken by force."

He blinked, caught off guard by her blunt statement, though he didn't deny it.

"The soldiers—it wasn't just Arboleda they destroyed," she went on, her heart twisting. "They—they hurt your mother, too."

"Yes! And I will not let it happen again!" Then his expression changed, and his hands dug more firmly into her shoulders. "How did you know about the soldiers at Arboleda, Lucy?"

It took her a second to realize how much she'd just revealed. "I . . . I . . ."

"I never told you that." He shook her. "*Dios mio,* how did you know?"

Her breath felt harsh and raw in her throat. "Rafael told me."

Diego thrust her away with a look of shock. "That day in the wardroom?"

"Yes."

"How much did he tell you?" he bit out.

There seemed little point in keeping it from him now. "Everything he knew. What the soldiers did to Arboleda and your father. What you vowed." She blinked back tears. "But he never told me about your mother. He didn't know, did he?"

Diego curled his fingers into fists. "When I get my hands on him—"

"I *asked* him to tell me!" she cried. "*You* should have told me. I would never have tried to seduce you if I'd known any of this about you."

"And that is why you refused me," he said, comprehension dawning. His eyes were dark pools of pain in the candlelight. "Because you did not want to be the cause of my losing Arboleda and breaking my vow to Papá."

"Not just because of that," she said hoarsely. "I knew you would eventually come to resent me for ruining your plans. For making you break your vow." She dropped her gaze from his. "I knew you would only be marrying me to assuage your guilt over taking my innocence. And I couldn't let you do that."

"That was not the only reason I offered marriage," he protested.

"No? I gave you the chance to give me another reason. You didn't."

"Oh, God, I have been such a fool." He caught her in his arms, drawing her close. "I swear to you, I was not just offering marriage to assuage my guilt." Cupping her cheek, he urged her to look at him. "I did not make myself very clear."

"You made yourself clear enough," she whispered. "You were furious about being trapped into marriage."

"No, no—"

"Diego, you said, 'Taking a woman's innocence levies certain obligations on any decent man, and I always honor my obligations.'" She tried to push herself from his arms. "You'd always said you couldn't marry. And I didn't want to be any man's 'obligation.' I still don't."

He flinched but refused to let her out of his embrace. "*Dios mio,* I bungled that proposal even more than I realized, *mi corazón bello.*"

My beautiful heart. Did he *mean* those lovely words? "You spoke your true feelings. I wouldn't have wanted anything else."

"But they were not my true feelings!" When she arched an eyebrow at him, he frowned. "Well, perhaps they were then. I spoke in anger—not at you but at myself. And perhaps you are right—at that moment, I was not eager for marriage."

He clasped her head between his hands. "But I have had time to reconsider, Lucy. Time to realize I cannot go on like this, yearning for you, not having you. Going mad at the idea of you being hurt by some other man."

The way his mother had been. That was the key to understanding him. "Tell me about your mother, Diego. Tell me what happened the day the soldiers came."

As the blood drained from his face, he released her. "Do not ask that of me."

"How can I be your wife if you can't talk to me of the things in your heart? That night on the ship, you asked me not to hide from you. And I didn't—not then, not ever." She caught his hands and lifted them to her lips, kissing each one. "Don't hide from me now, my darling. Please."

His eyes darkened at the word "darling." "*Cariño,* I cannot."

"You can." She drew him to the bed and urged him to sit on it beside her.

"It is an ugly tale."

"Tales of war often are," she said gently. "Tell me."

A shuddering breath wracked him, but then he began to speak in a low voice. "They came at night. Fifteen soldiers, desperate for whatever they could find. When they discovered our wine stores, they went mad, drinking and carousing and filling their bellies with our food. My father did not even attempt to fight. He kept saying, 'They are only hungry and tired, but they are on our side.'"

Diego's voice cracked a little. "He was so sure of it. Until, when they started getting out of hand, my mother cursed them for their destructive ways. That brought her too fully to their notice."

Lucy reached for his hand, and he gripped it so tightly she thought he might break it. "The one who understood Spanish got angry. He forced her into the storeroom, and then he . . . he . . ." He trailed off, his eyes haunted.

Tears welled in Lucy's eyes. So much tragedy for him to endure, and so young. How had her poor love borne this horror inside him all these years?

"Papa could do nothing," he went on in a bleak voice, "because a soldier held a pistol to his head. When I struck out at the others in fury, they laughed, calling me a little Spanish dog and locking me in the root cellar. It shared a wall with the storeroom, so I had to sit there listening while Mamá begged . . ."

Lucy hugged him tightly, tears pouring down her cheeks. He shook violently in her arms, transformed into the boy he must have been, the count's son who'd never witnessed such cruelties until then.

How had he stood it? She couldn't imagine having to witness such an awful thing being done to a person she loved.

She soothed him as best she could, rubbing his back, cradling him close, fighting not to let him see her own weeping. Her poor, dear love. This was at the root of all his honor and dignity, this dark secret that tortured his soul. His mother had lost her dignity and honor, and he'd spent a lifetime trying to reclaim it for her. For his father. For his family. Trying to blot out what had happened.

That was why he held his profession in contempt. He didn't see it as she did—an offering to other people who'd suffered, a way to help them forget the pain. He had a fine gift, but it didn't fit his image of what a gift should be, so he spurned it.

And that was why he always made snide remarks about her countrymen, why he'd never toured England with his conjuring act. With such memories festering inside him, how could he?

How could he ever bear to be married to her when she was English in her heart, even if not in her blood? She held him tighter, the pain of that realization threatening to overwhelm her. How could she ask him to give up so much when she had so little to offer?

Chapter Twenty-six

❧

Dear Charlotte,
*   Have you so little faith in me, after everything*
we have meant to each other the past few years?
Can you really think I would betray you for a few
pounds in rent? You wound me to the heart with
such an accusation. And what do you mean by
putting "cousin" in quotes?

*   Your equally outraged cousin,*
*   Michael*

Slowly, Diego became aware of where he was, of Lucy's arms holding him, her tears dampening his coat. He and his mother had never spoken of that night—not when it had happened and not when she had lain on her deathbed. He had never spoken of it to anyone else, either, not even Gaspar. He had spent half his life trying not to think of it. Until Lucy had forced him to.

And now that he had told her . . . he felt different. The pain was still there, but it felt less of a goad and more like something simply there. Part of him. Always part of him, making him who he was.

"Now I know why you hate the English so much," Lucy said in a small voice against his coat.

That made him start, made him realize something. Lucy was half English! How astonishing that nowhere during his frantic state in the past few hours had that occurred to him. After the duke had made his revelation, Diego had only cared about getting here to her. Saving her. Being with her.

"I do not hate *all* the English." Turning in her embrace, he enfolded her in his arms. "I certainly do not hate you."

"Only because you don't think of me as English, since I have Spanish blood. But Diego, I'm still English in every other way."

"I know, *querida*. And I do not care." He sought her mouth, brushing a kiss to her lips, giddy with the hope that had begun to swell in him. For the first time in his adult life, his virulent hatred of the English was gone. He still despised the soldiers, could never forgive those men for what they had done. But he hated them as he would hate any man with no honor—not as representatives of the entire English nation.

After all, *she* was English, too, and she was all that was good in the world. Later he would tell her of her real past, of her grandfather and her father and the other things that might hurt her.

But first he wanted to hold her and cherish her. He wanted to revel in the woman who would be his forever, the woman who had his heart.

She pushed him gently away, her beautiful eyes clouded by tears. Tears for him, for what he had suffered. The gift of her sympathy humbled him.

Her troubled gaze played over his face. "You say you don't care if I remind you of the English, but you will care later."

"No," he said firmly. "I will not." He knew it with a certainty as solid as Gibraltar. "English or Spanish, I don't care, as long as you are my wife."

Her breath caught. "How can I marry you, if it means watching you lose everything that matters to you—your estate, your future, your hopes?"

"Arboleda is not the only thing that matters to me anymore, Lucy. *You* are the only thing that matters to me. You said not to hide myself from you. Well, here I am, *cariño*. I need you. I cannot do it without you, any of it."

"But Rafael said—"

"To hell with Rafael."

He kissed her, to blot out whatever his well-meaning friend had told her. Now he understood why she had refused him the first time. She had probably been right to do so, given how he had bungled it. But he would be damned if he let her go again.

She tore her mouth from his. "My grandfather—"

"To hell with your grandfather, too." This time his kiss was more heated. Happiness and hope bled into his desire seamlessly as he plundered her mouth, especially when she opened to the kiss as sweetly as a rose opening to the sun. He wanted to touch her, to taste her, to remind himself of everything that was alive and beautiful.

Opening her nightdress, he swept his mouth down to kiss her breast, then suck it and lavish it with all the tender care he possessed. He had to make her understand what she meant to him.

"Oh, Diego . . ." she rasped as she realized what he was about. "This will not solve anything."

He nuzzled her nipple, then pressed a kiss to her other

breast. "It will solve everything." *It will show you that there is nothing to solve. Not now.*

"I don't see . . . how . . ."

She trailed off as he tongued her nipple to a hard little point. In a fever to be with her, he shucked off his coat and unbuttoned his waistcoat.

With a gasp, she closed her hands in his hair. "Good Lord, Diego . . . you mustn't . . . oh . . . my . . . word . . ."

For once, he was grateful for the profession that had taught him how to manage several actions at once. While he kept her focused on his mouth caressing her lovely breasts, he shed his waistcoat and unfastened his trousers and his drawers.

By the time she thought to push him away, it only remained to slip off his trousers and drawers, then drag her astride his lap. Fortunately, she wore no drawers underneath her nightshirt.

"Diego!" she cried as she gazed down at his cock, jutting hard against her bare belly. He could see the fascination on her face, warring with what appeared to be her righteous determination to talk herself out of this. "What do you think you are doing?"

"Trying to seduce you, *querida*." Time to appeal to the hoyden in her, the budding seductress who had tempted him so gloriously on board ship. When she tensed, he grabbed her waist with both hands and settled her more firmly against him. Then he used his cock to strafe her dewy center.

Her lovely eyes slid closed, and she clutched at his shoulders. "That is *very* wicked," she chided, yet she arched her back and gave in to the motion.

Ah, he loved how she responded to his caresses, with passion and eagerness and a sweet, fervent enjoyment. "Yes," he teased, "you only like me when I play the devil."

Her eyes shot open. "That's not true!" she said petulantly, then let out a heartfelt groan as he used his fingers to thumb her where it would rouse her most. "*Dios mio, Diego!*"

He laughed, damned near delirious with the pleasure of making her his. "You sound more Spanish by the day, *mi amor.*" Grinning, he filled his hands with her breasts.

He had not even realized what he had said until she drew back to stare at him in shock. "You called me your love."

His love?

The words rang in his heart. Why had he not accepted it before? Yes, she *was* his love. He loved her. Oh, God, how he loved her! "Is that not what a man calls the woman he loves?"

She swallowed. "You said love is an illusion."

He clasped her face in his hands. "For us, it is real. I love you, Lucy Seton, soon to be Lucy Montalvo."

For a moment, she looked as if she did not believe him. Then her eyes lit up, and a melodic laugh escaped her, transforming her already beautiful features, gilding them with a golden glow. "I love you, too, you wicked Spanish devil. I love you so much, *mi amor!*"

That earned her a heated kiss that had them both breathless by the time they drew apart.

"Then show me what you feel," he whispered. "Make love to me, *mi corazón bello.*"

"Make love to you?" A pretty confusion touched her face. "How?"

"Rise up on your knees, and take me inside you." He thrust against her to show her what he meant.

Though she blushed, her eyes smoldered. "I can do that?"

He chuckled. "Tonight, *mi dulzura,* you can do whatever you wish." He lifted his hands, showing her his palms in a classic magician gesture. "No tricks. I am all yours."

"Careful," she teased as she stripped his shirt from him, then ran her hands over his chest. "You may come to regret that offer."

"I seriously doubt that." But the way she was thumbing his flat nipples gave him pause, especially when she bent to tug one with her teeth, sending his blood into full roar.

She reached down to toy with the crown of his cock. "You were very high-handed with me the last time we made love, you know."

"Was I?" He struggled to remember it, his mind too fogged with his need for her to think.

"You said, 'My way or not at all.'" She ran her fingers over the shaft of his cock, making him shiver. "You said, 'I will pleasure you until you beg for more, even if it takes me all night.'" Still fondling him, she leaned close to whisper, "You said, 'I will taste and touch every part of you—as often as I wish, as thoroughly as I wish.' That is what I mean to do to you now, Diego."

He groaned. She wanted to punish him for waiting so long to tell her how he felt. And in truth, she deserved that and more. He had been such a fool not to appreciate what she had offered him.

"Do as you please with me, *querida,*" he managed. "Only do not take too long."

A vixenish delight lit her face. "Well," she said. "This could be fun."

Those words sealed his doom. For what seemed an eternity, she played with him, fondled him, caressed him, until he thought he might die if he could not be inside her.

Just when he was ready to break his promise and throw her down onto the bed, she lifted herself and came down on his cock with a slow descent that sent him into madness.

"*Dios Santo*, Lucy," he said hoarsely, his hands gripping her shoulders as he thrust up, trying to get her to move. "Please, *querida* . . ."

"Are you begging, Diego?" she whispered, undulating over him.

"Yes," he growled. "Take me, *mi amor*. Now. Before I die."

She uttered a luxurious laugh. "Even when you beg, you're high-handed."

Then she began to move, so deliciously that he caught her waist and held on for dear life. She was a goddess in motion, seductress and angel in one, the only woman he could ever imagine in his life.

He kissed her mouth, her breasts, her throat, reveling in the glory that was Lucy. And when the blood finally rose in her cheeks and the heat surged inside him until he feared he might not last another moment, she shattered atop him so beautifully that he could hold back no more. With one last deep thrust, he spilled himself inside her, uttering a cry of purest joy.

She was his now. His Lucy. For now and forever. And no one, *nothing*, would ever take her from him again.

Lucy didn't know what had awakened her. A noise? Diego's arm across her belly?

She twisted to look at him, glad that the moon was bright enough to illuminate the room through the open balcony doors. The breeze from the harbor cooled the room only slightly, since Spain in early June was quite a bit warmer than England in early June. His hairy chest glistened with perspiration, his black locks clung damply to his forehead, and he'd thrown off most of the sheet, leaving only a swath across his privates.

He was beautiful in his slumber, an orgy of golden skin and leonine muscle, like the painting of Endymion asleep that she'd seen at the duke's house.

And he was all hers.

Her breath caught. Diego loved her. She couldn't believe it. He loved her and meant to marry her, for herself alone and not out of any mere sense of honor. She couldn't even worry about what that might mean to their future. With him beside her, she was sure she could do anything.

A noise came from the balcony, startling her.

"Is someone there?" she whispered.

"Lucy?" called a familiar voice as the sound of boots landing on iron came to her, followed by a great deal of huffing and puffing. "Is that you, girl?"

"Papa!" she cried, and sat up straight in bed. Then she realized she was naked.

Swiftly, she dragged the sheet up around her. Just in time, too, for at that moment Papa appeared in the balcony doorway, still breathing hard.

"How did you get here so soon?" She fumbled under the sheets for her nightdress, praying it was too dark for him to see. "How did you know where to—"

"What is it, *querida?*" Diego mumbled as he roused from sleep.

Good Lord.

Papa cursed as his gaze shot to the bed beside her. "Who the hell is *that?*"

Diego shot up, glowering in the direction of the balcony. "I must ask you the same question, sir," he growled.

Too late, Lucy realized that Diego had never met Papa. "Diego, this is—"

"You bedded her, you damned whoreson?" her father shouted, stomping further into the room. "You kidnapped my daughter, and then you *bedded* her?"

"Papa, it is not what you think!" She found her nightdress at last and dragged it over her head.

"*Hostias,*" Diego muttered, as he, too, scrambled under the covers to find his clothes.

Now presentable enough, she leaped from the bed to prevent her father from launching himself at Diego. "We are going to be married," she said hastily as she grabbed his arm. "At once. Today. As soon as possible."

"Over my dead body!" Papa roared. "Were you his reward for dragging you back to the bloody *marqués?* Is that the devil's bargain he made?"

"No!" she cried. "And who are you to accuse him of anything? You're the one who helped the sergeant and his lover kidnap me. You're the one—"

"Um, Lucy," Diego began as he slid out of the bed, wearing only his drawers.

"You can't tell me you actually believed his lies!" Papa gazed at her with such hurt that it took her aback. Then he whirled on Diego. "And *you,* sir, trumping up some tale, portraying me as a villain just to further her wretched grandfather's plans. You ought to be ashamed of yourself."

"I believed it to be true!" Diego protested. "I did not know that Don Carlos was lying to me. He lied to everyone. How was I to know—"

"You . . . you mean it's not true?" Lucy broke in. She stared at Diego. "Everything you told me about Papa and the nurse is a lie?"

Diego sighed. "As it turns out, *cariño*, Sergeant Crawford really was your father. He married Doña Catalina, your real mother, against your grandfather's wishes. The story about the nurse was a lie."

She stared at Diego, stunned. So she'd been right about Papa's good character all along. He had merely helped two lovers escape a wicked father who didn't want them to be together.

Then something awful occurred to her. "Oh, Lord," she said, casting Diego an accusing glance. "When you came here tonight, you *knew* my grandfather was lying! That's why you sought me out." Her heart twisted. "All that nonsense about the duke and his key? You came because of your blasted honor. You realized you'd been tricked, and you wanted to fix it! It had nothing to do with *me*."

"No!" Diego cried. "I came here for you, *mi amor*, I swear it. You must believe me."

"Believe you?" Papa snarled. "After you lied to her about her own father?" He turned accusing eyes on Lucy. "Though I still can't believe you thought I could condone anyone stealing a child from her parents."

"Why not?" came a new voice from the doorway.

Lucy wanted to scream in frustration as her grandfather hobbled in, his eyes filled with rage. He'd obviously been drawn by the noise, since neither Papa nor Diego was being particularly quiet. Behind him came Nettie, who looked perplexed by the appearance of two men inside Lucy's room.

"You helped that sergeant steal Catalina from *me*," Don Carlos spat. "It might as well have been my granddaughter he stole."

"Ah, so the villain himself has joined the party, has he?" Papa answered.

Lucy instinctively went to Papa's side, but he didn't seem to notice her, his attention narrowed on the *marqués.* "Tom didn't steal Catalina, you ass, and you know it," he bit out. "You pushed her out by setting up that fool marriage to Álvaro. Catalina despised yer choice of a husband. She tried to do what you wanted, but once she found herself carrying my child, she told me she'd rather die than be his wife! *You* were the one who drove her out of here, damn you!"

A sudden silence fell across the room. Don Carlos hunched over his cane, his eyes stark with shock and grief, and Diego looked stunned.

But Lucy barely noticed. *My child.* Her mother had been carrying *Papa's* child? Not the sergeant's?

Suddenly everything fell into place. That was how Papa had known to come to this house. How he had known where to get in. That explained why an unmarried soldier with nothing but a deathbed promise to prompt him would have chosen to take on a little girl! Oh God oh God oh God, she was going to be sick!

"*You're* my father?" she said in an anguished voice. "My *real* father?"

"What?" Papa turned to her, his face blanching as he realized what he'd just revealed. "Lass! Oh, God, lass, I didn't mean for you to learn of it this way."

He reached for her, but she slapped his hand away, her world shifting so entirely on its axis that she didn't know which way was up.

"Apparently, you didn't mean for me to learn of it at all," she choked out. "You meant for me to live my whole life feeling like an orphan, like a woman without any family, like a stranger in my own country."

"Lass, no," he said hoarsely. "I did it for you! Because I loved you. Because I loved your mother."

"Not enough to marry her," she spat.

"You have to understand," he said, his eyes dark with remorse as words tumbled out of him. "I never meant for any of it to happen. I fell in love with Catalina the moment I first saw her at a ball in Gibraltar. I pursued her relentlessly and asked her to marry me. She gave herself to me the night I proposed, but afterward she got scared and refused to marry me, saying she couldn't go against her family." He shot the *marqués* a foul look. "She said her father would be publicly humiliated by the broken betrothal."

He threaded his fingers through his hair. "But when she realized she was carrying you, she couldn't endure her situation any longer. She escaped to the garrison in Gibraltar, meaning to marry me. Only I had caught the fever that swept Gibraltar in 1803. They told her I was going to die. I was unconscious."

His voice hardened as he glared at Don Carlos. "There was no time to waste. Sure that her father would drag her back to marry her forcibly to that bloody Álvaro, she turned to Tom, my best friend, for help. He'd been half in love with her himself, so he offered her marriage to provide a father for her child and protect her from the *marqués*. That way, she wouldn't have to marry a man who might abuse her once he discovered she was bearing another man's bastard."

Tears rolled down his cheeks. "The curse of my life is that I recovered a week later. By then, they were married, and there was naught to be done. I'd lost her, and I couldn't do a damned thing about it."

"Except adopt your daughter." Her heart broke for him. And for herself. "Your own daughter, whom you *lied* to all your life! Why didn't you tell me? After they died—"

"And brand you as a bastard for the rest of your life, the unmarried colonel's illegitimate brat? For all intents and purposes, you had legitimate parents. I thought it best to leave it that way. I made you my daughter in every way acceptable to society."

"But not to me!" she cried. "You could have told me privately. Don't you remember how many times I asked about them, and you would tell me nothing? I wanted a mother so badly, and you wouldn't even tell me about her."

The stricken look on his face tore at her, but she fought to ignore it. "Oh, lass, I was afraid if I told you, you'd go looking for the *marqués*. And when he wrote the regiment last year to ask about you, and they warned me, I—"

"Oh, God!" she cried. "That was why they put him off! How could you?"

"Lass, dearest lass—"

"No. Don't." She backed away from him. "I don't even know you anymore."

"He kept your family from you," the *marqués* cut in, edging closer. "You see, dear girl, he doesn't care about you."

She turned on him with a vengeance. "And you do? You didn't even come looking for me until after your son died and you had no more chance of an heir." How could she have been so blind?

More facts fell into place. "You had to have known my mother lived with the garrison; we were here for four years. She was just there across the border."

"You probably even knew the name of her damned husband when you sent me on my wild-goose chase in England," Diego snapped.

"No!" Don Carlos cried. "I knew she married a soldier but not his name."

When Diego snorted, Papa turned on him. "You have some nerve to question *him,* when you're the one who believed his nonsense and did his bidding. Or did you believe it? You're a famous magician, a master of lies. How do we know you didn't realize it from the first, that you didn't act out of greed?"

That was like throwing pitch on a fire. Diego drew himself up with offended dignity. "I will have you know, sir, that I acted on the purest of motives."

"To gain your property," her grandfather put in with a sneer.

Her father cursed. "*You* only acted to get yerself an heir, you bloody, selfish—"

"Enough!" Lucy shouted. "Enough, all of you! The whole lot of you have been lying and scheming and manipulating my life!" Suddenly, she couldn't bear to look at them. "Out! Get *out!* For once in your misbegotten lives, leave me *be!*"

They stared at her, shocked, then broke into a chorus of protests.

She ran onto the balcony, where Papa had used a grappling hook to attach a rope and climb up, and turned to glare at them. "If all of you don't leave, I will climb down the same way my *father* did, and none of you will ever see me again!"

She simply couldn't take any more! She had to think, had to figure out who she was, what this meant. She had to be alone.

"Lucy, *mi amor*—" Diego began.

"You, too, curse you! Nettie, get them out of here, and lock the doors. Or I swear . . ." She threw one leg over the balcony rail.

"All right, all right, lass, we're going!" her father cried as he backed toward the door. Between him and Diego, they muscled her grandfather from the room. Nettie followed, shooing them along.

Once the room was emptied, Lucy pulled the rope up and went back into the bedroom, closing and latching the balcony doors behind her.

Her eyes caught sight of the bed where she and Diego had made love. The bed where the man she'd considered a saint for adopting her had conceived her with the woman he'd loved but never told her about.

It was all too much.

Dropping to the floor, she wept.

Chapter Twenty-seven

❦

Dear "Cousin,"
    You know perfectly well why I put "cousin" in
quotes. In the past few years, I have sought out
every one of my late husband's relations. None
has your knowledge of society or your financial
capabilities. It is long past time that you admit you
are not my cousin, by marriage or otherwise. As
for being wounded by my accusations, you wound
me far more by continuing to protect your precious
privacy while I am fighting for my very future!

                          Your "relation,"
                          Charlotte

Two hours after Lucy had evicted the men in her life
from her room, she stood in the tiny parlor, staring up at
her mother's portrait.

So much of what she'd learned about her life in the past
two months now took on an entirely different meaning:
Papa's changes in regiment, the legal adoption, the fact
that he'd kept her at his side until the end of the war, so he
could remain close by in Great Britain while he packed her
off to a costly school in London. Had he been worrying
even then that her grandfather might whisk her away?

Not that it mattered. What mattered was he'd lied to her all these years. How could he? Surely he'd seen how desperately she wanted to know about her family. She understood his keeping it from everyone else—even with legitimate parents she'd had trouble fitting in. But to keep it from *her* ...

How could she ever forgive him, even if he *had* only done it to prevent her from falling into Grandfather's hands?

Her grandfather. God rot him, too. She'd fallen for his crocodile tears, been swept up in the long conversations she'd had with him about her mother. She'd been fool enough to believe that her dear *abuelo* was truly glad to have her here, to like her for herself. And after he'd said it was her choice whether to marry the duke, she'd acquitted him of bringing her to Spain just so she could bear his heir.

Hah! His behavior toward her had all been a lie, too. He'd known from the beginning that his daughter had run off with a soldier. He hadn't just discovered it a year ago, as he'd claimed. No, he'd sent Diego after her because his son had died and he needed his precious heir. In that respect, he was exactly the same manipulative, scheming scoundrel who'd ruined her mother's life

And he'd been well on his way to ruining Lucy's, too. He'd certainly packed Diego off swiftly enough, once he thought Diego might destroy his plans to yoke her to Don Felipe.

That brought her to Diego. She'd avoided thinking of him, because his was the most cruel betrayal. *I love you, Lucy Seton, soon to be Lucy Montalvo.* Had he meant it? Or had that been the only way he could force her to marry him? He'd just learned how terribly he'd wronged her by stealing her from her father. It would be so like him to try to fix it by marrying her—to salvage his honor at her expense.

Why else had he not told her what he'd learned when he'd first entered the room? He'd probably feared she wouldn't marry him once she realized he'd been duped by her grandfather. And since he had to make it right, as always, he had to marry her, even if it meant pretending to love her.

She sighed. Could he really not have meant any of that beautiful speech he'd given her? He'd never said things like that to her before. And he'd seemed rather desperate to marry her.

But then, he was always desperate to reclaim his honor. Just as Grandfather was desperate to produce his heir and Papa was equally desperate not to let him, even if it meant hiding the truth from her all her life.

God rot them all! How was she to believe anything they said? How was she supposed to know if she even mattered to them when they lied to her at every turn?

She gazed up into the face of the mother she had barely known. "They're all scoundrels, every single one of them. You were better off without them. Perhaps *I'm* better off without them."

"You don't really believe that, do you, miss?" asked Nettie, coming up to stand beside her.

Nettie was the only one she could trust. Look at how patiently she'd waited through Lucy's fit of weeping and her brooding. "I don't know, Nettie. I don't know anything anymore."

A knock came at the door, and Nettie headed toward it.

"I don't want to see any of them," Lucy called after her. "Don't you dare let a single one of those men in here!"

"As you wish, miss." The door opened, a few soft words were spoken, and then Nettie returned.

A female voice said, "I came as soon as your father summoned me from the ship."

Lucy whirled to see Lady Kerr standing there with Nettie.

"Since it wasn't one of the men, I thought you might like a friendly face," Nettie said.

Torn between pleasure at having another woman to talk to and wariness of Lady Kerr's purpose, Lucy stared at her stepmother. "Did you know about Papa all along?" She had to be sure whether Lady Kerr was friend or foe in this.

"About Hugh being your real father?" Her stepmother shook her head. "Not until the day we left for England to come after you."

That was all Lucy needed to hear. Lady Kerr opened her arms, and Lucy rushed into them, her tears spilling over again. Her stepmother held her close, soothing her, gentling her, crooning softly to her until Lucy could regain her calm.

"How could he lie to me?" Lucy whispered as she dashed tears from her aching eyes. "To both of us?"

"He thought he was doing the right thing." When Lucy frowned, Lady Kerr added, "He was being an idiot, of course. But men can be astonishingly blind when it comes to their women."

Lucy didn't know what surprised her more, that Lady Kerr had called Papa an idiot or that she'd taken Lucy's side. "How can you forgive him for hiding such a monumental secret from you?"

Lady Kerr smiled sadly. "I love him. It's either forgive him or cut him out of my life, and I can't bear to do the latter."

"That's what I ought to do," Lucy said petulantly. "I ought to cut them all out of my life, the lying, scheming scoundrels."

"Yes, sweetheart, they are that. But I think in their own twisted minds, they thought they were doing what was right for you."

"So they're lying, scheming, *arrogant* scoundrels."

"That, too. And yet I do think they love you."

Lucy snorted. "They have a funny way of showing it." She stared at Lady Kerr. "Do you know everything? How I came to be in Spain?"

Lady Kerr nodded. "Aside from the information we got from Gaspar, as soon as I arrived here, your father, the count, and your grandfather filled me in on what had happened since you left England." She smiled grimly. "Well, as best as they *could* fill me in, between all the squabbling."

Remembering how she'd been dressed when her father invaded her bedchamber last night, Lucy blushed. "Did Papa tell you where I was and what . . . that is . . ."

"Yes. I know you were with your young man. As it happens, the count . . . well, he's still in his drawers, since no one has thought to offer him any other clothes, and his are apparently up here. So when I arrived, his lack of appropriate dress necessitated an explanation about how he came to be that way."

Mortified beyond belief, Lucy dropped onto the nearby settee and hid her face. "You must think me a horrible wanton."

"Of course not, sweetheart." Lady Kerr came to sit beside her on the settee. "But you did *choose* to share his bed, didn't you?"

Lucy's gaze shot to her stepmother, her heart constricting to see the worry in her eyes. For the first time since Lady Kerr had entered, she noticed the pale cast to her face, the anxious lines about her mouth.

Her stepmother had worried over her? That was so sweet it made her want to cry again. "Yes, I chose to share his bed. I thought . . . we were going to marry."

"And you thought you were in love with him."

Lucy nodded. No point in telling her about the first time she'd shared Diego's bed. That would definitely make her sound like a wanton.

"Well, then, your behavior is understandable. People in love don't always behave rationally." She rubbed Lucy's back. "Do you still think yourself in love with him?"

She hesitated, then sighed. "Yes, but I'm not sure I can trust that he's really in love with *me*."

"If I had to judge from his behavior downstairs, I'd say that he is. He's ready to throttle your father and your grandfather both, just for hurting you."

"My feelings go beyond throttling. Right now, I want to murder them both!"

"While I imagine that would be briefly satisfying, it's rather too permanent a decision to make when you're upset, don't you think?"

The dry comment startled a laugh out of Lucy. "Yes, and it might get me hanged. There's that, too."

They both laughed. Then Lucy remembered why she wanted to murder them, and her amusement vanished.

"If it's any consolation," Lady Kerr said, "your father said he'd intended to tell us both the truth once you married." She took Lucy's hands. "He said that with your open and generous nature, he was afraid if he told you, you would reveal it to whoever offered for you, and the man might spurn you for it. But after you married, it would be too late, and there would be no danger of the truth ruining your future."

"That's absurd," Lucy snapped.

"Think of whom you've been in love with for the past few years, sweetheart. You had your heart set on Peter Burnes, and if you had told *him* . . ."

"Oh." She stared down at her hands. "I suppose that much is true. Not only would he have spurned me, but he probably would have spread the gossip far and wide. Although Papa needn't have bothered to protect me from Peter—even my false lineage wasn't good enough for him."

"Well, I'll admit we are both grateful that he's gone from your life. Your father never did like him. But he was willing to put that dislike aside for you."

She caught her breath. "And will he do the same for Diego? That is, if . . . well . . . assuming things work out?"

"You'll have to ask your father about that yourself, I'm afraid."

Even the thought of speaking to Papa made her throat close up. "I still don't understand why he never told me the truth. Why he couldn't see how much it would have meant to me. And I don't know if Grandfather meant anything he said to me, or if he just wants his heir. And I'm not even sure if Diego is marrying me because he truly loves me or if he just feels guilty because he believed Grandfather's lies and ruined my life as a result."

"Perhaps you should ask them."

"Why? I can't trust them to tell me how they really feel. They'll say anything to get what they want from me, whatever that is."

"Yes, clearly they are idiots, the lot of them. But they're downstairs driving each other to distraction with worry over you, and I don't think they mean to leave anytime soon." Her stepmother squeezed her hand. "You'll have to deal with them eventually. You can't very well stay up here the rest of your life, can you?"

"I suppose not. But right now I can't even face them."

Lady Kerr was silent a long moment. Then she put her arm around Lucy's shoulders. "What if I told you that I have a way to help you get your answers without having to ask directly? Generally, when your father—or any man—is pushed to the wall, you can get the truth out of him. And I think I know how to manage that. Would you be willing to try it?"

Lucy stared at the woman who, despite her many strictures, had never lied to her, had never withheld the truth from her, and had been as much of a mother to her as any woman other than Mrs. Harris could be.

She broke into a tremulous smile. "Yes. I cannot go on like this."

A look of concern passed over Lady Kerr's face. "Be careful, sweetheart. You may not like what you hear. Are you prepared for that?"

Lucy glanced up at the portrait of her mother, a woman who'd been made utterly wretched when she'd spent too long bowing to what her family wanted before fighting for what was important to her.

Lucy refused to do that. Turning back to Lady Kerr, she nodded. "I think I can handle it."

"Very well. Here's what I suggest we do . . ."

Diego paced the courtyard in a frenzy. His two companions were thankfully no longer speaking, after spending the past two hours accusing each other of everything from bad manners to bad fathering.

Diego had spent those two hours accusing himself. He should have told Lucy immediately what he'd learned about her father. He should never have tried to manipulate the situation to his advantage. *Dios mio,* if he could only go back and do it all over, he would do it differently.

It was bad enough that he'd bungled every aspect of this affair, but every other man around her had done the same. What a shock it must have been for her to learn that the man she'd clearly adored had kept such an appalling secret from her.

The devil of it was, now that Diego saw how deceptive the *marqués* could be, he understood the colonel's reasoning. Or partly understood it, anyway. The man had wanted to protect Lucy.

So had Diego.

Oddly enough, Gaspar's words to him the last time they'd spoken came to mind: *Did you ever ask me what I wanted?*

Diego sighed. He should have asked Lucy what she wanted, what she needed. Then he wouldn't be standing down here wishing he was up there with her, praying that he hadn't spoiled the best thing that had ever happened to him.

The door above them opened, and, as one, the three men glanced up at the gallery. But it was only Nettie. And she was alone.

She came down the stairs and hurried past them without stopping. The three of them rushed after her.

"Is my wife still up there with Lucy?" the colonel asked. It was an inane question, since they hadn't left their spot below the door since Lucy had thrown them out. Of *course* she was still up there. Where would she go?

"Is Lucy all right?" Diego asked.

The *marqués* couldn't keep up with the other two men, but he called out, "*Carajo,* girl, stop and tell us what's going on!"

Nettie just kept heading down the gallery. "Lady Kerr called for some tea and sumpthin' for them to eat. I'm fetching it."

"Tea?" the colonel said. He glanced at Diego. "That's a good sign, isn't it?"

Diego winced, remembering what Lucy had done with a teacup the last time she'd been furious at him.

The three of them followed Nettie into the kitchen, hoping to glean more information, but she remained stoic as a stone throughout her errand. She told them nothing, answered nothing, and made Diego curse Gaspar yet again for hiring the damned woman in the first place.

They kept trying to get information out of her as they followed her back to the courtyard—only to be arrested by the sight of Lady Kerr standing in the middle.

"Maggie!" The colonel hurried up to her. "Where's Lucy? How is she?"

"Lucy's fine," Lady Kerr said primly. "She's in the carriage headed to the ship."

They all looked at each other, perplexed.

Diego was the first to figure it out. Nettie had been a diversion to get them away so Lady Kerr could sneak Lucy out. *Hostias!* He was a magician, for God's sake. He ought to be able to recognize a disappearing act when it hit him in the face.

She was leaving. And without him? *Dios no lo quiera!* How could he bear it?

"*Our* ship?" the colonel asked, his voice pitifully hopeful. "She's going home with us?"

"She's going home with *me*," Lady Kerr said. "I'm afraid she's none too happy with you right now, Hugh. We both think it best that you return to England separately from her."

"The hell I will!" he roared. When Lady Kerr raised an eyebrow at him, he scowled. "All right, so I shouldn't have kept the truth from her. It seemed best at the beginning, when she was young and wouldn't know to keep quiet about it. Then, as the years went on, it got harder to tell her. I knew she'd hate me, and I couldn't stand that! I kept putting it off." He set his shoulders stubbornly. "I shouldn't have done that, but I did, and I can't do aught about it now, except make sure that she understands why I did it."

He glared at his wife. "And I'll be damned if I'll watch her sail off to England, nursing her anger at me, just because you and she think that's a grand idea. I'm going after her!"

He turned for the door, only to be blocked by the *marqués*. "You're not going without me," the old man commanded. "She's my granddaughter. I have just as much right to her as you."

"Why, so you can put her out to breed your heir?" Colonel Seton snapped.

"I don't care about my heir, you overgrown Englishman!" Don Carlos shot back. "I'll admit I made a mistake with Catalina. I should have listened to her, should have realized how unhappy she was. I should never have abandoned her. I have paid for that mistake my whole life!"

He clutched his cane as if it were a lifeline. "First, we found out about her death, and no one would tell us what had happened to her girl. It was hard to find out anything during those years. I thought maybe they'd died together, and I tried to forget about her. I kept thinking my son would give me a child I could dote on—not just an heir but a little girl like my Catalina." His face hardened. "Only he didn't. And when he died, and my wife died, I realized—"

"That you needed an heir," the colonel growled.

"Yes, that is true," Don Carlos admitted. "That is why I sent Don Diego after her." His rheumy eyes filled with tears. "But then she arrived, and she was the very picture of her mother—"

"Aye, she is that," Colonel Seton said softly.

"And all I wanted was to have her with me." Fierceness lit his face. "I have no one—don't you understand? No one to ease me into the next life, to be with me in my final days." He pointed his cane at Lady Kerr. "You at least have *her*. And now you'll have Lucy, too, and I'll die all alone . . ." He began to cry.

Diego was unmoved. "What about the duke? You were willing to marry her off to him against her will, just as you tried to marry her mother off."

"No!" the *marqués* protested. "Ask her yourself. I told her if she didn't take to him after a week in his company,

I'd send him packing. I meant that. I only wanted a good husband for her, someone worthy to marry the granddaughter of a *marqués*." He narrowed his eyes at Diego. "Not some jester with a run-down estate who barely holds a claim to a title."

"Ah, yes, the estate he kidnapped her to gain." The colonel fixed a malevolent gaze on Diego. "That's one thing we agree on, Don Carlos. He doesn't deserve to have her. He's naught but a lying, scheming devil."

"At least I know what an ass I've been," Diego said quietly. "That woman is the best thing that ever happened to any of us, and all you can think about is who deserves to have her. *None* of us deserves to have her, damn it! And she is not a possession. She has feelings, thoughts and dreams of her own."

He glared at them both. "We trampled over those for our own selfish purposes, and she has every right to tell us to go to hell. I do not blame her in the least for wanting to be well away from us, after what she has been through. So if she says she needs time away to think matters through, then by God she will get it—even if I have to tie you both down to make sure of it!"

With his heart in his throat, he clenched his fists at his sides. "I may love her beyond reason, but I know better than to think I deserve her. If I am ever fortunate enough to have her speaking to me again, to have her willing to accept my suit, I will drop to my knees and thank God for it!"

"Do you mean that?" said a soft voice behind him.

Diego whirled to find Lucy emerging from behind a pillar. For a moment, he could only gape at her, a torrent of emotions swelling in his chest.

She was the most beautiful sight he had ever beheld, even with her eyes swollen from tears and her cheeks pale.

"Did you mean it?" she repeated with a hesitant smile.

His heart constricted at the sight. "Every word, *mi amor*," he said hoarsely.

As she approached, he dropped to his knees and took her hand, kissing it with all the love in his heart. "Forgive me for not telling you right away what I learned from the duke about your father. All I could think was that I had to get to you, had to save you from him by marrying you."

Her hand tensed in his, but he didn't let go. "I told myself it was the least I could do after I had wronged you by believing your grandfather's lies. I told myself you might not agree to marry me if you knew how I had wronged you." He held her sweet hand against his cheek. "But the truth is, by then I would have sold my soul to make you mine. I finally realized I could not bear a life without you."

He lifted his gaze to her. "I will do whatever I must to have you in my life, *querida*. I will continue touring, sell Arboleda, restore it, move to England and work for Philip Astley, whatever you wish. Tell me what you want, and it's yours."

Her eyes filled with fresh tears. "I only want one thing," she whispered, and dropped to her knees in front of him. "I want *you*. None of the rest of it matters."

With a glad cry, he caught her to him, kissing her mouth, her cheeks, her hair. Laughing, she kissed him back so sweetly that he thought he might die of joy. For a moment, they were the only people in the courtyard, the only people in the world, kissing and murmuring endearments and rejoicing in each other.

That ended when something hard was thrust into his back. Startled, he turned to see her grandfather stabbing at him with his cane. Don Carlos was glowering, with the colonel standing right beside him doing the same.

Brought painfully back to the present, he and Lucy scrambled to their feet to face the two men. Diego put his arm instinctively about her waist.

"I can destroy you for this, you know, Don Diego," her grandfather growled. "And if you think you'll see a penny of her inheritance—"

"I don't care about her inheritance," Diego shot back. "She's all I want."

It was true. Somewhere in the midst of this tempestuous night, he had lost the driving need to restore his family's estate. If he and Lucy could manage it, then he would do it, but he now realized that Gaspar had been right. Fulfilling his impossible vow to his father would never wipe out what the English had done. It would never assuage his pain. Only Lucy could do that.

"What if I threaten to have you arrested for kidnapping?" the colonel asked.

Diego blinked at him.

"Oh, yes," Colonel Seton went on, his eyes unreadable. "I know my daughter didn't come here by choice. Your man Gaspar told me the truth. You drugged her to carry her off. I could have you hanged for that."

"You'll look a fool if you try it, Papa." Lucy clutched Diego tightly. "Because I'll be standing right next to him, swearing I came of my own free will." She frowned at her grandfather. "And I should think by now, *Abuelo*, you've learned your lesson about interfering in affairs of the heart."

Lucy glanced over at Lady Kerr. "You were right. I didn't like everything I heard." She gazed up at Diego with a soft smile. "Except for what *you* said, *mi amor.*" She kissed him, and he responded instantly, even though he suspected she did it only to provoke her idiot father and grandfather.

After prolonging the kiss long enough to have the other two grumbling under their breaths, she broke it, winked at Diego, then frowned as she faced her father and grandfather once more.

"Fortunately, I heard enough to tell me that while you're a pair of bull-headed fools, you do seem to care about me. And I can probably learn to forgive what I heard that I *didn't* like. As long as you meet my conditions."

The two men exchanged wary glances.

"Grandfather," she went on, "Diego is my choice for a husband. If you truly want to have me in your life, then you'll have to honor my choice. There will be no negotiation on that point. Do you agree to my condition?"

Her grandfather gazed at her, hope rising in his face. "You would stay in Spain then? Be a comfort to your old *abuelo?*"

She glanced up at Diego.

"I told you, *cariño,* whatever you wish," he said.

With a brilliant smile, she returned her gaze to Don Carlos. "I can't answer that yet. My husband is so talented, he could do absolutely anything he pleases, so we'll have to decide what's best for us both." Pride shone in her face. "But I'm sure we can visit here from time to time. I will be at your side when I can."

"Then I am content," the old man said, wiping away tears.

"As for you, Papa," Lucy said, "if you want me to forgive you for keeping the truth from me so long, you'll have to accept Diego as my husband. And agree at least to be civil to Grandfather. Can you do that?"

Colonel Seton scowled, his gaze shifting to Diego, then to Don Carlos.

"Hugh?" Lady Kerr demanded.

"I'm thinking, I'm thinking!" His gaze fell on Lucy, and a softness entered his eyes. "Oh, very well. As long as the bloody scoundrel doesn't keep you over here in Spain all the time."

"Very good." Lady Kerr beamed at her husband, then at Lucy and Diego. She headed over to kiss both their cheeks. "I'm so happy for you."

Casting Lady Kerr a smile, Lucy squeezed Diego's waist. "I've caught myself quite a fine husband, haven't I, Mother?"

For a moment, Lady Kerr looked stunned. Then tears welled in her eyes, and a glorious smile curved her lips. "Yes, sweetheart, you certainly have." She dropped her gaze to Diego's bare chest, and her eyebrows shot high. "Though I do think it long past time that he don more appropriate attire. It simply is not dignified for a count to go about in his drawers."

Lucy burst into laughter. As Diego frowned at her, she teased, "Given your gift for sleight of hand, I would have thought you'd have palmed the key to my bedchamber on the way out the door."

With an arch smile, he held out his hand. "I *did*."

She looked at the key, then at Nettie. "You said you locked the door!"

Nettie winced. "Weren't no key in the lock when I went to do it, miss. And I didn't think you'd be too happy to hear that at the time."

Lucy turned back to Diego with widening eyes. "You mean you could have gone in anytime and just carried me out if you'd wanted?"

"*If* I had wanted. But I figured you'd had enough of being carried off against your will. I decided to let something other than my head dictate my behavior for a change."

"Oh?" she said, taking his hands in hers. "And what was that?"

"My heart."

And as she beamed up at him, he realized what he should have known from the first. A man could never go astray if he followed his heart.

Epilogue

∞

Dear Charlotte,

    *Then perhaps it is time I remove myself from
your life. I have only ever asked one thing of you—
that you accept my condition of anonymity. If you
cannot grant me that, I fear there is no hope for us
continuing our correspondence.*

        Yours sincerely,
        Michael

*L*ater that year, Lucy watched from across the drawing
room of the Seton town house in London as her husband
made a card disappear from Lord Stoneville's hand. She
smiled. Diego would be doing a charity performance for
the Newgate Children's Fund at the Athenaeum Theater in
two hours, yet here he was entertaining guests at the reception her parents had thrown for them. He never could stay
still.

He fanned out the cards, caught her watching him, and
winked. There came that quiver in her belly again. Five
months married, yet he could still turn her into mush with
just a wink.

"Do you know how he does it?" murmured a familiar
voice beside her.

"Mrs. Harris!" she cried as she turned to greet her old friend and schoolmistress. "I thought you didn't expect to make it for the reception."

"And miss seeing you?" She kissed Lucy's cheek. "Never, my dear."

"How have you been?" Lucy asked.

Mrs. Harris flashed her a wan smile. "As well as can be expected."

She didn't look particularly well; her features were pale, her eyes sad. She'd been enduring the scandal of Lady Kirkwood's suicide ever since Lucy's abduction, as even more information came out about Silly Sarah's indiscretions.

Her death had gone hard for the school. Mrs. Harris's lesser competitors had dredged up older scandals of past elopements, along with Lucy's. People were saying Mrs. Harris could no longer be trusted to control her girls. Never mind that the elopements had resulted in happy marriages; society cared nothing about *that*.

And there were other problems. "Is it true that Mr. Pritchard has found a buyer for Rockhurst?" Lucy asked.

Mrs. Harris sighed. "I know as little about it as you do, I'm afraid. Right now, it's all rumors."

"What does Cousin Michael say?"

A frown touched the pretty widow's brow. "Nothing. We quarreled and are no longer corresponding."

"Oh, I'm so sorry. Not over me and Diego, I hope. I know you blame Cousin Michael for pressing you into letting me meet with Diego that day."

"That had nothing to do with it, dear. We fought over something else." She changed the subject. "But your husband's lovely performances on behalf of our charities are sure to counteract any bad press. It's very good of him."

"He's happy to do it. He enjoys what he does."

Astonishingly, that had become true. He'd begun to recognize how amazing it was to be able to entertain people so effortlessly. Though this would be his one and only tour of England, he'd clearly been having fun.

"So, *do* you know how his tricks work?" Mrs. Harris asked again.

"Are you mad?" Diego answered from behind her. He strolled up to gaze at Lucy with eyes gleaming. "Have you not noticed that my wife's tongue often runs away with her? The whole world would know how I do my tricks if I told *her*."

"That is not true!" Lucy protested, though it was.

"Fortunately," he went on, "I shall soon be curtailing my performing quite a bit. Then my tricks will not have to be such a state secret."

"You are planning to run Arboleda full-time?" Mrs. Harris asked.

Lucy laughed.

"It's not funny, *cariño*." But the corners of Diego's mouth were twitching.

"Oh, I believe it's quite amusing." Lucy leaned toward Mrs. Harris. "It took my husband only one long month in the remote mountains of León to realize that running a vineyard, far from any society, wasn't for him. You should have seen his expression when he learned that his favorite brandy could not be had within a day's ride, for love or money."

Diego sighed. "Nor my favorite newspaper, coffee, cigarillos . . ."

With a grin, Lucy tucked her hand into the crook of his arm. "Who could have guessed he was so particular about his creature comforts? And so grumpy without them, too."

"That is not why I sold the place," Diego protested. "I did not want you to give birth out there, with only an old midwife of dubious credentials to attend you."

"I know, darling, I know." She cast Mrs. Harris a sober glance. "I'm afraid Villafranca isn't fully recovered from the damage the British and French inflicted fifteen years ago. Raising a child there would be difficult, to say the least."

"You're expecting a child?" Mrs. Harris asked.

Lucy glanced at Diego, who beamed at her with adoring pride. "Yes. Sometime next spring."

"Congratulations, my dear!" Mrs. Harris said warmly. Then she looked perplexed. "But if I may be so bold as to ask, with your husband performing less and Arboleda sold, how do you intend to live?"

As Diego burst into laughter, Lucy explained. "Diego has bought a pleasure garden in Cádiz with the money he got from the sale of Arboleda."

"A pleasure garden!" Mrs. Harris exclaimed. "You're bamming me!"

"It's a joint venture with my grandfather, of all people," Lucy said. "It keeps us close to him while he's ailing, and we anticipate its being quite a success."

"And if it's not, we'll come back here and move in with you at the school," Diego quipped. "Have you any positions for teachers of the conjuring arts?"

"I somehow think that's not a skill for young ladies," Mrs. Harris said dryly.

"Oh, I don't know," Lucy said. "It might be useful to know how to make an unwanted suitor disappear."

"Unfortunately," Diego put in, "at this moment *I* must disappear. Gaspar awaits me at the theater, *mi dulzura*."

Gaspar was married to his cook now, and he and Diego

had repaired the rift in their friendship. Thank God. The more Lucy knew the man, the more she realized how he'd become a father to Diego over the years.

"You can come with me if you like," Diego told Lucy, "unless you'd rather stay here."

"And miss my chance to see how you do your tricks? Not on your life!"

They said their good-byes to her parents, who were planning to attend the performance later. Though Papa had reluctantly resigned himself to having a conjurer for a son-in-law, he'd been noticeably more friendly since he'd learned he was to be a grandfather.

As soon as they were in the carriage and off, Diego drew her into his arms and kissed her until her toes tingled. When at last he pulled back, his eyes were smoldering. "I am so glad you decided not to stay."

"Oh?" she teased. "I thought you didn't like me hanging about when you're preparing for a performance."

"That depends on the theater." He closed the curtains. "And on the performance." Drawing down the shoulder of her gown, he pressed a kiss to the upper swell of her breast. "And most definitely, it depends on the audience."

She knew her husband's appetites only too well. She reached for the buttons of his trousers. "So it's to be *that* kind of performance, is it?"

"If madam approves." He moaned as she swept her hand along his already stiffening "tallywhacker."

"Madam most definitely approves. As long as you don't rip anything. Nettie gave me quite a lecture the last time we had a . . . performance in the carriage."

"Nettie has turned into a prude since she became lady's

maid to a *condesa*." He drew up her skirts with a devilish smile.

"And I have turned into a hot-blooded hoyden." Her blood was already hot, and her heart racing with anticipation.

"No, *mi amor*. You are every inch a *condesa*." He grinned. "Except in the bedchamber."

"And the carriage," she added.

Then she showed him exactly how much of a hot-blooded hoyden she could be.

Author's Note

❧

Thanks to Bernard Cornwell's Richard Sharpe series, I have a fascination for the Peninsular Wars, with all their drama and pain. Everything that happened at Villafranca is true, except for the rape, which I took from similar incidents with the British army at Badajoz. The French were even more brutal, and the Spanish retaliated with equal brutality, so no one came out of that war entirely pristine, which makes for plenty of fodder for personal tragedy and triumph.

To create Diego's conjuring persona, I used Giuseppe Pinetti, a very popular eighteenth-century Italian magician. He extinguished and ignited candles with a pistol shot, he made eggs dance down a cane and cards dance in a closed glass container, and he removed a man's shirt without removing his coat. But more than his tricks, Pinetti was known for his panache onstage. So I put him in my magic hat, added a touch of David Copperfield, a dollop of Philip Astley (who invented the bullet catch), and the looks of actor Rodrigo Santoro, covered the whole thing with a handkerchief . . . and abracadabra! A guy Lucy could fall madly in love with jumped out.

Pocket Books
proudly presents a sneak tease into

Wed Him Before You Bed Him

The final novel in Sabrina Jeffries's
New York Times bestselling
School for Heiresses series

Available July 2009 from Pocket Books

Next month, the book everyone has been waiting for arrives—the romance between Charlotte Harris and the mysterious Cousin Michael. The question is, who is Michael?

Is he Charlotte's supposedly dead husband, Jimmy Harris, who ruined her life by dying and leaving her destitute? Was his death only a cover for something more sinister, forcing him to woo his wife from afar by making amends anonymously?

Or could Michael be the enigmatic Marquess of Stoneville, whose rakish enjoyment of anything in skirts might mask a deeper need for the one woman he can't have? If anyone could pull off a secret second life, it's the dashing marquess.

It might be the beleaguered Viscount Kirkwood, now conveniently unattached and ready to find happiness with a woman more deserving of him. Could something in his past have provoked him into creating a second identity with Charlotte?

Or perhaps it's the stalwart friend, Charles Godwin, owner of a radical newspaper that affords him an intimate knowledge of society's secrets. Has he been watching out for Charlotte in secret as well, sure that marriage is impossible between them?

You'll find out next month!

P9-DHM-850

Other books by Maylan Schurch:

Justin Case Adventures:
1. *The Case of the Stolen Red Mary*
2. *The Desert Temple Mystery*

The Rapture
Rescue From Beyond Orion

To order, call 1-800-765-6955.
Visit us at www.reviewandherald.com for information on other Review and Herald products.

REVIEW AND HERALD® PUBLISHING ASSOCIATION
HAGERSTOWN, MD 21740

Copyright © 2001 by
Review and Herald® Publishing Association
All rights reserved

The author assumes full responsibility for the accuracy
of all facts and quotations as cited in this book.

This book was
Edited by Randy Fishell
Designed by Tina Ivany
Cover art by Del Thompson/Thompson Brothers
Electronic makeup by Shirley M. Bolivar
Typeset: 10.5/14 Cheltenham

PRINTED IN U.S.A.

05 04 03 02 01   5 4 3 2 1

R&H Cataloging Service
Schurch, Maylan Henry, 1950-
      Beware of the crystal dragon.

      I. Title.

                    813.6

ISBN 0-8280-1610-0

This book is dedicated to the memory of

Vee Kuriger,

whose honest study of the Bible cut through
years of mystical confusion
to the heart of a really lovable God.

Contents

Chapter 1
Dangerous Spiral

"No."

"Dad, it's just—"

"No."

"—$39.95! Just—"

"No."

Justin paused. Dad's no had slapped right up against the sunny brown bricks of Seattle's seven-story Campobello Hotel and echoed firmly back. Still, Justin sighed and decided to make one more try.

"Dad, it's a *hunting* knife."

"With a five-inch blade."

"A hunting knife has *got* to have a long blade."

"So you're going hunting, is that it?"

"Dad—"

"Put a bookmark in it, guys," said the serene voice of Justin's mother, Tovah Case. "We've got to check in. Robert, the keynote address is in an hour. You're sitting at the head table, remember."

Dad glanced at his watch, uttered a startled "Yoy!", hoisted two heavy suitcases onto a cart pulled by a bellboy, and hurried toward the glossy wood-paneled doors of the Campobello's entrance.

Mom followed him. "Come on, kids."

"What gets me," Justin said in a low voice to

his friend Monique Walters (who was almost 13, within a few months of Justin's age), "is that *Dad* had a hunting knife like the one in the store window when he was a kid. He still keeps it in his desk drawer. But will he let *me* get one?"

"Of course not," said Monique.

"What do you mean, 'Of course not'?"

"For one thing, you wouldn't have any room for it in your belt pack."

Justin glanced down at the square black nylon pack on his belt. "Yes, I would. In this back zip-pocket."

"And also, my mom and dad are dentists, right?"

"What's that got to do with it?"

"They didn't feed me candy when I was a kid. They knew it could mess up my teeth."

"So?"

"So *your* dad used to be a police detective. And maybe he's seen too many punctured people. He knows a knife could get you messed up. Wow," she said, squinting upward into the sunshine. "What a cool old hotel. It's almost like a palace. See those arches and towers way up there? And the flags?"

The Campobello Hotel was built like a giant seven-story capital L lying on its side. In the inner corner of the L was the entrance, covered with a long green awning with white stripes so that if it was raining, cars could drive under it to let off hotel guests. Justin let his eyes sweep up the corner to the very top, where a tiny balcony hung out from the side of the wall, with an iron railing around its edge.

He frowned up at the bars of the railing. "It looks like a prison."

"It does *not* look like a prison," Monique objected. "It's like one of those romantic old English castles."

"And we've gotta stay in this prison," Justin continued, "all because Dad tried to make this writers' convention a family vacation."

"Hey," Monique countered. "You're lucky your dad takes you on vacations like this. And *I'm* lucky your folks brought me along."

"When are your mom and dad getting back from Africa?"

"Next week, probably. That's when another dentist is coming to take their place at the clinic."

"Well," Justin sighed, "I just hope we can find something to do around here."

As it turned out, activity would hardly be a problem.

"See?" Monique said as they entered the elegant lobby, crowded with people. "The Campobello is a *palace.*"

Justin didn't say it out loud, but he had to admit she was right. In the center of the crowded lobby a giant spiral staircase with stone steps curved grandly up to the second floor. A gigantic, brilliant chandelier hung from the high ceiling above it. Just beyond the foot of the staircase was a wide doorway. Through it he could see a large circular room with lamps and paintings on the wall, and soft chairs and couches around tables. Everything was brown and leathery and gold-edged and elegant. And old.

"Justin, look. Your dad's picture!"

Justin glanced around. Monique was pointing at a large slick brochure that had been unfolded and tacked to an easel near the door they'd just come through.

"'Robert Case,'" she read aloud, "'formerly a metropolitan police detective and now a freelance journalist, speaks on "Reporting and Writing on Crime."'"

Justin snorted. "That's an old photo. Mom calls it Dad's cuddly-writer picture." He scanned the rest of the brochure, then blinked. "Who's *this?*"

"Wow." Monique stared at the large color photo of a very blonde woman with large diamond earrings. The woman was smiling. Her eyes were closed and her lips were puckered humorously, as if she was going to kiss the object that she held in her hand: a little crouching dragon about three inches long. It looked as though it was carved out of glass or diamond.

This time Justin did the reading out loud. "'Angelica Fawkes, Sunday night's keynote speaker, has authored six best-selling books on New Age topics with the aid of Belisarius, her crystal "dragon guide." During the week she'll teach a class on writing with the aid of crystals and other channeling methods.'"

Suddenly Justin felt a motherly hand squeeze his shoulder.

"What, Mom?"

"No wisecracks," she said softly in his ear.

Justin snorted again. "But Mom, her dragon talks to her?"

"Justin." The squeeze tightened.

"But crystal dragons don't talk!"

"We don't have to agree with her, Justin, but we need to be respectful."

He shook her off. "OK, OK."

And that was the exact moment when everybody in the Campobello's lobby heard the horrifying sound of bone hitting stone.

Thump. Thlopp. Thumpity-bumpity-bump.

Justin and Monique whirled and stared at the staircase.

Halfway up, a boy lay sprawled on the steps head down. As Justin stared at him wide-eyed, two other things happened. There was a woody-metal whacking sound, and something bounced twice on the lobby floor. It was a white-handled sponge mop with a metal squeezer.

"Call 911!" Dad's voice barked above the gasps of the guests.

"Yes, sir," gulped the desk clerk, who picked up a phone and began dialing. "There's a hospital two blocks away," the clerk said.

Dad bounded up the stairs and bent over the boy, whose eyes were half open. Delicately

Justin's dad put his middle and index fingers on the boy's throat. All the people in the lobby held their breath until Dad gave a great sigh of relief.

"He's alive," he said. "But let's not move him. He may have broken his neck." Dad glanced around. "Does anybody know who this boy is staying with?"

Suddenly the boy smiled a sweet smile, but his eyes didn't move. A gabble of conversation arose, people asking other people whose boy he might be.

Sirens sounded in the distance.

"That was quick," Monique whispered.

Dad backed down the stairs, keeping his eyes on the limp form above him. "Clear a path to the door," he said, and guests and maids and bell-hops hushed and moved back.

Justin glanced at the boy again. He still had the smile on his face, and Justin noticed for the first time that his right hand was grasping a stick, round like a pencil and about twice as long.

The siren wailed very close now, and the lobby doors swung open. Two emergency medical technicians hurried in, and behind them came another, pushing a wheeled stretcher. The first two EMTs darted up the stairs and bent over the boy like Dad had. Finally they lifted him and slid him gently onto a plastic board. Justin saw, with a lurch of his stomach, that the boy's head was bleeding.

The EMTs began carefully strapping him to the plastic board.

"That's so his neck won't move," whispered Monique. "In case it's broken."

When they reached the bottom of the stairs, one of the EMTs noticed the stick. He gently removed it from the boy's hand and looked at it, puzzled.

Justin darted forward and reached out his hand. "I'll keep it for him."

"Thanks." The EMT handed it over.

The boy's smile had faded, but his eyes were moving as the EMTs placed the plastic board on the stretcher.

"Tory! Tory, my baby!"

The scream came from above. A very blonde woman in some kind of flowing green robe came hurrying down the stairs, her sandals going *clop-clop-clop,* and a large brilliant jewel dancing crazily on the end of her neck chain. She was going so fast that several times she nearly tripped. A long shawl or scarf of the same flowing green material streamed out behind her.

The EMTs glanced at her, and one of them moved in front of the stretcher to protect the boy. "Ma'am, don't touch him."

"What happened?" she gasped. "That's my son! Let me see him! Oh, what happened?"

Dad said, "I'm afraid he fell down the stairs."

The woman gave him a bewildered glance. "Fell down the—" She stopped, and her lips firmed. "Where's Cosmo?"

Dad's eyes stayed on her face. "Cosmo?"

"Well, then, where's Gwen? Gwen will know where—oh, Tory!"

"Ma'am, we'll need to take your son to the ER," said one of the EMTs. "Right away."

"I'm coming with you."

Dad glanced at the brilliant jewel on the end of its chain. It was a dragon. "You're Angelica Fawkes?" he asked.

She nodded. Then with an automatic motion she flipped her shawl over the dragon, hiding it from view.

"I'm Robert Case, one of the other presenters," Dad said. "You're the keynote speaker tonight, right?"

"Oh." She put her hand to her mouth.

"Go ahead," he said. "I'll explain everything. They'll just have to fit you in later in the week. Go along."

"Thank you. Thank you so much." She clasped the dragon between both her palms and quickly followed the disappearing EMTs.

"Justin," said Monique. "Look." She was pointing at a maid who had just picked up the sponge mop that had fallen when Tory had. "Did you see that?"

"I see she's got the mop."

The maid walked quickly toward the staircase and started up.

"No," said Monique. "I mean, did you see how she picked it up? It's like she was angry. She swooped down on it and snatched it."

"That mop is evidence," Justin said quietly. "Let's follow her."

"Evidence about what?"

"About who pushed him," he whispered. "Let's go."

"Justin, we can't just—"

"Let's go."

The maid and mop were now at the top of the staircase. Justin and Monique followed. By the time they'd reached the top, she was halfway down a long hall. When she disappeared to the right, they broke into a silent run, skidding to a stop just before the corner.

Justin peeked around. "She's taking it into the women's restroom." He turned to stare at Monique.

She stared back. "Well?"

"Go," he said. "Get in there. Watch her."

Chapter 2
Suspect Number One

Justin heard Monique take a breath as if she was going to say "Justin!" again, but instead she walked swiftly to the restroom door, opened it, and disappeared inside.

I've got to think of some reason for just hanging around here, he thought, and bent down to tie his shoe. Instantly the restroom door opened and the maid came out—without the mop. She glanced curiously at Justin as she walked by. He noticed that her mouth was very firm, and that her name tag read "Maria."

Ten seconds later Justin heard the sound of running water and then the *gallump-gallump* of a paper towel dispenser. The door opened, and Monique peered cautiously out.

"She's gone," Justin said.

Monique slid out through the door and let it close silently. She was breathing deeply. "You and your crazy ideas,"

"Where's the mop?"

"In some sort of a supply closet in there." She pointed toward the restroom.

Justin's shoulders sagged. "Locked?"

Monique nodded, and they began to walk back the way they came. "How come you think someone pushed him?" she asked.

"Look at the facts," Justin replied in a low

voice. "He's walking down the stairs. Suddenly he falls—hard."

"Maybe he just tripped."

Justin shook his head. "No. If you're going downstairs and you trip, you don't fall too far. You grab the rail. Maybe you'll lose your balance and fall a couple of steps, but that's all. You heard what I heard. This kid was *moving.*"

"So what does the mop have to do with it?"

"Somebody runs up behind him and rams him with it."

"Why?"

Justin shrugged. "I don't know. To stay out of sight, maybe, so they won't be seen by anybody in the lobby. And there'll be no fingerprints on the victim."

"Oh, brother. Here goes Superdetective again," Monique said with mild sarcasm. "Well, just for the record, there'll be fingerprints on the mop," she pointed out.

"Maybe the person let go of the mop by accident," Justin mused.

"But who would have done it?"

"Could have been that maid," he said. "She's got the key to the broom closet. She gives him a shove, then comes and takes the evidence away. You said she snatched up the mop."

"Yeah, but why would she do that?"

"Who else could it be?"

"I think it was Cosmo."

A crease appeared on Justin's forehead.

"Who's Cosmo?"

"Don't you remember? The boy's mom ran down the stairs, saw her son, and then said, 'Where's Cosmo?'"

"Oh. That's right. But—"

"Hey, here comes your mom."

Tovah Case appeared down at the other end of the hall, carrying a suitcase and garment bag. "Hey, you two," she said. "You're a couple of slippery customers. I thought you were going to help me get this luggage up to the room."

Justin hurried up to her and grabbed the suitcase. "Where's the other stuff?"

"Your dad's got it downstairs. He's talking with a police officer who showed up." She stopped in front of one of the door to their suite and inserted a key in the lock. "I want you two to be really careful on those stairs." The door swung inward. "That boy could have been killed," Mrs. Case continued. "I wonder what happened. Did he trip on something?"

"We think—" Monique began.

"Mom," Justin loudly interrupted, "may I have five dollars?"

"Why do you need five dollars? It's not for that knife, is it?"

"No, just for—for sodas and things like that while we're here."

"You just wait on that," Mom said. "What were you saying, Monique?"

"Well, Justin and I think—"

Justin glared at his friend. "You know what, Mom?" he said quickly.

"Don't interrupt," said Mom.

"You know what I think?" he continued. "I think we should go visit that kid in the emergency room."

Mrs. Case was a kindhearted woman. "Now *that,*" she said, "is the best idea you've had all week. Let's do it. Your dad's going to be tied up in the writers' meeting. Let's get settled in here; then we'll leave a note for your father and find out where the hospital is."

Mrs. Case glanced down, puzzled. "What's that stick you've got in your hand?"

Justin blinked. "Whoa. I forgot I even had it. It belongs to the kid. He still had hold of it when the EMTs got there."

"Good. You can give it to his mother when we see her."

✧   ✧   ✧

Half an hour later the three of them left the Campbello and walked to the hospital, which was just a block and a half away. Justin lagged behind. He held the stick in his right hand. Under his left arm, almost out of sight, he carried a large hollow rubber alligator, yellow and green and about two feet long from snout to tail tip. Its lower jaw dangled, jiggling from the motion of the walking. Suddenly Justin began making strange noises.

"Justin," said Mom, glancing around and

Beware of the Crystal Dragon

spotting the gator for the first time. "Did you really have to bring that to the hospital?"

"I'm just gonna try to cheer the kid up."

Monique tried to grab the alligator's tail. "Those corny jokes you tell are going to give him permanent brain damage."

Justin twisted away. He put the stick in his back pocket and then stuck his hand up through a slit in the alligator's stomach. Suddenly the mouth began to move.

"Knock-knock," said the alligator in a growly voice.

"Your lips are moving," Monique commented.

"Of course my lips are moving," said the alligator. "I'm talking."

"No. *Your* lips are moving, Justin," Monique said.

"Knock-knock."

"Nobody's home," Monique responded.

"Come on," Justin begged in his normal voice. "Just do it. Knock-knock."

Monique rolled her eyes. "OK, OK. Who's there?" she asked wearily.

"Oswald."

"Cosmo who?"

"I said Oswald," Justin said in his normal tones.

"Why don't you have InvestiGator talk in a different voice?" she asked. "I can't understand him when you growl like that."

Justin pushed InvestiGator toward her. "Look at his face."

"It gives me nightmares."

"That face," Justin went on, "is the face of a growler."

"I'll bet gators yap, not growl," Monique said.

"Shush," Mom said. "Here we are."

Inside, the emergency room receptionist glanced at a computer monitor and clicked a couple of keys. "Tory Fawkes?" the woman said. "He's been moved up to 326 East. Are you family?"

"My husband's a presenter at the same writing conference his mother is speaking at. We were in the hotel lobby when he fell," Mom said.

"So you saw it happen?" The receptionist shuddered. "Well, he's doing OK from what I hear. They'll probably just hold him overnight for observation."

Mom whispered as they paused outside room 326. "You two be friendly, but not too loud." She gave a discontented look at the gator, which quickly vanished around Justin's other side.

As they entered the room, the first person they saw was Angelica Fawkes. She was seated in a chair next to a bed, watching TV. Justin saw that her green shawl was thrown over her shoulder so it hid the crystal dragon.

Tory lay on the bed. His head was bandaged and his face was pale, but his eyes were open, and they flicked over toward his visitors.

"Hello," said Mrs. Fawkes, smiling uncertainly.

Mom introduced Justin and Monique and herself, and explained why they were there. "We just wanted to check in and see how your son was doing. I'm Tovah Case; Robert Case is my husband. He's one of the seminar presenters."

Mrs. Fawkes's smile widened in delight. Now that he was closer to her, Justin could see that her shoulders and neck seemed pink and sunburned. "Why, how nice of you to stop in," she said. "Tory, you've got company. I'll tell you what—did you say your name was Tovah? Let's you and me go over and sit in those chairs next to the other bed. It's empty. That way we can talk, and the kids can talk." Together they moved behind a hanging curtain and began to chat.

"Hi, Tory." Monique smiled her brilliant Monique smile, the one that always got results.

"Hi," Tory said with a small grin.

There was a pause. Justin, not knowing what else to do, brought InvestiGator out into view. "Knock-knock," he growled.

Tory drew back quickly.

"Justin, you dufus," Monique snapped.

"Sorry."

"No p-problem," Tory said faintly, pressing his hand to his bandage. "It just caught me by surprise, that's all." He stared at InvestiGator. "He's kinda cool . . . sorta."

"How are you doing?" Monique asked him. "I mean," she said with an icy glare at Justin, "up until just now?"

"OK, I guess. My head hurts."

Justin said, "You were really bleeding there on the stairs."

Tory nodded, then looked as if he was sorry he'd nodded. "I don't remember a lot of what happened. I think I sort of drifted in and out. I remember I landed kind of upside down. And then the ambulance people came."

"And," Justin said, "we think we know who pushed you."

Monique stepped on Justin's foot, hard. "But we don't need to talk about that right now, *do* we?" she said brightly.

Justin quickly shook his head. *"Ouch.* I mean, *no.* Not at all. Never. No way."

"Nobody pushed me," Tory said.

The other two eyed him thoughtfully.

"Mom thought my cousin did it. But nobody did."

"Are you sure?" Monique finally asked. "You were coming down pretty fast."

"I know." He sat forward excitedly. "I was almost doing it."

"Doing what?"

Tory paused, watching them for seven full seconds. Then he said, "Flying."

Monique snickered. "You're as bad as Justin."

Justin blinked. "What are you talking about?"

His voice was so serious that Monique paused again. "I mean," she said, "Justin's always cracking jokes too, and his jokes are so . . . I mean . . . "

In desperation Justin brought InvestiGator into sight again. "Knock-knock."

Tory blinked, and cleared his throat. "Who's there?" he asked timidly.

"Cosmo."

"You mean my cousin?"

Justin reddened. "Sorry. What I meant was 'Oswald.'"

"You said 'Cosmo'."

"I know, but—"

"I get it!" Tory smiled that sweet, heart-melting smile of his. "You're channeling! I never heard anybody channel through a rubber alligator before. Do it again!"

Justin's jaw went slack. "Channeling?"

"Sure. You just did it. I mean, how else could you have known Cosmo's name? I've never seen you before." He smiled again. "Who's your spirit guide?"

"You know what?" Monique said faintly. "I don't think Justin or I know what you're talking about."

"Magick," Tory said earnestly, "with a k. An ancient spirit told you Cosmo's name. And when I fell down the steps, I was trying to fly."

Monique's mouth popped open. "You mean like Potter? Harry Potter?"

He nodded energetically—and his face crumpled in pain. "Remind me," he gasped, "not to move my head." He took a trembly breath. "Yeah, I was trying to fly. And I almost had it." He patted the spot just above his stomach. "I could feel it—here."

"You were trying to fly with a mop?" Justin asked. "I thought Potter used a broom."

"I couldn't find a broom. So I found a mop and figured I'd try that. I straddled the mop and grabbed it in my left hand, and held my wand in my—" he broke off. A really worried look passed across his face. "By the way, you haven't seen my wand anywhere, have you? A sort of thin stick?"

Justin reached into his back pocket, and Tory's worried look vanished in a dazzling smile. He reached out for the wand with both hands, like a mother getting together with her long-lost baby. "Wow, thanks!"

Justin swallowed. "Um, you really were trying to fly? You're not kidding? Aren't you a little past that stage? I mean, you don't really believe in the Harry Potter stories, do you?"

Tory snorted. "Of course not. They're just made up."

"I'm getting more confused by the minute," Monique said. "You just told us you were trying to fly like Harry Potter. But now you say you don't believe in him."

"Look." Tory sat up and crossed his legs. "The Potter stories—they're just made-up, right? Everybody knows that. But magick wands have been around for hundreds of years. And brooms, too, to fly with."

In the dead silence that followed, they heard

the voice of Angelica Fawkes say, beyond the curtain, "And do you know what's really the most distressing thing about Tory's fall? It's that Belisarius didn't predict it, and Belisarius didn't prevent it."

"Interesting," Tovah Case said cautiously. "I wonder what the problem could be."

"I think I know what *my* problem is," Tory said softly to Monique and Justin. He stared at his wand and twirled it in his fingers. "I don't have enough power in my wand. See that?" He pointed to one end, which was wrapped in clear plastic tape. Justin could see what looked like a couple of black hairs sticking out. "That's a little piece of an eagle feather. I bought that feather from an Indian boy when Mom was on a reservation studying trickster stories. I split the wand and slid part of that feather into it. I thought for sure that this would give me enough power. I mean, eagles fly all the time, right?"

Justin's mouth felt dry. He wanted to change the subject. He wanted Mom to come out from behind the curtain.

"W-well . . ." he stammered.

"Wow . . ." said Monique.

Tory started tapping the wand against his palm. "But I've got a plan."

"A plan?" Justin repeated.

Tory glanced toward the curtain, then lowered his voice. "It's a secret, though. Can you keep—"

At that instant a tall, dark-haired boy came into the room, followed by a woman who looked a little like Tory's mother.

"Hello, hel-*lo!*" the woman said cheerfully. "What have we here? Some little guy must not be too terribly sick if he can have visitors already."

"Hi," Tory said. "This is my aunt, Gwen Delgado," he said to his two new friends. "Aunt Gwen, meet Monique and Justin. And this," he said with absolutely no expression in his voice, "is my cousin, Cosmo."

Cosmo Delgado looked them over and smiled vaguely. He looked as if he was about 15. The teenager had an earphone plugged into each ear. Justin could hear the faint clashing of music.

"We're just breezing through," Aunt Gwen said. "Really. Can't stay. I'm taking Cosmo to a movie." She moved over behind the curtain, where voices greeted her. "Oh, *Angie,*" they heard her say. "Look at your *sunburn.* We stayed out in the park too long yesterday."

"I guess I'd better stay home from the harbor boat tour tomorrow," Mrs. Fawkes said.

"Oh, no, come along. Just cover up. I'm so glad," Aunt Gwen said breathlessly, "that Tory wasn't badly hurt."

Cosmo, who had stayed on Tory's side of the curtain, spoke to his younger cousin. "Hey, Tor," he said. He had a deep, quacky voice.

"Hey, Coz."

"Don't forget."

Tory glanced at Justin and Monique, then back at Cosmo. "Forget?"

"You know."

Tory's mouth became thin and firm.

"*You* know," Cosmo repeated. "About Puff. Don't forget." He began to hum a little tune. "Dah dah-dah-dah dahhhh dahhhh . . ."

Tory's face darkened.

"I *told* you this visit would be quick," said Aunt Gwen, hurrying out from behind the curtain. "Gotta go. We'll be late." She grabbed one of Tory's feet and gave it a squeeze. "Take care of yourself, kid."

"Dah dah-dah-dah dahhhh dahhhh . . ." Cosmo hummed thoughtfully in his quacky voice as he and his mother disappeared through the doorway.

"What's that song?" Monique asked.

"'Puff the Magic Dragon,'" Mrs. Fawkes said from behind the curtain. "I didn't know you kids paid any attention to old songs like that." She began talking to Mom again.

Tory lifted his wand and beckoned Monique and Justin close with it. "You know what?" he whispered.

"What?" Justin whispered back.

"I need your help."

"What kind of help?"

"I need you," Tory hissed, "to help me steal Belisarius."

Chapter 3
Tory's Secret Place

It was almost comical: both Justin and Monique backed away quickly, at the same time and to the same distance. Monique giggled uncomfortably, then quickly sobered up as she saw the desperate look on Tory's face.

"You want us," she said, "to help steal your mom's dragon?"

Tory glared at her, his fingers on his lips. The three of them waited in terrible silence, listening to see if they'd been overheard. But the conversation on the other side of the curtain flowed on with no interruption. Finally Tory nodded.

"But I'm surprised you know about Belisarius," he whispered.

"Your mom mentioned the dragon back at the hotel," Justin explained.

Monique stared at Tory. "But why would you want to steal it?"

"Don't give me that weird look," he replied. "I'm not the only one who wants that dragon. But I *am* the only one who'll give it back once I'm done with it."

Justin cleared his throat. "Who else wants it?"

"Maria."

"Maria? The maid?" Justin asked, remembering the name tag he'd seen earlier.

Now it was Tory's turn to lean back cautiously. "Whoa. How did you know who she was? But yeah. Maria's the maid on our floor. She cleans our rooms and shoes and everything." He shook his head in amazement. "So you're channeling again. And this time you didn't use your alligator. And no trance. How do you *do* that? Are you a wizard? What's the name of your spirit? He must know Belisarius or something."

"I'm not channeling."

"You've *gotta* be channeling. You channeled my cousin's name, and now you know that Maria is a maid. If you're not channeling, how could you know all this stuff?"

"How come she wants the dragon?" Justin asked.

Tory shook his head. "You won't believe this, but she's one of those totally weird Christians. She told me that Belisarius is a heathen idol, and she told me that God wants to destroy all idols, including my mother's."

"Whoa," Justin said.

"Maria is dead serious."

"Who else wants Belisarius?" Monique asked.

"Cosmo does. He got acquainted with a gang member at a music store he goes to. Someone called 'The Man.'"

"'The Man,'" Monique said in a mock-dramatic voice. *"Tough* guy."

"Don't laugh. He's a bad one."

"How come he wants the dragon?"

Tory glanced at the curtain, scowled, and

lowered his voice even further. "Did you see last Sunday's paper? If you didn't, you ought to read its article about Mom. She had to go and brag to the reporter that it's totally impossible for her to write without help from Belisarius, and that he's the reason she's written six best-selling books. He's why we can live year-round in a suite in the Campobello. Well, The Man read the article last week and told the other gang members. Now they're putting pressure on Cosmo to steal it for them. And Cosmo wants *me* to do the job."

"So the gang wants to sell it?" Monique asked.

"Hold it hostage," Tory replied. "For money. Mucho money."

"Your mom better put it in a safe or something."

He shook his head. "Belisarius never leaves that chain, and that chain never leaves Mom's neck. She sleeps with it on. She even wears it in the shower."

He paused again to listen to the conversation on the other side of the curtain. Mrs. Fawkes was talking about the harbor boat tour again.

"I want to go on that," Tory said softly.

"So who's 'Puff'?" Justin whispered.

"That's Cosmo's code name for Belisarius. Puff the Magic Dragon."

Justin glanced at the curtain, then back at Tory. "And you want the dragon too, right?"

"Yeah," Tory whispered. "But I'm going to give it back once I chip a piece of it off to put in my wand." He glanced longingly at the curtain. "If I had even one tiny chip off Belisarius' tail scales, and if I could glue it inside my wand, *wow*, what power I'd have!"

Monique flicked a google-eyed glance at Justin, which Tory spotted.

"No, it's *true*," he said. "Belisarius is a really powerful crystal. Mom got him in a New Age crystal shop in Germany's Black Forest. Remember, he's the reason we can afford the Campobello year-round—and now, unfortunately, Aunt Gwen's suite too. She and Cosmo have been here a couple of weeks," he said darkly. "And I hope they get out after this writers' conference is over."

Behind the curtain the voices began saying goodbye. A few seconds later Mom and Mrs. Fawkes appeared. "We'd better go," Mom said. "Tory needs his rest. Come on, kids."

They said goodbye. Tory looked wistfully after them as they left the room.

✧   ✧   ✧

"Can I get you anything else?" the elderly waiter asked kindly. He paused for a moment to carefully straighten the two elegant cut-glass salt and pepper shakers on the glossy, dark wood of the table.

"Uh, no thanks," Monique replied, and handed him her well-cleaned plate.

It was dinnertime that same evening. Down at the other end of the hotel's huge dining room, the writers chattered and called to one another. Justin, seated across from Monique, could see Dad and Mom at the head table. Somebody pointed a finger at Dad, and Dad raised his hands in comical terror, as though he was being held at gunpoint.

"Justin," Monique said, "what are we going to do? About Tory?"

"He really believes that stuff, doesn't he?"

She sighed. "Well, I guess it's no wonder since his mother believes in it. When you get right down to it, it's basically her fault he tried to fly down the stairs. She's been planting that 'magick with a *k*' stuff in his head all these years."

"I don't like what he said about other people wanting the dragon."

"Neither do I."

Justin folded his napkin on the table and stood. "Let's keep an eye on him. I'll give you one of my walkie-talkies tomorrow."

"OK. Your mom said we could go on the harbor boat tour tomorrow afternoon, didn't she?"

"Right. And if Tory is well enough to go, that's where we need to be."

✦ ✦ ✦

The next morning Justin and Monique went to the hospital to walk their new friend back to the hotel. When they arrived at his hospital room, Tory was already up and dressed. His head bandage was smaller, but his face was still pale.

And his grin had a cautious look to it. His wand with the tape on one end was stuck into his belt.

He didn't say much until they were out on the sidewalk. Then he suddenly handed Monique a little crumpled pamphlet. "Merry Christmas," he said bitterly.

"Happy New Year," she said, taking it. "It's June. What calendar are you using? What's this?" She smoothed out the paper, and then her hand jerked and she almost dropped it.

"FLEE IDOLATRY!" screamed the pamphlet's headline in blood-red letters. "Thou shalt have no other gods before Me!" says the God of Israel. "Destroy the Baals, cast down their altars, cleanse My land of the abomination of images!" Then there were lots and lots of Bible texts, some of them underlined in wavy blue ballpoint ink. The person who'd done the underlining had pushed hard on the pen, and it had cut through the paper in a couple of places.

"That," said Tory flatly, "was what I found on my pillow this morning. Right beside my head. I rolled over and felt paper under my cheek, and there it was."

Justin's skin crawled. "Maria."

Tory nodded. "Who else could it have been? I think she waited until my mom left for the hotel last night. Then she came down here and wormed her way into the hospital, probably through the emergency room doors, and somehow got into my room and laid this beside my head."

"But wouldn't security have caught her?"

Monique shook her head. "Not in her maid's uniform. It probably looks enough like a hospital worker's uniform to let her go anywhere she wanted. She could've grabbed a broom or mop as she went along, and she'd have looked even more real."

Justin fake-punched Tory's shoulder encouragingly. "At least she's not after you. She's after—"

"I *know* what she's after. Belisarius. But she's looney. Who knows what's going on in her scrambled Christian brain?"

Monique gave a quick glance at Justin and another at her watch. "Tory, are you still going on the harbor tour? It's in a couple of hours."

"We're going on it," Justin added quickly.

Tory looked relieved. "Cool. I want to see Seattle from the water."

But when they came in sight of the green-and-white awning in front of the Campobello's entrance, Tory suddenly stopped. "I don't believe it," he said in a tiny voice.

"What's wrong?" Justin asked.

Tory's shoulders slumped, and he turned his back on the hotel. "Over there, on the street corner. It's my cousin and another guy. They're waiting for us. I'm not sure who the other guy is, but I can guess."

"Let's just walk right past them," Monique said. "I need to get in there. Justin's dad said I could use his laptop to check my e-mail. I should be getting word from my parents about when they're coming back."

"I don't want to see those guys," Tory said.

"Get out your scope, Justin," Monique said. "Maybe it's not The Man after all."

Justin unzipped his belt pack and removed something that looked like half a binocular. He put it to his right eye and focused it. "Shaved head," he said. "Baggy black pants. Skateboard. Lots of chains around his neck. Big silver cross hanging from one of them."

"The Man," Tory said bitterly. "I've never met him, but it's gotta be him. They're going to hassle me about that stupid dragon. Go on ahead," he said to Monique. "They're not after you. Maybe Justin and I can figure something out."

"Here," said Justin, handing her a yellow walkie-talkie from his pack. "You remember how to work this, don't you? I showed you when we went to Carnera Bay for outdoor school. Keep the unit turned on, but keep the volume low. I might need to ask you to find Dad."

"OK." She scanned the walkie-talkie's controls with an expert eye. "Channel 6. Squawk if you need me. And be careful." She put the device in her purse and sauntered toward the Campobello.

Tory gazed at Justin's belt pack. "Got a switchblade in there?" he asked, half comically.

"No." This time it was Justin's turn to sound

bitter. "Dad won't even let me get a clasp knife."

"Too bad. Would've made me feel better. They're walking this way."

"What do we do, run?"

"Just do what I do. Follow me."

Tory started walking toward the approaching duo, and Justin followed. When they were within 20 feet of each other, Cosmo Delgado and The Man stood so that they blocked the sidewalk.

Tory kept moving toward them. Suddenly he yelled, "Split!" and darted around them to the right. Justin dashed around to the left, and the chase was on. The two younger boys made it to the hotel doors just as Cosmo and The Man were entering the courtyard.

Once in the lobby Justin slowed to a quick walk so he wouldn't attract as much attention, and headed for the staircase.

"No! Follow me." Tory hissed. "Fritz, don't tell, please," he said to the desk clerk, grinning and putting a finger to his lips. The man smiled a startled smile and nodded. Tory darted for a door beside Fritz's desk, and he and Justin dashed through it and closed it behind them.

Right in front of them was a steep circular iron staircase that ascended high above. Justin decided that they were now in one of the Campobello's castle-like turrets. The only light came from tiny round windows in the curved turret walls.

"We've gotta tiptoe up this," Tory whispered,

starting to climb. "If we don't, it makes a booming sound you can hear out in the lobby."

"Doesn't Cosmo know about this staircase?" asked Justin from behind him.

"No. Like I said, he's been here only a couple of weeks." Tory glanced at the doors they passed as they climbed. "We're going all the way to the seventh floor. Those guys are using the staircase, and they're gonna try to catch us near our suite, which is on the sixth floor."

"So we're OK."

"Not yet," Tory said. "If they think we made it inside, and Coz asks Mom about us, she'll tell them she hasn't seen us. Then one of them will probably hang around the suite door, and the other will start exploring. Don't worry though. They won't find us."

At the very top of the staircase it was dark, but Tory found the door handle. He cautiously pulled it open a crack and peered out into the hall. "All clear," he said, and they slipped through the door and closed it behind them.

Tory led the way into a large open suite. "They have parties here," he said. "Mom rents it once in a while for Belisarius' channeling sessions. And it also has—" he said as he reached one end of the room, "—an unlockable window." He twisted a little handle, jerked upward on the window frame, and finally slid it open. "Come on. We've got to be quick."

Justin saw to his horror that the window

overlooked the Campobello courtyard seven stories down. "What are you *doing?*" he asked.

"Calm down. It's safe. We just have to climb through, like this." Tory wriggled out onto a wide ledge. "Come on."

Justin's heart felt as if it were slamming against his tonsils, but he scrambled out onto the ledge.

Tory slid the window shut. "Hope we can get this open again," he said. He began creeping along the ledge toward the left. Justin followed, not looking up or down, but close to the soles of Tory's sneakers. Suddenly his friend climbed over an iron railing, and Justin realized that it was the railing of the little balcony he'd seen from the courtyard the day below. He scrambled over and landed beside Tory.

"Isn't this cool?" Tory asked enthusiastically, leaning back against the brick wall. "There used to be a big window in the wall here behind us. People used to be able to walk right out onto this balcony. The window was bricked in years ago, but they didn't take down the balcony. It's a perfect place to hang out. And it's so high that nobody can see us from below unless we stand up and lean over the railing. And nobody can see us from the window we just came through."

Justin scrunched his back up against the wall and shuddered. Now that he was safe, he actually came up with the courage to look at the scenery. It was awesome. Tall silver and copper and steel-blue skyscrapers loomed up around him, and from far below he heard the rumble and squeaking sounds of traffic.

"And here's my trunk." Tory dragged a large wooden box around in front of them. "Just like Harry Potter had." He spun the dial on a combination padlock and lifted the trunk's lid. Justin saw a lot of black cloth and the end of a stick.

"My robe," Tory explained. "And this is my other wand," he said, grasping the stick and holding it out to Justin. "You can have it. It's older and it doesn't work as well. But you're a channeler, so you can probably get it going. You might even be a wizard and not know it, like Harry Potter at first. Here."

"I'm *not* a channeler," Justin responded.

"Sure you are. You proved it a couple of times."

"No. Look, my dad used to be a detective. He taught me how to keep my eyes and ears open. After you fell in the lobby, your mom happened to mention Cosmo's name. And when that maid picked up your mop, we followed her, and I saw her name tag."

Tory's shoulders sagged a bit. "Oh." He held out the wand again. "But here, take it anyway."

Justin looked at it in silence.

"Don't you want it? I'm *giving* it to you." Tory's voice sounded hurt.

"Thanks, but—"

"It's yours." Tory dropped it in Justin's lap. "You can use it to help me put a spell on Coz and

The Man. And listen. You said your dad wouldn't let you get some kind of a knife you wanted?"

Justin, his head spinning, nodded.

"All you gotta do is to get something from his body. Like a few of his hairs, or his fingernail clippings. We split your wand open, stick those things in there, and figure out the right spell, and he's in your power. He's got to do what you want him to."

"Tory."

"What?"

"You're serious? You really believe this?"

Tory stared at him. "Of course."

"That wand you've got. Have you ever been able to—*do* anything with it?"

"Sure. The first day I had the eagle feather in it, I pointed it at a bird, and the bird flew away."

Justin discovered that a jagged brick had been poking into his back, so he shifted position. "Are you sure the bird didn't just get scared when you moved your arm? Are you sure it wasn't just a coincidence?"

Tory snorted. "Now you're sounding like Cosmo. Listen, Justin. You're a cool dude. You're smart. But you gotta remember that there's a whole world of magick you just don't know about. Like in the Potter books. There are all these wizards, and nobody knows they're wizards, because they cast spells to keep themselves secret."

"I thought you said the Potter books were

just made-up stuff."

Tory nodded, annoyed. "Yeah. But remember that the person who wrote those books didn't *invent* wands or brooms or wizards. They've existed for centuries. And I think that I'm a wizard too. Otherwise, why would I be so interested in magick?"

Justin said timidly, "We all want power."

The other boy scowled. "So you think I'm power-hungry? Is that it? You think I wanna just—" He broke off and began rummaging in the box. "OK, let's try something." He began to wrestle himself into a long black robe, and when his head finally popped through at the top, he put on a black cone-shaped hat that had white cloth stars sewn onto it. He dug around some more, brought out a school notebook, and started thumbing his way through it.

Justin slowly unzipped the zipper on his belt pack.

"OK, here it is." Tory held the notebook in one hand and grasped his wand tightly in his other fist. He stood up and loomed over Justin, pointing down at him with his wand. "I'm going to levitate you; make you float in air."

Justin's heart crashed up against his tonsils again. "Uh, maybe you shouldn't do that." *Dear Jesus,* he prayed silently, *drive back the demons if demons are here.*

"It's not going to hurt. And I'll do it just a little bit. Remember when I fell down the stairs? I was just starting to fly. I knew it because I felt something funny right here." He patted the part of the robe just above his stomach. "So if you feel something there, you know it's going to work."

"People can see you down below if you're standing up," Justin said desperately. "Especially with that hat on."

Tory flicked a glance down over his shoulder at the courtyard. "I don't care."

This kid, thought Justin to himself, *is crazy.* He put his thumb into his belt pack's walkie-talkie pocket, ready to grab the unit if necessary. *But how am I going to give Monique directions to this balcony?* he wondered. He scrunched his spine back against the bricks.

Tory concentrated on the notebook and pointed the wand at Justin's nose. *"Levitato,"* he commanded.

Justin pressed himself hard against the bricks. He felt a funny feeling in his stomach.

Chapter 4
Missing Magick

Dear Jesus, Justin prayed again, *I don't know what's going on here, but please keep me safe.*

Tory shut his eyes and concentrated harder. *"Levitato,"* he said again.

The hairs on Justin's legs prickled.

After a couple of seconds Tory peeked with one eye. "I can't figure it out," he said. "It worked before."

Justin's scalp tingled. "You've actually *levitated* something?"

"Myself. A little." Tory flipped a couple of notebook pages. "A couple of weeks ago I pointed the wand at a chair and said the spell. I felt that funny feeling in my stomach. Then I realized I had the front end of the wand pointing at me instead of the chair."

"But you didn't float upward?"

"I'm not sure. Did you feel anything?"

"Well," Justin said, "I felt a funny feeling in my stomach."

"Yes!" Tory slashed the air triumphantly with his wand.

"But I think I was just nervous. Like I was getting butterflies in my stomach."

"Oh, all right. Let's try something else," Tory said. "Would you like to . . ." he flipped through some pages ". . . become a goat?" He pointed the wand. *"Capra capella.* Feel anything?"

"No." Justin took a deep breath. "Tory, I don't think any of this is going to work, especially on me."

Tory cocked his head to one side. "How come?"

"Because I'm a—"

"A what?"

Justin swallowed. "I'm a Christian."

Tory dropped his wand and backed away. "You're a *Christian?* Like Maria?"

"No, no. Not *that* kind of Christian."

"So what kind are you?"

Justin looked doubtfully at him. "How much do you, uh, know about Christians?"

"Well, nothing, really." Tory glared at him. "Except that they sneak into hospitals and put pamphlets by your head."

"Have you ever heard of Jesus?"

"I've heard of him."

"Do you know anything *about* Him?"

"No. Except that if he really had power, he was probably a channeler."

"So you never went to Sunday school or anything?"

Tory shook his head. "Mom's been into New Age since she was a teenager. She told me that being a Christian is only one path to the true light. She says that other paths work a lot better because they don't have all the extra 'baggage' that Christianity does. She likes channeling with crystals. It's simple." He chuckled, then changed the subject. "I wonder what Coz and The Man are doing now?"

"Do you think they're still in the building?"

Tory nodded. "They've probably even come and looked out the window we crawled through. When they finally leave, we'll be able to see them from up here." He leaned cautiously forward and peered down through the rails into the courtyard. "When's that harbor tour starting?"

"We've got to be down in the lobby at one o'clock."

Tory glanced at his watch. "Hmmm. I've got to be on that tour. With so many people after that dragon now, I've got to keep an eye on it. But we've still got an hour."

And when half of that hour had passed, they saw The Man come out from under the awning, alone. He slinked across the courtyard and disappeared around a corner.

Tory wriggled out of his robe. "Let's go."

❖   ❖   ❖

The harbor tour boat, named *Happy Times II*, was painted brilliant white. It was a large two-level craft with a big dining room on the first level, and you could go up inside or outside stairs to the open-air seating on top. As it rumbled away from the pier, everybody ooohed and aaahed about how beautiful Seattle's skyscrapers and Space Needle looked against the hazy blue sky.

"Where *were* you guys, anyway?" Monique asked Justin in a low voice as they stood side by side at the rail on top of the boat. Tory and his mother sat in twin deck chairs at the far end of the boat. They seemed to be talking seriously about something.

Justin told her about Tory's secret balcony hideout.

"Well," she said, "you sure fooled Cosmo and his nasty buddy. They were roaming all around the hotel, getting grouchier and grouchier."

"Did they harass you at all?"

"No," Monique said grimly, "and they better not try. Actually, I checked my e-mail and then went right down to the writers' seminar and listened to a few of the speakers. I even caught a bit of your dad's class, but it was a little over my head."

"Did you hear any of Mrs. Fawkes's presentation?"

Monique nodded, and stared at him solemnly. "Justin, she was talking the purest baloney I have ever heard in my life. At first I thought she was just joking, but then I realized that she really does believe that her dragon talks to her."

She glanced over at Mrs. Fawkes, who was now lying back in her chair, a blue baseball cap covering her eyes. The dragon dangled from its chain, sparkling in the sunlight. Tory was gone now. "It turns out," Monique continued, "that Belisarius was a real person, a military general or something who lived about 1,500 years ago. He fought battles in North Africa. And Mrs. Fawkes thinks it's his spirit who's talking through the crystal dragon."

"Weird." Justin shuddered. "Well, I apologize for thinking this vacation was going to be boring."

"Yeah. Anyway, Mrs. Fawkes says that she keeps the dragon around her neck at all times, even when she's sleeping. But she never looks at it."

"Never *looks* at it?"

"Not much, anyway. She says it's bad luck. She just holds it between her palms and thinks. And whatever comes into her head is supposedly from Belisarius."

"Well," Justin said, "Tory now knows that I'm a Christian."

"Uh-oh. Does he think you're like Maria?"

"He's suspicious. But he had to know sooner or later."

"Yeah."

The tour boat was crowded. Justin drifted away from his friend and explored both levels of the boat, threading his way through the sightseers and up and down the stairways. He passed his mother, then Cosmo, then Aunt Gwen. Often he saw Tory, sometimes sitting with Mrs. Fawkes and sometimes scowling at Cosmo.

At one point Tory found him. "Good news," he said, with a look of relief on his face.

"What about?"

"Belisarius. I told Mom everything—about Maria, about Cosmo, about The Man. So she held Belisarius in both hands and said a spell that will keep him close to her forever. That takes a load off my mind."

Justin looked at his friend sideways, then stared out over the water, silently praying hard.

An hour later the boat nudged up against the pier it had started from, and everybody stood up to leave. Tory walked watchfully beside his mother, who was blinking as if she'd been asleep. She looked more sunburned than ever, and she was squinting in pain as she clutched a beach towel around her shoulders. She was muttering to Cosmo and Gwen about how she needed a cold shower.

✦ ✦ ✦

Dinner that evening, now over, was held in the Campobello's large dining room. Warm yellow light, like candles, glowed against the wood-paneled walls. Again Monique and Justin were at a table off to the side of the large group of writers. Tory was sitting with them, but he had his back to the crowd.

"Tory," Justin said as he folded his napkin and set it beside his plate. "Want to come up to our suite and surf the net with Monique and me? I've got to check my e-mail."

Tory puffed air out from between his lips in

a sigh. "You go ahead. I've got to keep an eye on Mom."

"I thought you said your mom said some kind of a spell over Belisarius to protect him."

"I know. But I want to make sure." He glanced at Mrs. Fawkes, who was seated at one of the tables, staring into space. "Mom's not feeling too well. She tried to take a nap after the harbor tour. She's a light sleeper, but she must have finally dropped off, because Aunt Gwen had to wake her up. Mom barely had enough time to get down here."

"Why bother?" asked Monique. "Belisarius didn't keep you from falling down the stairs."

He scowled at her. "Hey, watch it. I don't always know why Belisarius does what he does, but you've gotta admit that he keeps Mom's best-seller money rolling in."

A few tables away, one of the male writers got to his feet and said, "May I have your attention please?"

Tory glanced around at the writers for a moment. "Tonight," he whispered, "they're going to give Mom some sort of writing award. So don't knock our dragon, OK?" He glared at Monique. "What are you, a Christian like Justin?"

She nodded.

Tory's jaw fell. "You guys are *everywhere,*" he yelped. "That's not fair. Two against one."

"Your attention, please," said the speaker again. Justin saw that he was holding a dark wooden plaque with a brass plate attached to it. "As you know, at this yearly convention we present a Writer of the Year award. This goes to someone whose writing has had wide acceptance, and has deeply influenced his or her readers with mind-changing ideas."

He paused and smiled. "And I know I speak for the committee when I say that the recipient of this year's award should come as no great surprise to any of us. For her great personal faith in her abilities, and for the use of her talents to challenge and improve the lives of her readers, I would like to present our Writer of the Year award to Angelica Fawkes."

Tory glanced around again, watching his mother rise gracefully to her feet. This time she was wearing a misty-blue robe, with a shawl of the same pattern across her shoulders and hanging down in front. "By the way," he said, looking straight at Monique with a superior little grin, "that's the fifth award like this she's gotten this year. How about a little more respect for Belisarius?"

Monique smiled politely.

"Thank you so very, very much," Mrs. Fawkes said, accepting the plaque. She gazed humbly at it for a few seconds, and then raised her eyes to her audience.

Justin saw that Tory's smile had widened to a grin. With his back to his mother, he now began mouthing silently what she said aloud.

While she paused he whispered, "I know this speech by heart."

"As most of you know," she said—and Tory lip-synched it perfectly, even shaping his face into his mother's humble expression—"writing is not easy. Writing is terribly difficult, if you wish to do it well, and if you wish to have eternal impact." Tory placed both hands on his heart.

"Tory, stop that," Monique choked. "You're making me laugh."

"Writing," Mrs. Fawkes (and the silent Tory) continued, "requires far more than the reserves of love and goodwill one has been able to store within one's heart. Writing requires"—and she (and Tory) paused dramatically—"something from beyond." Tory flung out his arms in ecstasy.

"Don't, Tory," Monique gulped, trying to keep a straight face. "You'll get us in trouble."

Now Tory's eyes went reverently shut, and his whole body began to quiver.

"I," said Mrs. Fawkes, her eyes closed, "have been tremendously honored to have been chosen to be one small echo of a voice from the past. Why I was chosen for this I do not know." (Tory lowered his head modestly, and so did his mother.) "I only know that responding to wisdom's chime from across the centuries has changed and enriched my life forever." (Tory raised his head and pointed his finger first at Monique, then at Justin.) "And I would encourage each of you—yes, you and you—to open your own hearts to the call of eternal wisdom, wherever it might find you."

The writers applauded enthusiastically. Justin was wishing he could see the expressions on Mom's and Dad's faces.

"Here," whispered Tory, "is where she shows them Belisarius." He cupped his hands together close to his heart, and Mrs. Fawkes reached beneath her shawl and did the same.

"I would like to introduce to you the one who has made my work possible," she said. "This is, of course, only a crystal, only what you might call a radio receiver. But my little dragon never leaves me. He is always next to my heart. He is the reason I write. He tells me what to say. Even the words I am saying to you now are his. If he was not with me tonight, I would have neither the wisdom nor the courage to address such an intelligent, creative group of people as you are."

She—and Tory—paused dramatically. "So now let me introduce to you the one whom you should really thank—Belisarius!"

Tory uncupped his hands and held one of them up, fingers pinched, swaying an invisible dragon on an invisible chain. Mrs. Fawkes was doing the same, only her chain was real, and what was on the end of it flashed and sparkled.

There was a smattering of applause from the writers, and then a puzzled silence.

Tory's face sobered. He glanced around.

One of the writers said, "Ooohh," and someone else giggled nervously.

Mrs. Fawkes screamed.

And even from where he was sitting, Justin could see that what was dangling from Angelica Fawkes's chain was not a crystal dragon but a beautiful cut-glass saltshaker!

Chapter 5
Pike Street Danger

With a choking gasp, Tory tumbled off his chair and darted over to his mother. Justin and Monique followed. As they came near, they saw that Mrs. Fawkes had collapsed onto a chair with her hand to her mouth, sobbing. Several adults crowded close. Justin and Monique walked closer to the activity.

"Look," Monique whispered in Justin's ear. "That saltshaker. It's just like the ones in this dining room. But it's empty."

The saltshaker was dangling back over Mrs. Fawkes's left shoulder. Justin studied it closely. "That's a paper clip threaded into the holes at the top," he whispered back. "That's what attaches it to the chain."

Dad was kneeling close to Mrs. Fawkes's chair. "Angelica," he said gently, "Angelica, just breathe deeply. That's it, just like that. Monique," he said, "get her a glass of water, could you?"

Monique grabbed for a water pitcher and began to pour.

Tory was kneeling too. His face was numb with shock, and he reached out for the saltshaker.

"Don't touch that," Dad said quickly. "Fingerprints." Tory snatched his hands away. Dad gently removed the chain from Mrs. Fawkes's neck and placed it carefully in the center of the table, with the saltshaker standing upright. "Watch that, guys," he said to Justin and Tory. "Don't touch it, and don't let anyone else touch it. Angelica, do you think you're strong enough to walk to the elevator?"

"I'm all right," she said weakly. "I'll be all right."

"Your pulse is a little quick," Dad said doubtfully. "Do you have high blood pressure?"

Mrs. Fawkes nodded. "My sister has had nurse's training," she said.

"Maybe we'd better get her to check you out," Dad said. "It's been awhile since I had EMT training, so maybe I'm wrong, but I don't think we'd better take any chances."

The writers who had gathered around her table parted to make a path. Justin's mom and dad led a dazed Angelica Fawkes up to her large seventh-floor suite. Tory followed right behind them, carefully holding the chain with the saltshaker at arm's length, with Justin and Monique bringing up the rear of the procession.

"Gwen's in suite 612," Mrs. Fawkes murmured faintly.

Upon the group's arrival, a wide-eyed Gwen Delgado listened to the facts with a horrified expression. She patted her sister's hand a lot, then made shooing motions at the kids. "Tory, take them to your room. Angie needs some peace."

Tory led his two guests into the next room.

Justin saw that every wall was covered with Harry Potter posters. A model of Harry Potter flying a broom hung from one corner of the ceiling, and an owl from the other.

"Tory, your poor mom," Monique said sympathetically.

Tory shook his head, still dazed. "Somebody's magick is a lot more powerful than ours is."

"It's not magick," Justin said firmly. "Somebody stole it."

"I *know* somebody stole it!" Tory snapped. "Somebody stronger than Belisarius."

Two quick knocks sounded on the door. It opened, and Aunt Gwen stepped in. Her face was tight with anger. She closed the door behind her.

"Sit down on the bed," she told them.

They stared at her, then quickly obeyed.

"OK," she said, "you've had your joke. Let's see the dragon."

Tory's jaw dropped.

"Tory, I'm waiting."

"I don't have it!" he sputtered. "I've been *guarding* it all afternoon!"

She snapped her fingers twice. "Come on, come on. Get it over with."

"I didn't take it!" he wailed. "Why would I take it?"

Monique flicked a glance at Justin. *I know why he'd take it,* the glance said.

Aunt Gwen suddenly turned to them. "And you two. You probably don't realize how important this dragon is, but if you've got it, cough it up. *Now.*"

Justin cleared his throat. "Mrs. Delgado, I promise you that we don't have it."

Monique nodded. "How could we have taken it? Tory told us his mom never takes it off, not even at night. Not even in the shower."

"Better ask Cosmo," Tory said in a small voice.

Aunt Gwen frowned. "Cosmo wouldn't do something like that and you know it."

Tory opened his mouth, but a look of fear sprang into his eyes, and he closed it again.

"All right then," she said. "Tory, stand up and turn around." She watched his pockets as he turned, and poked him here and there. When his back was to her, she saw the scotch-taped stick in his belt. "You and that wand of yours," she said sourly. "You'd better wave it around and say another spell. And make it a juicy one, because Angie's didn't work. Now," she said, "get out. Go somewhere and play." She paused. "And if you see Cosmo, send him right up here. *On the double.*"

Out in the hall Justin gave Tory's shoulder a fake punch. "Come on down to our room," he said. "We've gotta talk."

Nobody said anything as they thumped down the stairs to the Cases' suite. When they got to the door, Justin unlocked it and pushed it open. "Go ahead," he said to his friends.

Monique stepped into the suite, and something crackled under her foot. She bent down and picked up a folded piece of white copier paper. "Somebody's left us a note." She handed it to Justin.

He unfolded it and glanced at it, then stepped into the room and tipped it toward a window so he could see it better. And his heart skipped a beat. "Tory, look."

Tory took the paper. Justin saw his face sag.

"What is it? What does it say?" Monique asked.

Tory cleared his throat. "'Where is Puff? Answer phone.'"

A few seconds of silence. Then the phone rang.

"Don't answer it," Monique said.

"Could be Coz," Tory said anxiously.

"Could be The Man," Justin said.

"Oh."

Justin swung the door shut and twisted the deadbolt into place. The phone rang a few more times and then quit.

"Call your dad," Monique said to Justin. "This is too big."

"No, wait," Tory said quickly.

"Dad'll be over, but it won't be for a while," Justin said. "He told me he was going to give your suite a good going-over for clues," Justin said. "But Monique's right. This is too big for us. Cosmo knows the dragon's gone. He thinks we have it. We're safe if we sit tight here."

"Or Cosmo could be just faking," Tory said. "Maybe he got it somehow, and he's trying to throw us off the trail."

"I'm hungry," Justin said suddenly.

"You just ate," Monique said.

"I'm a growing boy." He went to the refrigerator, got out some strawberries and ice cream, and dished up three bowls.

Monique sighed, but took hers too. She eyed Tory closely. "So you didn't take it?"

He scowled. "Of *course* I didn't take it. If I had it, I wouldn't be sitting here. I'd be someplace in private, chipping one of its scales off and figuring out how to return the rest of it without getting caught." He scooped up a strawberry too quickly with his spoon, knocking it onto the tabletop. Retrieving the strawberry, Tory said, "You know what this means, don't you?"

"What?" Justin asked.

"Mom's going to be a mess, and she'll stop writing. And then she'll start spending all her time seeing a psychiatrist or dragging me around Europe this summer trying to find another crystal with that much power. You wouldn't believe how long it took her to find Belisarius. We were living off canned food until then." He gazed moodily around the room. "And you just watch. Until she finds Belisarius or some other crystal just as good, there'll be no more best-selling books. And no more Campobello suite."

"*Somebody's* got that dragon," Monique said.

He glared at her. "Brilliant, Sherlock. However did you come to that amazing conclusion?"

Justin fumbled in his belt pack and brought

out a small black notebook. "We'd better get a suspect list going," he said.

"I don't need a suspect list," the other boy said. "I know who took it. Cosmo. Or The Man. Or maybe even Aunt Gwen."

Monique looked startled. "Why Aunt Gwen?"

"She's a writer too. But she's never been as good as Mom. Maybe she stole Belisarius to see if he works for her."

"But she doesn't believe in him."

"That's what she *says.*"

"I don't think it was your aunt," Monique said. "Didn't you see that look on her face when she came into your bedroom? She wasn't faking how she felt."

Justin nodded. "I agree with that."

"But Aunt Gwen's smart," Tory insisted. "She can see how it works. Wear Belisarius around your neck and you write best-sellers. You get to travel all over the world. People clap when you come into a room. But no Belisarius means no bucks. And if we don't do something quick," Tory said darkly, tapping himself on the chest, "you're looking at a member of Seattle's latest homeless family."

"Do you know what I think?" Monique said.

"It'd better be good."

"I think we need to pray."

Tory carefully laid his spoon in his bowl and got to his feet. "Thanks for the ice cream," he said calmly. "I'll see you around."

"Hold on," Justin said.

The other boy started toward the door, then paused. "Hey, I've got an idea. Why don't you just run off and find Maria and get her to pray too? She's also a suspect, in case you didn't know it. But of course, she's a *Christian.*"

"Guess what," Monique said. "You're going to be a whole lot safer with the Christians than out there in the hall."

Tory stood silently.

"Just wait here till my dad comes at least," Justin begged him. "I don't like Maria's methods any more than you do. Who knows, she might have mental problems. We're better off together. If we even have a hope of finding Belisarius, we've got to compare notes."

Tory gazed down at his knuckles.

"And look, Tory," Monique said in a pleading voice, "Belisarius has had his chance. I'm saying, let's give Jesus this next chance."

"What can Jesus do?"

"Anything He wants to."

"Except," Justin said, "He won't force us to believe in Him."

Tory flicked his gaze from Justin to Monique and back to Justin. He then came slowly back over to his chair and sat down. "I don't have to close my eyes, do I?"

"You mean when I pray?" Monique asked. "No, not if you don't want to."

"I don't have to get down on my knees?"

"No."

"I don't have to roll around on the floor?"

She stared at him. "What kind of TV programs have you been watching, anyway?"

"I can sit right here?"

"Sure."

"Let me get this straight. A Christian is going to pray that Jesus will help find a New Age dragon?"

Monique shrugged. "Sure. The Lord can answer it however He wants."

"I like magick better."

"How come?"

"With magick you just say a spell and things happen."

She grinned. "Except in the case of Belisarius."

He scowled. "OK. Make it quick."

"Make what quick?"

"Your *prayer.*"

"Oh, right." Monique and Justin bowed their heads. "Dear Lord," Monique said, "thank You for loving us and being our friend. Please help Tory's mom find her dragon. In Jesus' name, amen."

Tory blinked. "That's it?"

"That's it."

"No spells?"

Monique smiled and shook her head. "No spells, no wands, no robes. All that stuff would just get in the way. Jesus is my close friend."

"Was he a wizard?"

"No."

"But you said he can do anything. So he must

be a wizard."

Justin said, "He's not a wizard. He's God. That's better than a wizard."

"How?"

"I don't know much about magick, but doesn't a wizard have to reach out for power?"

Tory nodded. "Sure. Wizards connect with power by saying spells."

"That's one difference between Jesus and a wizard. Jesus doesn't have to reach out for it. He's got it already. He's God."

Tory blinked once.

"And when you want His help," Monique said, "all you have to do is ask for it—in ordinary words."

Tory's nostrils suddenly flared with fear. "I can't believe that I'm sitting here letting someone talk Christianity at me. Whatever you do," he said earnestly, "don't tell Mom. She'd have me in counseling first thing tomorrow morning. But what do we do now? You've talked to Jesus. So when do you hear back?"

"Who knows?" Justin said. "He'll figure something out. It's like your mom. You ask her for something. Does she always give it to you right away?"

"No."

"Why not?"

Tory rolled his eyes and said in a high voice, "'It's not good for you, Tory.' 'You're not old enough, Tory.' 'Be patient, Tory.'"

"God is power, Tory," Monique said. "But He's also a *parent.*"

"And," Justin said, "He's given us minds to think with when we have problems to solve. Which reminds me, we'd better start checking out the suspects." He started drawing columns in his little notebook and labeling them down the left side. "Cosmo," he said, writing busily. "The Man. Maria. You still want to put your aunt on the list?"

"Yeah."

Justin wrote "Aunt Gwen" on the page. Across the top he wrote "Means," "Motive," and "Opportunity." "OK. Let's go through it," he said. Who had the means?"

"What's 'means'?"

"Means is what it takes to do a crime. A crowbar is the means you use to break through a door and rob somebody's house. In this case the means is access to your mom."

"Oh, you mean who could get close to her." Tory thought for a minute. "Everybody on your list, I guess. We've all got keys to our suite. I know Aunt Gwen has one. Maria would too. She's the maid who cleans on our hotel floor."

"When did you last see the dragon?"

"Mom always has it around her neck. She never takes it off."

Monique said, "The boat. I'll bet somebody stole it on the harbor tour. Your mom seemed to be dozing off a lot."

"That's impossible," Tory said. "I was with

Mom all the time."

"*All* the time?" Justin asked. "What about when you came up beside me and told me how your mom had said a spell to keep Belisarius safe?"

"Well, *almost* all the time," Tory admitted. "But I stayed pretty close to her."

Justin held his pencil over the notebook. "OK, who was on the tour?"

"Mom, Cosmo, Aunt Gwen. And me."

"Maria?" Monique asked.

Tory thought a moment. "I didn't see her. But maybe she was. Fritz will tell me if I ask him."

A couple of hours later two quick raps, then two more, sounded on the door.

"Dad's knock," Justin said. He ran to the door and wrestled with the deadbolt. Finally he got the door open. Dad was standing outside with another piece of white copier paper. There was a tight, puzzled look on his face.

"Who's leaving us notes?" he asked. He stepped into the room and closed the door. "Threatening notes." He handed the paper to his son, and Justin stared at it.

"Where is Puff?" said the note. "Answer the phone, or I will hurt you."

Chapter 6
Knives and Wands

"First question," said Dad, "who is 'Puff'? Second question, who in this household is mixed up in all this?" He glanced quickly at Justin. "Or maybe this is a joke? A game?"

Justin shook his head, a frightened lump in his throat. He glanced at Tory and Monique, then back to Dad. "OK, we'll tell you."

"We'll tell you what we *know,*" Monique said. "There's a lot more we *don't* know."

Tory glanced from face to face. He looked as though he wasn't sure where all this was going, but he didn't say anything.

Dad took a small black notebook like Justin's from his pocket, clicked a ballpoint pen, and listened to the kids. Twenty minutes later they'd almost finished telling the story, when the phone rang.

"Dad," Justin said in a quivery voice, "will you get that?"

"How come? Oh, right. The note." Dad glanced at his watch and reached for the phone. "Hello," he said into the receiver. A pause. "Hello. *Hello?*" Holding the receiver to his ear, he jotted down a few more notes, then set it back in its cradle. "Hung up," he told them. "I heard the click right away. So whoever it is—probably Cosmo or The Man—wants somebody else besides me. Now, kids," he said firmly, "listen up. This is out of your hands. Let the professionals take it from here. We've called in the police, and they'll be checking the pawn shops and putting pressure on the locals that they know pay cash for stolen goods. That little dragon's important to your mom, Tory, and we'll do our best to get it back to her."

Tory nodded sadly.

✧　✧　✧

A bright sun poured into the Case suite the next morning at breakfast. Mom glanced at it gladly.

"A beautiful day for a trip to Pike Place Market," she said to Justin and Monique. "Are you two coming?"

They stared blankly at her.

"Oh, maybe I didn't tell you," she said. "Tory's mother and his aunt want me to come with them to the market so that Angie can try to find a temporary crystal to use until she finds Beelzebub."

Justin and Monique collapsed with laughter. "Mom," Justin gasped, "it's Belisarius!"

Mom put her hand over her mouth and sputtered out a couple of snickers herself, but then her face got serious. "Don't you dare let it out that I said that. It was just a slip of the tongue. I wouldn't ever want to hurt Angie's feelings. She really believes in channeling. But she and I have had a couple of really interesting talks."

Dad grinned too, but then sobered up. "You

kids come along. I'm coming too—my seminar's not until 2:30. We've got to stick together until we get some answers to this thing." He glanced uneasily at the door to the hall. "I found another note this morning. It said somebody's going to get hurt 'bad.' I'm going to give the note to the police. Paper's not too good for fingerprints, but maybe they can get a partial."

It was a seven-block walk to the market, but as Mom had said, it was a perfect day. Aunt Gwen had decided to come along with her sister, so the adults and Monique walked together, talking. Justin hung back with Tory—but not too far back—so they could keep an eye out for stores with interesting display windows.

"Monique," Justin said once they'd made it to the market, "check your walkie-talkie battery, OK?" He unreeled a length of cord from his belt pack and plugged an earphone into his ear.

She gazed at him doubtfully as she got the walkie-talkie out of her purse, turned the unit on, and pressed the talk button. "I don't really want to carry this walkie-talkie around," she said into the walkie-talkie.

"Sorry," Justin squawked back at her. "But I'd like you to keep it with you, just in case."

"Hey," Tory said. "It just struck me. That's your name. Justin Case!"

Justin rolled his eyes.

"At least they didn't name him 'Suit,'" Monique said.

"Knock-knock," Justin said to change the subject.

"Who's there?" Tory asked.

"Oswald."

"Where have I heard this before?" Monique murmured.

"Oswald who?" Tory asked.

"Oswald my gum," Justin replied. "Can I have a piece of yours?"

Monique and Tory groaned loudly.

Monique drifted off to join the women, who had paused in front of a display of wind chimes. Justin and Tory each bought a white paper bag of caramel popcorn and started to munch. Dad, who didn't enjoy shopping, had purchased a couple of newspapers and was sitting in the sunlight at a little metal café table glancing through one of them. He flicked an alert glance around him from time to time. A helmeted policeman pedaled by on a black mountain bike, and Dad waved to him.

"Justin, look." Tory pointed. "Knives."

"Ooohhh." Justin gave a guilty glance at Dad, and he and his friend walked toward a little shop. The shop sold kitchen supplies, but there in a glass case was an impressive display of hunting knives with glossy leather sheaths.

"I want that one," Justin said through the popcorn in his mouth. He pressed his finger on the glass just above a large clasp knife with a wide blade.

"Why? Do you like to go camping?"

Justin shrugged. "Once in a while."

Tory glanced discontentedly around him. "I wish they had a case full of wands. I wish they had a wandmaker's shop like in Harry Potter."

Justin looked at the price of the knife, and his heart sank. "My dad's got a clasp knife," he said. "But he won't let me get one."

"Duck!" Tory suddenly hissed, disappearing from sight.

"What?"

"Just duck!" Tory's arm appeared, grabbed Justin by the elbow, and pulled him down behind the knife case.

Justin crouched down and massaged his elbow. "Ouch. What's wrong?"

"Cosmo." Tory peered cautiously around the case. "He just came through that door. He must have been downstairs on the lower level of shops."

"Anybody with him?"

"No, I don't think so. But let's stay down here till he goes away."

"OK." Justin knelt on one knee.

"What would you use it for?"

"What would I use what for?"

"That knife."

Justin shrugged again. "Oh—just for anything. And it would be handy to have with me, just in—" Too late he stopped.

Tory grinned. "'Just in case?'"

Justin fake-punched him in the stomach. Tory doubled over in mock pain, then pretended to reach through the glass and grab a knife. He thrust his fist toward Justin's chest. Justin blocked him with a karate move.

"Hey," Justin said as he glanced around the case, "we'd better be careful or Cosmo's gonna spot us."

"Wands," Tory said, "are safer than clasp knives. Forget a knife. Get a wand."

"You can't defend yourself with a wand."

Tory looked at him curiously. "You want to *stab* people?"

Justin shook his head. "Well, no. But let's say The Man suddenly showed up right here and wanted to hurt us."

Tory stared at Justin in amazement and then exploded in a sputtery laugh.

"What? What's wrong?"

Tory lowered his voice and glanced around. "Listen, if The Man showed up here, it would be with a .357 Magnum, and he'd have half the bullets inside you before you could even get that knife out of your pocket."

Justin paused. Then he said, "My dad used to carry a Smith and Wesson Model 439 when he was a police detective."

"Whoa." Tory glanced over to where Dad was sitting. "Does he have it on him now?"

Justin shook his head. "He sold it years ago."

"How come?"

"He says it's too dangerous. People get hurt when guns are around."

"Well then, how would he protect himself if somebody tried to rob him?"

Justin thought a moment. "Pray, I guess."

Tory chuckled. "So your dad, the former detective, uses prayer to protect himself. And you"—he tapped the wood at the back of the case—"wanna use a knife."

Justin suddenly felt hot and uncomfortable.

"And I," said Tory, reaching around to the back of his belt and pulling out his wand, "want to use *this.*" He pointed it around the case, and said, *"Levitato,* Cosmo, you big bully."

"Can you see him?"

"No," Tory said, shifting his position. "So which one is more powerful? A knife, a wand, or a prayer to Jesus?"

"A prayer, I guess."

Tory turned his back on the knife case. "Then save your money."

"Yeah, but—"

"And *this* thing," Tory said, holding up his wand. "If I thought this thing was useless, I'd snap it over my knee and pitch it. But wands have been around for centuries."

"Prayer has been around for centuries."

"Then what's the difference?"

"Prayer," said Justin, "is—talking to somebody."

"So?"

"Somebody who knows a lot."

"So?"

"I mean," Justin said, "like when my dad helped your mom last night just after she found out the dragon was a saltshaker. Dad took some EMT training when he was a policeman. He knew what to do."

"So?"

"So God is like that. I mean, my dad isn't God, or anything like that. But God knows a lot—everything, in fact. God created us. And all I'm saying is, why don't we ask Him for advice? He tells us we can talk to Him."

Tory's eyebrows went up and down a couple of times. Justin could tell he was thinking, because even though he pointed his wand at a couple of things and mumbled, *"Levitato,"* he didn't even watch to see if the things rose into the air.

"That's fine," he finally said. "But it's not good enough." He spun his wand between his thumb and finger. "When I need power, I need it *now.*"

Justin was silent.

"Just like you," Tory said flatly.

"What are you talking about?"

Tory jerked a thumb at the knife case. "That knife is like my wand. Get it in your hand, and you've got power. It won't stop a bullet, but it's great against an unarmed person. And you can use it whenever you want to. Just like Harry Potter." He waved his wand. "You don't have to *pray* for strength. You just say the spell. Or give somebody a stab."

Justin's lips were getting dry. He ran his

tongue over them.

"Admit it, OK?"

Justin nodded shamefacedly, his conscience urging him to acknowledge to Tory that he'd been wrong to want to get protection from a knife.

"I suppose," Tory continued in a kinder voice, "that if you could be sure that God, or Jesus, or who- ever, was really cool, really on our side, then—"

A shadow fell across them. Justin looked up, then winced. Tory looked up too.

Cosmo towered over them.

Chapter 7
Crystal Clear

Tory straightened up. "Hey, Coz."

This time Cosmo didn't have earphones on. They were dangling from his pocket, sending out little clashes of music near his knees. There was something that looked like worry in his eyes.

"Hey, Tor," he replied. "What are you guys hiding from?"

Tory shrugged. Justin straightened to his feet and shrugged too.

"Your friend, the girl," Cosmo said to Justin. "She's hurt."

"Monique? What happened? Where is she?"

"Through there." Cosmo swallowed, and pointed to where they'd first seen him. "You go a little bit and come to some stairs. She fell down them."

"Whoa. I'll get Dad," Justin said. He glanced at the little café table.

Dad was gone.

"I tried to find him, but I couldn't," Cosmo said. "She twisted her ankle. I couldn't carry her by myself."

Justin glanced at Tory. *Did The Man get to her?* his eyes asked. Tory raised his eyebrows.

Then they both started to run toward the stairway. Cosmo, after inserting his earphones into his ears, jogged casually after them. As they

ran, Justin unzipped his belt pack and fished out
his yellow walkie-talkie. He pushed the earphone
further into his ear and squeezed the talk button.
"Monique, hang on," he said. "We're on the way."

"Justin," Tory gasped as they rumbled down
the stairs. "Where is she?"

"Not at the foot of the stairs." Justin's gaze
flickered from a line of parked cars to the huge
pillars holding up the upper level of stores.
Suddenly the back of his neck crawled. Still running down the stairs, he jerked the earphone out
of his ear and shoved the walkie-talkie, along
with the earphone cord, deep into his caramel
corn bag.

Tory and Justin got to the bottom of the
stairs, and Cosmo finally descended too.

"Where's Monique?" Justin asked. He turned
to see Cosmo, whose face had stiffened.

"Come on, Justin," Tory said. "Let's go find
your—"

Cosmo suddenly began to sing in a loud
but wobbly voice. "Dah dah-dah-dah dahhhh
dahhhh . . ."

Justin froze. "Puff the Magic Dragon."

There was a metallic rattling, and Justin
glanced in its direction. There, with neck chains
gleaming, stood The Man beside a brown wooden
fence back under the stairway. Through a gate in
the fence Justin could see a rusted dumpster.

The Man's hands were thrust deep into the
pockets of his baggy faded-denim pants. His right

fist emerged for just an instant—just long enough to reveal half of a deadly black revolver—and then jammed into his pocket again.

"Get through there," he said in a deep, sinister voice. He jerked his elbow toward the fence door.

Tory backed away.

"Be cool, you little unprintable," said The Man softly with a wide smile. People passing probably thought they were old friends. His voice was elegant in a deadly way. "I did a drive-by in April, and I can do you." He then said some unprintable things himself, mainly to describe what he thought of Justin and Tory, and what he planned to do to them if they refused to go through the gate.

Justin and Tory went through the gate.

"Pat 'em down," he said to Cosmo. "And don't miss anything."

Cosmo hesitantly approached Tory. Tory started to twist angrily away, but then caught the cobra-like gaze of The Man, and he went limp. Cosmo searched him from top to bottom.

"Now the other one," said The Man. "Quick."

Cosmo, who seemed to be doing his best to impress The Man, was rougher with Justin. He grabbed Justin so hard that the bag of caramel corn fell, emptying half its contents on the ground, and revealing the walkie-talkie earphone and an inch or two of bright-yellow cord.

Justin struggled a little so that the attention

would stay on him and not turn to the caramel corn bag. He was hoping Cosmo wouldn't notice how badly he was sweating.

After Cosmo had searched completely through Justin's belt pack, he backed off, and Justin humbly bent to gather up the bag and what was left of the popcorn. He hid the bag with his body and flipped the earphone back into the bag. Then he stood up, turned around, and gazed sorrowfully down into the bag for a moment, as though he was sad that most of the popcorn was gone. Then he carefully began to squeeze the paper around the walkie-talkie. Tight.

"I want to go home," he said in a clear, child-like voice. "Just let me go home."

"Shut up," Cosmo said.

"I want to go back up those stairs into the market."

The Man shot him a look so deadly that Justin's voice box almost froze.

"I don't like it down here by this dumpster," Justin said earnestly, in a clearer voice than ever. "What if the cops come here?" He glanced rapidly out through the gate. "What if somebody comes out of the Sailor's Tavern and sees us?"

The Man was in front of him with a single bound. In his right hand he now held a long knife. "Shut that mouth of yours," he said, "or I'll use this to help persuade you."

Justin's mouth began to quiver, and this time he wasn't faking. He nodded several times rapidly, and said no more. His hand still squeezed the paper bag.

"OK," The Man said to Tory. "That dragon. Where is it?"

Tory was silent.

"You got till I count to ten. One. Two."

"I don't *know!*" Tory yelped.

"Three. Four."

"I don't *have* it. I didn't take it!"

"Five. *You.*" Suddenly The Man turned his attention to Justin. "Tell me. Six. Seven."

Justin couldn't speak. He shook his head.

"Maybe they don't know," Cosmo said timidly.

"Eight."

"Please, *please!*" Tory said desperately. "I promise. We don't know. We've been looking for it, but we can't find it."

"Look," Cosmo said quickly. "They don't have it."

A rumble from above froze them all. The Man looked up. Two people were bounding down the steps. Justin's heart leaped up in hope, but it was just two teenage boys. The Man held up his knife and glanced from Justin to Tory to keep them quiet. Finally the teenagers disappeared in the direction of the Sailor's Tavern.

The Man stopped counting and glanced at the dumpster. Then he fumbled in a gigantic pocket. Out came a small roll of silver-gray duct tape. He grabbed Tory around the throat, and squeezed hard for a moment. Then he quickly released his hand, ripped off a foot-long piece of duct tape, and plastered it across Tory's lips and behind his head. Tory's eyes were bright and fearful.

In a few more quick motions The Man had taped Tory's wrists together behind his back and bound his ankles together. Then he turned to Justin, grabbed his arm, and yanked him forward.

The caramel corn bag fell again, and this time the bright-yellow walkie-talkie skittered out of the bag's opening into full view.

"Please, *please!*" Justin said rapidly, staring into The Man's eyes. "Don't, don't." *Anything to stall, anything to stretch out the time, anything to keep The Man's attention off what was on the ground.*

Suddenly The Man smiled and stepped back. And suddenly his roll of duct tape disappeared.

And suddenly something crashed against the fence gate, and the blue shirt and black helmet of a bicycle cop appeared.

"*Freeze!*" he shouted. "*Reach!*"

✧   ✧   ✧

"But this still hasn't gotten us the dragon," Tory said moodily to Justin.

It was an hour later. The two were sitting with their backs against the brick wall on Tory's balcony, watching the clouds reflected in the copper and blue and silver skyscrapers looming over them.

Their ears were still ringing with "Freeze!" and "Reach!" and "Why in the world did you two kids let somebody talk you into slipping off after I told you to stick together?" and "Now that you're back safe in this hotel, thank the Lord, you're staying inside it until we leave Friday morning. Do you understand that?"

The mood brightened when Mrs. Case said, "It was smart thinking to transmit your location on the walkie-talkie. Monique picked it up perfectly and we heard all about the dragon. I got hold of the bicycle police, and he came right down to the Sailor's Tavern. Now The Man is locked up for violating his parole."

"Is your stomach still aching?" Tory asked Justin.

"A little."

"I got you these." Tory searched in his pocket and pulled out a half-used roll of antacid tablets. Justin took them from Tory, but didn't take out a tablet. Instead, he dropped them in his shirt pocket, and pulled out his black notebook and opened it to the suspect list. "We can cross Cosmo off," he said.

"Yeah. Otherwise he wouldn't have had to trick us into coming down those stairs."

"Your Aunt Gwen too."

Tory nodded. "Like Monique said, that look in her eye when she got us all into the bedroom and demanded to know where the dragon was. That was real."

"And we can cross your mom off too. How's she doing?"

"OK. She's acting really quiet," Tory said gloomily. "Next week she'll probably go into counseling, and won't write anything for six months. That's what happened last time, just before we bought Belisarius." He glanced at the turrets of the Campobello Hotel. "So it looks like we'll have to kiss this place goodbye."

Justin flicked a glance at the locked wooden box beside them. "How are you going to get your wizard's trunk back inside the hotel? It's really heavy with all that stuff in it."

Tory blinked, as if it had been a long time since he'd thought about the trunk. "Oh, that. I'll probably have to bring things in a little at a time."

Justin grinned. "You could levitate it. Maybe it's lighter than I am."

Tory smiled sadly and half-slugged him.

"But look," Justin said. "We've got to follow the trail of that dragon. It could have been stolen on the boat."

"Naaaahh. Not with all those passengers. Remember, somebody had to not only get the dragon off the chain but also get the saltshaker onto it. And then take the risk that somebody would notice the switch."

"Good point." Justin thought for a moment. "So if it wasn't stolen on the boat, it was stolen in your mom's room when she took her nap after the tour. Who did you say had keys to your suite?"

"Mom. And Aunt Gwen. And maybe Cosmo, but I'm not sure."

"And Maria."

Tory nodded. "So if it wasn't Aunt Gwen, and wasn't Cosmo, and wasn't me, it's got to be Maria."

"Whoever it was had to get rid of the salt."

"What salt?"

"In the saltshaker. Remember, it was empty when we saw it hanging on your mom's neck last night. And the thief had to empty it quick, before your mom woke up again."

Tory shrugged. "She could have dumped it in the wastebasket. But no, your dad would have found it. Mom told me how careful your dad was. He didn't miss a thing. He checked all the drawers, even the underwear drawers. Dumped everything out. He emptied all the purses—took everything out himself and looked inside them with a flashlight."

Justin leaned back. He reached into his shirt pocket for the half-used antacid roll, unfolded the paper, and took one.

"Yuck," he said. "How old are these?"

"I don't know."

"They're salty."

"You wanted salt," Tory said absently, "and you got—"

"Whoa!"

Both of them said it together, and turned their heads until they were staring into each other's eyes.

Justin broke the silence. "Tory, where did you get these?"

Tory turned pale. "Aunt Gwen. She got them . . . from her purse."

"The purse Dad emptied and searched last night?"

Tory nodded. "It's the only purse she's got."

Justin's fingers trembled as he peeled back some more paper from the antacid roll. "Salt grains, Tory," he said softly.

✧ ✧ ✧

The boys found Monique and told her. Then the three of them went to the suite where Dad still had half an hour to go with that day's writing class. When he was done, they hurried him to a quiet place and told him everything. And then the four of them headed toward the suite where Angelica Fawkes was teaching a class. Her sister was distributing handouts.

When Gwen had distributed the last sheet, Dad beckoned to her, and she joined them just outside the room, closing the door after her. At first she didn't see the serious looks on their faces.

"Isn't Angie brave?" she said proudly. "I can remember the time when losing Belisarius would have sent her into a breakdown. And add to that Tory's kidnapping, or almost-kidnapping . . ."

Then she looked at their eyes for the first time. "What is it? What's wrong?"

Dad held up the antacid roll, and for about

five seconds she still didn't get it. Then her face went loose. She glanced from Tory to Justin and back to Dad.

"Th-those are mine," she said.

Dad nodded. "Where's the dragon?"

"I don't know."

"Come on, Gwen."

Suddenly she burst into loud, wobbly sobs. "All right, I took it!" she wailed, trying to get control of her voice, "I took it, but it's gone. And I don't know where it is!"

Ten minutes later, in her suite, Aunt Gwen was calmer but still sobbing. "Angie has always been such a talented little snot," she said. "I don't have a tenth of her abilities. And what got me so mad was that she thought—or pretended she thought—it was because of those stupid little crystals she went around trying to find. She spent so much on those rocks, and made so much because of them, that I said to myself, 'One of these days, Angie, I'm going to show you."

Dad said gently, "You took it to *help* her?"

Aunt Gwen shook her head sadly. "No, to get back at her. I thought, 'I've had to struggle, Angie. Now it's your turn. I've had to work hard to stay above the poverty line. Maybe you need to feel the pinch.'"

"When did you take the dragon?"

"After the harbor tour, when we came back to her suite. Her sunburn had gotten worse, so I rubbed some pain ointment on it, and she tried to get to sleep. I watched her, but every time I thought she was asleep, she'd move, and her eyes would open. A couple of days before that I had taken the saltshaker from the dining room and had carried it upstairs in my purse. I'd even put a paper clip through the holes in the top."

Dad shook his head. "I checked your purse and Angie's thoroughly for salt grains. Or I thought I did."

She nodded. "I cleaned that purse like no purse has ever been cleaned before. But I didn't consider that some of the salt grains might have fallen into the open end of the antacid roll."

"So she finally dropped off and you made the switch. What did you do with the dragon?"

"On the floor were some walking shoes Angie had worn to a park on Sunday. I reached down and dropped Belisarius into one and slid him out of sight. I remember that one of the shoes looked really muddy—we'd walked too close to a stream in the park, I guess. Then I glanced at my watch and saw that we only had a little time before the dinner. I knew that she didn't like to look directly at Belisarius, and I thought I was safe for a while. I had no idea they were going to give her an award that night, and that she'd make that speech where she reveals Belisarius to the audience."

Dad said, "So your idea was to go get the dragon later and hide it someplace safe?"

Aunt Gwen nodded. "Angie got really upset when she saw that Belisarius was gone. Well, *you* saw how she behaved. We all got her up to her suite. I slipped into her bedroom and felt around in the shoes to make sure it was safe, and it was gone." She glanced at Tory. "I figured maybe one of the kids had snitched it, so I went and asked them about it. And I never saw it again."

"Maria," said Tory promptly.

"Who's Maria?" Aunt Gwen asked.

"The maid. She does our floor."

"I thought of the maid," Aunt Gwen said, "but I didn't dare ask her or talk to anybody about her, because then I might be suspected myself. But maids don't do shoes, do they?"

Tory nodded. "The Campobello's an old-fashioned European-style hotel. Maria does shoes. When she comes into your suite and straightens things up, she'll look at your shoes. And if they need cleaning, she'll take them away and do it, right then."

"Well, let's get her in here," Dad said, reaching for the phone.

Ten minutes later a courteous but firm-lipped Maria joined them.

Dad got right to the point. "Maria, we know that you found a crystal jewel carved like a dragon in the toe of one of Mrs. Fawkes's walking shoes. What did you do with it?"

She stared steadily at Dad for about five seconds. "I do not say."

"You mean you *won't* say?"

"I do not say."

"Maria, if you say nothing, I must call the police."

Fear widened her eyes, and some of the firmness went out of her lips. "I do not say. Ask—"

"Ask who?"

"Ask—" and her eyes traveled to Aunt Gwen's face. "Ask—your sister."

✧   ✧   ✧

"Yes," said Angelica Fawkes calmly.

Dad had stopped by the Case suite to collect Mom, and Cosmo had been located too. They all found Mrs. Fawkes sitting on a sofa in the large open suite where Tory said she had often held channeling sessions with Belisarius. It was the same suite that had the window leading to Tory's balcony.

"Yes," she repeated. "When all was said and done, I stole my dragon from myself. Maria found it in my walking shoe and took it away for safekeeping. She was surprised to discover it in so strange a place, but since it was in my suite, she thought I must have placed it there for some private reason. So later, after everyone had gone, she knocked softly on my door and returned it to me." She smiled at Maria, who smiled back. "Crystal dragons are definitely not a part of Maria's beliefs. She has spoken to me several times, very earnestly, about Belisarius, and she has given me literature, too. Once she had found him, she could hardly bring herself even to touch him. But her honest Christianity brought her to my room that night. And since the dragon was now back in its owner's hands, she agreed to keep my secret with me."

Justin and Monique glanced at Tory. His face was a bit pink, and he looked at the floor.

Aunt Gwen sputtered, "But why didn't you tell us you'd found it? Why keep it secret?"

"Because," Mrs. Fawkes said, "Belisarius had become a heavy weight on my neck in more ways than one. Half of me believed that he was the source of my power. But half of me knew that I needed to try working without him. So I decided to put him out of my life."

"But where," Aunt Gwen asked, "is he hidden?" "You've searched for him, haven't you?"

Aunt Gwen nodded guiltily. "Over and over and over."

Angelica Fawkes smiled mischievously. "Next time you walk down the main staircase into the lobby, look up among the hanging crystals of the chandelier. You just might see him." Her voice took on a grim note. "I'm calling the newspapers to give them the scoop that I don't need Belisarius like I thought I did. That should get any would-be thieves off our trail."

Monique said, "So he's hanging out there in plain sight?"

"If you know where to look," Mrs. Fawkes said. "I'm taking him down to sell him over at the market, but I thought I'd just let him dangle there for a while—right there where my son nearly fell to his death."

Tory swallowed. "Mom? Don't you believe in Belisarius anymore?"

Mrs. Fawkes glanced at Tovah Case and then back at her son. "Let's say that there is a greater and friendlier Power than a dead general," she said. "And I'm only now beginning to learn about Him."

"Then I know what *I've* got to do," Tory said.

He smiled a sweet, heart-melting smile at them, then got up, crossed to the window, and raised it. The sounds of the city's rush hour boomed in upon them, and the silver and copper and blue skyscrapers glowed in the afternoon light. He put one leg on the window ledge.

Mrs. Fawkes screamed, and leaped to her feet.

"No!" Justin shouted—not to Tory but to Tory's mother. "No! It's OK, really. Just watch."

"You're gonna have to help me, Justin," Tory said, and disappeared.

"Sure." Justin ran to the window. Out of the corner of his eye he could see Dad getting to his feet.

"Justin!" Mom said warningly.

Out on the balcony Tory was wrestling with his wooden wizard's trunk. "It's not really too heavy," he called to Justin. "I can get it over the railing, if you can lower it down on the other side."

Beware of the Crystal Dragon

Soon they were back in the room. The wizard's box lay in a corner, a snapped wand lying across the black robe. And everybody was hugging and laughing and crying and giggling. And when Justin told the Oswald knock-knock joke again, everybody roared, and asked him to tell it two more times.

Discover more about
Justin's real-life
supernatural friend,
Jesus,
by visiting

www.justincaseadventures.org.

The Justin Case Adventures

Meet Justin Case. He never knows what adventure he'll stumble into next. So he keeps things handy. Scope. Walkie-talkies. Pencil and paper. You know, just in case. His dad, a police officer turned journalist, provides him with the chance to explore new territory—and land smack in the middle of another mystery.

1. The Case of the Stolen Red Mary

A cherished painting belonging to Justin's friend, Tessa, has been stolen. Will the criminal now destroy the work of art as well? In the end, the truth about the painting and life after death becomes crystal clear.
0-8280-1611-9.
US$6.99, Can$10.49.

2. The Desert Temple Mystery

A full-scale replica of ancient Herod's Temple—in the Arizona desert? Yes, if businessman Orville Frazier has his way. Justin joins his dad, who's going to help provide publicity for the tourist attraction. Soon Justin and his friends find themselves on a dash to discover hidden gold. En route they learn just how dangerous racial prejudice can be.
0-8280-1612-7.
US$6.99, Can$10.49.

To order call: 1-800-765-6955

Watch for more books in the series coming soon!
Price and availability subject to change. Add GST in Canada.